Rise of the New Race

Rise of the Giants Series: Book 8

Theo Mann

The Invisible Publishing Company

Rise of the Giants Series

Contents

Chapter 1

Blackjack stood off to one side and watched his younger brother Maeno say goodbye to Mora and Thena in front of their shelter. Four years had passed since the Godless band had come to live in the Angler Valley.

Everyone still called it the Angler Valley even though no Anglers lived here anymore. Everyone still kept a close watch for them, but no one ever saw any Anglers again. The band really had wiped them all out.

Maeno stood taller than both Mora and Thena now and he wasn't even fully grown. He'd only started to shoot up this past year. He would probably get bigger and taller than Blackjack.

Blackjack waited at a distance for his brother to say his last goodbyes to his mother and sister. Oracle, Pyro, Smash, and Chief waited with Blackjack. Loso, Kabi, and Zakra had all initiated and become Rebel, Cyclops, and Cloud.

Carnage's son, Fortune, Red's two sons, Cyclone and Landslide, Viking's grandsons, Reaper and Diamond, Butch's son, Iron, and Jolt's sons Arrow and Torch completed their party.

Blackjack and all his men stood at the edge of the camp near the entrance opening between the rocks while they waited for Maeno to join them.

He was the oldest of the younger boys, so he would be the first to initiate. The younger, uninitiated boys had to stay behind. They weren't allowed to attend Maeno's initiation.

Hangman, Kuvik, Red, Viking, Bantam, Lock, and the rest of Red's men sat across the camp. The older men didn't get involved. They didn't even stand up to approach the younger men who would go out with Maeno.

Hangman had already said goodbye to Maeno in private. Blackjack and his men would initiate Maeno. Maeno and the uninitiated boys spent all their time with Blackjack's men nowadays anyway.

Hangman had started following the same pattern with Blackjack that Hangman followed with Hammer. Hangman let Blackjack run his own internal band of younger men with Blackjack in charge.

The younger men went hunting, patrolled outside the valley, and took responsibility for eliminating any enemy Clans that made it this far.

The younger men also went on longer journeys deeper into the canyon country to find these enemy incursions before they got anywhere near the valley.

The older men still ran their own operations. They still went out the same way they always used to, but the older men kept their business separate from the younger men.

The younger men took responsibility for training the uninitiated boys. The boys went out with Blackjack's men all the time. He and the other men treated these boys as part of their band. Today was the only exception.

Mora said goodbye to Maeno with a smile on her face. She didn't cry over him. Maybe she would save that for when he came home.

Thena, on the other hand, said goodbye with tears pouring down her cheeks. She kept bursting into sobs, throwing her arms around his neck, and holding him so tightly that he couldn't leave.

He finally had to tear her arms away by main force. She really started bawling when he walked away to join up with Blackjack and the other men. Maeno didn't look back at anyone.

Blackjack saw him coming and headed out of the camp. This core group of families were the only people who still lived in the camp among the rocks.

All the freed captives that Hangman had rescued from the Red Riders had moved out to different parts of the valley. They lived in four separate bands, but they rejoined once a year for gatherings.

The band had started to follow a tradition of holding smaller gatherings once a year inside the valley. Anyone who didn't find a spouse at the valley gathering could travel south to the bigger gathering to bring in someone from outside.

Hangman had ruled that the four bands could do it this way temporarily. The bands would probably have to change things once the four smaller valley bands started to become too closely interrelated.

Then everyone would have to go south and take spouses from other Clans and bands in different parts of the country.

The four valley bands weren't likely to become too closely interrelated for a long time. The freed captives had brought in enough new blood to keep the band diverse for years to come.

Oracle, Pyro, Smash, and Chief followed Blackjack out of the camp first. Maeno caught up with the group and the other men surrounded and followed him outside. None of them looked back or said goodbye to anyone.

They walked a long way through the jungle before Blackjack stopped in front of his brother. "Do you know where you're going?" Blackjack asked.

Maeno nodded at nothing. He didn't make eye contact with Blackjack. Maeno stared off into the distance somewhere past Blackjack's shoulder.

Blackjack didn't try to bring his brother back from out there. Blackjack understood this mental state only too well from his own initiation.

"You go ahead. We'll follow you and watch from a distance." Blackjack couldn't stop himself from squeezing Maeno's shoulder and the side of his neck, but Maeno didn't notice. "I'm proud of you no matter what happens. I know you're going to make us all proud."

Maeno didn't respond. He was already gone. Blackjack gave him a subtle push and steered him away into the jungle.

Maeno took off running much faster. The other men ran behind him to keep up with him. He sprang into the branches in just a few minutes and kept going at a breakneck pace until he came to a certain place the bands knew of.

A high stand of rock stood out in the middle of the jungle. The trees grew right up against the rock. The canopy surrounded its highest crown and shielded its sides almost the whole way down.

Gorlocks nested in the rock's many fissures and hollows. Mother Gorlocks laid their eggs in there and perched right on top of the hollows to protect both the eggs and the young from any other creature trying to attack.

The father Gorlocks stood guard around the nest site at a distance from the rock itself. The mothers could get murderously protective even against the males if the males ventured too close to the nests.

The male Gorlocks patrolled the area and went hunting to bring back food for both the mothers and young. Some of the males stayed behind on guard while others went hunting. They never left the rock unguarded anytime day or night.

Maeno slowed down when he got near the rock. He didn't go too close too soon. Blackjack and his men backed off. Blackjack didn't try to talk to Maeno again.

Different boys handled initiation in different ways. Some got terrified or agitated or even aggressive toward the men around them. Others checked out of reality and went into another plane of consciousness where they didn't talk to anyone.

Some of these boys took a long time to come out of it after the initiation ended. Blackjack had learned to leave these boys alone and let them go on their own internal journey until they were ready to come back to reality.

Maeno advanced toward the rock much more slowly. He acted as though he was already alone. He wiped the men out of his awareness.

Blackjack and his men retreated into the canopy where Maeno and the Gorlocks wouldn't see them. Blackjack and his men inched forward to match Maeno's pace so they could keep him in sight at all times.

Blackjack felt himself getting nervous as the time came closer. His instincts told him to jump in and rescue his younger brother from danger if Maeno got hurt or pinned down.

Blackjack wouldn't be able to do that today. Maeno had to fight his own fight. He would rather die than suffer the humiliation of failing his initiation. All initiating boys said the same thing and Blackjack had felt the same way.

No boy ever came home from initiation saying he'd failed to defeat his creature. That would have been intolerable. No one would be able to respect the boy ever again. He would become an outcast.

Blackjack wouldn't have wanted that and Maeno certainly wouldn't be the first. That was the whole point of saying goodbye to his family. He might not come back at all, and when he did, he would come back as a completely different person.

Maeno already seemed to have shed the trappings of his boy self. He drew his weapons while he skirted the rock to pick out his target Gorlock.

He fought with two blades carved from long Crusher thigh bones. He had fashioned the weapons himself and he was rightfully proud of them.

He was the only person in the whole valley who fought with bone weapons. Hangman, Viking, and the other older men insisted that they'd never even heard of anyone fighting with weapons like this.

Not even Kuvik's jawbone kukris came close. They certainly didn't require as much workmanship as Maeno's blades.

They curved backward in swooping convex arcs instead of inward like kukris. He kept his blades sharpened to a razor edge and he fought with them exceptionally well.

He stopped in the canopy when he spotted a large male Gorlock alone on one side of the rock. The other Gorlocks circled the other side of the rock. They wouldn't see Maeno approaching.

He didn't hesitate for an instant. He balanced through the branches on a dead run for the Gorlock. Maeno made enough noise to get the Gorlock's attention before he got there.

The Gorlock turned around, narrowed its eyes at Maeno, and then roared out in fury when the Gorlock saw Maeno raising his blades.

Maeno launched himself out of the branches in a flying leap to intercept the Gorlock. The creature had all the time in the world to raise one of its wings and club him to the ground.

The feathers slashed Maeno down the arm, side, and part of his chest. He slammed down hard on the ground, bounced up, and faced the enraged creature on his feet.

Blood poured down the side of Maeno's body, but he didn't notice. He brandished both his weapons in front of the Gorlock to meet the creature.

It stalked closer and made him back off—or it looked like it. He wound up circling closer to the rock, but he didn't back right up against it. He stayed at a distance where he would have enough space to move around.

Maeno cast one glance up toward the nest hollows. That was the moment when Blackjack understood. Maeno was deliberately trying to antagonize the Gorlock into overstepping.

The strategy worked. The Gorlock rushed him and swiped its wing at him again. Maeno jumped clear of the stroke and then leapt straight back in as soon as the Gorlock started to pull its wing back.

Maeno grabbed onto the Gorlock's feathers and it pulled him up along with the wing. His weight infuriated the Gorlock even more. The creature roared in fury and flapped its wing farther outward and higher than normal to try to shake him off.

He rode the stroke to its highest point, let go, and flipped around in midair to land on the creature's back. The Gorlock screeched and spun around trying to get to Maeno and shake him off at the same time.

He used that moment to raise his blade and hack it down into the back of the creature's neck, but the Gorlock's sudden movement threw Maeno off balance.

His blade cracked into the side of the Gorlock's shoulder instead—right at the point where it met the Gorlock's neck.

The Gorlock roared in pain, reared all the way back to its full height, and pumped its wings in one mighty stroke before it realized one of its wings was injured.

Maeno went sailing off into space again, but he landed on his feet this time. The Gorlock spun around much faster and attacked much more ferociously than before. Rage and pain drove the creature out of its mind.

Maeno tucked and rolled to get away from it and the Gorlock ran headfirst into the rock. Maeno reacted just as fast, dove in, and impaled the creature through the ribs right behind the shoulder blade.

The Gorlock whipped around fast enough to tear the blade out of Maeno's hand. He didn't have time to pull it free. The Gorlock carried it away and kept fighting with the handle sticking out of its side.

That left Maeno with one weapon. The Gorlock reared in front of him and raised its other wing to club him again.

Maeno leapt forward impossibly fast, got inside the wing before the Gorlock could move it, and chopped his one remaining blade into the inner shoulder joint this time.

His blade stuck in the bone and severed a major blood vessel there. The Gorlock bellowed again and reared away, but Maeno hung onto the blade handle and his weight tugged the weapon free.

He collapsed back, sprawled on the ground, and had to scramble to get out of the way before the Gorlock came after him. He barely got to his feet before the Gorlock rushed him again.

Pain and fury wiped all restrain from the Gorlock's mind. The creature flexed both its injured wings, rose off the ground, and pounced on Maeno to grab him with its claws. He rolled again and the Gorlock landed right on the spot where Maeno had just been lying.

He vaulted to his feet behind the Gorlock's shoulder, pulled his second blade from out of the Gorlock's body, rotated in a complete circle, and stepped up onto the Gorlock's wing while the creature was still crouched there close enough to the ground.

Maeno clambered up the Gorlock's back, hacked it one last time across the side of the neck, and sprang clear to land on the ground at a safe, fighting distance. The creature lunged for him again, but that last stroke had broken a blood vessel in the creature's neck.

Maeno circled, backed away, and kept a distance from the Gorlock while it stalked and hunted him down everywhere. The creature kept making lunges to snap him with its beak and rushes to grab him with its claws.

He always evaded. Blood saturated the creature's feathers all over. More blood kept gushing from the wounds in its neck and shoulder. The Gorlock couldn't survive much longer.

Maeno didn't try to engage again. He stayed in front of the Gorlock—just enough to keep it coming after him. He already knew he'd won.

The Gorlock's actions kept its blood pumping harder and faster than necessary. Its own efforts drained its blood more effectively than anything else Maeno could have done. The Gorlock started to weaken and missed its strokes more often.

He waited just long enough for the Gorlock to stumble once. It made another dive to snap its beak at him, missed its footing, and crashed down onto its stomach.

He sprang forward just as fast and delivered the killing stroke to the back of the Gorlock's head. Maeno hacked his blade down so hard that he embedded it all the way into the creature's skull. The skull cracked and the blade stuck there.

Maeno staggered away staring at the enormous body lying in a heap on the ground. He still didn't seem to be thinking clearly. He started to turn away, fell against the rock behind him, and gaped at the Gorlock like he couldn't remember how it got here.

Blackjack and his men moved in. They had to get Maeno away from here before the other Gorlocks smelled the blood and came around to investigate.

Blackjack hurtled out of the trees heading for his brother. Maeno's knees gave out and he slumped onto his seat still staring at the Gorlock in mindless disbelief.

Blackjack squatted in front of him. Maeno was almost as drenched in blood as the Gorlock. It was a miracle Maeno stayed on his feet as long as he did.

"You're hurt, little brother," Blackjack murmured. "I'll take you into the branches and get you cleaned up. You can't stay here. The other Gorlocks will find you."

Maeno didn't respond. He kept staring at the dead Gorlock even when Blackjack's body blocked Maeno from seeing.

The other men gathered behind Blackjack's back and stared down at Maeno in concern. "Did he get hit in the head or something?" Chief asked. "I didn't see that."

"He'll be all right," Blackjack replied. "He's just exhausted. Butcher the Gorlock and let's get away from the rock." He bent over and started to pick up Maeno. "Come on, little brother. I'll help you."

Maeno burst back to life instantly and pushed Blackjack away. "Wait a minute, Blackjack."

The men stood back and watched Maeno stagger to his feet. He stumbled over to the dead Gorlock and looked down at it for a second.

Then he cleaved his blade out of the creature's skull, carved a bunch of the sharpest feathers from the creature's wing, and hacked four enormous fangs from its mouth.

Maeno stared down at them and then glanced around at the other men. "Sorry," he mumbled. "I guess I kind of lost my mind there for a while."

Blackjack couldn't even bring himself to smile. He walked up to his brother and gripped his shoulder. "You did your Clan proud today. You're a brave, powerful man and your name is Bone. It's an honor to call you brother. Now come on. You're covered in blood and we don't need to fight another Gorlock today. We have enough meat."

Chapter 2

The men got busy sectioning the dead Gorlock and carried it off into the jungle away from the Gorlock's nesting rock. Blackjack stayed near Bone. He started out by walking straight. Then he started weaving and then staggered.

Blackjack got under his arm and supported his brother to a safe distance from the Gorlocks. Bone could barely walk at all by that point, so Blackjack lowered him to the ground near a stream buried deep in the jungle.

Bone didn't actually pass out, but he drifted in and out of a stupor for a while. Blackjack wound up carrying his brother to the stream and lowering him into the water to wash all the blood off him.

Blackjack even had to wash blood out of Bone's hair. The Gorlock's blood had splattered everywhere. The gashes on Bone's body were a lot worse than Blackjack initially realized. The other men gasped when they saw how deep the cuts went.

"He fought the Gorlock like that?!" Rebel exclaimed. "Those cuts would have killed another man!"

"You should have named him Slash or something like that," Reaper added. "He'll carry those scars with him for life."

"He'll carry them with pride." Blackjack pulled a bowl of leaf paste out of his bag. "My father will be very proud."

"He should be," Oracle returned. "Your family seems to favor initiation scars."

Blackjack laughed. "It does seem to be a kind of family tradition, doesn't it?"

"I better go gather some Gooji sap for him." Cyclops headed out of camp. "He's going to need it tonight."

The men built a fire and started cooking the Gorlock meat, but no one celebrated Bone's victory. The men kept it subdued while he recovered. He fell into a black sleep and didn't wake up.

He barely roused when Cyclops dumped gallons of Gooji juice down Bone's throat and then did it again six hours later at midnight.

The men stayed up talking about initiations, life in the valley, and all their shared adventures. Blackjack kept glancing over at Bone.

Blackjack wished now that Hangman and the other older men had been here to witness Bone's initiation. Hangman should have been here at least.

Blackjack understood why Hangman didn't come. He didn't want to cast doubt on Blackjack's leadership.

Blackjack and his father had talked at length about how things had gone down between Hangman and Shadow. Hangman didn't want to make the same mistakes Shadow had made.

Hangman didn't want to wait until he died before a new Kral took over. He would remain Kral until he did die, but he wanted Blackjack to start taking the lead in this band before that.

Bantam didn't have any sons and Lock had never married, so Blackjack would become Kral after his father unless something went disastrously wrong.

Blackjack could think of at least six older men in Hangman's party who would have been qualified to take over as Kral after him. All of them were young enough, strong enough, smart enough, and had enough authority to lead the band.

They all seemed to be of the same mind about letting the younger generation step up and grow into the older men's places. Neither they nor Hangman ever overruled Blackjack's decisions.

They discussed the band's situations in private, but they always supported Blackjack in everything.

The men woke up early the next morning and started packing up the meat to take back to the band. Bone didn't wake up until hours later.

He groaned and winced when he sat up. "You should have woken me up sooner," he croaked.

"You needed to sleep." Blackjack glanced down at his brother's injuries. "How do you feel?"

"Sore." Bone blinked and then stared into the fire. "It's over. I'm a man now."

"Yes, you are. You did very well yesterday. We're all proud of you."

Bone glanced around at the other men. They all stood around the fire staring at him. "I thought I would die," Bone murmured.

"You conquered. You fought a good fight and played it smart. Are you ready to take your kill back to the women?"

Bone nodded. He still seemed like part of him was somewhere else. Blackjack could understand that.

Bone didn't use his arms or upper body to stand up. His legs were fine.

He stopped when he picked up his weapons to tie them back onto his waistband. He studied the two blades. Blood had seeped into the bone and permanently stained the grain. It would stay like that forever.

"Maybe in time these blades will turn black with the blood of your enemies," Blackjack told him. "It's a perfect name for you."

Bone didn't answer. He took a long time before he brought his mind back to reality enough to tie on his blades and accompany the other men back to the camp. They carried the meat for him so he didn't have to.

Mora and Thena really did cry when the men came back and Blackjack announced Bone's new name to the band. The two women took turns hugging him, wailing over his injuries, and sobbing all over him until Blackjack pulled himself away from them.

Hangman even got tears in his eyes when he came forward to congratulate Bone. All the older men gathered to do the same thing. Then everyone sat down to cook, eat, and share Bone's kill.

He sat with his parents for a few hours, but he didn't talk much. In fact, he hardly talked at all and barely responded when anyone spoke to him. The older men treated him gently and didn't make a fuss over him.

He left in the afternoon and started building his own shelter across the camp near the other single men. He winced a lot when he used his arms, but he didn't stop until he finished the job.

Blackjack stayed with the men. The older men, younger men, and uninitiated boys all sat together while Blackjack and his friends told the story of Bone's fight against the Gorlock. The older men all exclaimed over his bravery, speed, and quick thinking.

He came back in the evening and sat with the men, but he still didn't engage them very much. He took out the Gorlock teeth and feathers and started fashioning them into weapons.

The feathers' long, razor-sharp edges made perfect blades. Kuvik gave Bone some tips on how to attach the feathers to long, curved pieces of carved, polished wood. The wood ran the length of the feather's spine to support it and make it stronger.

The Gorlock's teeth didn't have sharp edges. They came to recurved needle-sharp points. Bone studied them for a long time before he decided what to do with them.

He went out into the jungle alone without saying a word to anyone. Everyone in the camp fell silent when he came back carrying a young male Demonex. No one commented on Bone fighting this creature while he was still injured from his initiation.

He butchered the creature in front of everyone, skinned it, boned it, and started building tripods to dry the meat. No one understood why he did any of this until he took out the Demonex's thigh bone, scraped it clean, and fashioned it into a club.

He stayed up late into the night drilling holes in it and seating the six Gorlock fangs in the club head. They stuck out at angles that would impale his enemies when he hit them with the club.

He spent the rest of the evening preserving his kill and removing the Demonex's teeth. He handed them around to the other men to use as different weapons. They all thanked him profusely.

Blackjack stayed up and kept watch over Bone until he went back to his shelter alone. Mora gave him another dose of Gooji juice which he drank without any protest or complaint. He also didn't complain when Reaper applied another layer of leaf paste to Bone's injuries.

Blackjack followed Bone to his shelter. Bone didn't go inside right away. He stood outside looking up at the stars. "The world looks different now," he murmured. "I didn't think it would be this different."

"You're different," Blackjack remarked. "You're a different person. I've seen it before, but never as strikingly as with you. The boy really did die today. None of us knows who you are now except that you're a powerful man. You'll just have to start learning who you are the same as the rest of us will."

"It doesn't seem real," Bone murmured. "I remember it all, but it doesn't seem real. It seems like it happened to someone else. I felt like I was watching from somewhere else."

"It did happen to someone else. It happened to the boy who died."

Bone turned and stared up at him. "Was it like that for you?"

"Not during the fight. I was too focused on killing the thing. Things didn't start to change until afterward. Then I had to find out who I was just like you are now."

Bone shook his head. "You didn't change that much. I remember how you were before. You were like this before your initiation."

Blackjack looked away. "I guess so."

Bone looked around him like he didn't recognize where he was. "It's hard to believe I'll sleep here alone tonight."

"You're strong for building your own shelter and coming here immediately instead of staying over there with Mother and Father. Everyone respects you for it."

"I couldn't stay there!" Bone breathed. "Are you kidding? Thena wouldn't leave me alone."

Blackjack laughed and turned away to his own shelter. "You'll always be her little brother just as you'll always be mine. Try not to stay up too late thinking about it. You need sleep. I'll see you in the morning."

Blackjack went into his own shelter. Whatever Bone would go through to get used to being this new man, he would go through it alone. He had slept long and hard last night. He might not sleep at all tonight. He had too much on his mind.

Blackjack stretched out on his bed and found himself lying there awake with plenty on his own mind. He cast a glance around his shelter. He'd lived here alone ever since the band moved to the Angler Valley.

He wouldn't live here alone much longer. He would go to the gathering this year. The four valley bands didn't have any girls his age that he could marry, so he had to go south.

Rebel, Cyclops, and Cloud were all a year younger, so Blackjack would be the only person from the entire valley going to the gathering this year.

He would also be the first young person from the valley to go. The others had all paired off within the valley itself. They didn't have to leave.

He and his men had scouted the route south and established a much safer, quicker, more direct way to cover the distance. The journey should take a month in each direction.

Hangman had decided to take only the barest minimum of people to the gathering. Hangman, Mora, Thena, Bone, Bantam, Lock, and Viking would accompany Blackjack.

No one else would go. Any additional people would slow the band down and put everyone in danger. They might miss the gathering entirely and then Blackjack would be out of luck. No one wanted that.

He felt no nerves or panic or embarrassment or any other feeling of misgiving about going to the gathering. Some part of Blackjack's innermost gut told him that he would find a wife there. He wouldn't come back to this shelter alone.

Some part of him had always known he would get married. Maybe it was part of his gut feeling that he would become Kral of the band after Hangman.

A Kral needed a wife. Blackjack had always known he would get married and have a family of his own. He would raise his own sons in the band. It was inevitable.

He even sensed that his sons would become Kral after him. He didn't understand why or how he knew this. Maybe this band would get so big that it would have to split again.

All the valley bands kept growing as couples had children and the children grew up. Everyone needed more space. They would eventually leave the valley and go back out into the world. Maybe the other bands would take up residence in the surrounding valley systems.

Or maybe Blackjack would be the one to do that. Maybe he and some of his men would take their families to another valley and start a separate band while Bone and his family stayed here—or maybe Bone would never marry. Who knew what the future held?

Blackjack knew what the future held for him. He would be a husband, a father, a Godless warrior, and a Kral. He already was all those things. He just had to go get his wife, whoever she was.

He could imagine a lot of possibilities. She might be soft, retiring, quiet, and restrained. She might be brassy and exuberant. She might be tough, practical, and driven.

He would welcome her no matter who or what she was. She might even come from another Clan. He wouldn't care if she did. He wouldn't even have cared if she came from the Followers.

She would get a big surprise when she found out he could read and write as well as she could and that he knew so much of the Followers' information. This would be the perfect Godless band for a Follower girl to marry into if she couldn't marry another Follower.

Blackjack wound up drifting into fantasies about what it would be like to actually have a wife of his own. He couldn't think about that or he would drive himself crazy. He forced himself to roll over and go to sleep. The future would have to take care of itself.

Chapter 3

Blackjack squatted on a high rock overlooking the country to the south. He and his closest relatives had spent three weeks traveling south to the gathering grounds.

The journey had gone much quicker than anyone anticipated. The band had been able to take more time on the way, relax, and camp in certain protected spots.

Blackjack stared across the open country to the plateau in the distance. Tonight was the night. He would leave the gathering with a wife tonight. He found himself withdrawing from his family as the time got closer.

His family treated this as normal and didn't try to engage him. They kept their conversation casual. None of the married people in the party talked about their own experiences at the gathering.

Bone came out of the jungle behind Blackjack, advanced to the rock, and squatted down next to his brother. "Father says for you to come back," Bone announced. "It's time to go."

Blackjack only nodded, but he still lingered—not because he was nervous or reluctant. He only sensed himself approaching a window of time that would change his whole life. Tonight would be the most important night of his life.

Tonight would determine everything that happened after this. The wife he chose would affect every day and night of his life from now on.

He finally got to his feet. Bone stayed with him on their way back to camp. Everyone else was ready to go and waiting for the two brothers.

The band headed off to the plateau. Some of the others talked on the way. Blackjack didn't hear them. He went somewhere else—into that faraway future land where he already saw everything that would happen to him for years to come.

The band arrived at the gathering ground first. Viking, Bantam, and Lock built a fire in the middle of the plateau. The men had to travel a long way back to the jungle to gather enough wood to build it into a bonfire.

Blackjack's nerves really started kicking into high gear as the sun went down. No other bands came to gather. His relatives talked in low murmurs when they talked at all. What if his feeling turned out to be wrong and he didn't get a wife at all?

Another two hours passed before a band of Whisperers showed up. One of their older men approached the Godless. Hangman stood up to meet him.

"Are we the only ones here?" the other man asked.

"It looks like it," Hangman replied. "We've been here since mid-afternoon. No one else has come. I suppose we can just get started by ourselves. What do you say?"

The other man nodded and held out his hand. "My name is Manoso. What's yours?"

"Hangman," Hangman replied. "Who did you bring?"

Manoso jerked his thumb over his shoulder. "Just my daughter, Narina." He glanced over at Thena. "Is that your daughter? This must be the first time in history that any girls have come to the gathering and left without husbands."

"My daughter isn't of age," Hangman replied. "We brought my son, Blackjack. That's him there."

Manoso gave Blackjack a hard look. "He looks like a fine, strong man."

"He is," Hangman replied. "If your daughter and my son are the only two here, then there isn't a lot we have to do, is there?"

Manoso frowned and rubbed his chin. "I guess not. I guess we don't have to go through the whole process. Bring your son out and let's see him."

Hangman turned around and waved Blackjack forward. Manoso did the same thing and his daughter stepped forward.

Blackjack felt his worlds colliding when he stopped next to his father and the girl stopped next to her father. She and Blackjack leveled each other with a long, measuring stare.

She wasn't tall. She wasn't even as tall as her father and he was considerably shorter than Hangman. She had a very round, almost childlike face, but the hard cast of her eyes and the firm set of her features told a different story.

She had a strong, athletic build like she was used to hard work and even hunting in the jungle. She carried two long dagger-like blades tied in sheaths, one on each hip.

Blackjack liked her instantly. She looked more like a friend than his fantasy dream girl. She wasn't retiring, shy, brassy, or aggressive. She just looked friendly, practical, and straightforward—exactly the kind of woman he needed.

"Well, what do you have to say for yourself, young man?" Manoso demanded.

"Only that it's an honor to meet you and your daughter here," Blackjack replied. "I swear I'll do everything in my power to protect her and our family. I'll work to give her a good life and welcome her into our Clan as one of our own. I hope I can be worthy of both of you. I'll never stop working every day to build a family that you, your daughter, and your Clan can be proud of."

Manoso nodded. "Well spoken." He turned back to Hangman. "I guess we don't have to do anything else. We can go."

"Are you satisfied?" Hangman asked. "You can always bring your daughter back next year if you want to."

"I'm satisfied." Manoso turned to his daughter. "Are you satisfied?"

She nodded, made eye contact with him, and said, "Yes, Father." She had a soft, musical voice, but it didn't waver in the slightest. She said it smoothly like she had been preparing herself for a long time to marry a totally stranger.

Maybe she had been getting these gut feelings the same way Blackjack had. Maybe she already sensed that she would meet her husband here tonight. Maybe she got that sense just from looking at him—the way he got it from looking at her.

Her father hugged her and choked back tears. "I'll miss you, my precious child. I love you. Make your family and your Clan proud."

"I will, Father," she replied. "I love you. Take care of the family for me."

He tried to smile. Tears streaked down his cheeks. "Maybe we'll see you here again in future years."

"I hope so. I love you. Thank you for everything."

He kissed her on the cheek and pushed her forward. "Go on, then. Travel safely."

Manoso shook hands with Hangman and Blackjack. Everyone from both bands was already getting to their feet. That went so much more quickly than most gatherings.

Hangman and Blackjack escorted Narina back to the band. Blackjack didn't know how to act around her. He wanted to walk next to her, but he didn't want to crowd too close.

Mora and Thena moved in and started talking to Narina about everything.

"I'm Mora. I'm Blackjack's mother," Mora shook Narina's hand. "This is my daughter, Thena, and my son, Bone."

Narina only murmured, "It's nice to meet you."

Mora went around the circle introducing everyone else. Then she started telling Narina about the Angler Valley and everyone waiting for the band back there.

Narina remained silent. She didn't say anything for the rest of the evening. The band camped in the jungle on the way back north. They had a long way to travel.

Mora went to extra pains to find Narina a comfortable place to sleep that night, but she only said she was used to sleeping on the ground, curled up by the fire, and slept there.

Blackjack stayed awake again that night. He tried not to stare at her and eventually found a place for himself on the opposite side of the fire where she wouldn't think he was horning in on her.

He knew the story about his father completely turning his back on Mora during their first nights married to each other. Blackjack didn't want to do it that way, but he didn't want to parade his marriage in front of everyone else. He wanted to keep it special.

He would have enough time to deal with all of that on the journey north. He would find time to talk to Narina alone, get to know her, and get comfortable with her before they wound up getting close.

Chapter 4

Mora woke up the next morning and spotted her new daughter-in-law squatting across the camp. Narina and Thena worked together to butcher a Dushag. Bantam was busy untying one of his blades from a long branch, so he must have been the one who had killed the creature.

Narina and Thena chatted endlessly exchanging gossip about everyone in their respective bands. Mora got to her feet to go over there and join the conversation, but she stopped herself.

Mora had been building up such a huge expectation of what meeting her first daughter-in-law would be like. Narina was nothing like what Mora anticipated.

Mora expected a girl coming from another Clan to be uncertain and out of her depth. Narina worked effortlessly to butcher the Dushag, put the meat on the spit, build a tripod, and slice the meat to dry it.

She even laughed when she went around the camp serving the meat to all the men. She didn't shy away from approaching any of them or even smiling at them.

Blackjack sat off to one side watching her as closely as the others. She smiled at him, too, when she went over there to give him a bowl of the food. He thanked her and her eyes twinkled.

Narina served Mora the same as everyone else, but Narina was in the process of holding a lively conversation with Thena right at that moment. Narina barely responded when Mora thanked her.

Narina went back to the same fire, squatted down, and went on with her work. She was in the middle of telling Thena a funny story about Narina's older sister's husband's sister's baby.

The little one had been born with some kind of deformity that made him look strange. Narina described in detail how her sister-in-law had to modify her nursing technique to accommodate the baby. Both young women found this story intensely funny for some reason.

Mora sat back down and started eating the food that Narina had given her. Hangman stood off to one side talking to his brothers and Viking about something. That left Mora on her own.

She decided to leave Narina alone unless Narina needed help with something and specifically asked Mora to do something. Narina seemed perfectly capable of taking care of herself right now.

She and Thena talked the whole time they worked to dry the meat. Then they packed up and the band headed off north on the way home. Narina carried her share of the supplies. She traveled well and never once asked to stop. She didn't even break a sweat.

The band camped on the ground again that night. "Do you know how to travel through the trees?" Hangman asked her by the fire that night.

All the color drained from her face. "Uh...no. What does that mean?"

"I'll show you tomorrow. We can travel faster that way."

She gaped at him with her eyes hanging out of their sockets. "You travel....through the trees?"

"All the time," Bone added.

"It's easy," Thena interjected. "You'll learn in no time. It's much faster and safer than traveling on the ground."

Narina spun around to stare at Thena. "You know how to do it?!"

"Sure. We learn when we're children. It isn't hard. You just have to get used to it." Thena pointed at the supplies of dried food. "The men can carry your bundle until you get used to it. You'll pick it up and then you'll be fine."

Narina gulped. "I guess I....I guess I could try it."

"I had to learn, too," Mora interjected. "I came from the Follower Clan, so I had to learn a lot. Now I can do it easily. Things will be much easier for you."

Narina glanced back and forth between everyone in the party. "What else do I have to learn?"

"You seem to already know everything else," Hangman pointed out. "You seem to know everything about hunting and making camp. You should be fine with that."

"Everyone knows that, don't they?"

"Not everyone," Mora replied.

"How good are you at fighting your enemies?" Viking asked.

Narina shrugged. "I guess I'm as good as I can be for a girl my size."

"That's all you need," Hangman told her. "As long as you aren't helpless."

Mora shoved him. "Watch it."

Everyone laughed around the fire. Narina stared at them all and then her eyes locked on Blackjack across the fire. He laughed at the joke, too, and she caught him grinning. His eyes sparkled.

Narina stared at him extra hard. He didn't look away. He hadn't gone near her all day.

Mora sure hoped he and Narina would like each other. They would have to find a way to work together if they didn't. Mora didn't want that for him.

She would have liked to speed up time and get Blackjack and Narina to the point where they could appreciate each other the way Hangman and Mora did now.

Blackjack and Narina would just have to take their time and work it out for themselves. Mora had to step out of the process. It didn't concern her any longer.

Mora hardly saw Narina the next day. Thena and the men took it upon themselves to teach her how to travel through the treetops. The band split up Narina's supplies so she could travel hands-free.

She didn't have any shoulder bags and she didn't bring any possessions with her from the gathering. Mora used some extra pieces of hide from her bundle to start making Narina a collection of her own bags to carry her things.

She started out traveling extra slowly through the branches. Thena, Bone, Lock, and Bantam stayed near her, coached her, and encouraged her until she got the hang of it. She couldn't run as fast as the Godless, but she still traveled well.

She laughed and enjoyed herself while she took her first explorations through the canopy. She didn't complain or get scared. She showed no uncertainty about it at all.

She treated her own incompetence as a joke and made all the others laugh, too, including Blackjack even though he stayed out of it.

Mora felt herself getting shunted farther and farther into the background. She wasn't part of this. She didn't even feel like she could go near Narina without dampening the younger woman's enjoyment.

Mora didn't want Narina to think Mora was judging her, criticizing her, or calling anything she did into question. Mora didn't want that for Narina. Mora could only feel happy that Narina fit into the band so well.

The band camped in the treetops that night. Narina didn't make a squeak of complaint or even comment on eating dry food. She treated it as normal.

She only commented on how strange it felt to be sitting in the treetops so high above the ground and to think about sleeping here all night long.

Thena gave Narina a detailed description of all the places Narina could sleep to make herself more comfortable. Thena explained about sleeping in the cleft of tree trunks or pulling smaller branches together to make a nest.

Narina laughed herself silly over that. She compared the Godless to creatures and blushed when she remarked that she was one of them now. It was impossible not to like her.

Mora was really starting to wish now that she wasn't this young woman's mother-in-law. Their social positions created an unbridgeable gap between them. Mora would never be on those friendly terms with Narina—not for a long, long time at least.

Chapter 5

Blackjack raced through the canopy in a wide circle to surround his family's camp. The band traveled even faster on the way north than they did on the way south.

Narina was the only person who slowed the party down and she barely even did that anymore. She traveled much faster through the branches than anyone expected her to.

Her lively sense of humor had won over everyone in the band, especially Blackjack, but he still kept his distance. He sat, ate, and slept apart from her.

He didn't know how to approach her, but he had already made up his mind to do it when they would be alone together. He wouldn't do it in front of his family. He didn't even want his family to see him talking to her—not yet.

He circled the camp at a distance and met back up with Bone, Lock, and Bantam. "It feels strange to be traveling through country where we might encounter enemy Clans, doesn't it?" Lock remarked. "We're used to the valley."

"You spend too much time in the camp, Uncle," Bone countered. "We encounter enemy Clans outside the valley all the time."

Lock made a face. "*We* encounter enemy Clans outside the valley all the time, too, little brother. I meant it figuratively. We don't have to worry about enemy Clans coming near our women and children. They don't come near our camps the way they do here."

"The valley is making us all soft," Blackjack remarked. "We're Godless. We weren't built for safety."

"Why don't you leave the valley, then?" Bantam asked. "Why do you stay if you think it's so bad for us? I think it's the best thing that's ever happened to us."

"You're right. It is." Blackjack looked away. "It can't be a good thing, though, if our strongest warriors aren't used to thinking of their women and children in danger. It's unnatural for anyone to live that way, especially Godless warriors."

The four men set off back to the camp together, but they made multiple wide sweeps of the area just to make sure no enemy Clans snuck up on the party.

They were on their way back when they encountered Hangman and Viking down on the jungle floor. Viking sat on the ground with blood streaming down his arm.

"A Krakelow attacked us," Hangman explained. "We got away, but one of the segments stuck to Viking's arm. I cut the segment off, but we need one of you to go gather some Gooji sap while we clean this up and I take him into the treetops."

"I'll go get it," Blackjack offered and jumped up into the branches. He had to travel a long way before he found any Gooji trees. He scraped the sap off into a folded piece of hide from one of his bags.

He was just turning away when Narina came up to him. She grinned a huge, bright, cheery grin. "Hi. You're Blackjack, aren't you?"

"You know I am. Why are you so far away from the camp? You shouldn't be out here alone."

"Mora cut herself. I said I would come out and get her some Gooji sap." She practically elbowed Blackjack out of the way. "I didn't know you were going to be here."

"I should take you back to the band. I don't like you being out here alone."

She beamed up at him. "Are you protecting me?"

"Of course," he countered. "What did you think I would do—leave you unguarded?"

She smirked again and turned back to the sap. She scraped it off the bark with her knife, but she scraped it into her hand.

"Here. Put it in here." He held out his folded piece of hide. "We can take it back for both her and Viking."

Her eyes popped. "Viking got hurt?"

"He got a Krakelow segment stuck to his arm." Blackjack studied her and made up his mind in a heartbeat. He probably wouldn't get a better chance than now to talk to her alone. "You're doing well moving through the branches. I feared the worst when I got a wife from another Clan."

She burst out laughing and started following him back toward the rest of the band. "Why is your territory so far away?"

"My father led us north to a valley that no one can get into or out of. It's totally defensible. We just had to get rid of the Anglers to make the valley safe to live in. Now we have to leave the valley to find other enemy Clans invading our territory."

"That sounds amazing," she breathed. "What's an Angler?"

He took a deep breath and made another snap decision. He pulled her down onto the branch next to him. "It's a long story. Sit down here and I'll tell you."

He told her the whole story. That led to another long story about the conflict between Shadow and Hangman, the incident that had led to Hammer's band leaving, and even the whole journey from Renegade country to the northern mountains and back south to rendezvous with Shadow's band.

Narina gasped and exclaimed through the whole tale. She couldn't get enough of it. Her enthusiasm and attention loosened Blackjack's lips. He told her all about the band's campaign to exterminate the Anglers and more about the war against the Red Riders.

She nodded at the end. "We have Red Riders in my father's territory."

"You might think we're cowards for laying ambushes for them, but it sure beats watching our families butchered and carried off into captivity."

"I don't think you're cowards at all. It's really smart. I wish I could tell my father about that. He could really use that information. How did you find out about it?"

"My mother came from the Follower Clan like she told you. She learned ancient ways and she taught us." He hesitated for a second and then blurted out. "She taught us how to read and write, too."

Narina's jaw dropped. She had exceptionally big, bright, deep, soft eyes. Blackjack felt himself falling for her. "You know how?!" she gasped. "Could you teach me? I would love to learn."

"You actually want to?!" Blackjack countered. "I didn't think the Whisperers were interested in that."

"We aren't—but I've always wanted to learn. A Follower woman married into our band. She knew how, but the others never thought much of it. They never thought to ask her about Follower ways." She looked away. "I wish we had."

"I'll teach you if you want me to. It isn't hard." Blackjack pulled out one of the tooth blades Kuvik had given him at his initiation. Blackjack scratched the tree bark next to his leg. "This is the letter A. It makes the sound—ahhh."

She blinked at it and then burst out laughing. "Aahhh!"

Blackjack laughed with her. She made it infectiously impossible not to laugh at her constant jokes. "Practice that for a week and I'll teach you the next one."

She blushed and grinned at him. Then she looked down at the weapon in his hand. "This is so interesting." She grabbed his hand and turned it over and over so she could examine the blade from all sides. "It's a Demonex tooth, isn't it?"

Blackjack experienced a rush of heat to his guts when he felt her touching his hand. He had to fight himself to stay calm. Was she trying to get close to him by acting so familiar with him? He was trying to get close to her, so why not let it happen?

"I killed the Demonex for my initiation. Kuvik made the took into a weapon."

"Whose Kuvik? I thought all the men of your Clan took other names?"

He launched into Kuvik's story and finished by explaining why none of the Godless used Kuvik's real name.

Narina stared up into Blackjack's eyes through the whole story. He became aware of her studying him at close range. They were married now. She was his wife. Why did he hold back?

He stopped talking at the end of the story. She didn't pick it up by asking another question or making a joke. They wound up staring into each other's eyes for a minute.

He threw caution to the wind and leaned in to kiss her. She must have been expecting it because she kissed him back. That kiss built to a deep, hot torrent of smoky passion. He didn't stop it or slow it down and neither did she.

He wrapped his arms around her and lifted her onto his lap. He planned to sit her sideways on his lap, but she twisted around, straddled him, and wrapped herself around him. She didn't shy away from it at all.

Her whole body quivered in his arms. He sank into kissing her as deep and hard as he possibly could. He didn't plan to take her all the way—not right now—but he felt himself starting to lose control with her the longer this went on.

She threw herself at him just as hard. Her mouth opened and his brain exploded when their tongues met. Her breasts compressed against his chest through her top. He had to hold himself back from tearing her clothes off right this minute.

He opened his eyes at the same moment when hers floated open right in front of them. They stared deep into each other's eyes while they kissed.

She suddenly pulled off his mouth and burst out laughing. She turned bright pink. "I was so scared!!" she exclaimed.

"You were? You didn't act scared."

She blushed, lowered her eyelashes, and waved that away. Her loose hair swam all around her angelic face when she smiled like that. "I thought you would be an ogre or maybe a scrawny weakling. I thought I might get stuck with someone I didn't like."

He found himself stroking her cheeks and running his fingers through her hair. "I like you."

She got serious and gazed deep into his eyes. Her expression overflowed with passion, desire, and deep, heart connection. He had never expected to feel this way about anyone.

"I like you, too," she whispered. "I like you a lot."

They both fell into a much deeper, more connected swoon of kissing. He held her tighter. She was all his. He would never let her go—not ever.

He felt his body running away with him again. He wanted her right now and he felt that she wanted him, too. He could take her right now if he wanted to.

Just thinking that made him stop and pull back, but he couldn't stop stroking her face, neck, arms, and rubbing her back. She mesmerized him with her beauty except that this was unlike any beauty he'd ever seen in any woman.

She wasn't as strictly beautiful as some women he'd seen. Her beauty came from the inside. Her personality made her irresistible to him. He already felt himself loving her. Thank the stars in Heaven he hadn't gotten stuck with someone else.

"I want to take you home," he murmured and dove in to steal one more kiss. "I don't want to do it here or in front of the band or anything like that. I want to take you home where we can be alone in our own shelter. I don't want you to think I don't want to because I do. I want that more than anything, but I want it to be private between us."

"I want that, too," she breathed. "I was so worried about what it would be like between us, but I'm not worried about it anymore."

"We can slip off on the way home if we want to be alone together. I just don't want to take it any further than this—not until we can do it in private. I don't want to do it out here."

Her face pinched for the first time. That was the first sign of distress he'd ever seen from her. "Thank you!" she choked. "I thought I would have to do it with you that first night in front of everyone."

"I would never do that to you. You're too important to me."

She sank into him, but he couldn't even kiss her. He just held her in his arms and felt her near him. This turned out to be so much better than he ever dreamed.

He eventually pushed her back. "You're going to be just fine in our Clan. Everyone in the family already loves you. You have nothing to worry about."

"What about your mother? My mother told me a bunch of horror stories about the way her mother-in-law treated her when she first came to live in our band."

"My mother would only ever try to help you. If she keeps her distance, it's because she sees you spending so much time with Thena and my mother doesn't want to intrude. My mother is one of the nicest people alive. She would only want to help another young woman who had to leave her Clan and go live with strangers. My mother went through that. You should go to her if you have any problems at all. She's smart and kind. She'll help you."

Narina nodded, but he saw her starting to lose her grip on her emotions. She had never shown anyone before that coming to a new Clan bothered her at all. Was that just her way of covering up how nervous and uncertain she really was?

He hugged her close for another minute. "Everything is going to be all right," he breathed into her hair. "We'll be home soon and then you can settle into our own house. No one will bother you. Everyone in our band is really nice. They welcome outsiders."

"Thank you." She kissed him on the neck. That sensation shot a lightning bolt into his brain. He couldn't stay here with her—not without losing control.

He picked her up, stood her on her feet, and kissed her a few more times just because. "We're going to be doing a lot of that in future years," he told her. "I just want you to know."

She laughed. "We should probably get back. The others are probably waiting for the sap."

They set off through the canopy together. No one paid any attention when Blackjack and Narina showed up together and he delivered two portions of Gooji sap out of one package.

She sat next to him that night and she didn't joke around the way she had been these last few days. The men talked about the strategic situation back in the valley. She and Blackjack both listened without interjecting anything.

The band stayed up late around the fire until Viking and Mora both got enough Gooji juice. Everyone slept around the fire. Blackjack and Narina stretched out next to each other on the ground.

He turned on his side facing her and she did the same thing so she faced him. He stared deep into her eyes and remembered everything that had passed between them today.

This was his wife—the mother of his children—the mother of generations. She was so perfect. He couldn't imagine a better wife. He put his hand out in front of her and she took it. They laced their fingers together.

This was it. It was happening. His vision was coming true in front of his eyes. She was right here in front of him.

He could almost imagine her as an old woman—a grandmother or even a great-grandmother of dozens of families. He could almost imagine that they had lived together for decades and seen the worst of everything together—and they still loved each other for it.

The electric warmth coming from her hand spread to the rest of his body. He really wanted to kiss her right now and pull her into his arms, but he wouldn't do that in front of his family.

Everyone could see them holding hands and lying close like this. That was enough—for now.

He would have no problem doing it once they got behind closed doors in their own shelter. Then he would explore all there was to explore about her. Nothing would hold him back then.

Chapter 6

The band woke up early the next morning—or at least Mora did. The very first thing she saw when she got up was Blackjack and Narina lying on the ground next to each other. They were both asleep, but they still held hands in their sleep the way they did last night.

She found herself smiling at them. They were going to be just fine. Mora had never doubted it, but the sight still made her wistful. At least Blackjack and Narina didn't have to go through the nightmare that Mora and Hangman had to go through.

The noise of everyone else waking up woke up Blackjack and Narina in a minute. Everyone pretended not to notice them holding hands and sleeping next to each other. They broke apart immediately and went to work doing things separately.

Narina came over to Mora and Thena to help them tie up their bundles of supplies. Narina smiled at Mora once and looked away.

Mora read so much in that one brief smile. It wasn't the fake smile of a much younger woman who thinks she needs to placate her mother-in-law with false manners. Narina actually looked embarrassed about smiling at Mora at all.

Mora understood everything in that instant. Narina must have felt nervous about getting along with Mora. Narina must have come to the gathering expecting her new mother-in-law to make life hard for her.

Mora really hoped Blackjack had been reassuring Narina about that. He must have been if she made an overture like smiling at Mora for the first time. Maybe there was hope for the two women after all.

Blackjack and Narina traveled together when the band set off through the canopy again. The two of them stayed near each other when the party came to open country pretty soon and had to descend to the ground.

Hangman didn't suggest that they return to the treetops once the band came to the next patch of jungle. The band traveled on the ground for a while. No one talked. Everyone drifted with their own thoughts.

The men split off two at a time to scout the area, but they always came back reporting that the territory was clear of enemy Clans. The band had the area to themselves.

The party took a break at a stream crossing to get a drink of water. "This country is as empty as the northern mountains," Hangman remarked. "What do you make of so few bands coming to the gathering?"

"It was like this two years ago when my sister went to the gathering," Narina piped up. "She married a man from our own band, so they didn't have to do anything. They just went home together, but there was only one other band there that time, too. They brought one young man. He had to leave alone. My sister was the only girl there."

Hangman frowned. "I wonder what's happening. I'm used to the valley where we have too many people."

"You'll have to spread the word that the south country is empty," Viking suggested. "Maybe we can send a scouting party down here and find out whose territory this is. It might be up for grabs—and the enemy Clans aren't around."

"I might have to do that."

The band moved out and everyone fell into another thoughtful silence. Mora found herself looking around at the terrain. The Followers lived south of the gathering grounds. Were the Followers even still there? Was her family band still there?

The enemy Clans might have wiped her family out and then moved on. The Renegades, Bounty Hunters, and Red Riders didn't stick around where they couldn't take captives and loot their victims' goods.

The enemy Clans wouldn't stay in any country where they couldn't find enough people to attack. The enemy Clans would have moved on, too. That would leave the territory relatively safe—from them at least.

Almost as if her thoughts made it happen, a Krakelow dropped from the treetops right then. The creature couldn't have been trying to attack the party. The Krakelow would have landed on top of one or more of the Godless if it really wanted to.

It landed on the ground a dozen yards in front of the party—and then five more fell out of the canopy and landed right next to the first. All the men lunged forward to protect the band from danger.

The men really lunged forward to protect the three women. They were the only people here to protect. Blackjack pivoted in front of Narina and pulled both his axes—and just in time.

The Krakelows sensed movement, burst into dozens of segments as soon as they hit the ground, and the segments flew at the Godless. The men had to slash their weapons everywhere to protect themselves from flying segments.

One extra long segment hit Hangman in the leg and wrapped itself around his thigh and knee, but he was fighting all the other segments too fast to get it off. He roared in pain as it sank into his flesh.

Mora tried to move forward, but another three Krakelows landed on the ground behind the party right then. These didn't divide. They coiled themselves off the ground and hurled themselves at the women.

Mora spun around, yanked her blades, and slashed one of the Krakelows in half, but that only doubled the number of segments flying around.

She didn't have time to hit another Krakelow flying straight at Narina. Narina pulled both her daggers, but she wouldn't be able to defend herself with those.

Mora took a flying leap and tackled Narina out of the way just as Blackjack pivoted out of the group of men and chopped the Krakelow to the ground with one blow of his axe. The creature shattered into dozens of segments.

He hit it close enough to Narina's face for one of the segments to land on her arm. She screeched in pain as the thing sank its hooks into her flesh.

Mora landed hard on top of Narina, scrambled upright, and wound up straddling her. Mora seized the segment with her bare hand and Narina screamed again when Mora ripped the segment off.

The segment immediately strapped itself around Mora's forearm. She yelled out as the thing sank into her arm next. She raised her blade and used the sharp edge to scrape the segment off, but not fast enough to stop the bleeding.

Another segment hit her in the back just then. She scrambled to get off of Narina in time. "Get up!" Mora practically bellowed. "Hurry! Get up!"

She pulled Narina to her feet and pushed her behind her to get Narina away from the Krakelows. Thena wound up on that side of the fight, too. All three women faced the chaos with drawn weapons.

Thena rushed up behind Mora and used another blade to scrap the segment off. The thing had latched onto Mora's top. It didn't eat through it that fast to harm her.

The women all pivoted into line together and backed away from what looked like dozens of Krakelows attacking the men. Almost all the men were bleeding. Segments flew thick and fast.

The women got separated from the others, but not far enough to protect the women from the danger. One of the Krakelows came whipping toward the women again only to get cut down by Bone.

Mora backed Thena and Narina away. "Get into the branches!" Mora yelled over her shoulder. "Climb up! Hurry!"

Thena climbed up and helped Narina scramble up there, too. Mora stayed on the ground. Hangman saw the women retreat. "Get out of here!" he bellowed. "Take them up to the treetops—now!"

Mora didn't stick around to hear any more or even to sheath her blades. She clambered into the branches and met up with the two younger women at a safe distance where they could see the men fighting.

Most of them had Krakelow segments stuck to them. The men all still fought tooth and nail to get themselves out of the area.

Mora forced herself to look away. She turned to face Narina. "You're bleeding," Mora rasped. "We need to get you cleaned up."

Narina's features convulsed. "Will they be all right?"

"We can't help them if they aren't." Mora sat down, took down her bundle, and used a water gourd to clean the blood off Narina's shoulder. "We'll put leaf paste on it now and get you some Gooji sap later. The men will need it as soon as they finish....."

She broke off when the noise died down on the ground. The men had fought their way to one side of the battle, but the Krakelows didn't back off. They came after the men and would have probably killed every last Godless man present.

One of the Krakelows accidentally hit a tree trunk nearby and shattered it to spill countless Abnormits onto the ground. The men sprang into the branches to save themselves, but not without getting a bunch of Abnormit grubs attached to their bodies into the bargain.

The noise of battle died down. The men didn't climb up to join the women. The men stayed near the ground to tend their own wounded.

"You see? Blackjack is all right. He's probably injured, but he'll heal along with the others." Mora turned to Thena. "You're the only one unhurt, my love. You go into the canopy and get enough Gooji sap for all of us. Bring a lot."

Thena murmured, "Yes, Mother," and headed out into the thick foliage.

Mora turned back to Narina. "You saved my life!" Narina choked. "I thought you were going to be horrible to me!"

Mora found herself chuckling. "You should have met my mother-in-law."

Narina's eyes widened. "Was she horrible to you?"

"She was extremely hard on me and she was extremely insulting—but I wasn't like you. I was helpless. I couldn't do anything for myself and I had a terrible attitude toward the Godless. She had to be hard on me to teach me how to fight and make me stronger. She saved my life in other ways. She taught me what I needed to know to become Godless—but you don't need any of that. You're fine the way you are."

Narina looked away and flinched when Mora put leaf paste on the younger woman's shoulder. Mora sat down on the same branch and grimaced at her own arm. "Now let's see about this."

"Let me do it!" Narina grabbed the water gourd out of Mora's hand. "I want to."

Mora started to smile at her and then gasped when Narina poured water over the wound. Mora tried not to whine and moan so much while Narina cleaned the wound and then put leaf paste on it.

"We should go down and see if the men need help," Mora suggested. "I'm sure they do."

"Let me check your back first." Narina stood up on the branch and moved behind Mora. The Krakelow segment had torn the hide of Mora's top, but that was it.

The women climbed down the branches and met up with the men. They did need help—a lot of help. Almost all of them had both Krakelow segments and Abnormit grubs attached to them.

Hangman wouldn't let any of the men take any of the segments or grubs off. That would make the men bleed too much. He ordered everyone to move a long way away from the spot before they did anything.

Bone, Lock, and Viking were both too injured to walk. Hangman wasn't much better off. Bantam supported Lock. Mora did her best to support Hangman.

Blackjack had a segment wrapped around his upper arm and multiple grubs attached to his legs, but none of the others were able-bodied enough to support Viking, so Blackjack and Narina had to do it together.

They got on either side of him and almost had to carry him through the treetops. They only made it a short distance before they cleared far enough away from the Abnormits.

The whole band collapsed by a stream. Mora got to work on the men starting with Viking. Narina started working on Lock.

Hangman had to drag himself over to Bone. Bone writhed and bellowed through gritted teeth while Hangman carved the segments and grubs out of Bone's legs. Viking passed out completely while Mora did the same thing to him.

Hangman killed all the grubs and chopped the segments into pieces too small for them to reattach.

Then he dragged Bone down to the stream, submerged him to wash off all the blood, smeared leaf paste on his wounds, and hefted him over his shoulder to carry him up into the branches.

"How is he?" Mora asked when Hangman came back down.

"He's unconscious. He needs Gooji juice—badly."

Mora glanced down at Hangman's leg. "Sit down before you fall over."

Hangman sat down. "Finish working on Viking first."

"I'll need some of you to help me move him. I can't lift him by myself."

"I'll do it." Blackjack dragged himself to his feet.

He had been sitting off to one side shaking like a leaf. No one could help him, Bantam, or Hangman until they treated the most serious, life-threatening injuries first.

It took Blackjack, Bantam, and Hangman all working together to move Viking even though all three men were almost as severely injured as he was. They washed the blood off him, sealed his wounds with leaf paste, and carried him into the branches.

Hangman insisted that Mora treat Bantam first, so she did. Narina started working on Blackjack. Mora didn't dare to look in their direction. She didn't want to know how bad Blackjack's injuries were.

Bantam remained conscious through the whole agonizing ordeal of digging the grubs and segments out of him. He washed himself off, put leaf paste on his own injuries, and climbed up into the branches to watch over his injured relatives.

Hangman stayed conscious, too. Mora got sick to her stomach when she saw how bad his leg was under that segment. It was a miracle he could still walk at all.

Thena came back while Mora and Narina were still working on the last two men. Thena took one look at her father and brother, built a fire, and stayed on the ground alone to brew Gooji juice for the whole band.

Hangman cleaned himself up and vanished into the branches. Mora almost followed him, but Blackjack passed out just then. She stayed to help Narina carry Blackjack down to the stream and clean him up.

They had to get Hangman and Bantam to help carry Blackjack up to the branches. Then Mora and Narina went back down to the ground to help Thena. "How bad is it?" she asked.

"It's about as bad as it can be," Mora replied. "We won't be going anywhere for a while. You better go out there and get another load of sap before it gets too dark. Narina and I will keep an eye on things here until you come back."

Thena only nodded and left. Mora and Narina settled down by the fire to heat the rocks and boil the juice from the sap Thena had already brought. The two women wound up sitting down together and eating while they waited.

"You're nothing like what I expected," Narina remarked without warning.

"What did you think I was going to be like?" Mora asked.

"I don't know. I guess I thought Godless women would be hard and tough and unfeeling. I didn't expect you to be so caring—toward everyone."

"Well, these men are my family, aren't they? They're my husband and sons and brothers-in-law and Viking is their cousin. Besides, Godless women can be hard and tough and still caring. They don't cancel each other out."

"I don't know," Narina went on. "I thought you would be snapping orders and telling me what to do all the time." She shook her head. "I don't know what I thought. I mean—I do, but it was nothing like this."

Mora frowned at her. "Just remember that I'm not Godless."

"You are!" Narina exclaimed. "You're as Godless as any of the men. I saw you around the Krakelows. You were amazing."

Mora made a face. "I'm just trying to say alive out here like everyone else. We all would have been dead without the men. They're the ones who protected us while we ran away and left them in danger."

"But your own husband told you to. He told you to take me and Thena into the treetops—and he is your Kral, isn't he? It isn't like you could disobey."

"I don't know what I am anymore," Mora murmured. "We've all been through so much. Maybe none of us are really Godless anymore. Anyway, I couldn't see these men in pain or in danger without trying to help them. We've seen it all."

"Blackjack told me about all your travels together," Narina replied. "It's an amazing story. It doesn't seem possible that anyone could survive all of that."

Mora looked up. "He told you all of that?"

Narina nodded. "It's such an honor to be a part of this band. You're all so.....so much more than I ever thought people could be."

Mora looked away. "We aren't anything special. We've been through a lot, but we only did what anyone else would have done in the same situation. We just did our best to survive."

"I hope I can do your band justice. I hope I can do Blackjack justice—for all of you."

Mora smiled at her. "I'm sure you will. I have absolutely no doubt of that. You're a credit to this Clan already. You have nothing to worry about."

Chapter 7

Hangman glanced around at his closest relatives. None of them was uninjured except for Thena. The men had been hiding out in the branches for three days drinking one dose of Gooji sap after another. None of them was much improved for the rest they'd gotten.

At least they were all conscious—for whatever that was worth. He didn't like to think about what it would be like for them all to start traveling again.

The three women had been doing all the work. They'd been down on the ground alone and unprotected brewing tons of Gooji juice and even hunting for themselves and the men.

The women kept climbing up to deliver food, water, and Gooji juice to the men so the men didn't have to move. That time was rapidly coming to an end.

All the men sat up and he read the same truth in their eyes. The party had been sitting in one place for too long already.

At least Hangman didn't have to worry about Mora and Thena getting along with Narina. The three of them talked together around the fire. Mora and Narina tended each other's wounds. They got along as though they'd known each other all their lives.

The three women worked down there right now, but they climbed up pretty soon. The party sat around eating the last of their food.

Someone would have to go hunting again soon and it sure as hell wouldn't be any of the men. Most of them could barely move at all.

Hangman finally struggled to his feet. Everyone else got moving without a word of complaint, but the men still gasped and flinched a lot when they tried to move their limbs.

They took a long, long time to lower themselves to the ground. Then the men set off limping extra slowly through the jungle. No one could move faster than that.

It never once crossed Hangman's mind to hurry his people any faster. They would be lucky to make it back to the Angler Valley within the next month. The men would have to move if anything else attacked them.

Mora and Narina left together sometime in the middle of the day. They returned with the joints of a full-grown male Gurlg. Hangman called a halt and the party camped right there on the ground.

The three women did all the work of cutting up the creature, feeding the men, and drying the rest of the food. The party had only walked half the day and they stayed there on that spot for another three.

The journey improved after that, but no one suggested traveling through the branches. No one wanted to move very much or very fast.

"Why do you think there were so many Krakelows on that one spot?" Viking asked one evening.

"They might have been nesting there," Blackjack suggested. "They obviously weren't trying to attack us—not at first. They just fell out of the trees by accident. That's what it looked like to me."

"I agree with you, little brother," Bantam agreed. "They only attacked after we surprised them."

"I think it's more interesting that we're the only people in this country," Bone added. "The Red Riders were in the south. If they aren't here, then they aren't here to travel north to the Angler Valley."

"That's a little too much to ask, isn't it?" Lock asked. "They've been coming around the Angler Valley for four years straight. They won't stop now."

"They might have come from the south initially, but they come from the west now," Blackjack pointed out. "We run enough scouts on the west side. We would know if the Red Riders stopped coming."

"It's nice to know there's an end to them somewhere," Mora pointed out. "It's nice to know they aren't absolutely everywhere."

"It sure felt that way for a while, didn't it?" Viking mused. "I thought for a while that we would never get rid of them."

"Maybe if we kill enough of them they'll get the message that being a Red Rider or any other marauder Clan isn't a good idea," Hangman suggested.

"We would have to wage a much wider campaign against them if we did that," Blackjack replied. "We would have to launch one of our overwhelming attacks on a much larger band or maybe even their territory itself."

Hangman stared into the fire. "Maybe we should."

"I sure hope it isn't like this when I go to the gathering," Thena remarked. "The Krakelow and Abnormit attack, I mean—not there being no enemy Clans around."

"Why don't you find a man in the valley?" Blackjack suggested.

"There aren't any," she pointed out. "None my age, at least."

"Ask Father to keep you in the valley until one of them comes of age," Bone suggested.

Thena sneered at him. "Are you out of your mind? The nearest boys are more than five years younger than I am. I would be old and grey by the time they came of age."

"I'm sure you'll find someone," Hangman told her. "Look at how fast we got to the gathering this time. This Krakelow attack was just a fluke."

"We could be the only band there next time," Thena countered. "Maybe no one will come and I'll have to go home alone."

"Then you'll go back the following year," Blackjack told her. "You'll keep going back until you find someone."

"That's easy for you to say when you're sitting right here with your wife," Thena fired back. "What if no one is ever there again? What if this whole country emptied out and I never find anyone?"

"Then you'll marry one of the men from the other valley bands when they get old enough," Hangman told her. "I'm sure it won't make that much difference once you all come of age. You won't be marrying a thirteen-year-old boy—or you might wait even longer than that. You'll find someone eventually—or you might marry one of the older single men. It isn't as though the country is completely devoid of men."

"Practically," Thena grumbled. "You saw what it was like at the gathering this year. Blackjack was the only man there—and you heard what Narina said about when her sister got married. Her husband was the only man there and the other girl had to go home alone."

"Actually, I said the other person was a man," Narina interrupted. "*He* went home alone—which isn't unusual. There have been years in the past where only three people went to the gathering and two paired off and the other one left alone—and I've even attended gatherings where all three of the young people were men and they all went home alone."

"I've seen that, too," Viking replied.

"Let's not start thinking about the worst that can happen," Hang-man told Thena. "Heaven knows we have enough problems without coming up with new ones."

Chapter 8

Blackjack limped down to the stream, squatted there, and very delicately and carefully scooped some water onto the wounds on his legs, side, and arm. They hurt like anything, but at least he could walk—barely.

This journey was taking forever, but he didn't give himself the option to complain. The other men were just as bad if not worse.

At least the three women were okay. Mora and Narina kept working as though they weren't injured at all. They had gotten off much more lightly than the men—thank God.

He was still squatting there when Narina came down to the stream and squatted down next to him. She smiled at him. "How are you feeling?" she asked.

"I feel much better now that you're here." He put his arm around her shoulders and kissed her for a long time. "I miss you."

She laughed at him. "I'm right here. I've been here the whole time."

"I miss being with you. I miss holding you and kissing you—like we are now."

She blushed. "You said you wanted to wait."

"I said I wanted to wait before we did anything. I didn't say I wanted to wait on kissing you and holding you. You don't sleep near me anymore."

"I can't sleep near you when we sleep in the branches. It isn't like we could do anything there—and you were too hurt and out of it even to know if I was there."

He shrugged. "It isn't because I don't want to."

She opened her mouth to say something, but he silenced her by kissing her again. She sank into that kiss. All the energy between them came back with a vengeance. Getting hurt didn't change that.

She blushed and looked away when their lips parted. She looked so intoxicating when she blushed like that. He loved seeing her all vulnerable and unguarded like this.

She turned back to the stream and got busy filling the water gourds she'd brought. "You might not be ready to do anything even after we get back," she suggested over her shoulder. "You might be bedridden for months."

Those words set off a chain reaction in him. He grabbed her arm, spun her around, and in that moment, all his restraint evaporated. He was already married to her and they were alone out here with no one around.

He pulled her in and steered her onto his lap to straddle him the way she did before. He mauled her mouth and pawed all over her body. He grabbed her breasts and thighs, and in one last burst of desperation, he pulled the ties on her loincloth.

He had to lift her to move it out of the way and he tore off his own loincloth at the same time. He kept kissing her through it all right up until the moment when he sat her back down on top of him and slid all the way in.

They both gasped in torrential shock when their bodies met like that—and then the rhythm took over. Her squeals in his ear rose to shrieks and screams. That sound set off his primal madness.

He crushed her into his stroke, buried his face in her neck, and felt himself biting her like an animal. She surged in his arms, but she didn't fight him. She touched him all over and even gripped some of his injuries.

The energy spiked off the charts and then she let out one high-pitched wailing scream in his ear. She didn't sound like she was in pain. He didn't recognize that sound, but it detonated the last shred of his defenses.

He exploded into her in a rush of heat and mind-blowing pleasure. He buried his mouth in her neck to silence feral roars and snarls. He wanted to devour her—and then it was over as quickly as it had begun.

Neither of them let go. They both clung to each other in the calm after the storm. Sweat drenched both of them and they gasped and panted in each other's ears. Blackjack couldn't let go of her to save his life. Thank God she didn't want to let go of him, either.

He took a long time before he could bring himself to relax his arms, but he didn't pull her off. She stayed where she was straddling him with his flesh still buried deep inside her. He didn't want to be anywhere else.

Her hand flew to his hair and she hugged him tighter. He clamped his arms around her and she did the same thing.

They both finally eased off at the same time and looked up to stare into each other's eyes.

Blackjack's mind felt dizzy. He had to focus extra hard on her eyes. She glowed with some kind of inner light. Her eyes looked especially big, deep, soft, and magnetically inviting.

She didn't laugh, blush, joke, or even say anything. She hovered there in front of his eyes. Overwhelming emotion flooded him for her. His wife. She was his wife. His hands migrated to her face and hair. He couldn't stop touching her. God, she was so beautiful!

She finally passed her hand across her eyes. She looked like she was having trouble focusing, too.

"Are you okay?" he whispered and became aware that he was still inside her.

She nodded. "That was.....that was not what I expected."

"What did you expect?"

She shrugged. "I'm not sure."

He leaned in and kissed her—and that kiss led to another unstoppable wave of overpowering energy building up between them. He kissed her harder, crushed her in deeper, and felt her matching his rhythm to slam herself down on top of him.

Both of them kept their eyes open this time. Blackjack couldn't yell out, not even when the cataclysm hit him the second time. He could only gasp and stare into the forgotten depths of her soul.

Had he known her all this time? Had she been with him all this time? Had she just been invisible so he couldn't see her—or maybe he *could* see her? Maybe she was there in his visions and she was the one he'd been dreaming about all these years.

She panted into his mouth while they kissed. Her body rocked and quaked in his arms. Her vision kept blurring when she lost focus and swooned in delirious bliss. Then she locked on him with brutal power and spiraled his desire for her out of this world.

He couldn't stop until they both released and sank back into each other all over again.

He pulled her back and stretched out on the ground with her on top of him. She tried to pull away. "Am I hurting you?"

He pulled her right back down. "Don't even think about going anywhere."

She laughed at him then. "You said you wanted to wait."

"I changed my mind based on new strategic information. I can do that, you know."

She giggled, broke out of his arms, and sat up still straddling him. "Don't you think we should go back to your family?"

"No." He grabbed her thighs and pulled her in again. "Not for a long, long time."

She laughed again and jumped all the way off him. She scampered away, grabbed her loincloth, raced down to the stream to wash herself off, and even clambered up the opposite bank so she could tie on her loincloth at a safe distance.

He took much longer to get to his feet. She knew he couldn't catch her in his condition. "You're going to pay for that," he muttered.

She only smirked at him, jumped over the stream, snatched up her water gourd, and took off running through the trees to rejoin the band. She only yelled, "You'll have to catch me first," before she vanished out of sight.

Blackjack limped down to the stream, washed off, and put his loincloth back on. He took his time going back to the band.

Narina sat with Mora and Thena where Blackjack couldn't get to her. That was okay. She wouldn't be able to avoid him forever. They would get home to the valley eventually. Then she would be living in the same house with him and sleeping with him every night.

He could wait for that. He lowered himself to the ground near his brother and uncles. No one had to know about him and Narina. His whole family probably already knew anyway or they were already thinking he'd done it even before he did. He had no reason to wait.

He caught her casting blushing glances at him all evening, but she didn't talk to him. So she must have been embarrassed or maybe a little excited. Holy crap, she felt so good! He couldn't wait to get his hands on her again.

Chapter 9

Hangman's party entered through the secret tunnel and headed across the open ground to the jungle. Narina couldn't stop gasping and gaping at everything.

Mora and Blackjack hadn't told her about the tunnel. No one had. Blackjack filled her in on the details on the way to the camp among the rocks. The rest of the band welcomed the family home and then Narina had to meet everyone.

The introductions took a long time. She only met those people living in this band. She probably wouldn't meet everyone from all the other valley bands—not in any close personal way. The bands didn't really mingle except at gatherings.

Blackjack sat with his family and waited for the commotion to die down. All the men still had to recover from their injuries, but Blackjack's restlessness started to get the better of him, especially when he caught up with his men and the uninitiated boys.

"We were just about to go on a scouting run outside the valley," Chief informed Blackjack. "Did you see anything out there?"

"We didn't see a single person all the way here, but that doesn't mean they aren't there." Blackjack made up his mind. "I want to go with you."

Diamond raised his eyebrows at Blackjack's leg. "Something tells me that isn't a good idea."

"I can still run," Blackjack insisted. "I can run and fight as well as I ever did."

"Have you run even once since you got hurt?" Cyclops demanded.

Blackjack tried to shrug that away. "Well, no, but I guess I can start now as well as another time."

"If you hurt yourself again or slow us down, we'll send you back," Reaper insisted.

"I won't hurt myself again or slow you down." Blackjack heard himself almost pleading. "I promise."

None of his men looked convinced. They looked even less convinced when Bone found out what they were doing and wanted to come, too.

"I won't slow you down," he insisted. "I promise."

Fortune rolled his eyes to Heaven. "I can't believe I'm actually going along with this. If you two old women mess up even once, we're sending you back."

"Of course," Blackjack replied. "We'll be the first to turn back. Won't we, Bone?"

"Yes, absolutely," Bone agreed.

"You should be staying home with your wife," Landslide countered.

"She's busy." Blackjack waved behind him. The men could all see Narina talking to everyone. "Are we going or not?"

The men left the camp and took off running their fastest through the jungle. They ran faster than usual to test Bone and Blackjack. They both struggled to keep up. Maybe this wasn't such a great idea after all.

They kept pushing to the top of the cliffs where Bone doubled over, propped his hands on his knees, and gasped for breath.

"You better go back, brother," Rebel told him.

"No way," Bone panted. "I'm just out of practice because I've been sitting around for so long. I'll be fine."

The others looked away in disgust and the men split up to scout the area. No enemy Clans should have been nearby since the men had been scouting here and much farther afield for so long already.

The men set off running in ever-widening concentric circles to cover the whole territory. They finally clambered into the highest canopy where they could see everything.

Bone and Blackjack caught their breath there. They both needed to get their condition back—not to mention spend a whole lot more time healing up.

Blackjack didn't want to wait any longer. He pushed himself to climb up just as fast as the other men even though his body ached.

The men froze when they scanned the horizon. A long dust trail rose out of the distance. It was the unmistakable sign of Blastidons running—a lot of Blastidons.

"Do the rest of you see what I'm seeing?" Oracle snarled.

"There are a lot more of them than before," Cyclone murmured. "Maybe it's an illusion of the distance."

"We should go check," Blackjack suggested. "We have to report this to Hangman. We need to know exactly how many are coming."

The others nodded. Blackjack no longer cared that he was signing himself and Bone up for more running and probably a lot more climbing.

The men traveled through the canopy this time, which presented a whole new set of problems because Blackjack had to use his arms. He ignored that, too.

The men caught up with the Red Riders at sunset just as the Riders stopped their mounts to make camp for the night. The Red Riders had come out in force this time. They had brought over two hundred mounted men. They'd never brought this many before.

Blackjack and his men watched from the treetops. "Should we ambush them?" Iron asked under his breath.

"We don't have time for that," Blackjack replied. "We need to make sure we get back to the valley undetected so the Riders don't find the tunnel. We'll be able to attack them much better if we bring out the whole band—and maybe everyone from the other valley bands. Come on."

He took off back through the jungle the way the men had come. They stayed in the treetops and even diverted in a wide detour so they could stay in the treetops. They didn't even dare to return to the cliffs in case the Red Riders followed the men's footprints down to the tunnel.

The men didn't get back to camp until long past dark. Blackjack, Bone, and Chief went to find Hangman. He sat in his old place with the other men his own age.

His head shot up when Bone and Blackjack returned. "Where have you been?" Hangman demanded. "Your wife is worried that something happened to you."

"The men were going on a scouting run up to the cliffs, so we went with them," Blackjack replied. "There's a much bigger force of Red Riders moving in, Father. They have over two hundred mounted men all coming on their Blastidons. We had to find out how big their force was and then come back and report it to you."

Hangman's features hardened. "Sit down, my sons. You sit down, too, Chief."

The three younger men sat down in the council of their elders. Meetings like this happened so rarely, but Blackjack felt like he belonged here.

"We'll have to rally all the other valley bands," Red began. "We'll need a lot more men to counter that many Riders."

"We'll send out word in the morning," Hangman replied. "I don't suppose you carried out an ambush on them, did you, my son?"

"No, Father," Blackjack replied. "We didn't want them to detect us and we didn't want to run the risk of them following us to the tunnel."

Hangman nodded. "Good thinking. Maybe it's time to stop playing the cowards with these fools. Maybe it's time to go out into open warfare against them."

"How would we do that when they're so much more powerful than we are?" Chief asked.

"They're just men," Hangman replied. "We know we can kill their Blastidons. That brings the man down to the ground where anyone can fight him. Fighting one of them would be the same as fighting any man who's bigger, stronger, and more heavily armed. We use speed and brains. They're used to fighting mounted and they're used to overpowering their enemies with strength. We'll have to use that against them—both of them."

The party talked for another two hours. Hangman assigned the younger men to patrol the cliffs and keep the Red Riders under surveillance until they made it that far.

"We should use the cliffs to our advantage," Wildling suggested. "We've done it before. We can do it again. The Red Riders don't know which direction we'll be coming from. We can go through the outer valley, get into the jungle, climb up there, and come at them from the west. They won't be expecting that. We can drive them toward the cliffs and off it."

"We would have plenty of fresh meat then," Carnage pointed out.

"The ants and Abnormits can have the Red Riders," Hangman added. "We'll take the Blastidons. Now we all better get some sleep. We have a big day tomorrow."

The party split up. Blackjack went to his shelter. He didn't know where Narina was. He hoped someone had told her where to go.

She met him coming the other way. She must have been coming from the shelter.

"Where the hell have you been?!" she demanded. "We've been married less than a month, you're already injured, and here you are worrying me that something happened to you! What were you thinking running off like that?"

"I'm sorry. I wasn't planning to be out so long, but something important came up and I had to talk to my father about it."

Her eyes popped. "You've been talking to your father—and not to me?! You told him you were back and left me to worry?"

"I'm sorry. It concerns the fate of the whole valley. I had to."

She compressed her lips. "Couldn't you at least have told me where you were going? You didn't tell anyone where you were going."

"I'm sorry," he repeated. "You were so busy talking to everyone else and I really didn't plan to stay out this long. I thought I would only be gone for a few minutes at the most. I thought you would still be talking to everyone when I got back. I didn't think you would care or even notice."

"Well, I did!" she snapped. "I did notice and I did care. I kept thinking the worst."

He slipped his arm around her waist and steered her back toward his shelter. "Never mind about that. Tonight is our first night together. We can forget all that."

She tried to look behind her. "Are you sure?"

"I'm sure. Come on. I thought I would have been home hours ago. I just want to spend some time with you." He led her into the shelter and pulled her down next to him to sit on the bed.

They were alone now in their own house. He didn't know what to do with her first, but he didn't want to rush it. He just wanted to appreciate finally being with her with nothing standing between them.

He turned to look at her at the same time she looked up at him. Her eyes communicated so much doubt, longing, and even fear of what was about to happen.

She never showed that to anyone but him. She always acted so smooth and confident around everyone else. No one would ever guess she was as fearful, nervous, and out of her depth as she could possibly be.

The look in her eyes cracked his heart in half for her. He was her one safety—the one person who saw her at her most vulnerable. He was the one who would make her life here a blessing or a nightmare.

He pulled her into his arms and stretched out on the bed with her by his side. He steered her head down onto his chest and held her there. He didn't need anything else—not now.

He would have all the time in the world to explore her body and fill her up with his children. The passion, energy, and intensity between them would always come back. Its own strength wouldn't let him or Narina avoid it for long.

He didn't need to do it now. He did need to make her feel safe and comfortable. He couldn't let her live in that fear. He needed her to feel that smooth and confident around him all the time.

He wanted to erase that fear and uncertainty until she felt that nothing in the world could possibly go wrong. Then he would feel that he'd succeeded as a husband. He wouldn't feel he'd succeeded as a husband as long as she worried about anything—especially not him.

He shut his eyes planning to just sleep next to her tonight. Hangman would take everyone out of the valley to deal with the Red Riders tomorrow. Blackjack would go with the other men. He might not make it home for days after tonight.

She twisted onto her side, shifted her head farther up his shoulder, and turned over to look up at him. He angled his head in that direction and kissed her just because she was there and because he could. He didn't open his eyes.

He only planned to kiss her once and let her go back to relaxing in bed with no other expectations or obligations, but she kissed him back. Her lips softened more than he expected, so he kept kissing her.

Their mouths opened and they both sank into that dark, warm, swirling place where he no longer felt any separation from her at all. He couldn't tell anymore where he ended and she began or even if they were two separate people.

She gave him no warning before she rotated on top of him and stretched her body all the way down his. Her petite frame didn't crush him or hurt him in the slightest. Her weight felt incredibly good.

She kissed him harder and faster. The torrential heat and passion of their time by the stream came back with a vengeance and they both started breathing harder.

She spread her legs to straddle him. Her body rippled and undulated under his hands anywhere and everywhere he touched her.

This feeling in his body brought it all back. He *was* separate from her. He was a man and he wanted her. She obviously wanted him back. She was his wife—the mother of his children.

His relaxation evaporated. He reared off the ground, seized her in his arms, and rolled her onto her back with her legs still wrapped around his waist. He might go out to war against the Red Riders in an exhausted state tomorrow morning.

He didn't care. He wouldn't rest until he felt everything with his wife and made her his own.

Chapter 10

Hangman strode through the group of warriors assembled in front of the camp entrance. Rebel had returned at dawn to report that the other valley bands were assembling to confront the Red Riders, too.

"We aren't going out to fight them," Hangman insisted. "We're just going to check and see where they are and maybe try to figure out how they're planning to attack us. We can't engage a group that big without more men anyway. Our one goal will be to preserve the secrecy of the tunnels. That's all that matters. Run off into the jungle and lead the Red Riders away from the tunnel if something goes wrong. Is that understood?"

Everyone nodded.

"We'll travel fast, we'll travel silently, and we'll stay in the branches as much as possible to conceal our movements," he went on. "We need to play to our advantages. Numbers isn't one of them."

"Do you plan to lay another ambush for them?" Red asked.

"I don't have any plans until I see where they are and what they're trying to do," Hangman replied. "I won't know what to do until I see that. Now let's go. We can bring the information back to the other valley bands. Then the other Krals and I will decide what to do. Now let's go. We're only speculating as long as we keep standing around here."

He turned away. The women and children stayed on the other side of the camp. They pretended not to notice the men leaving. The men had all taken leave of their families before this meeting. No one needed to go through that again.

The men all came armed and ready for war even though they wouldn't be fighting the Red Riders today. Anything was possible when it came to the Red Riders.

Hangman led the way to the camp entrance. He planned to start running as soon as he got there. He stopped dead in his tracks when he saw a whole army of Red Riders coming through the jungle toward the camp entrance.

They didn't come mounted on their Blastidons. The Red Riders came on foot this time. This was only the second time he'd ever engaged them on the ground like this.

Their presence here conflicted with everything he knew about living in the valley. Did they find their way through the tunnel? Did one of the younger men leave enough of a trail for the Red Riders to follow?

That shouldn't have been possible. Everyone from all four valley bands knew the importance of keeping the tunnel a secret. No one would give it away.

Blackjack's group had deliberately avoided engaging the Red Riders to preserve the tunnel's secrecy. Everyone who went into or out of the tunnel did exactly the same thing. It was the Godless' most important rule.

Hangman even forgot to draw his weapons. He stared at the Red Riders in shock. How did they get here?

They saw him at the same moment and charged forward to engage with him. He drew his kukris and rushed the entrance just as Kuvik and Blackjack got there at the same moment.

The camp's fortifications worked against the Red Riders just as the camp's walls had worked against the Anglers. The Anglers had been even better able to breach the camp's defenses. The Anglers could up the walls and jump down from above.

The Red Riders couldn't have ever seen this camp before. They could only attack from one direction. The opening created a bottle-neck so only two of them could approach at a time.

The Red Riders charged in without stopping. Each man tried to fight his way inside only to get cut down by the Godless standing guard.

Hangman, Kuvik, and Blackjack killed so many Red Riders that the bodies blocked the entrance, too. Hangman didn't think about anything but killing as many of these enemies as possible.

He probably could have completely blockaded the camp by leaving the bodies where they were. The bodies would have stopped any other Red Riders from entering.

The other men and uninitiated boys must not have been thinking that, either. They hustled in behind the men and dragged the dead Riders out of the way to let more of them enter.

More men got involved and created a fire line identical to the one they'd used against the Anglers. Hangman, Kuvik, and Blackjack attacked each man as he came through.

More Riders invaded while the three men were busy. The other Godless engaged and took down these new invaders just in time for Hangman and those nearest him to take on the next attackers coming through the entrance.

Everything about this attack copied the band's campaign against the Anglers. Hangman's brain switched gears.

He could almost see his war against the Anglers as a rehearsal for fighting the Red Riders. He and his men used the same techniques and strategies.

He didn't think about how many Red Riders he had already killed until they stopped coming through the entrance. He found it and had to come back to his senses enough to see what was going on.

A few dozen Riders stood off in the jungle eyeing the entrance. They didn't come near it. They stood there talking.

Hangman's instincts took over. These bastards would withdraw to launch another battle against the Godless. They had invaded his valley and attacked his people. He wouldn't let them get away with that.

He rushed outside with his weapons raised to attack. All the rest of his men and boys charged out with him. The Godless spread out to surround the Red Riders.

They fled into the jungle, but they weren't used to running fast on foot. They always rode their Blastidons everywhere. They couldn't have brought their Blastidons through the tunnel. The Blastidons couldn't fit around all the machinery.

The Godless overtook the Red Riders and took them down in seconds. Hangman left the bodies there to rot. He didn't care about these men. He had to find out if the Red Riders knew about the tunnel.

He might have to wage war against their entire Clan after all if they had found out about the tunnel. He might have to wipe out every Red Rider everywhere to preserve the secret and keep the valley safe.

He just had to know. He couldn't let the sun go down on today without finding out once and for all if the Red Riders did know about the tunnel. Then he could start making his plans. He wouldn't do anything until he knew for sure.

He waited just long enough to assign Oracle's men and the uninitiated boys to guard the camp. Then Hangman took off running, but he didn't go straight to the tunnel.

He swept the area until he found the Red Riders' tracks leading through the jungle. They didn't know how to conceal their presence. They led him right to their source.

The tracks didn't lead to the tunnel. They headed north. The trail became even more obvious as soon as it left the Godless camp. That many men couldn't travel through the jungle without leaving a giant swath of footprints and other signs.

The men picked up speed to cover the distance. They ran along the ground. They didn't need to hide their movements here.

The trail led all the way to the far northern end of the valley. The men stopped in sight of the cliff walls Hangman had taken so much trouble to climb down to find Mora and the children.

He halted inside the tree line and stared out at the open space between the jungle and the waterfall. What looked like a hundred Red Riders stood around talking, sharpening their weapons, and arranging their baggage for war.

The Red Riders had constructed some kind of giant scaffold at the very top of the cliff. Hangman couldn't see the scaffold clearly from this distance. The structure extended over the side with a long rope on some kind of pulley. Maybe Mora would have been able to understand it.

The structure creaked and screeched as the Red Riders wound the rope up and down. It ended in a sling that carried one Red Rider at a time from the top of the cliffs down to the ground.

The process took a long time, but the Red Riders kept lowering one man after another. They must have been working all night to lower this many men to the ground.

Hangman's mind went into a tailspin trying to understand everything he knew about this situation. Blackjack and his men had just checked the clifftop yesterday. The Red Riders hadn't been here then. They hadn't built any kind of structure there.

The structure must have been huge for anyone to be able to see it from so far down on the ground. The Red Riders couldn't have built that in one night.

Even if they did build it in one night, they wouldn't have been able to lower this many men to the ground just in one morning. They would have had to work all night to lower this many men—plus all the men who had just attacked the camp.

He couldn't imagine how they could have accomplished all of this, but the result turned out to be the same in the end. They really did get all these men down inside the valley.

The Red Riders already had too many men standing right here for the Godless to defeat them—not without using the camp's defenses.

Hangman opened his mouth to order his men to fall back to the camp. He needed to regroup with the other valley bands. No one could deal with this alone. The Red Riders put all four Godless bands in danger. They would all have to work together to defeat this enemy.

He didn't get a chance to say anything before one of the Red Riders spotted the Godless watching from the undergrowth. That one man raised the alarm and all the Red Riders charged forward to attack.

The Godless bolted into the jungle, scrambled into the branches where the Red Riders couldn't follow, and took off at high speed to return to the camp. The men would be safe there. They could always defend that camp no matter what.

The Red Riders didn't give up so easily. They followed the Godless from the ground. The Red Riders yelled back and forth to each other to track the Godless' movements through the trees.

The Red Riders couldn't do anything as long as the men stayed in the branches. The Godless had to descend to the ground to get inside the camp.

Hangman's first instinct told him to stay in the branches potentially forever and wait for the Red Riders to leave. He only had to glance behind him to see how dangerous that would be.

More and more Red Riders poured out of the undergrowth heading for the camp. They may have realized that the Godless had left the camp only partially guarded.

More Red Riders would come. Oracle and the others wouldn't be able to defend the camp alone. Hangman and his men had to get back inside at all costs.

He plummeted out of the trees, landed on the ground between the Red Riders and the camp entrance, and spun around to stand his ground. He had to carve out an opening for the rest of his men to get inside.

His men had the same idea and dropped out of the canopy all around him, but not fast enough to escape the Red Riders. The Riders swarmed the area and overwhelmed Hangman in seconds.

He got into a battle against seven of them before his men caught up, but none of them could overcome these numbers. The Red Riders wound up pushing the Godless back toward the entrance.

Hangman's men yelled back and forth to the men and boys inside. Red bellowed for Oracle and the others to stay where they were and guard the entrance. The Godless couldn't let the Red Riders breach the camp. That would have been disastrous.

Hangman spun one way to block the blow of one Rider's massive axe. The others struck just as fast and one of them hit him a glancing blow across his thigh. The blade cut him down to the ground. He couldn't stand anymore.

The others moved in and raised their axes to annihilate him right there on the ground. He scrambled to roll from one direction to another and crawl between the Riders' legs to avoid their strokes. They had to keep turning one way and then the other to keep up with him.

He had to drag his injured leg behind him, but desperation to save his own life gave him all the energy he needed. Adrenaline wiped the pain out of his mind.

The Red Riders kept hacking their axes down and chopping deep cuts in the soil all around Hangman. He didn't get out of the way of all of these blows in time. One of them struck him in the ribs and he felt them crack.

The blade also carved off a big swath of flesh going back to his shoulder. He would have been dead if his ribs hadn't protected him.

He tried again and again both to get to the safety of the camp entrance and to lead the Red Riders away from it. He barely saw what the other men were doing. He heard bellows, screams, and the clash of weapons all around him.

Kuvik appeared out of nowhere, took down two Riders with his jawbone kukris, seized Hangman by his injured arm, and dragged him clear of the fight. The Red Riders attacked just as fast, but Kuvik's sudden attack got Hangman out of the way in time.

Kuvik pulled him to the camp entrance, flung him inside, and spun backward to face the oncoming enemy alone. Four of the original seven remained. He eliminated one of them in the first swing and then backed the rest of the way through the entrance.

The Red Riders tried to follow and fell to Oracle and the others. The uninitiated boys did the same thing by dragging the dead Red Riders inside the camp.

That left room for all the other men to battle their way around to the camp side and then to retreat through the opening, too.

Chapter 11

Blackjack and the other men collapsed all over the ground as soon as they got inside the camp. Oracle's men, Kuvik, and the uninitiated boys were the only uninjured men in the party.

Mora rushed forward when she saw how bad Hangman's injuries were. She tried to touch him, but he thrashed and bellowed so loudly that she couldn't get near him.

Half the men who were injured had to go back to the entrance opening to help defend the camp from more Red Riders assembling from all over. They kept throwing themselves into the opening again and again and dying by the dozen.

One of them finally realized what was going on and pulled the others back, but that didn't remove the threat to the band. The Red Riders assembled at a distance from the camp where they could see everything and discuss how to get inside.

The men on guard had to stay there while the women moved in to tend to everyone's injuries. Hangman finally stopped flailing enough for Mora to get close enough to assess his injuries.

The axe cut on his leg was more than bad, but the wound on his ribs was by far the worst. She straightened up and looked around. None of the men were available, so she waved to some of the women who weren't doing anything.

"Get a piece of hide and help me carry him to our shelter," Mora told them.

Blackjack came over just then. "I'll take him, Mother." Blackjack went down on one knee and compressed his lips when he saw Hangman's injuries. "This is bad," Blackjack muttered. "It couldn't have happened at a worse time."

Hangman lunged off the ground and grabbed Blackjack's arm with his uninjured hand. "Take over, my son," Hangman choked. "Take over as Kral."

Blackjack's eyes widened, but only for a minute before Hangman passed out completely. He buckled onto his back and his head lolled to the side.

The women brought back a big Stalkion hide, spread it next to him, and Mora directed them to roll him onto it. The women carried him to his and Mora's shelter where they transferred him to his bed.

Mora worked over him for an hour to clean his wounds, put leaf paste on them, and wrap them in clean hide strips to hold him together. He would heal from this, but not for a while. He wouldn't be going out to fight the Red Riders anytime soon in this condition.

She rummaged in her possession, found a packet of Gooji sap she kept for times like these, and took it outside to boil some Gooji juice for Hangman. She would probably have to wake him up later tonight to help him drink it.

She stopped when she got out there. Another battle raged outside the camp entrance. The uninjured men and boys stood around the opening watching killing any Riders who came within weapons range.

Women surrounded all the other injured men trying to treat their injuries and stopping the men from going over there and getting involved in the fight.

Mora didn't see Blackjack anywhere. Narina must have hauled him off to their shelter so she could treat him away from all of this.

Men from the other four valley bands assembled outside the camp. The Godless outnumbered the Red Riders now, but Mora didn't hold out any hope that it would stay that way. How many men did the Red Riders bring against this one valley?

The Godless overwhelmed the Red Riders pretty soon, killed half of them, and forced the rest to run for it. A posse of Godless pursued the Red Riders away to hound them through the jungle and reduce their numbers as much as possible.

The rest of the men from other bands entered the camp and all the men stood around talking. Their talk would go on for a long time while they all decided what to do. Mora turned away, built up the fire in front of her shelter, and placed a flat rock in the embers.

She and every other woman in the camp kept these rocks in their shelters for exactly this purpose. The women also kept basins on hand for boiling the juice and sticks for lifting the rocks into and out of the coals.

Everyone in the band kept extra supplies of Gooji sap in storage just in case. No one wanted to get caught without it.

Mora tipped half of her sap into the basin. She had enough for four batches, but she wouldn't be able to go out and get more—not with the Red Riders prowling around and potentially besieging the camp.

None of the other women would be able to spare any sap, either. They would need it for their own men.

Bone came over to the shelter while Mora was still working. All the other men dispersed pretty soon. The men who lived in this camp went to their own houses. The visitors relieved Oracle's men and the other boys at the entrance so they could take a break.

"How's Father?" Bone asked.

"Not very good. He hasn't regained consciousness. He won't be participating in this campaign any longer." She glanced over at the visitors. "What's the decision? Is anyone going out after the Red Riders?"

"Not now. The men want to wait for Hangman to come around so they can include him in their councils. Too many of our men are injured and not here. No one feels comfortable talking or making any plans until everyone is present, even if they're too injured to take part."

Mora eyed him. "You're injured, too, my son. Let me take care of you."

He looked away. "I'm all right. Blackjack and Father are much worse."

She didn't ask how Blackjack was. His wife would look after his injuries. Neither he nor Narina needed or wanted his mother sticking her nose into their business.

She squatted down next to Bone and put leaf paste on his injuries. "These aren't that deep, but you should still have some Gooji juice."

"Save it for Father and the others. They need it more."

"We'll see. It would be better to kill any infection now than let it go all the way through you and maybe get so bad that we couldn't heal it at all."

He only shrugged. "At least the Red Riders didn't come through the tunnel. That would have been terrible."

She didn't ask again what anyone planned to do about the Red Riders. She shared her food with him. They ate alone that night and he helped her dump Gooji juice down Hangman's throat in the middle of the night.

Bone slept on the ground outside the shelter that night. A hush hung over the band. The visitors stood guard all night until Oracle's men relieved them in the morning.

Bone woke up and sat outside in silence until Mora got up and went out there to make another batch of juice. "We'll have to wake your father up to give him this dose," she told him.

"How is he?" Bone asked again.

She shrugged. "He isn't feverish. He seems to be sleeping normally. He'll recover. It will just take time. He isn't young anymore. His body takes longer to heal and this might affect how well he can move around in the future. He slows down more and more each year."

"I guess everyone has to get old," Bone murmured. "He's still one of the strongest men I know. It's a miracle he's held up as well as he has considering everything he's done and gone through."

She smiled at him. "I think the same thing all the time when I see how beaten up his body is. He's been through a lot in his life—even more than most other Godless men. He's a risk-taker and it shows."

"It was all worth it to get the band here. We're here because of him. We've had four years of peace thanks to him and we'll have who knows how many more years of peace after we get rid of the Red Riders. He knew what he was doing when he brought us here. Sometimes I wonder if the next generation will even understand how great he was and what he did for them."

"You and the others will just have to tell them." Mora set the juice aside to cool and went about her work for another hour before the juice cooled enough to drink.

She and Bone went into the shelter. The noise of their movements and out in the camp didn't rouse Hangman. He also didn't rouse when she laid her hand on his forehead to see if he had a fever. He didn't. She didn't know why he was sleeping so soundly.

She shook him by his uninjured shoulder. "Hangman! Hangman, wake up!" she called. "You need to drink another dose of Gooji juice! We're going to sit you up."

She and Bone picked him up and heaved him into a sitting position. Hangman yelled out and woke up enough to jolt from the pain of moving his body around. He stayed awake long enough to drink the juice they gave him.

Bone and Mora lowered him back down on the bed. He broke out in a sweat and his face went pale. His eyes raced around the shelter.

"What's happening out there?" he gasped. "What's happening with the band and the Red Riders?"

"The men of other bands came to help us," Bone told him. "They're helping defend the camp. They want to meet with you and all the men who got injured yesterday. No one wants to decide anything unless you and the others are there. Everyone plans to wait until you're ready to talk about what to do next."

Hangman gasped again. "I have to get up." He spoke in a rasp. "I have to meet with them. We have to decide what to do and get back out there."

"You aren't going back out there." Mora bent over to check the bandage on his side.

He roared when she touched him. "Don't! It hurts too much!"

"You shouldn't be in this much pain," she told him. "Did you injure something internally?"

"My ribs." He winced again. "Some of them are broken." He grimaced and forced himself to sit up.

"You should stay where you are, Father," Bone told him. "You're no good to us like this."

"You said the men won't meet unless I'm there." Hangman hauled himself off the bed. He wouldn't stop flinching and making faces. "I have to at least show them that I'm still alive and functional enough to think about what's happening even if I don't participate." He started to stand up.

"At least wait until I wrap up your ribs." Mora pulled out a long strip of hide. "This will stabilize them so they don't hurt as much."

She started wrapping the strip tightly around his chest and the bandage on his side. Hangman yelled a lot. Bone left before she finished.

Sweat drenched Hangman's hair and body by the time she tucked in the end of the strip. "There. Does that help?"

He nodded, but he was panting too hard to answer. He hobbled on his injured leg to get to the door. He could barely put his weight on that leg.

She opened the door for him and held it for him while he limped outside. Bone stood there talking to Blackjack. Leaf paste covered wounds all over Blackjack's arms, chest, and back, but he didn't show any sign of distress or inability to move around.

Blackjack opened his mouth when Mora opened the door. No doubt he had come over here to ask how his father was doing. Blackjack shut his mouth when he saw Hangman.

Hangman grimaced at his sons. "Call the men over here, my son," Hangman croaked. "Tell them we're meeting to decide what to do about the Riders. Tell them to come now. We shouldn't delay."

Neither Bone nor Blackjack left right away. They stood there and watched Hangman lower himself to the ground. He gasped and sucked air through his teeth when he sat down.

He held his injured leg out to one side and yelled out again when he used his uninjured arm to support himself. He finally slumped against the shelter wall with his leg stretched out in front of him and his one good arm clasped across his ribs.

Blackjack left. Bone stayed standing where he was. Mora sat down next to Hangman. He shut his eyes and tried to catch his breath. She couldn't do anything more for his broken ribs than she'd already done.

He would just have to get through this meeting. Then the rest of the men would carry out whatever decision the men came to about how to deal with the Red Riders.

He would go straight back inside, lie down on his bed, and stay there for the rest of the campaign. His fighting days were over for now.

Chapter 12

Blackjack came back in a little while. The rest of the men assembled from all over the camp. Injured men limped out of their shelters and dragged their aching bodies over to Hangman's shelter.

The Red Riders weren't attacking or even standing around the camp, so the visitors came, too. A lot more of them showed up than Hangman expected. He expected fifty or maybe a hundred men.

A hundred men crowded into the camp, but more stood guard outside it. The other three Krals came forward and sat down around Hangman. Mora got up and moved away into the crowd.

He would have liked to keep her here, but she vanished before he could bring himself to say anything. She hardly ever participated in these councils when they happened. She stayed out of it and let the men handle everything on their own.

Bone stayed standing close to his father. Blackjack went over there and stood next to his brother. They weren't Krals. They weren't even the oldest men here—not by a long way. Bone was one of the youngest.

Viking, Kuvik, Hangman's brothers, Red and his men, and some of the older freed men from the Red Riders' camp surrounded the Krals.

The younger men stood behind the older men. The uninitiated boys came, too. The visitors from the other valley bands had brought their uninitiated boys. This policy had spread to all four bands.

Hangman didn't look forward to talking—to anyone. He really didn't want to preside over this meeting, but it sure looked like everyone else wanted him to.

Blackjack spared Hangman the effort by speaking first. Blackjack raised his voice so everyone could hear him clearly. "My father called you all here so we could discuss our strategy against the Red Riders. As you all know, they're lowering men down from the clifftop to attack us. They attacked our camp yesterday. We can expect more of these attacks in the future. They're probably over there right now lowering the rest of their men so they can attack us with their full force. This is the northernmost camp in the valley. The Red Riders probably plan to finish us off and then work their way south to all of your bands, too."

"We came here to meet with your father—not you," a man from one of the valley bands countered. "You're one of the youngest men here. You have no authority to decide anything."

"You can all see that my father is too injured to take part in whatever campaign we decide to launch," Blackjack replied. "Someone has to lead the men from this band. It won't be him. Each of you will follow your own Kral, so it isn't up to you who takes over as Kral of this band at least until my father regains his strength. The men of this band will decide who takes over—and I suppose I can speak as well as any man. I haven't made any decisions. I'm only telling you what the situation is."

"You might as well take over as Kral," Red interjected. "You've been in charge of our men all this time. I see no reason to change it now." He gave the other speaker a murderous look. "I don't see that a man's age has anything to do with it. I would rather take a younger man with the strength, experience, will, and intelligence to destroy our enemies. Blackjack has all that. He's proven it a million times."

"I agree," Chief chimed in. "We might choose someone else, but we would all follow Blackjack anyway."

One of the other valley Krals turned to Hangman. "Are you okay with this?"

"Of course," Hangman replied. "I told him after I got hurt to take over as Kral. He's the best we have."

No one answered. Blackjack pretended not to hear the doubters. "I suggest we wait until all the Red Riders descend into the valley and no more remain on the upper cliffs."

"Are you insane?" one of the other Krals fired back. "They'll amass a gigantic army right here in the valley! No one will be safe."

"They'll amass a gigantic army right here in the valley, but our women and children will be safe," Blackjack pointed out. "Once the Red Riders descend into the valley, one of us can sneak out through the tunnel and destroy their hoist structure. The Red Riders will be trapped here. They won't be able to get out of the valley—but they won't realize that because they'll be too busy fighting us. We can sneak our women and children out of the valley through the tunnel. We'll do this under cover of darkness so the Red Riders don't know where the women and children are. The Red Riders can attack all they want. They'll never find our women and children."

"And then what?" Yeoli asked. He was Krals of the southernmost valley band. "How do you suppose we defeat such an army when they'll outnumber us so heavily?"

"We'll wage a campaign of annihilation against them exactly the same way we waged one against the Anglers. I don't see the Red Riders as more powerful than the Anglers."

"We defeated the Anglers by wiping out their nests and their young," Kavis pointed out. "Defeating fully grown men armed with battle axes will be a lot harder."

"Hey, if we really wanted to, we could even build another bottle-neck at the far end of the valley and lead all the Red Riders into it. They won't be able to get out and we can kill them two at a time when they try." Blackjack shrugged. "We used our wits against the Anglers and we can do it now. We have everything going for us and nothing to lose. This is our valley. We fought hard to win it and we're going to keep it. These fools made their last mistake by coming here. They just don't realize they're already trapped here and ripe for the slaughter. That's our advantage. They don't know they can't get out. We can engage them and then run from them to make them think we're scared of them. They'll follow us south—away from their hoist structure. They'll get farther and farther away from any ability to escape. They won't have supplies nor will they be able to rearm or reinforce themselves. They won't stand a chance."

The other men exchanged glances. Yeoli and the other Krals turned to Hangman. "What do you think?"

"I think it's a brilliant idea," Hangman replied. "I only wish I could be there to take part."

"You should go through the tunnel, too, Father," Blackjack added. "We can expect the Red Riders to capture any women and children left behind and to kill any men they find, especially wounded ones."

Hangman looked away. He wasn't prepared to listen to that.

Chapter 13

Blackjack looked around at all the men gathered in conference. "Does anyone have any other suggestions to make about how we should do this? Does anyone have a better idea—or any idea?"

No one said anything. The older men scowled and rubbed their chins. The Krals all looked at Hangman. They had all gotten used to following his lead, but he couldn't help them this time.

He really didn't see any better plan to defeat the Red Riders. If they thought for two seconds about how they would get back out of the valley after lowering themselves into it, they would leave a few men up on the cliffs to guard the hoist.

The Red Riders would expect these men to be able to pull their comrades up once they finished the assault against the Godless. Whichever Godless went to destroy the hoist could easily overcome these men and kill them into the bargain.

The Red Riders probably thought the Godless were trapped in the valley, too. The Red Riders didn't know the Godless had another way out of it.

"If no one has any suggestions to make, then we need to start arming to carry out this plan," Blackjack went on. "The first stage will be to launch some dummy skirmishes against the Red Riders to distract them while our women and children get out through the tunnel. We'll plan to attack the enemy at the cliffs before the Red Riders spread any farther south. Our camp is the closest so our women and children will leave first. The rest of you should send one or two scouts south to your bands and bring all your women, children, and fighting men up here. That will take time. Then we'll be able to strategize about when and where to attack the Red Riders to draw them away from the tunnel so the women and children can get out. We can attack from the west. That will turn the Red Riders that way so they don't see the women and children moving into position."

His words sparked a wave of movement and talk among all the other men. None of them raised any objection. Hangman expected the men to at least ask a few clarifying questions. The men didn't even stick around long enough to do that.

The meeting broke up with everyone talking to everyone else. The Krals stood up, returned to their men, and gave orders for the scouts to leave right away. The uninitiated boys went through the camp spreading the word to all the women and younger children.

The men left Hangman sitting there alone. Relief flooded him. It was over. He didn't have to get involved in this again. He only had to hobble out through the tunnel. Then he could rest while he healed up. He didn't want to move ever again.

Mora returned in a little while, squatted next to him, and then sat down on the ground in her old place. None of the men noticed. They didn't return or ask Hangman's opinion on anything.

Bone and Blackjack stayed where they had been standing through the whole meeting. Blackjack frowned at all the men like he might be waiting for one of them to come back and challenge him—or at least question him.

They didn't. He'd made it so clear already what he wanted everyone to do. None of them came back. They dispersed.

Narina finally hustled out of the crowd. "Is it true? Are we going through the tunnel to get away from the Red Riders?"

"Yes, it's true," Blackjack told her. He turned around and came over to squat on Hangman's other side. "Maybe someone should carry you out, Father. I don't want to see you walking around like this."

Hangman snorted. "No one is going to carry me, my son—not unless I'm unconscious."

"You *will* be unconscious if you try to walk all that way," Bone pointed out. "You might reinjure yourself."

"Someone has to help defend the women and children against creatures that might attack," Hangman pointed out. "The women and children will still be in danger even out there."

"You won't be able to defend anyone from anything," Blackjack told him. "You're one of the people who needs to be defended."

"Can I make a suggestion?" Mora asked.

"Of course, Mother," Blackjack exclaimed. "Please."

"I suggest that you keep any able-bodied women around who don't have young children to take care of. You could use us as bait to lure the Red Riders into attacking in certain places to lead them into ambushes. We could set up dummy camps with these able-bodied women—women who can fight—and any older children who want to participate and who know how to handle a weapon. We could pretend to be camping somewhere—somewhere other than here so it looks like we're fleeing from the invasion. Then the Red Riders will try to capture us and you can hit them unawares."

Blackjack frowned. "That's an excellent idea, but what if they do actually capture you?"

"That's exactly what I was going to suggest. They'll take us to their camps—or wherever it is they plan to stay during the campaign. Then we can kill some of them from inside their camps."

"Yes!" Narina exclaimed. "I want to participate! This would be great!"

"You've never done anything like this!" Blackjack pointed out.

"But all of you have." Narina turned to Mora. "I want to help. Just tell me what you want me to do."

"That will be for Blackjack to decide," Mora replied and turned to him. "You just need to tell us where you want us to camp and what you want us to do."

He frowned at her for a minute before his expression cleared. "Why don't you and Narina go around the camp and round up anyone who you think will be good for this? Don't mention it to the mothers or young children. Just ask the people who might be able to participate and find out if they want to. We won't take anyone who doesn't want to. Everyone else can go through the tunnel."

The two women left together. Blackjack turned to Hangman. "Are you going to be all right, Father? Maybe you should go back inside and lie down."

Hangman snorted. "I won't be going anywhere, my son, not until it's time to walk out through the tunnel. Just leave me here until then."

"I almost wish you were staying," Blackjack murmured. "I need your help and advice on this one. No one is better at carrying out these campaigns as you are."

Hangman opened his eyes and locked onto his son. "You're the best man for this job. Everyone respects you and listens to you. Do what you think is best. I'm sure you'll succeed. The Clan needs you. I'm proud of you, my son." He turned to Bone. "I'm proud of both of you. You're both ready to step in and lead in my place."

"Don't say that, Father," Bone croaked. "You're still Kral."

"Not like this, I'm not." Hangman turned back to Blackjack. "Do it, my son. Do it your way. You're already doing it. The band will follow you. Do exactly what you said. Lead the Red Riders south, build the bottleneck, and destroy them. You'll succeed. I'm certain of it."

Blackjack didn't look happy about Hangman's comments. The commotion in the camp distracted everyone. The women and children started packing up everything to leave. The men armed for the next stage of battle.

Bone and Blackjack both stood up. Some of their younger men came over to discuss their first maneuvers. Smash, Viking, Carnage, and Landslide were all too injured to go on the campaign. They would be leaving the valley with Hangman and the others.

Viking hobbled over to Hangman and collapsed on the ground next to him. The two cousins exchanged a knowing glance. "It looks like this is the end of the road for us, little brother," Viking murmured.

Hangman tried to smile at him. "The next generation is in good hands."

Viking nodded and turned to look out at the rest of the band. Blackjack was just giving orders to Bone, Rebel, and Cyclops to leave right now, go up to the clifftops, and lie in wait for the Red Riders to finish lowering their men to the ground.

Then the three men would kill any Red Riders standing guard over the hoist, destroy the structure, and leave no trace of what happened to them.

Bone and his men left immediately and vanished into the jungle. The rest of the camp was in too big a flurry of activity for anyone to notice the three men gone.

The women and children gathered in the center of camp with all their baggage and any spare food supplies they had left over.

Some of Smash's female relatives had to carry him on a big piece of hide. Hangman didn't see what was wrong with him. He looked unconscious. Landslide wasn't much better. His female relatives had to carry him, too.

Carnage could barely walk, but he forced himself to.

Blackjack and the other men assembled in a different place. They didn't stop talking all evening. Hangman and Viking stayed where they were. They weren't part of the men's conference.

This would be the first time in Hangman's life that he removed himself from the men's company and business. He wasn't part of this anymore.

This moment gave him a glimpse of things to come. He would keep aging. He would get less and less able to take part in the other men's maneuvers and even their conversations.

He shouldn't even technically be Kral right now. He wasn't Kral. A Kral had to make decisions on his people's behalf. Now someone else performed that job while he sat on the sidelines.

He'd spent years thinking that Shadow ought to hand over the position of Kral to someone else. Hangman had even told his father straight out that Shadow should do that.

Hangman hadn't expected to step in as Kral while his father was still alive. The circumstances that had caused that to happen weren't Hangman's choice.

He'd worked hard all these years not to be like Shadow. Hangman had gone to extraordinary lengths to conduct himself and lead his people in all ways opposite from what he saw as Shadow's worst mistakes.

Now Hangman saw himself facing the hardest task of all. He might not ever recover from these injuries—not enough to actively take part in any hunting or warlike activities.

If this injury didn't disable him permanently, then the next one would. Every injury made it more and more certain with every passing year that he would be able to do less and less.

He shouldn't be Kral now. Blackjack should take over. None of the older men would challenge him. They all supported him anyway and he would have been able to beat them in a fight even if one of them had been stupid enough to challenge him.

He was already Kral. Everyone in this band knew it. Even Hangman knew it. He just had to step aside. He already was. He was already out of the picture.

Night fell over the jungle. Blackjack sent men out to scout the terrain. They came back to tell the women and children that the coast was clear. The men escorted the women outside in a long, silent column heading for the secret tunnel.

Viking and Hangman had no choice but to get to their feet and go with the others. Both men limped painfully.

The column filed out of camp. The able-bodied men flanked the column all the way through the jungle. Hangman and Viking weren't the only people moving slowly. The youngest children whimpered and some had to be carried.

The ones who could walk walked slowly. The relatives carrying Smash and Landslide had to keep stopping to rest their arms and hands. Hangman and Viking had no trouble keeping up.

The men didn't hurry anyone along. The men kept splitting off, scouting the area, and heading off north to make sure no Red Riders spotted the party. The jungle sounded quiet except for the usual night creatures.

The trip to the cliffs took a long time at this speed. More children fell apart from lack of sleep. Some even outright cried and their mothers had to silence them by one method or another.

The band finally came to the cliffs. The armed men stood guard while the column of women and children filed through the tunnel. Hangman limped inside. He had to grope along the walls with his hands to find his way in the dark.

One person after another squeezed through the narrow spaces between the machinery. The whole party wound up on the other side of the tunnel facing the next valley adjacent to the Angler Valley.

"We'll stop here," Hangman told everyone. "Everyone settle down right here inside the tunnel. We'll camp here tonight and then see about where to go and what to do in the morning. We won't go anywhere tonight. We're safe here—much safer than we'll be walking around outside."

The families around him responded instantly to his decision. Everyone sat down. The women started nursing or rocking their children, reassuring them, and encouraging them to go to sleep now.

Viking sat down against one of the tunnel walls, but Hangman didn't. He found himself going from person to person and checking on everyone. He and Viking were some of the only men here.

He was still Kral. He was still responsible for these people and they all looked to him to make decisions for their benefit. He owed them that much. He wasn't dead yet. He could still do this Clan some good for as long as he lasted.

Chapter 14

Bone, Rebel, and Cyclops raced through the trees, dove into the secret tunnel, scooted between the machinery, came out the other side, and sprang into the branches to make it through the canopy to the high cliffs.

The men traveled a long way out of their way to conceal their approach from the Red Riders. The three men didn't make it to the cliffs until sundown.

The three friends skirted farther north so they could get into the jungle adjacent to the clifftops. The men approached the hoist scaffold from the same direction the Red Riders always used to approach the cliffs.

Sure enough, the Red Riders had left ten men to guard the hoist. The men sat around next to and in some cases actually sat on the lower parts of the hoist. The men had built a fire there. They were in the process of cooking some dead creature while they talked.

Bone and his men searched the area and found all the Riders' hundreds of Blastidons tethered at a distance from the cliffs. The ten guards weren't close enough to keep an eye on the creatures.

The Red Riders didn't think to check the surroundings for anyone sneaking up on them. Blackjack had read the Red Riders' strategy down to the letter. It never occurred to them that the Godless had another way out of this valley.

"How do you want to do this?" Rebel murmured under his breath.

Bone shrugged. "I suppose we could just wait for them to go to sleep, kill them all, and throw them over the side along with the hoist. Do we need to make it any more complicated than that?"

"I don't see why we should," Cyclops added. "Your brother needs us down below. Why should we hang around up here showing off when we could do the job more quickly?"

"That's what I think," Bone agreed.

The men fell silent and waited for full dark to set in. The Red Riders didn't stay up late. They made camp at a distance from the hoist and left that unguarded, too. Some of the men stayed up longer while others stretched out and went to sleep right away.

The rest crashed out soon enough. The Red Riders snored loudly enough for the Godless men to hear them even over the pounding noise coming from the waterfall.

Bone and his comrades snuck down to the ground and tiptoed closer. Each man approached one sleeping Rider.

Bone stood over his victim for a minute. He wouldn't normally have felt right about stabbing a defenseless man in his sleep—except that these bastards were trying to kill or capture his mother, sister, and every other woman and child in the whole valley.

The Red Riders would even kill or capture little babies. The Red Riders would sell infant girls into captivity for life. He didn't even want to know how bad it got for the captives in the Red Rider camps. His father, Red's men, and the freed captives never talked about it.

It didn't matter how bad it got because Bone and his friends would never let that happen to any Godless woman, girl, or child—especially not the ones who had already escaped from the Red Riders thanks to Hangman and his men.

Bone drew his weapon and drove it into his victim's throat. Rebel and Cyclops both struck at the same instant. Rebel skewered his target through the eye. Rebel's kukri split the man's skull and made a cracking sound.

It echoed much louder than anyone expected. Bone's victim startled awake and struggled around the blade lodged in his throat. He choked and spluttered with blood pouring down his throat into his lungs.

He tried to grab the blade to pull it out, but the damage was done. He only cut his hands on the sharp edge.

Bone wrenched the blade to one side and tore out the other great blood vessel in the man's neck, but it was too late. The noise woke up the rest of the Riders in camp.

Cyclops killed his victim by hacking his axe down across the Rider's neck. The blow severed the man's head and killed him instantly. The guy didn't make a sound.

The other seven Red Riders shot to their feet, grabbed their weapons, and looked around for the source of the disturbance. They saw the three Godless warriors standing over the three dead Riders. The rest of the Riders charged in to attack.

The Red Riders had to split up. Two went after Cyclops, another two advanced on Rebel, and the remaining three came after Bone. He couldn't fight them all.

He felt the situation slipping through his fingertips. The whole valley and all its hundreds of Godless residents depended on him and his friends killing these men and destroying the hoist.

Bone made a snap decision, sprang sideways, and then pivoted behind the Riders to back toward the hoist and the cliff edge. "Over here!" he yelled.

He meant to signal Rebel and Cyclops to come with him, but the Red Riders must have thought Bone meant for them to go over there. They turned around and widened their formation. They probably thought they could drive him over the cliff edge to his death.

He braced himself for what he knew he had to do. He hadn't spent the last fourteen years growing up with Blackjack, Hangman, and Mora without learning a few dirty tricks to pull on his enemies when it suited him.

Rebel and Cyclops knew all the Godless tricks, too. The two friends realized what Bone was trying to do and they pivoted over to the cliff edge, too. They wound up on the other side of the hoist.

It actually wound up working in the friends' favor to separate themselves from Bone and his adversaries. The hoist kept the Godless men apart from each other. They couldn't come any closer for the Red Riders to surround them.

The hoist also stopped the Red Riders from consolidating against the three men. The Riders might have won if they could have found a way to do that.

Bone's adversaries moved in on him. He didn't let himself back all the way to the edge. He couldn't even see it in this darkness. He planted himself there next to the hoist and resolved not to back up any further.

The Red Riders read his body language instantly and all three rushed him at once. He dodged left—away from the hoist. One of the Riders moved in on him from that side. The man's momentum kept him moving toward the spot where Bone had just been standing.

Bone got on the other side of the guy, hurled all his weight against the Rider's shoulder, and sent the guy pinwheeling over the side into open space. He vanished into the dark as his screams faded into silence.

The other three Riders spun around to face Bone, but he knew now that he could take these two. They didn't have a shred of guile or cunning in them. They didn't have the first clue about how to combat his techniques.

They charged him again. They tried to be smart by coming at him from two different angles, but he veered one way and then lunged between them at the last second. He wound up behind them with his back to the hoist.

They pulled exactly the same maneuver a second time. They weren't used to their victims thinking creatively. Bone sidestepped out of their way and wound up with his back to the cliff again.

This position gave the Red Riders a surge of confidence. They didn't think they could miss catching him this time. They changed their positions again and dove in to pounce.

He dropped into a crouch and both of them wound up bumping their knees against his shoulders. He jerked upright instantly, toppled one of the Riders across his back, and pitched the guy over the side. That left one.

The guy bellowed in a rage, raised his huge axe, and tried to chop it down at Bone's head. Bone sprang out of the way and the axe clanged against the stone right at the edge of the cliff.

Bone rotated behind the guy even before he picked up his weapon. Bone kicked the man from behind and sent him over, too.

Rebel and Cyclops fought back and forth with their own opponents on the other side of the hoist. Bone didn't see what his friends were doing. He couldn't wait any longer.

He raced around the hoist studying it as well as he could in the firelight. The Red Riders had constructed it right there on top of the rock. The structure didn't have any wheels or anything like that.

He went back to his own side of the scaffold, picked up one of the Riders' fallen axes, and used it to chop away the structure's lowest support members. None of them was big enough to stand up to his assault.

He splintered four different supports before the thing started to collapse. It toppled toward him. He had to jump out of the way so it didn't crush him.

The hoist falling over distracted the remaining Red Riders. That gave Rebel and Cyclops all the time in the world to finish off their enemies.

"Help me push it over!" Bone called to his friends.

All three got behind the broken structure. The friends heaved and puffed, but in the end, they had to hack it into even smaller pieces. The friends couldn't lift anything bigger than that.

The men worked for an hour before they pitched everything over the side followed by the bodies. Bone and his friends built up the fire and searched the area to remove every splinter of wood from the rock ledge.

The men returned to the Blastidon herd and slaughtered every last one of the creatures while they slept. Their tethers made it easy. The Blastidons couldn't have gotten away even if they'd realized they were in danger.

Then the men scoured the whole site and erased all trace of their own presence. They even erased their own footprints after they pushed the burning coals over the side and retreated into the jungle.

Bone didn't worry about erasing the dead Blastidons. The ants and Abnormits would find the creatures as soon as the sun came up. The ants would do the job of erasing the Blastidons more thoroughly than Bone and his friends ever could.

The men clambered into the branches, climbed all the way up to the highest canopy, and sat in silence to watch the site and listen.

Bone didn't understand why he stayed. He should have beat it back to the band to help Blackjack and the others. The Red Riders weren't here anymore. The band needed him more right now.

Rebel and Cyclops didn't hurry away, either. Whatever kept Bone here held them back, too. Something about this didn't feel right.

That was the moment when all three of the friends heard voices in the distant jungle behind the men's hiding place. The noise coming from the falls made it hard to hear, but they were definitely human voices.

Bone stiffened. Then all three men turned around, stared into the dark, and strained their ears to listen. The voices didn't sound like Red Riders. The voices didn't sound like men at all. He could barely hear them.

He and his friends advanced through the treetops without discussing it first. The men moved slowly from branch to branch homing in on that sound. Bone didn't want to take anyone by surprise. He didn't want anyone even to realize that he and his friends were here.

They stopped in another patch of foliage a few miles from where they started. The three men stared down into a Red Rider camp dotted with all the usual tents.

This one was nowhere near the Blastidons and the camp didn't look like a Red Rider camp at all. It didn't have any men in it.

Chained captives moved back and forth from one tent to another doing something or other. They all looked extremely busy even at this time of night. The captives worked extra hard as though the Red Riders really were here.

Bone and his friends exchanged glances. "What should we do with them?" Cyclops asked.

Bone squirmed in his skin. "I have no idea. The Red Riders won't be coming back for these people. I say we set them free. I don't feel right about leaving them here alone, especially not when they're chained like this. We should unchain them, tell them the Red Riders are gone, and that the captives are free to go." He squinted at the camp. "They have men down there. They can protect the women and children. What do you think?"

"I agree with you," Rebel added. "The only alternative is to take them down to the valley, but there's no one down there who can take care of these people right now. Our own people are in hiding from the Red Riders. We couldn't take all these people there—not without putting our own in danger."

"You're right," Cyclops added. "Taking these captives to the valley isn't an option—not with the Red Riders down there. They'll have to stay up here and that means they have to go free." Now he was the one who squinted at the camp. "Do you think they have weapons down there? Your father and his men armed all the captives with weapons stolen from the Red Riders. We could do the same thing—if they have any weapons."

"Let's find out." Bone stood up. "We can unchain them either way. They'll be better able to defend themselves with their hands free even if they can't take weapons."

His friends followed him to the ground. The captives went into fits of agitation when they saw three armed Godless warriors coming toward them. Bone didn't know how to react, so he stopped there at the edge of the camp.

"You have nothing to fear from us!" he called out. "The Red Riders are all gone! They won't come back! You're all free to go! We're here to free you! You can arm yourselves with the Red Riders' weapons, form your own band, and travel away from here wherever you want to go! You're free people. You and your men can defend you from creatures or any enemies who come after you. You should leave the area and get as far away from the Red Riders as possible. They may send out another band to reinforce the men who went down the valley. We're here to free you! We won't harm you! We only want to help you take back your lives and leave here as free people!"

His words got through to someone, at least. A few men and a handful of women came forward to meet Bone and his friends. The freed captives clasped his hands in theirs even though they were all still chained.

"We should have searched the dead Riders to find the keys to these chains," Cyclops muttered.

"I know where the keys are," one of the men offered. "The Red Riders threatened to kill all of us if even one person tried to escape. That's their way. I can find the keys."

He hustled away to one of the tents, came back with a set of keys, and placed it in Bone's hands. Bone didn't ask any questions about why the guy wanted Bone to unlock the chains instead of this man doing it himself.

Bone went from person to person and unlocked all their chains. He even unchained little children, including girls covered in bruises. Bone tried not to look too closely at them.

He told the men to locate the Red Riders' extra weapons and to arm everyone, including the children. Then he ordered the women to rifle the Red Riders' tents for food and other supplies the captives could take on their journey.

The freed captives responded much better than he expected. They all got to work, tore the camp apart, and the men armed everyone. The

Red Riders had enough weapons for all the captives to carry more than one.

The freed captives took way too long to thank the three Godless. Bone tried to tell them more than once to go on their way and get out of the Red Riders' path before another band came along.

The freed captives kept pressing the three men's hands, thanking them, and even crying and kissing the men's hands even though all three men told everyone not to.

The freed captives finally, finally filed out of camp and left the tents standing. Bone and his men didn't have to do anything to erase their presence here. None of the men had entered a tent. They hadn't done anything.

Bone waited until all sound of the freed captives faded into the night. Then he dropped the keys right there on the ground in the middle of the camp.

If anyone came along and found this place, they would find the keys right out there in the open along with all the unlocked chains. Maybe the Red Riders would think that the captives had freed themselves and escaped en masse.

Bone and his men took off at high speed through the canopy with nothing to stand in their way of rejoining their own people.

Chapter 15

B lackjack pointed down at a large clearing buried in the jungle. This one wasn't too far from one of the old Angler breeding sites.

The site had been a charred, blackened scar on the landscape after the Godless' last big push to exterminate the Anglers.

The jungle had grown back in the last four years. Lush foliage surrounded the spot. Vines and creepers blocked out the canopy all around the clearing.

No trees grew on that spot. Thick trees and dense undergrowth surrounded a wide, grassy area with nothing in the middle.

"Make your camp there," Blackjack murmured to Mora and Narina. "Build temporary shelters for yourselves. Make it look like you plan to move on pretty soon—like you're migrating south to get away from the invasion."

Mora nodded. "That shouldn't be too hard. Where will you be?"

"The men and I will station ourselves in the trees surrounding the clearing. We'll drop out of the canopy to attack the Red Riders from all sides, but we'll have to wait until they actually enter your camp. Bury your weapons in the grass so you'll be able to grab them easily and fight back. Do whatever you have to do. Just don't let them take you out of the clearing."

"We will." Mora nodded to Narina and the women climbed down from the trees. The uninitiated boys went with them.

These boys usually went out on maneuvers with Blackjack and the other men. All of these boys were between eleven and fourteen years old—not old enough to initiate as men but old enough to know how to fight.

All the women and boys came armed. Most of them carried their usual weapons with as many more concealed inside their clothes as each person could reasonably carry.

The whole party entered the grassy clearing and started working to make camp. Everyone went about their tasks in the usual way as if they really had been traveling south and just stopped here temporarily.

Everyone worked together to trample the grass over most of the area and then to rip it out from certain places to build shelters. The women gave the boys instructions on how to construct the shelters.

Some of the boys went hunting, butchered their kills, tore out more grass down to the bare dirt so they could light fires, and started cooking the food while the women finished working on their shelters.

The smell of smoke and roasting meat drifted through the camp and gave it an inviting, comfortable atmosphere. Mora kept casting glances around her when her work allowed and when she could do it without making it too obvious that she was looking around.

She didn't see any men hiding in the surrounding trees. Blackjack must have brought two hundred men with him, but they hid themselves too well even for other Godless to detect.

She didn't see any Red Riders approaching, either. How long would they take to get here? She sure wished they would hurry up.

She and the other women finished their shelters. Some of the boys had killed large animals. The boys worked to prepare the meat for travel, so the women helped out and then everyone sat around to eat while they waited for the meat to dry.

Narina sat down next to Mora. "Did you see anything?" Narina murmured under her breath. She kept her head turned and faced front to make it less obvious that the women were having a conversation.

"No, nothing," Mora replied in the same undertone. "I don't know when they'll come."

"Is it always like this?" Narina asked. "How long does it usually take for them to attack?"

"I don't know because I've never done anything like this before. I just hope they don't come while we're sleeping tonight."

"I don't think I'll be able to sleep." Narina's voice trembled with the tension. "I suppose we have to sleep to make it look like everything is normal."

"At least we'll be sleeping in these open, three-walled shelters instead of......" Mora broke off when she heard movement in the surrounding jungle. The sound set off a shockwave among the other women and boys. Everyone stopped talking to listen.

Every person's hand moved to his or her weapons, but no one moved yet. Everyone sat in place around the fire as before while they strained their ears to hear.

The noise came from north of the camp—the direction the Godless had traveled to get here. The noise only came from that one direction. Then it spread out to surround the camp.

The lack of conversation should have been a dead giveaway to the Red Riders that the women and boys weren't as helpless as they seemed, but nothing stopped the Red Riders from moving in. The noise spread all around the camp. None of the Godless moved a muscle.

Mora prayed to High Heaven that Blackjack and the other men really were there watching. She didn't want to face the Red Riders again—not alone with a bunch of other women and uninitiated boys.

This was the same nightmare all over again that cost Shadow his life.

She couldn't outright draw her blades without giving everything away. She put the rest of her food into her mouth and chewed it while she waited so she would have both her hands free.

The boys squirmed. They had to fight themselves not to grab their weapons, too. The other women had the same problem.

Narina glanced over at Mora. Mora gave her a warning look even though Narina wasn't doing anything. She held herself perfectly still exactly the way she should. Narina handled this well considering she'd never done anything like this before, either.

Mora faced front. How long would the women have to wait before the Red Riders attacked? The Godless couldn't handle the waiting for much longer.

The Red Riders answered her question by attacking right then—before she even finished thinking that. They charged in from all sides. The women and boys would have been done for if they hadn't been expecting this.

The Red Riders gave the Godless even more warning by bellowing in thunderous voices when the enemy charged in from outside. That must have been the Red Riders' way of scaring their enemies into panic and maybe trying to run away.

The Red Rider's war cry only gave the Godless a few extra seconds of warning before the Red Riders actually got close enough to capture anyone. All the women and boys sprang to their feet, drew their weapons, and turned outward to face the attackers.

The Red Riders swung their enormous battle axes at the women and boys, but the Red Riders couldn't make it more obvious that they were trying to capture these women instead of killing anyone.

Two huge Red Riders came after Mora. She tried to stay near Narina, but the confusion separated the two women. One of the Riders swung his axe at Mora's head, but he deliberately missed.

She dove behind the shelter she'd just worked so hard to build. His axe hit it and demolished it in seconds. The pile of branches fell between them and gave her a few more seconds to back away, but more Riders invaded the camp from all sides.

The Red Riders made another strategic blunder by ignoring the boys. The Riders must have been in the habit of focusing all their efforts on defeating men and capturing women. They didn't usually have to worry about children.

The boys ran from Rider to Rider killing, stabbing, slashing, and impaling while the Riders paid all their attention to the women. The boys took down dozens of Riders before the Godless men sprung their trap.

Mora was too busy running for her life even to land one hit on the Red Riders. More of them assembled from all over. They drove Thena and Narina into a cluster with Mora. The three women turned back to back aiming their weapons outward.

The Red Riders saw their targets trapped and moved in to capture the women. Mora didn't want to engage any of these men. They would destroy her weapons and maybe even kill her to get to the younger women.

That was the moment when the Godless men swarmed out of the surrounding trees and closed their dragnet around the camp. The men came by the hundreds and flooded the area. All the Riders turned away from attacking the women.

Now the women were the ones to jump in and kill, slash, stab, and impale the Red Riders while they fought their hardest to protect themselves from the Godless.

The band rampaged through the camp killing as many Red Riders as possible. Their bodies covered the clearing. Their numbers dwindled as more and more Godless ganged up on each Rider and took them down in minutes.

Mora paused and looked around for any other Red Rider to attack. She didn't see any at first.....and then she did see them. Another wave of Red Riders poured out of the northern jungle. How did Blackjack and his men not see these Riders before now?

They must have just showed up to reinforce their friends. The new arrivals surged into the camp and swept the Godless before them. The Godless crowded to the other side of the camp. The men moved to the front and pushed the women and younger boys to the back.

"Get into the trees!" Blackjack yelled over his shoulder. "Get to safety!"

She would have liked to stay and help him, but the overwhelming numbers of Red Riders made it impossible. She didn't even see how the men would be able to defend themselves against this many.

She hesitated a minute longer before she and the other women turned tail and raced away into the treetops. The uninitiated boys stayed behind, but they couldn't help the men, either.

The Red Rides formed ranks on one side of the camp and pushed the Godless back toward the south. A few men on either side broke out of line to engage the other side, but both had to retreat back into their own ranks pretty soon.

None of the Red Riders could get close enough to kill the Godless men and none of the Godless men could get close enough to kill the

Red Riders. The Red Riders had force and numbers on their side. They pushed the Godless back into the jungle.

The Godless men retreated farther and farther. They would have backed all the way out of Mora's sight. She stopped in the branches to watch her sons and the other men fighting the Red Riders every step of the way.

The Godless men could have jumped into the branches and gotten away. They led the Red Riders a long way away from the grassy clearing—a lot farther than the Godless needed to lead them.

The men stopped there and held their ground for a minute. Mora didn't see why. Was something wrong?

Without warning, two of the boys sprang out of line and the men closed ranks to protect them. The boys grabbed a braided length of vines from some nearby branches and pulled. The boys had to lean all their combined weight against the rope to pull it hard enough.

The line twanged and then whistled when it stretched tight. Its other end cinched around a thick tree trunk high in the canopy. The rope severed paper-thin bark and snapped the trunk in half.

Abnormit grubs poured from inside and enveloped the Red Riders. The Godless men launched into the treetops just in time and left the Red Riders to their fate.

Chapter 16

Blackjack climbed up into the canopy and squatted in front of Mora, Narina, and Thena. "Is anyone hurt?"

"I don't think so." Mora passed her hand across her eyes. "Thank you. I was really worried there for a while."

He pretended not to hear her. "Follow me to the next campsite. We're going to scout the area to find out where the Red Riders are. Then you can start setting up for the next attack."

She nodded and he left. The uninitiated boys climbed up and joined the women in readiness for the next ambush.

"Is it always like this?" Narina asked after he left.

"Always like what?" Mora asked. "I told you we've never done this before."

Narina looked away at nothing. "I've never heard of this style of warfare before."

"I learned about it in the Follower Clan. I told Hangman about it and he started using it against our enemies." Mora shrugged. "I guess he might have been using it before then. He's smart that way. He fights with his brain when muscle and courage won't get the job done. He's the one who convinced everyone else to do it this way."

"It's better this way," Thena chimed in. "We wouldn't have defeated the Anglers without this way of fighting."

"Your father is one of the few Godless men I can think of who would actually consider doing something like this," Mora went on. "Shadow and Butcher never would have dreamed of striking their enemies without warning or using a booby trap like that. Most Godless would consider it cowardice."

"The Whisperers wouldn't consider it cowardice," Narina remarked. "They just never would have thought of it."

"The Followers only know about it because we study the ways of the ancients," Mora replied. "Not that knowing this information does the Followers any good. They never put it to use."

"But you brought it with you," Narina pointed out. "The Godless benefited from it thanks to you."

"Benefiting the Godless Clan is the least I can do. I only ever tried to do right by this Clan. That's all anyone can....."

Mora trailed off when she heard the sound of more movement in the jungle. The rest of the party fell silent and stayed perfectly still while a different group of Red Riders came out of the trees from the northeast.

Blackjack and his men had spread out to the northwest. They must have missed this party of Red Riders or maybe the Red Riders had come from a completely different direction.

They didn't try to conceal or mask their approach. They trooped out of the jungle and made as much noise as they wanted to. They almost seemed to want to announce their presence.

They searched the area and eventually discovered the women and boys hiding in the treetops. The Red Riders couldn't get to the Godless as long as the Godless stayed in the canopy.

Mora settled down to wait for them to leave, but the Red Riders didn't leave. They set to work at strategic locations all around the women's hiding place.

The Red Riders cut branches from the jungle and formed them into mounds in a circle and at a distance from the spot.

None of the women moved. It didn't occur to any of the women or boys to leave the area—not until the Red Riders set fire to their mounds. The Riders used the most flammable branches. The piles roared in flames and the fire spread into the canopy.

Mora jumped up and called the other women to get out of the area, but it was too late. The Red Riders set fire to certain trees to surround the women in clouds of choking smoke. Flames ate away at the canopy and started working inward toward the Godless hiding there.

Mora squinted through the smoke at the women and boys around her. All of them choked on the smoke and tears streamed down their cheeks. There was no way out.

"Let's go down to the ground," Mora called to them. "It's time to implement the next part of our plan."

She led the way and climbed down out of the trees. All the women and boys went with her. They assembled on the ground where the Red Riders would have no trouble capturing the party.

The Red Riders moved in and shoved everyone into a tight bunch. She expected them to start manhandling the women right then and there, but the Red Riders had other plans. They disarmed everyone and marched the whole group away into the jungle heading north.

Mora didn't know what to expect. She actually expected to be one of the first women the Red Riders killed. She was too old to have any more children. The Red Riders seemed to favor the younger women who could get pregnant.

The Red Riders marched the group a long way to a loose, crude camp the Red Riders had pitched for themselves. They obviously hadn't been able to bring down any tents, beds, or other comforts for themselves.

Mora couldn't tell what kind of accommodation the Red Riders were used to, but this definitely wasn't it. She didn't see anything in their camp except a bunch of fires.

The Red Riders kept these fires burning all the time even in the middle of the day when the men weren't cooking anything. All the Red Riders standing around glared at each other, the women, the surroundings—everything.

The Riders directed their hostility mostly toward each other. Their circumstances put them in a foul mood. They snapped or grumbled at each other when they engaged in conversation at all.

One of the Riders carried all the Godless' weapons back to the Red Riders' camp. That one man dumped all the weapons on the ground to one side—right where the women and children could see them.

Mora knew enough from talking to the other freed captives who lived in the valley. The Red Riders obviously hadn't planned to take captives here—or they hadn't planned it very well. They didn't bring any chains to restrain the captured women and boys.

The Red Riders had to stand guard over the Godless captives—which worsened the Red Riders' mood if that was even possible. They had to assign fourteen men to surround a group this big.

The other Riders lowered their guard the minute they got into their camp. Most of them put their weapons down, sat down around the fires, and ate whatever food their comrades had been cooking.

Mora surveyed the scene with a critical eye. These men must plan to sleep on the ground tonight—something they were definitely not used to. That could work to the Godless' advantage.

In fact, all of this could work to the Godless' advantage. The Red Riders wouldn't be able to watch all the women and boys all night long—not without someone slipping up somewhere.

Three of the Riders came over to the women, leered in their faces, and tried to grope them. One enormous guy grabbed Narina, scooped his arm behind her back, and pulled her against him while he pawed at her breasts through her top.

He laughed at her when she tried to struggle. He kept growling, "Huh? Huh?" in her face while she struck at him and tried to yank herself out of his grasp.

Mora dove between them, shoved her arms against Narina, and tried to push the guy off, but he was too strong and solidly built.

She wound up tearing Narina out of his arms. She stumbled behind Mora and Mora stepped between them to face the guy. "Leave her alone!" Mora snapped.

"What are you going to do about it?" the guy fired back and back-handed her hard across the face. He hit her with such force that her head snapped aside and she tasted blood in her mouth.

The guy reacted just as fast, seized her by a big fistful of her top, and yanked her upright to face him. He raised his fist to punch her even harder in the face.

The insult of getting hit in the face triggered something in her. She didn't recognize herself. She barely registered what she was doing when she grabbed a long knife the guy wore at his belt.

This one was much longer than the hunting knives the Godless carried. This one more resembled a long dagger or short blade almost as long as the Bounty Hunters' spearheads.

She snatched the weapon from his belt and plunged it into the hollow space right at the cleft of his ribs. Fury overpowered her senses and she stabbed him again and again multiple times before she even realized what she was doing.

The guy groaned and folded at the knees still holding onto her top. He would have torn it off, but his grip gave out and he let go before he hit the ground.

All the other Riders surged inward to attack her. One of them struck the blade out of her hand, shoved her back into the crowd, and all the surrounding Red Riders raised their weapons to threaten the Godless women and boys.

One Rider called out from the back of the mob. "Leave them alone!" Mora didn't even see who it was who spoke. He had a deep resonant voice that carried a heavy edge of authority. "All of you back off! Leave them alone!"

None of the Red Riders backed off or stood down. One man shouldered his way through the crowd, glared at his men, and then narrowed his eyes at the Godless captives.

The guy clenched his jaw and compressed his lips before he waved at nothing and turned away. "All of you go back to what you were doing. Don't go near them until we can chain them and give them the time and attention they need. Go on. Don't mess with them anymore unless you want the same thing. They're too raw right now. They'll fight back too much. Go on."

He waved his men away and they finally obeyed him. None of the women calmed down or relaxed. They couldn't. The Red Riders didn't even let the women sit down.

The guards still stood around with their weapons raised for a long time. Hours passed before any of the men lowered their guard.

The other Red Riders took the dead guy away. Mora didn't regret killing him. Her mind went into a tailspin about how she could kill even more Riders and get away with it.

The Godless were at war with these people. This camp was one battleground in that war. The Red Riders just didn't seem to be aware of that fact.

Chapter 17

The Red Riders all went back to their fires. Even more of them sat down, ate, and generally relaxed for no reason that Mora could see. None of these men acted too interested in hunting down the Godless men or attacking the other valley bands.

She mentally traced the Godless movements all over the valley. The men of her band would engage the Red Riders at certain points around the area.

The Godless would draw the Red Riders away so the women and children from other bands could make it through the tunnel to safety.

Hangman was out there and he was hurt. She had to find a way to rejoin him—and that meant killing every last mother's son of these Red Riders in front of her.

She didn't give herself the option to glance at the stack of weapons on the other side of the camp. One person.....only one person from the Godless group had to get away from the Red Rider guards.

One person could slip away into the darkness and kill these men while they slept. Mora glanced around at the boys nearest her. She knew them all. They were the sons and grandsons of her neighbors and friends.

Two were Vulture's grandsons. Vulture's son Ghari had been born after Vulture's death. Ghari and Vulture's older son Nubos both idolized Hangman and Blackjack. The two boys did everything in their power to be just like them.

Another two of the boys were the sons of captives that Kuvik had freed from the Bounty Hunters. These boys had grown up in the band.

They had been old enough to remember the campaign against the Anglers and all the band's ambushes and maneuvers against the Red Riders on the journey here. The boys' names were Calv and Urdis.

Urdis was the oldest of the four and hands down the strongest and the most skilled with a weapon. Ghari was the youngest and the smallest, but also the quickest and the most ruthless. Mora liked him a lot.

The evening wore on. More Red Riders assembled from all over the jungle. They must have been out on patrol or maybe engaged in skirmishes against the Godless. A hundred Red Riders gathered at this one camp alone. How many other camps had the Red Riders set up around the valley?

Some of the Red Riders came back injured. Others came back exhausted or enraged. They took a long time to calm down.

The Red Riders didn't treat each other's injuries with leaf paste and Gooji juice. Mora watched these men extra carefully. She didn't see them treat each other's injuries in any way.

They just washed off the blood and occasionally wound a hide bandage around the wound to hold the torn flesh in place. She frowned at them more and more as the evening wore on. Did they really not even know about leaf paste? How was that possible?

The more severely injured men would wind up just as dead if and when their injuries got infected. Didn't the Red Riders even know that much? Didn't they know they had to drink Gooji juice?

They must not have. Some of the injured men collapsed. Their comrades made them as comfortable as possible and then left them alone. Mora didn't understand it at all. The Red Riders didn't even cover up their injured comrades.

The sun sank behind the jungle. None of the Red Riders paid the women and boys any attention apart from leaving the men to stand guard. Even they started to let their guard down and didn't watch the women and boys as carefully.

Some of the women got too tired to stand any longer. They sat down on the ground. The men didn't try to stop them. Then a few more people did it.

Mora shot the guards a death glare, gathered up the four boys, and steered them to the back of the ground. "Come sit down over here," she murmured under her breath. "We're going to have to sleep somewhere tonight. Here is as good a place as any."

"What are we waiting for?" Urdis asked. "Aren't we here to attack these people?"

"We can't attack them without weapons," Mora replied. "Now settle down and try to relax. We have a long night in front of us."

He started to glare at her. She gave him a pointed look and his expression changed. He should know by now that she wouldn't give up on something like this—not with the fate of the whole valley hanging in the balance.

Ghari curled up on his side on the ground first, heaved a sigh, and tucked his arm under his head. Urdis kept glaring at everyone around him. He and the other two boys took a long time before they could bring themselves to stop watching the Red Riders.

The three boys were still sitting up in a guarding posture when Mora lowered herself to the ground. She positioned herself right in front of Ghari and curled up facing him where she could look straight at him from inches away.

Her position got his attention enough for him to open his eyes. His gaze darted down to her mouth. "You're hurt, Mora," he murmured.

"Listen to me very carefully, Ghari," she whispered. "As soon as it gets dark enough, I want you to sneak out of camp while the guards' backs are turned. Get out into the jungle, sneak around the other side of camp, get yourself a weapon, and then use the shadows to kill as many sleeping Riders as you can. Do you understand?"

Urdis heard her. So did Calv. Urdis spun around and glared down at her with his eyes flashing.

Ghari stared at her and then shut his eyes and snuggled down like he'd never been more comfortable in his life. He barely breathed, "I understand. Don't worry about me."

He didn't move again. Mora watched him. This kid was going to grow up to become a great warrior. She just knew it. He was Godless to the marrow of his bones. He didn't care what he had to do as long as he killed his enemies.

Mora finally let herself close her eyes, but she couldn't sleep. She eventually pushed herself up on her elbow and tugged Urdis, Calv, and Nubos down to the ground.

"Lie down," she murmured. "Come on. Lie down. You don't have to go to sleep, but you do have to lie down."

She said it in a way that told them more than she said. They had to lie down to make the guards think they didn't have to watch the Godless as closely as before. The guards had to believe all the Godless were asleep.

The boys obeyed her much better now. They all curled up. The other Godless did the same thing. They packed the area so tightly that they had to lie body against body just to give everyone enough space.

Silence descended over the camp as the Red Riders finished eating and curled up on the ground to go to sleep, too. They built up their fires extra big and bright for some reason. Maybe these men were afraid of the dark.

They grumbled a lot, cursed the Godless horde, and vowed to exterminate everyone in the valley so the Red Riders could get the hell out of here and go home.

They all eventually went to sleep. They left the same fourteen men on guard for hours. Fatigue and boredom eventually got the better of these men. They turned aside, paced around, and barely glanced at the captives.

None of the captives moved. They all breathed evenly in sleep. They must have been faking extremely well if they weren't asleep for real.

The hours dragged until close to midnight. Then one of the guards left to go through the camp and rouse some of his comrades to change the guard. Waking them up took a long time. The new men grumbled even more.

Even after they woke up, they took even longer before they actually came over to relieve their friends. Their comments and activities distracted the guards. Ghari took that moment to spring to life and dart into the shadows where no one could see him.

Mora planned to move into his place to hide the fact that someone was missing, but the other boys did it first. The three of them adjusted their positions to fill Ghari's place. They left no extra space between themselves. No one would have known someone was missing.

The new guards came over just then. The first shift of men on watch had been staring at the Godless all this time. These guards might have recognized that someone or something was different. These new men didn't.

The shift changed. The original men went to get something to eat. Then they lay down and went to sleep, too. The same impenetrable silence fell over the camp. Nothing happened for a long time.

Mora didn't hear anything no matter how hard she listened. Ghari made no noise. Was he even doing anything? He must have been being incredibly stealthy if he was doing something.

The hours of tedium and isolation got the better of the new guards, too. They paced around and turned in every way other than to watch the sleeping captives.

Urdis took advantage of one of these moments to leap to his feet and dive into the shadows, too. Mora didn't waste her breath telling him not to.

She and the remaining two boys adjusted their positions again. Their movements got the guards' attention, but they only noticed the captives shifting in their sleep. The guards hadn't committed the captives' positions to memory. The guards didn't see anything wrong.

Mora fought to stay calm. Now what? What were the boys doing out there? Were they doing anything? She really, really hoped they didn't get caught.

Chapter 18

Mora didn't see or hear anything all night long. She was still lying there waiting by the time grey dawn light spread through the jungle and the sun started to come up.

The guards headed back into camp to rouse the next watch. They shook their comrades, but the men didn't wake up.

A horrified yell rang through the camp. "He's dead! Someone killed Goutan in his sleep!"

All fourteen of the guards ran to the spot—and then they searched the whole camp.

"They're all dead!" one man husked in a shaky undertone when the fourteen guards reassembled. "Someone must have snuck into camp in the middle of the night and killed them all! They're all dead! The fourteen of us are the only ones left."

A different, much bigger Rider shot a glance around at the trees. "They're out there!" he croaked. "The Godless are out there! They must be the ones doing this! They must have come in here by stealth and killed all our men!"

The first guard barged across the camp and raised his weapon to threaten the captives. "Everybody get up! Get up—all of you!"

He pushed and even kicked the women and boys to stand up. The other guards gathered around and they all crowded the women and boys into another tight group. None of the surviving Red Riders noticed Ghari and Urdis missing.

Mora didn't know what to expect. Would the guards kill all of these women and boys right this very minute?

"Get moving!" The biggest man shoved the women and boys into the jungle and took off walking through the undergrowth.

Mora looked around her everywhere. Were Ghari and Urdis watching the party right now? Did the boys go and get the Godless men sometime during the night?

The party only made it a hundred yards before some unseen force yanked one of the Red Riders down into the undergrowth. Mora didn't see what got the guy. He screamed out once in blood-curdling agony before he fell silent.

The other Riders rushed to the spot and found his body lying there on the ground in a pool of the man's own blood. A giant gash cut him open across the middle of his upper abdomen.

Blood poured from the cut. He was already dead with no sign of who or what killed him. The other Red Riders searched the area and couldn't find a single footprint or even any sign of a creature nearby.

The men reassembled near the remaining women and boys. The Red Riders held a hasty conference and cast terrified looks all around at the jungle.

"I'm telling you this valley is cursed," one of them mumbled. "We never should have come here."

"Shut your mouth!" the biggest man snapped. "We're already here. We aren't going to let these vermin defeat us."

"We're all gonna die here!" the first man countered. "Don't you get that by now? Every party we've sent after these Godless has vanished without a trace. The same thing will happen to us."

"We're already here and we're going to finish the job," his comrade returned. "Now get in line and keep moving."

The column kept going, but the same thing happened a few minutes later. One of the men at the edge of the line toppled into the nearby undergrowth, shrieked out in mortal terror, and fell silent. His friends found him gutted and bleeding to death. No one could save him.

The Red Riders didn't stick around as long to debate the situation. There were only ten men left. The women and boys probably could have overcome the surviving Red Riders, but it somehow worked out much better not to.

Whoever or whatever was attacking these men used the women and boys to distract the Riders. They didn't guard themselves, each other, or the captives.

The party kept walking south. The Red Riders might want to meet up with another group out there on maneuvers. Mora couldn't explain their behavior any other way.

She wouldn't have been so concerned about taking a bunch of captives with her if she had been in the Red Riders' position. She would have been more concerned with staying alive.

The party walked for half an hour before the third man went down. The group had to stop again while the Red Riders checked the situation out to determine that their friend really was dead.

Mora stood there waiting for the Red Riders to get everyone moving again. Out of nowhere, a knife dropped from the trees above her head. The weapon fell right in front of her and embedded its point in the soft soil at her feet.

She started down at it for a second. It really was a knife. It wasn't as big as her usual blades. She wouldn't have been able to conceal that.

She didn't dare to look up to see where the weapon came from. She probably wouldn't have seen anything anyway.

A dozen other weapons fell right at that moment. They all dropped strategically so they didn't hit any of the Godless captives. The weapons buried their points in the dirt right where the women had no problem picking them up.

The Red Riders' discussion escalated into another argument. One of the men outright panicked and started screaming that they were all going to die and that they had to get out of the valley as quickly as possible before the Godless killed every last one of the Riders.

Mora took that moment to snatch the knife out of the ground. She wiped the dirt on her leg and stashed the weapon inside her top.

The other women did the same thing. They made a show of turning the boys away from the argument to conceal what the women were doing.

Thena and Narina both got weapons for themselves. The Red Riders came back, but instead of marching the women and boys southward, the Riders turned the whole group around and headed straight back north in the direction from which they'd come.

Thena and Narina moved closer to Mora in the line. The three women stuck close together and shared meaningful glances on the way. There were only eleven Riders left and far more women and boys.

When should the party strike? Leading the Red Riders around by their noses felt so much more satisfying.

The men met up with another, much larger party of fifty Red Riders after another hour. These men had just come from a major skirmish against the Godless.

Half the men here were injured. They were on their way to the camp where the captive women and boys had just spent the night.

The two parties came to a halt again while all the Riders discussed what had been going on. The surviving guards started to lose control of themselves explaining how all their men had gotten killed in the middle of the night.

That one guy kept saying over and over again that the valley was cursed—or that this particular band of Godless was cursed. He even speculated that the Godless might be ghosts from the other side and that they couldn't be killed at all.

The others hurled insults at him, called him crazy, and told him to pull himself together and use his head.

Their certainty wavered when he reminded them about all the Red Rider patrols that had gone out to look for this band and vanished into the landscape as if they were never there.

The Red Riders could count on one hand the number of men who'd gone out to hunt this band and lived to tell the tale. Hundreds of Red Riders had met their deaths compared to those rare few who survived any encounter with this band of Godless.

The biggest man who seemed to be in charge of the captives went on to say that he had decided to take the women and boys back north to the cliffs and fall back to the valley rim to regroup.

He told his comrades that they couldn't risk losing any more men by staying down here—not until they came up with some better plan to defeat the Godless. The Red Riders couldn't afford to sit around waiting for the Godless to ambush them in the dead of night.

The others didn't want to accept this—not with other patrols still out there fighting the Godless. The sheer panic in the original guards swayed the second party to go along with this. Everyone headed north.

Mora no longer worried about what would happen to her or the other women and boys. Enough of the women were armed now. They would strike as soon as the sun went down.

The Red Riders never thought the women might be the ones responsible for these deaths. The Red Riders defended themselves and kept watch against everything other than the captives.

None of the women could act with so many more men standing guard.

The Red Riders surrounded the party of captives and escorted everyone through the jungle in a guarding posture—as if the women and boys needed protecting from whatever was out there hunting the Riders.

Mora settled in for a long hike to the cliffs. She had no idea what the Red Riders would find when they got there. Blackjack was running this campaign now. Anything was possible.

Out of nowhere, an overwhelming force snatched one of the Red Riders off the ground, yanked him into the air at high speed, and he shot away into the branches. He vanished before the other Riders even realized what was happening.

Everyone halted in their tracks and looked around. Even the women and boys stopped to look around. No one understood what was happening—no one except Mora. She knew this trick. She was the one who had introduced it to the Godless in the first place.

She couldn't remember if she'd ever told it to Bone and Blackjack, but Hangman might have—or he might have told one of the other men who passed it on to Bone and Blackjack.

Mora knew one thing for certain now. Urdis and Ghari weren't the ones killing these Riders. The men were the ones doing this. They would hound the Red Riders all the way to the cliffs picking off one man at a time.

The Red Riders got moving again pretty soon only for the same thing to happen three more times in rapid succession. The first time alerted the Red Riders enough for them to see what was happening after that.

They saw their comrades getting ripped off the ground by ropes cinched around their necks. Mora didn't see the bent-over saplings springing back to pull the Riders away. The surviving Red Riders couldn't have seen the saplings, either.

Not understanding what was happening sent the Red Riders into a panic. Even some of the most rational and skeptical members of the second patrol finally got the message and hustled everyone to walk faster, but it didn't help.

More men kept sailing off into the canopy at strategic points. Mora didn't see how the Godless men could be laying these ambushes so quickly or how the men knew the Red Riders would come this way.

The Riders lost all sense of restraint and pushed everyone into a dead run for the cliffs—as if the Riders could find safety there. The Godless couldn't noose their victims at this speed, so running for it actually did work out for the Riders in the end.

The party burst out of the trees and ran the rest of the way to the walls—only to stop dead when the Red Riders saw a pile of bodies and broken timbers lying there.

A ripple of tension went through the captive women and boys. Mora heard a few women snort with suppressed laughter before they silenced themselves. Some of the women even had to turn away to hide their delight over the Red Riders' fate.

The Red Riders stood rooted to the spot staring at their dead comrades. One glance up at the clifftop told these men all they needed to know. This broken, splintered wood had come from their destroyed hoist. The Riders were trapped here in this valley with no way out.

More Riders panicked, turned away, and came face to face with the Godless men coming out of the jungle behind them.

The Godless came in overwhelming numbers this time. A massive line of warriors stepped out of the trees all the way to the right and all the way to the left as far as Mora could see.

The Godless ranks curved around at both ends to trap the Red Riders here. There was no escape. Blackjack stopped at the center of the army and halted there in open confrontation with his enemies.

The Godless drew their weapons and so did the Red Riders. Mora saw another battle about to break out—and now all the Red Riders stood with their backs to the women and boys.

She pulled her knife and attacked the Red Riders from behind. They were all too focused on the Godless men. She stabbed three Riders to the ground before any of the others saw what was happening.

Her actions set off an answering wave through the other women. Those with weapons dove in to attack, too. They slashed the Riders' throats, stabbed them in the back, hamstrung them, and snapped their necks one after the other.

The unarmed women surged forward, snatched unused weapons from the Red Riders' belts, and even grabbed fallen axes from their dead enemies.

The women struck fast and furious and leveled half the Red Riders before any of the Godless men moved out of line. The men stood off in formation against the tree line. None of them intervened to help or hinder the women's attack.

The few Red Riders who survived the attack had to turn around to defend themselves against the women. That's when the Godless men charged forward. Not even all of them had to attack to finish off the Riders.

Chapter 19

Blackjack led the women and boys back to the camp in the rocks for the night. A celebration broke out among all the freed Godless captives, especially the women who had attacked and killed Red Riders today.

The celebration really got out of hand when Urdis and Ghari returned from the jungle. The women made a huge fuss over the two boys, hugged them, and exclaimed over their victory. The women did everything except carry the boys around on their shoulders.

Blackjack watched from afar while Mora, Thena, and Narina celebrated with the others. They told the story over and over again. Their cheeks glowed in the firelight.

Some of the men went hunting, brought back their kills, and everyone ate as much as they wanted. The party had to sit down and keep quiet while they ate, but the conversation picked up again pretty soon.

"Will you bring the women and children back inside the valley now?" Mora asked.

"There are still a lot of Red Riders running around loose," Blackjack replied. "We need to get rid of them first. Then we'll bring everyone home once we know it's safe."

"How will you get rid of the Riders—by hunting them down?" Thena asked. "Will you use the bottleneck again?"

"We're already planning our campaign," Blackjack replied. "Yeoli's people are building the bottleneck and getting it ready for us. We'll need all of you women to help us spring the trap."

"How do you want us to do that?" Mora asked. "Please please please tell me your plan involves us keeping our weapons now."

He laughed at her. "It does. Oh, that reminds me." He waved over his shoulder. Two men from one of the southern valley bands entered the camp just then and deposited all the women's and boys' weapons in a stack near the fire.

The women crowded around separating their weapons from each other. The women all talked and laughed about what they would have done differently if they'd only had their weapons with them in the Red Riders' camp.

"So what's your plan?" Mora asked again after the noise died down and everyone resumed their places.

"My plan is exactly the same as it was before. I want you to make yourselves visible to the Red Riders and get them to come after you. You'll lure them to follow you and we'll lead them south to the bottleneck. We'll use the same staggered approach. Some of you will run from them until you feel yourselves starting to get tired. Then you'll get into the branches and someone else will take over to lead the Riders farther south. They can't resist the chance to capture a woman."

"It's risky," Thena remarked.

"Not as risky as letting them stay in the valley," Blackjack returned. "This will be the quickest way to get rid of all of them in one battle."

"How will you know all the Red Riders will take part in this?" Mora asked. "You said there was more than one group."

"There is, but their numbers are dwindling. They'll have no choice but to rejoin into one group just so they have enough men to attack us."

Narina scooted close to him, put her arm around him from behind, and rested her head on his shoulder. She didn't join in the general conversation nor did she laugh and joke around the way she used to when she first joined this band.

She seemed to have gotten a lot more serious since she came to the valley. This was the real Narina. The other casual, joking version was a façade to protect herself from people she didn't know.

Blackjack would spend tonight with her in their own shelter before they went straight back out to war tomorrow. No one could escape from that.

Everyone else present seemed to be thinking the same thing. Mora left early and went off to her shelter alone.

Blackjack didn't blame her. Hangman wasn't here. That had to sting. He wouldn't come back until the band defeated the Red Riders and rid the valley of all of them.

Blackjack took Narina away long before the others went to sleep. He didn't want to socialize.

He and Narina didn't talk. They just went back to their own shelter, went straight to bed, and held each other in the dark. She'd been in enemy hands for barely two days and she would go straight back out into danger tomorrow morning.

He couldn't even be glad that she'd participated in killing those Riders at the base of the cliffs. He didn't want them anywhere near her.

They both fell asleep without doing anything. He wasn't in the mood. Just holding her for one night was all he could ever really ask for.

They woke up in the morning and spent a long time just kissing, looking into each other's eyes, and knowing. He didn't have to ask and neither did she.

They eventually got up, went outside, and ate breakfast while they waited for the rest of the band to wake up and get ready to go. Mora was one of the first to come outside. Thena showed up not long after.

The family ate together—except that Hangman wasn't here. His absence cast a shadow over everyone.

Blackjack didn't like to think of his father as collateral of war. Blackjack continued to maintain the illusion that Hangman was and always would be Kral of this band. He would recover. He would regain his strength. He would take charge again.

The rest of the band assembled, ate, talked, and the conversation finally turned to the coming campaign. "We have a long way to travel south to get into position," Blackjack announced. "Let's get moving. We can work out the finer details on the way."

The others obeyed him and headed out. He sent out scouting parties to sweep the valley from north to south for any trace of the Red Riders.

The few remaining patrols had already traveled beyond the pass in the hopes of ambushing the southern valley bands. The scouts returned to announce that the northern end of the valley was clear.

The party kept traveling for the rest of the day. The scouts canvased the whole valley to make sure no Red Riders remained north of the pass.

The band camped in the open that night, fell asleep early, and hiked up to the pass by midmorning on the second day. Blackjack stopped there to look down. "It seems like only yesterday when we fought the Anglers here."

"These aren't Anglers," Mora pointed out. "The Red Riders will be able to fit through the escape holes we plan to use ourselves."

"We're planning for that," Blackjack replied. "Let's move out. You scouts go ahead, find out where the Riders are, and we'll send in the women to take over for us."

The party set off down the other side of the pass and picked up speed the closer they got to the jungle. Two bands lived north of the pass and two bands lived south of the pass.

Mora didn't know what Blackjack had been planning and doing while she and the other women had been the Red Riders' prisoners. She was about to find out.

She spotted both camps from the downward slopes of the pass. Columns of smoke billowed from both camps. They looked inhabited to lure the Red Riders there.

Blackjack followed the same strategy that the Godless had used against the Anglers. He cut wide to the west and followed the cliffs until the scouts came back and told him where the Red Riders were. He kept going to get in front of them.

He eventually came to the westernmost camp. A skeleton crew of men worked from shelter to shelter keeping fires going and making the place look as inhabited as possible without any women and children living here.

Blackjack divided up the women and boys, put ten women and two boys here in the camp, and then stationed all the other women and boys at key locations along the route south.

He posted the women who were the fastest runners at the front and kept back the slower ones for the final push to the bottleneck.

He accompanied all the women into the jungle, pointed out to them where he wanted them to wait, and where he wanted them to get into the branches to let the next person take over.

He barely got the first runners in place before his scouts returned to tell him that the Red Riders were moving in on the western camp. The separate Red Rider groups had already rejoined into a much bigger force.

He had to race after that to get all the women into position. He only prayed they could run and climb fast enough to save themselves.

He retreated all the way to the bottleneck to make sure the men and boys concealed themselves in the jungle. The Red Riders wouldn't see the trap until it was too late.

Blackjack rushed through all of these preparations and charged back to the jungle canopy to catch up with the women. He had to be there to help them in case anything went wrong—*when* something went wrong.

He got there just as Yonna, Bantam's wife, came perilously close to getting caught by the Red Riders. She scrambled into the branches just in time.

She barely got out of their reach before Thena pretended to be passing through that part of the jungle right at that moment. She screamed when she saw the Red Riders, turned away, and ran for it.

Her behavior sparked them to run after her exactly the way Blackjack wanted them to. She ran a long way before she came to the next checkpoint. The Red Riders gained on her and almost caught her, too.

She vaulted into the branches only for the Red Riders to get distracted by a scuffle in the undergrowth. They went to investigate and spotted Narina and Ghari scrambling to get away.

They both took off into the jungle. Blackjack didn't realize until that moment that Narina could run so fast. Blackjack and every other Godless he knew considered other Clans weaker and less capable.

He should have posted her in the very front. She was one of the fastest runners of all the women. He wouldn't have posted her in the very front. She was his wife. He had to protect her—or as much as possible.

She and Ghari easily stayed ahead of the Red Riders. Blackjack noticed them both slowing down so the Red Riders wouldn't fall too far behind.

Narina ran around a thick tree and Thena sprang out to run in her place. The Red Riders didn't notice. They only saw a woman running away from them and ran after her.

Ghari did the same thing and Urdis took over. The Red Riders chased him, too, even though he looked nothing like Ghari. Thena and Urdis came together and so did all the Red Riders. Thena and Urdis made their last desperate sprint for the edge of the trees.

They barely got into the branches in time for the Red Riders to see all the older, slower, less able-bodied women standing right there in the open—right in front of the bottleneck. The Red Riders couldn't resist the temptation.

Chapter 20

The Red Riders blasted out of the trees and all the women screamed and ran in the only direction left—straight inside the bottleneck. The women flooded inside with the Red Riders closing fast.

The last women barely squeezed through the opening before the Red Riders crashed into the fences. The Red Riders couldn't get inside straight on. Each man had to turn his shoulders sideways to wedge himself through the narrow gap.

The women ran shrieking for the walls and crowded into the corners as the first Riders broke into the enclosure. The women started clawing their way through the exit holes on either corner against the cliff walls.

One woman after another made it out, but not fast enough. Three Riders barged over there and grabbed the women still waiting to get out. Screams echoed from inside.

The women's voices electrified the rest of the Riders. They shoved their way inside. Blackjack and his men leapt out of the trees and rushed the fence. All the Red Riders were trapped inside—but so were the women.

One of the Riders caught Narina just as she was about to crawl through the hole. He dragged her kicking and screaming back inside the enclosure.

The women the Red Riders had already captured distracted the Riders from going after all the other women. More and more women crawled out. The Godless warriors stationed themselves at the holes.

The Red Riders tried to crawl through only to get skewered by the Godless as soon as the Riders showed their faces. Blackjack, Bone, and the others stayed around the bottleneck. The Red Riders couldn't escape.

That one man flipped Narina over and tried to grab her around the body. She kicked him in the knee hard enough to make him bellow, but that only enraged him. He pounced on her.

Blackjack couldn't stand here and watch that. He dove through the gap into the enclosure. He wasn't the only one. A dozen Godless men charged inside and attacked the Riders inside the enclosure.

The Riders couldn't hold the women and defend themselves at the same time. The Godless killed seven Riders before the survivors abandoned the women and closed ranks against the Godless.

The women scuttled away and through the side exit points. A few Riders tried to follow only to meet their deaths outside. Blackjack saw it all working out according to his plans.

"Fall back!" he called to his men. "Fall back and get out!"

The men backed away and defended each other one at a time to leave the enclosure. That left the Red Riders trapped inside.

They turned out to be a lot smarter than the Anglers. The Red Riders figured out instantly the predicament they were in. They didn't try to leave the enclosure. They gathered in one spot and put their heads together to decide what to do.

Blackjack nodded to his men. They set fire to the grass from either escape point. The Red Riders crowded closer to the center and choked on the smoke, but they still didn't run out through the bottleneck.

The long grass didn't create flames high enough or hot enough to put the Riders in danger. They just jumped over the flames and the fire burned itself out without harming them.

"Is that all you got?!" one of the Riders bellowed over the fence. "You'll have to do better than that if you want to kill us."

"You'll never leave this valley alive!" Blackjack yelled back. "Every one of your kind who comes after us will disappear! It's been that way for years and you won't be the last!"

He turned to the uninitiated boys who stood there watching with their weapons drawn to kill any Riders who left the enclosure.

"Go out into the jungle and bring the ants here," Blackjack ordered. "Lead the pollen trail to the enclosure entrance."

Urdis looked back and forth from Blackjack to the tall fence. "How will we get away once we bring them? They'll tear down the fence and we'll be stuck here."

"Bring the ants to that Denofus tree over there," Blackjack told him. "We'll gather our own pollen and lay the trail from here to that tree. Lead the ants to that tree, join the two pollen trails, and get up into the branches. The ants will follow the trail."

"Won't the Riders leave the enclosure as soon as you leave?" Ghari asked.

"We'll post guards to watch for the ants and give us warning. Go now. Bring the ants here. It will be all right."

The two boys took off running. Blackjack sent Calv and Nubos into the jungle to bring a different load of pollen. They spread a pollen trail from the bottleneck to the Denofus tree. Blackjack ordered all the women and boys to get up into the canopy now.

The Red Riders fell silent listening to Blackjack give these orders. He didn't give a crap if they heard or not. They wouldn't get out of here alive one way or the other. He had them trapped and he planned to keep them that way until they perished.

He waited a while and then posted Red and Wildling in the canopy to signal when the boys were bringing the ants. The time passed.

"You don't have to do this," one of the Red Riders finally blurted out.

"I'm not doing anything, you moron," Blackjack snarled back. "You're the ones who invaded another Clan's territory. You did that even knowing the outcome. You're the ones who did this, so don't come crying to me now. You got exactly what you asked for."

Blackjack glanced over his shoulder to see Red and Wilding waving at him. He ordered everyone else into the canopy.

He couldn't resist the urge to turn around and grin at his victims. He actually saw them as people now for the first time.

He'd always considered them little better than animals. He never thought of them as people who might feel fear at the thought of going down to the ants.

"See you men in the next life." He burst out laughing at the horrified looks on their faces. "I'm sure your deaths will be much more pleasant than the fate of all your captives. Just remember that. I'm doing you a favor."

He turned away and sprinted for the trees just as the ants came in sight. He was the last person on the ground except for the boys leading the ants.

His every instinct rebelled against running straight toward such a massive army of the creatures. He had to force himself not to run in the other direction. He wouldn't have been able to take refuge back there.

He bolted into the jungle and sprang into the trees just as the boys vaulted up there with him. They threw the last handfuls of pollen onto the ground in front of the Denofus tree.

The ants kept marching on an unbending course out of the jungle. They headed straight for the bottleneck. The Red Riders came forward to the gap, now that they didn't see any Godless standing guard there.

They saw the ants instead and instantly retreated back to where they were. They held an even more frantic discussion about what to do. There was nothing to do. It was all over.

The Riders even tried to climb the cliff walls. When that failed, they climbed up on the fence to scale over it.

The ants made it to the gap and entered the enclosure a few at a time. The rest of the army swarmed the walls and started chewing their way through it. The Riders inside drew their weapons and backed away to escape from the ants.

The ants homed in on their next meal. The Riders' movement drew the ants to them. The Riders hacked at one ant after another. The Riders defended themselves just fine against one or two.

The overpowering tide of ants outside the walls ate through the timbers in no time. The ants discovered the thick ropes binding the timbers together. The ants brought the fence down and all the men perched on top of it fell into the mass of swarming bodies.

The rest of the ants flooded the enclosure and took down all the rest of the Riders in a few seconds. Their screams drifted on the breeze and then faded to nothing.

The ants teemed all over the area, consumed everything they came across, and even ate the grass down the bare dirt. Blackjack and the others watched from the branches. He didn't have to do anything else. It was over. He could finally take his people home.

The others sat in silence for a long time. No one moved or said a word. Everyone just watched the cataclysm take the last Red Riders out of this world. Peace and quiet settled over the valley again, but no one got up to leave.

Life would return to normal after this—or as close to normal as possible. The four valley bands would go back to scouting the area outside the valley to keep watch for any other enemy Clans coming around.

These Red Riders just didn't learn. If Bone and the others were right, then the Red Riders would return to the top of the cliffs. The Riders might try to build another hoist. Blackjack would have to prepare his people for that.

The sun started to sink toward the west. "Let's get on our way home," he told everyone. "We have a long way to travel. Bone, take your men west and scout the area to make sure we got all the Riders. Oracle, you take your men to the east side. We'll travel straight up the middle of the valley. I'm sure we'll find any Red Riders if they're there to find."

The men split up. The women and boys descended to the ground, but the sun went down long before the band made it very far. The Godless who usually lived in the southern valley camps split off early to go to their own homes.

That left Blackjack with his core of closest supporters. They camped in sight of the pass on the southern side this time. The same silence blanketed the group.

Blackjack remembered this from the journey south to defeat the Anglers, but the silence only happened the night before the battle. The tension had lifted as soon as the Godless eliminated the Anglers.

That didn't happen tonight. Narina sat next to him, held his hand, and rested her head on his shoulder, but she didn't talk. No one talked beyond the bare minimum of a few words at a time.

Blackjack didn't feel like talking, either—not tonight. He tried to pinpoint exactly what the problem was. Some gut feeling gave him a vague sense of unease. This wasn't the end. The Red Riders were still out there.

They would come back. They always came back. They never went away. He wouldn't likely be able to trap the whole Clan in this valley. He would never be able to eliminate them all.

He would have thought someone in charge would have made the decision to leave the Godless alone after the band had killed so many Red Riders. Did the Red Riders still want revenge that badly? Why? The Godless weren't the ones who had started this.

He didn't know when or how the Red Riders would return, but his innermost gut told him they would. Everyone else in the band must have felt it, too.

Defeating the Anglers had been a decisive, permanent victory. The Anglers wouldn't come back. There were no more Anglers anywhere. The band had won this valley and made it safe from all enemy invasions—until now.

The Red Riders would come back and Blackjack would have to deal with them all over again.

Chapter 21

Hangman limped from one family to another. The women, children, and injured men had made camp by a stream a short distance from the tunnel's outer entrance. Everyone seemed comfortable here.

Landslide had died that very first night in the tunnels. The band had buried him in the adjacent valley. Smash wasn't far behind them.

Viking didn't seem to be improving from his injuries as well as he should have. He had become less mobile in the days since the band had been staying here. He felt worse and his energy drained way too quickly.

Hangman dosed his cousin with gallons of Gooji juice, but nothing seemed to help. The women helped Hangman immensely by gathering Gooji sap and firewood for him, Smash, and Viking.

All the Gooji juice in the world couldn't save Smash. Hangman had begun to fear as the days wore on that the same thing would happen to Viking. Hangman couldn't stand that.

He spent every evening sitting next to Viking talking to him. Hangman had faced the deaths of his closest comrades. He had to clasp every possible second with his cousin that remained before it was too late.

Viking seemed to come to the same conclusion. He spoke much more gently with Hangman these last few days and expressed both his admiration and affection more easily. These last precious days brought the cousins closer than ever.

Viking didn't get up and move around during the day. He couldn't stand. He had made it down to the stream the morning after the band had moved here. Then he'd sat down at the base of a tree and stayed there.

Hangman didn't see how Viking would ever make it back to the Godless camp without someone carrying him. Hangman didn't care how Viking got back there as long as he made it back—and then what?

Viking wouldn't live forever. Viking was more than fifteen years older than Hangman. Viking was already old by Godless standards. He wouldn't last much longer even in the peak of health.

These injuries took their toll on Hangman. The effects on such an older man would be even more profound. Hangman just hoped and prayed that Viking wouldn't die from them.

He would die from something. Hangman had to come to grips with that. His parents were dead. All his uncles and other cousins were all dead. Viking was the last of his generation.

Hangman could look forward to a lot more of this in the coming years. Red and his men were all older than Hangman. He would probably have to watch them die, too. He just couldn't bear that, but he would have to.

He would have to sit with them by their fires at night and talk to them about old times. They would talk about their children and grandchildren and how the younger generation was running the band in their place.

He would have to grapple for every single second of the time he had left with his friends. He couldn't waste any of that time.

They weren't here now. Were any of them dying right now inside the valley? He would have given anything to go in there and help them, but he couldn't.

The women and children needed him more. He couldn't take care of them, but they needed his guidance and leadership.

The women and children from the other three valley bands had joined Hangman's group outside the valley. The band had swelled to hundreds of people all clustered together by family.

The women took turns taking care of each other's children while some of them went hunting to feed the party.

He had selected a spot under the trees where the dense canopy would hide the smoke from the band's cooking fires.

He had convinced the band to sleep and spend all the rest of their time in the treetops—all except Smash and Viking. The women left the two men on the ground.

Viking kept his axe handy to defend Smash against anything that came along, but Viking wouldn't have been able to fight anything in his condition. The two men were either a liability to the band or already gone. Everyone treated them as if they were.

Hangman spent his days going from person to person helping the women and children as much as possible. He offered them his advice, encouragement, and straightened out any disputes between neighbors. Everyone had to get along here or die.

He also carried water, ground leaf paste, helped the women with their sewing, or whatever else they needed. Sometimes he got waylaid in the middle of camp and stayed there for hours before he went on with his usual rounds.

He usually made three circuits of the camp—once in the morning, once at midday, and once in the evening. He spent the rest of his time with Viking. Any of the women who needed Hangman could come and get him there.

The little children usually came to visit him there, especially the boys. They liked to pretend to fight him or ask him to teach them how to fight. He obliged just to keep them entertained.

He returned to Viking's side and lowered himself painfully to the ground. Hangman's injuries still hurt as bad as ever, but he pushed through it to keep helping his people wherever and whenever possible.

Viking made a face at him. "You would heal faster if you rested more. You know that, don't you? You're only making it take longer."

"I'll heal when the war is over." Hangman picked up a length of hide he was sewing. He was making a miniature shoulder bag for one of the little boys to carry pebbles and pieces of dried food that his mother gave him.

"How long do you think it will take Blackjack and the others to finish off the Red Riders?" Viking asked.

Hangman shrugged over his stitching. "I suppose that all depends on when the Red Riders finished bringing all their men down to the valley floor. That could have taken a while. I guess we won't know until the men send someone out to tell us it's safe to go back inside."

Viking grimaced at the people around him. He must have been in pain. It made him surly. He didn't tolerate it well when anyone except for Hangman went near him.

Viking turned away to pick up his water gourd. He had become insatiably thirsty since he'd gotten hurt. Hangman didn't like what that might mean.

Hangman glanced out at the band—and froze in his seat when he saw another band approaching the Godless camp. Hangman struggled to his feet and limped out there as quickly as he could to meet the strangers.

Women stood up all over the area when they saw these people moving in on them. Hangman took a second before he recognized the strangers' clothes.

A group of armed men stood at the front of the group. More armed men arranged themselves on both sides of a column of women and girls in the center. The women and girls far outnumbered the men.

Hangman didn't see any pregnant women in the group, but that didn't mean anything. Their clothes gave them away. These people must have come from the Red Riders. These people must be escaped captives.

"Can I help you?" Hangman asked. "Who are you and where do you come from?"

The men glanced all around the area at the women and children camping under the trees. "You're Godless," one of the men blurted out. "Do you know the young men?"

"What young men?" Hangman asked.

"Three Godless men.....they came to the top of the cliffs..."

"They were all very young," another man added. "One of them was younger than the others. He was hardly more than a boy."

"He said his name was Bone. I didn't catch his friends' names," the first man explained. "They came to the top of the cliffs over there. The three of them freed us from the Red Riders and sent us on our way." The guy looked around nothing. "Then we came here."

Hangman raised his eyebrows. "Bone freed you from the Red Riders?! When did this happen?"

"About three days ago," the first man went on. "He said we were free to go, but we have nowhere else to go. We would be wandering around out here forever."

"Most of us have spent our lives as the Red Riders' captives," another added. "We don't know how to hunt or fight or how to survive out here. You have to help us! We'll all die if you don't."

Hangman stiffened. "I won't be able to take you if you don't know how to do anything. Part of accepting my help is that you're prepared to defend yourselves against any enemy. The Red Riders would come back and try to retake you. Are you just going to stand there and let it happen—even when you're holding a weapon in your hands or maybe two weapons?"

The freed captives exchanged glances. Hangman decided to press his advantage.

"I'm only one of two men here and we're both injured. Everyone else here is a mother with young children. Do you really expect us to protect you? You could only join us if you brought something with you that we could use—like you're willing to protect us from our enemies instead of putting all of us in danger."

The men didn't seem to hear him. They looked around at all the women and children. "Why are you out here with women and children who can't defend themselves?" one of the men asked.

"That's none of your business because you aren't part of this band. You're going on your way unless you can give me some reason to let you stay."

He gave the men a hard look. They exchanged glances again.

"All right. We'll do it," the second man replied.

"You'll do what, exactly?" Hangman asked.

"We'll help you defend this band. We'll contribute. We'll pay our own way. We'll help you take care of the band instead of making you take care of us."

"You better or I won't take you at all," Hangman countered. "You'll accept me as your Kral and my word as law. Anyone who disobeys or betrays the band will go to the ants. Is that clear to you all? Anyone who disagrees can leave right now."

The freed captives exchanged glances again before they nodded.

"Then your first task is for all of you men to stand guard around the camp. I'll set up a watch later today so you can work in shifts. Any women who aren't taking care of children can help hunt for food and help the mothers who are taking care of children."

"How do we do that?" one of the women chimed in.

"Which part?" Hangman asked.

"How do we take care of children if we don't have any of our own?"

He shrugged. "I'm sure the mothers will tell you what they need. If you don't want to do that, you can help by bringing water from the stream and tending the fires to cook food for everybody."

The freed captives exchanged glances again. Something about this gave him a bad feeling. He'd never encountered any freed captives who agreed so reluctantly.

Most couldn't wait to join up with the Godless band. The captives knew the Godless would protect them from their enemies. So why did these people hesitate?

Chapter 22

The freed captives split up and settled in with the rest of Hangman's band. He kept an eye on them. At least none of them knew about the tunnel.

He realized too late that he should have warned his people not to divulge where the band really lived or how the band got into and out of the Angler Valley. It was too late now.

It probably wouldn't make any difference in the end. These captives would probably stay in the valley just like all the others. These people would become as Godless and committed to the valley's safety as anyone.

He returned to his place next to Viking. "This place draws them like moths to the flame," Viking remarked.

"At least Bone didn't invite them to come into the valley. That would be the last thing we needed."

"What about when these people do come to the valley?" Viking asked. "It's going to get a lot harder to manage all these people."

Hangman only shrugged. He had bigger things to worry about—like all these people living in one place. Now another group added their numbers to the band.

Things settled down after that. The new men patrolled the area. Some of them actually did know how to hunt and brought their kills back to share with everyone.

Actually the men brought their kills back for their own women. Hangman had to intervene and point out that any food they brought back would be shared by everyone. If the men didn't like it, they would have to make sure to bring back enough for everyone.

"How do we know our own women will get enough?" one of the men grumbled.

Hangman waved at the people around him. "Do you now see the situation I'm in? Our women have been hunting for us all this time. If you didn't hunt, our women would have to hunt to feed your women and children. Do you call that fair? If you want to keep your women separate and eat your own food separately, then go your own way. You don't need us for that."

"What *do* we need you for?" the same guy shot back.

"You don't need me for anything, brother," Hangman countered. "You're the ones who asked us for help. I never asked you to come here. Go your own way if that's what you want. We won't lose anything from you leaving."

The man turned away grumbling. His attitude sparked Hangman's temper. He dove forward on his one good leg, grabbed the guy by the arm, and spun him around.

"You accepted me as your Kral," Hangman snapped. "Make that the very last time I hear you complain about anything going on around here. You'll do your work and follow my orders or I'll feed you to the ants." He raised his voice so all the newcomers could hear him. "This will be the last time I give you the option to leave. Leave right this minute or accept my rule. Those are your only options. You'll share your kills and everything else you bring in. You'll defend our women and children as your own. Any betrayal after this will be punished accordingly—or you can keep on walking. No one will miss you."

Dead silence hung over the band as those words rang through the jungle. The new women and young girls settled in much more quickly than the men. The men stayed on watch, but they didn't guard the band as well as Godless men would have.

Hangman tried to distinguish the difference between these people and the captives he'd freed from the Red Rider camp. They had all been ecstatically relieved and happy to join up with him and his men.

The men he'd freed had been the staunchest allies he could ask for. They showed no qualms about taking up arms that very minute to kill as many Red Riders as possible. None of those freed men had ever questioned Hangman's orders—ever.

They had given him no reason to question them in all the four years the four bands had been living in the valley. The other bands had been the first to respond when Blackjack called on them for aid.

These people asked for his help and then seemed to throw it back in his face. They didn't seem to understand the concept of a Kral and that they had to obey him in everything even if they disagreed with him.

That business about not sharing their food struck him as the most offensive. What did these idiots think—that they could hunt for their women and leave everyone else to fend for themselves?

These people would gladly have eaten the band's food if he had let them. These people would have moved in and let the Godless do everything to take care of them.

These men making trouble right now—they would have thought nothing of eating food provided for them by another band's women—provided even by women who had their own children to take care of.

These people wouldn't have lifted a finger to contribute if he hadn't insisted on it. He never doubted that. Now they had the nerve to protest doing their part and helping take care of this band's most vulnerable people.

He kept a close watch on the men all day. He couldn't find any fault with their conduct. They guarded the camp the way they were supposed to, but they might have done that only to protect their own women.

He would have divided them into watches a lot sooner if they hadn't complained and protested like that. He would have made it easier for them to take turns so some of them could rest.

Now he delayed doing it. He didn't want them to rest. He didn't want to take it easy on them. He would have liked to drive them into the night.

Viking didn't say a word about the situation. His hard, sharp eyes told Hangman everything he needed to know. He even caught the women shooting the newcomers side glances.

Some of the newcomer women socialized with the Godless women. These more social newcomers and children settled in the easiest, but Hangman still didn't feel right.

What exactly was he supposed to do with these people once Blackjack came to tell Hangman that it was safe for the Godless to return to the valley? Would Hangman take these people with him? Was he really prepared to do that?

He didn't trust them enough to take them into the valley. He couldn't explain why except that their behavior raised too many questions.

The women's behavior didn't raise any questions. Only one man had complained against him so far. He couldn't hold that against everyone.

The day wore on and the sun started to go down. Some of the newcomer men approached Hangman and Viking. The guy who'd grumbled didn't come.

"Should we stay on watch all night long?" one man asked. "You said you would divide us into watches."

"You know these men better than I do," Hangman replied. "Go around and ask for volunteers for anyone who is willing to stand the first watch. If you don't find enough people, then assign some. The rest of you get some sleep."

The guy's eyes widened. "You're not going to do it yourself?! You want us to do it? You want us to assign ourselves? Isn't that what you're here for?"

Hangman gritted his teeth not to lose his temper with this man. Hangman leveled him with a brutal stare. "Would you like it better if I assigned everyone against their will and didn't ask for volunteers at all? Would you like it if I assigned you to the first watch instead of asking for volunteers?"

"I don't care if I stand the first watch," the man fired back. "Someone has to do it."

"Then you're the most qualified to go around and ask for volunteers. If you don't get anyone and no one agrees to you assigning them against their will, then come back and tell me and I'll make them do it—and tell them that if I catch even one of them sleeping or slacking off on watch, he won't survive until morning. I don't know which of these men have women and children in the group, but tell the men that these women's lives depend on the men standing watch, staying alert all night long, and being ready to fight if anything comes to threaten us."

Hangman turned his head away to dismiss the guy. The guy scowled at Hangman for a second and then stalked off back to the other new men.

"This is like nothing I've ever seen before," Viking remarked under his breath. "Why are these people even here?"

"That's what I keep asking myself. We'll see if they come around. They can all go die somewhere else if they don't."

Chapter 23

Hangman and Viking watched that one man go through all the freed men. The stranger gave them orders, collected ten volunteers plus himself, and assigned another twenty to stand the first watch whether they liked it or not.

Hangman distinctly heard the guy tell these dopes that he would go get Hangman if they didn't pull it into line real quick.

Hangman had to turn his head away and bite back a grin when he heard that. None of the other new guys argued when that one man mentioned bringing in Hangman to do the job.

Hangman was really starting to regret not asking this man's name. Some of these new people were bound to be good ones. They were bound to be people the Godless would be glad to welcome into their ranks.

Hangman would just as soon feed the rest to the ants or send them out into the wilderness to die. This whole situation didn't give him a good feeling at all.

The sun went down and the jungle grew dark. Hangman sent the Godless women and children into the canopy to sleep. That one new guy just happened to be standing close enough to hear Hangman's order.

"Why did you do that?" he asked.

"It's safer than sleeping on the ground," Hangman replied. "It conceals the women and children from detection and they can get away from any threats better if they're up there. Krakelows are the only real threat in the canopy and we can hear them coming."

"That's amazing." The guy stared up at the women and children scaling into the branches and settling down for the night. "I wish we could do that."

Hangman studied the guy from the side. "What's your name?"

The guy jolted. "My name is Yiatu." He frowned. "What's yours?"

"My name is Hangman. That's Viking over there."

Yiatu frowned back at him. "That's a strange name. Why don't you have a real name?"

Hangman took a deep breath and launched into an explanation of how Godless men change their names at initiation and leave their childhood names behind forever.

Hangman explained that the childhood name is considered an insult and the new name is a mark of status and respect. Then he explained exactly what initiation was and how each boy or newcomer initiates into the Godless Clan.

"Any of you men who choose to stay with us will go through the same thing," Hangman finished. "We've had a lot of new people initiate into the Clan. Some of my best friends came from other Clans and initiated as adults. It isn't that common in other bands, but it is in ours."

Yiatu gaped at him with his jaw on the ground. "That sounds incredible," he murmured. "I want to do that."

Hangman found himself beaming at the guy. "You have to get really good at hunting and fighting. Then you can initiate. I'll take you back to my band and introduce you to some of my men. They can tell you all about it."

Yiatu looked away shaking his head. "I don't know if I could ever be good enough to do something like that." He spun around and stared at Hangman. "What did you fight in your initiation?"

Hangman took another deep breath. "I fought a Crusher. That's how I got these scars. I wanted to make a statement and earn my older relatives' respect, so I chose the hardest creature I could think of. I barely survived."

Yiatu shut his mouth with difficulty and gulped. He could barely speak above a whisper. "I don't believe you."

Hangman laughed. "Go ask Viking. He was there. He can tell you what it was like—and he can tell you what a mess I was afterward. My mother cried for days when she saw me."

Yiatu shot a glance over his shoulder toward Viking. Then he scowled at Hangman like Yiatu had to think about whether he really would accept Hangman's story.

Yiatu suddenly spun the other way, stormed across the camp to where Viking sat, and squatted down next to him to talk to him.

Hangman walked off the other way chuckling to himself. These new people would be in for a rude surprise when they finally met up with the other Godless men. Hangman could just imagine what Viking was telling Yiatu right now.

Yiatu was all right. He was more than all right. He was one of the good ones. Hangman couldn't say anything about these other new people.

Hangman started his nightly rotation through the camp to check on all the new people—mostly the women and young girls. They shrank from him at first. Then they figured out that he was offering to help them.

He wound up putting leaf paste on a bunch of old injuries. They looked like blade cuts or just suppurated bruises that had never healed.

Almost all the women here had been brutalized in one way or the other. Even the young girls showed signs of rough treatment.

The men weren't in much better shape. Hangman worked late into the night making Gooji juice for the new people. He wouldn't know until much later if it worked or not.

His activities gave him plenty of opportunity to watch the new guys on watch. Yiatu had to monitor them practically every single second to make sure they did their jobs.

Hangman caught Viking keeping an eye on the new guys, too. Hangman could just imagine how the second and third watches would go without Yiatu supervising everyone.

Hangman was still helping the women by the time Yiatu went through the camp and roused the second watch. He took the new guys on duty, assigned them to their posts, and sent the first watch to sleep.

Hangman took that opportunity to pull Yiatu aside. "Do you remember when I said that anyone I caught shirking or sleeping on the job wouldn't survive until morning?" Hangman asked.

Yiatu gulped again. "Yes, I remember."

"This is the Godless way. I want you to go to sleep right now and be prepared for some of your men not to survive until morning. Some of them wouldn't have survived the first shift if you hadn't been there."

Yiatu looked away. "I know. That's why I did it. Are you angry at me for that?"

"Not at all. I'm not angry at you for anything. I'm extremely pleased with you. That's why I'm telling you. I gave these men a warning. Some of them obviously don't take my word seriously. These men know better than anyone what dangers are waiting for us out here and the men still would have left the women and children unprotected. We don't need anyone like that around. I just don't want you to be offended when you wake up tomorrow morning and find some of your men gone."

Yiatu nodded down at the ground. "I understand and you're right. I.....I just don't know if I would have the balls to do that. I'm.....I'm not Godless."

"You will be if you really want to be. Now go to sleep. This is my job—not yours. Go to sleep and leave it to me. No one will attack the band tonight."

Yiatu nodded and walked away. Hangman waited until Yiatu found a spot for himself, curled up on the ground, and went to sleep. He didn't sleep with any woman or interact with anyone in any significant way. He didn't have a woman.

Hangman shared a glance with Viking. Viking sat against his tree and watched the whole exchange. Viking showed no inclination to go to sleep, either.

Hangman returned to the spot where he usually sat next to Viking. The two cousins usually slept here, too. Hangman remained standing, surveyed the camp one last time, waited until the new guys turned their attention elsewhere, and slipped into the shadowy jungle.

He had to move slowly on his injured leg, but he still knew how to move silently. None of the new guys knew how to use their ears to track night creatures through the jungle.

The new guys wouldn't have heard Hangman even if they had been listening to the night noises.

He skirted the camp to the side where the new men stood guard. Hangman hid in the shadows and watched them. Their vigilance started to slacken the instant Yiatu shut his eyes.

Hangman hardened his heart against all these useless idiots. Who the hell did they think they were—asking for his help and then turning their backs on defenseless women and children the minute someone stopped policing them?

These bastards turned their backs on their own defenseless women and girls. That was the most sickening part of it. He might have been able to understand the men turning their backs and failing to defend total strangers.

These were the women with whom the men had escaped from the Red Riders. These were the women these men should have most wanted to protect.

Hangman knew for a fact that some of these men were in relationships with some of these women. Some of them might even have been as good as married or hoping to be. These men knew enough to provide the women with food.

Sure enough, the new men confirmed Hangman's worst fears by leaning against trees, yawning loudly, looking at everything other than the surroundings, staring into space, fiddling with their weapons, or in some cases, outright going to sleep on watch.

Seven of the fifteen men on watch stayed alert. They listened intently to the surroundings, strained to see anything in the darkness out there, and even glared at their comrades. Hangman had his people. He didn't need anyone else.

He would rather have seven alert, upright men on watch than fifteen bad ones. The bad ones would only drag the band down. They would keep questioning his authority and poisoning everyone else.

He snuck through the undergrowth, hid in the shadows, and waited for everyone else to turn away and pay attention to everything else. Then he tiptoed to the first sleeping man.

This waste of human flesh actually had the nerve to curl up on the ground in the undergrowth where he thought no one would be able to see him. No one could see Hangman here, either.

Hangman lowered himself onto his knees above the guy and slashed his kukri across the man's throat. The guy choked and grabbed at the blood pouring from his neck.

Hangman reacted instantly, shot to his feet, grabbed the man by his shirt, and dragged him off into the jungle. The rest of the men on watch heard the rustling, rushed over to the spot, and looked around, but they didn't see anything. Hangman was long gone.

He stopped thirty feet away still holding his unconscious victim by the shirt. The guards on watch searched the area and found blood-stains, but they found no other evidence of foul play. They came to the conclusion that some creature must have come near the camp.

None of the men on watch noticed their comrade missing. He'd already been missing before. His absence didn't change anything.

Chapter 24

Hangman deposited the guard's dead body near an Abnormit mound farther up the riverbank, but he didn't break into the mound just yet. He snuck back to camp and killed the next sleeping man in the same way.

This one had fallen asleep leaning against a tree where everyone could see him. Hangman used the tree to cover his approach, tiptoed up behind the guy, and snapped his neck so he wouldn't make any noise.

Hangman pulled the guy into the undergrowth before anyone saw or heard. No one realized the man was gone until one of the more alert, responsible guards turned around and frowned.

"Where's Huri?" he demanded.

Everyone paced around looking for the missing man. That's when everyone noticed Hangman's first victim gone, too. Hangman became aware of Viking watching everything, including everything Hangman was doing.

The remaining guards paid a lot more attention after that, but Hangman really didn't give a damn anymore. Their movements and pacing gave him the perfect opportunity to ambush all the rest of the slackers and drag them off to their deaths.

He threw all eight of them in the same pile near the Abnormit nest, but he still didn't feed the bodies to the creatures. He would add more dead men to the pile before he finished tonight's work.

He re-entered the camp in exactly the same way and sat down next to Viking as though Hangman had always been there.

The seven remaining guards couldn't fail to notice all their men disappearing. Those seven stayed on high alert until the time came to change the watch. One of them woke up the next fifteen men.

The second watch explained to their comrades about the other men disappearing. The men of the third watch offered a range of reactions from outright concern and suspicion to some of them saying it was nothing to worry about.

The shift changed. More of the third watchmen stayed alert and paid attention, but some slacked or went to sleep even after the second watch's warning.

"You're going to have a busy night," Viking remarked once the second watch had bedded down and shut their eyes.

"Maybe now everyone else will take my warnings seriously." Hangman got to his feet and went through the same process to leave the camp.

He eliminated five men from this shift. The others stayed alert enough. Their behavior definitely gave Hangman a crystal-clear view of which ones dedicated themselves to the task and which only went through it for the sake of putting in an appearance.

He planned to tell Yiatu to divide up the watches differently tomorrow night. Hangman would put all the dedicated men on the first shift with Yiatu. Hangman would assign everyone else to the later shifts.

Hangman would be able to weed out the shirkers that way. He would whittle their numbers down until he only kept the dedicated men alive. He would get rid of everyone else.

He threw the bodies to the Abnormits, returned to Viking's tree, and both cousins crashed hard until long past sunrise. Hangman dragged himself to his feet and started working his way through the camp again.

Smash had died in the night. Hangman couldn't do anything about that, so he didn't do anything about it. He left the body there until he figured out what to do with it.

The Godless women managed the new women and girls better than he could. The men who had been on watch last night took way too long to get up. The dedicated men woke up early even though they had been on watch last night, too.

The noise of everyone moving around and talking woke up the slackers. Then everyone went into a frenzy when they realized so many of the men were missing.

"I told you anyone caught sleeping or slacking on watch wouldn't survive until morning," Hangman told them over his shoulder. "What did you think—that I was just blowing hot air out of my mouth to make a bunch of noise?" He turned around and leveled an accusing finger at the remaining men. "The rest of you got one night's reprieve thanks to Yiatu. You can thank him that you're still alive. I'll be watching all of you. If I see anyone else shirking or yawning or chewing their fingernails, that man will disappear without a trace and you'll never see him again."

He went back to what he was doing and pretended not to see all the men staring at him behind his back. They finally pulled their heads out of the clouds and got to work.

Hangman sent some of the new men out to hunt for the whole band. He made sure to send the dedicated men. He kept the slackers in camp where he could keep an eye on them. He made it glaringly obvious that he was keeping an eye on them.

They cleaned up their act and started behaving themselves, but he still didn't like it. He shouldn't have to smack these fools down like children to make them behave. Grown men shouldn't need that kind of incentive to protect women and children.

The day wore on. Everyone had too much to do to worry about the men. Hangman got occupied with checking on the new women and young girls. Some of them didn't respond to the Gooji juice, either.

He really started to wish Mora that was here. She would have been able to tell him more about these women's condition than he could see from the outside. She knew more about injuries and illnesses than anyone he'd ever met.

He sure hoped the men of his band came to get him before any of these women died—which brought up the problem of what he would do when the time came to take these strangers into the valley.

He hoped he would get a chance to consult with Blackjack and the others before that happened. Hangman found himself not wanting to make that decision on his own—not when it could affect all four bands.

The sun started to slope toward the west. He was just getting ready to rendezvous with Yiatu to organize tonight's adventures when a whole crew of Godless men came out of the jungle from the west.

Hangman jolted out of his skin when he recognized Blackjack, Bone, Oracle, Chief, Rebel, Cyclops, and Reaper.

"What in the world is going on here, Father?" Blackjack breathed.

"These are the freed captives I told you about," Bone interjected. "These are the people Rebel, Cyclops, and I freed at the top of the cliffs. They must have wandered down here."

Hangman opened his mouth to ask Blackjack about whether to take these people to the valley or not. A gasp interrupted him. "Bone?" one of the women exclaimed and scrambled to her feet. "Bone?! Bone is here! Look! Bone is here!"

She pointed at him and all the other women took up the call. Dozens of women and girls leapt to their feet and surrounded Bone, Rebel, and Cyclops, but the women made the biggest fuss over Bone.

They all wanted to touch him and some even kissed his hands with tears streaking down their cheeks. They all thanked him again and again even when he told them it was nothing.

He tried again and again to get out of the crowd and to pull his hands away from them, but they wouldn't let him go until Hangman broke in on the commotion.

"All right! All right!" Hangman yelled over the noise. "All of you go back to your places! We have to talk about what we're going to do. Go over there. Leave him alone. He's a man like any other. You can see that. Clear off!"

He shooed everyone away and steered Bone to the other side of the men's group where the women at least couldn't see him as well.

"I better go back to the valley," Bone murmured. "I shouldn't be here if I'm going to cause this kind of trouble."

"Don't go anywhere for a minute." Hangman turned to Blackjack. "What's happening in the valley? Is it clear to bring the women and children back?"

"Yes, but....." Blackjack's eyes darted to the newcomers. "I didn't realize *this* was going on."

"That's what I wanted to talk to you about. I thought I should talk to all of you—Red's men, Yeoli—all the men from all four bands. We should be having a major strategy meeting about bringing strangers through the tunnel. We could be putting everyone in danger."

"These are freed captives," Rebel pointed out. "How can they put anyone in danger? They're helpless."

"They might be helpless, but these aren't freed captives like the ones we know," Hangman replied. "These people are nothing like the men and women we rescued from the Red Riders. I mean.....some of them are and some of them definitely are not. I've already had to eliminate quite a few of them for bad attitudes."

Blackjack raised his eyebrows. "Bad attitudes like what?"

Hangman gave him a rundown on last night's events. Blackjack listened with his mouth hanging open. "You can NOT be serious!" he finally husked.

Hangman nodded. "I was planning on doing the same thing tonight to get rid of anyone too stupid to pull their heads out of the sand. They're still lurking around—and that's saying nothing about the women. I don't know what their attitudes are alike. We wouldn't find out until after we took them through the tunnel."

Blackjack cast a much more critical glance at the captives behind Hangman's back. "I don't like leaving them out here on their own even if they are rotten."

"I know," Hangman replied. "That's why I felt I needed to consult with you first."

Blackjack frowned. "That's a tough one. Maybe we should wait and discuss it with the other men—or at least the other Krals."

"That means leaving the captives out here," Bone pointed out.

"Exactly," Hangman agreed. "We can't win."

"Then I say we take them with us," Blackjack decided. "We'll keep an eye on them and eliminate anyone who doesn't fall in line. We'll give these people an ultimatum right now to either fall in line or die. No second warning—no second chances. They join us or die. That's the only choice. Then we see who rises to the occasion and who doesn't. We'll at least get some good people out of it."

"I'll leave that decision to you, my son," Hangman replied. "I don't see a right or wrong in any of this."

"Leaving them out here *would* be wrong," Bone interrupted. "That's the one thing we do know. If we left them all, we would have to leave the good with the bad and we don't even know who the good and bad are. We either take them all or leave them all—and we can't leave them."

"You're absolutely right, brother. Well spoken. Let's go." Blackjack turned to Hangman. "Do you want to tell them or should I?"

"I'll tell them." Hangman turned around and faced the whole crowd. "All of you get up and get ready to move! We're going back to our own camp. You can all come with us."

His words sparked a commotion of activity. All the women and children got busy collecting whatever possessions they had brought with them.

The new women did the same thing. They got all mixed up with the Godless women. None of them kept apart. All the women acted as those these new women had been here the whole time.

Viking didn't get up. Reaper went over there to check on him and then Rebel and Cyclops went to see what the problem was, too. The younger men were probably over there planning on how to carry Viking back to the camp.

Hangman didn't turn around. He faced the crowd and waited for everyone to assemble in front of him. Their talk died down when they realized he wasn't leaving to go anywhere.

"Now listen to me very carefully!" he announced to the whole crowd. "I'm going to take all of you new people back to our territory. We have defenses in place to protect us from enemy Clans that might invade, attack, and try to kill us. One of these enemy Clans is the Red Riders who would recapture you if they found a way past our defenses. Your own lives and the lives of everyone you see around you right now depend on you keeping our secrets, joining our band, and committing yourself to fighting and defending our Clan as your own. I won't take you back to our territory if you don't make this commitment right now. If you cross that line—if you enter our territory—you're agreeing to become Godless and follow our laws. Any transgression—no matter how slight—will be punished harshly including a possible death sentence if your Kral deems it necessary to protect the whole Clan. Do I make myself clear? You join us as fully Godless, you walk away right now, or you die. We'll eliminate anyone who breaks our laws, betrays our people, or puts us in danger. We won't give you a second chance or a second warning. You make your choice right now and you ride with the consequences either way."

Silence answered him. No one moved to leave. He measured some of the shirkers in the crowd. They didn't leave. They didn't contradict. They didn't argue back. They just stood there as though they really did plan to fully commit themselves to the Godless Clan.

He didn't trust any of them as far as he could throw them, but Bone's words sealed the deal. The Godless couldn't leave these people outside the valley to perish. Hangman refused to leave Yiatu. Hangman would take the whole group for Yiatu alone.

Reaper came back over to Blackjack and Hangman just then. "My grandfather can't walk. We have to carry him home."

"Take Smash out into the jungle and give him a decent burial," Hangman ordered. "Then you can use the Stalkion hides to carry Viking home."

The younger men got busy carrying out his orders. They took Smash into the treetops. Hangman couldn't go with them and he didn't really know Smash that well anyway. The younger men would give him a better send-off.

They came back in a little while and rolled Viking onto the Stalkion hide. Reaper, Rebel, Cyclops, and Bone carried Viking in front of the rest of the group.

Blackjack called out, "Follow me, everyone!" and waved the party forward.

Hangman stood off to one side. He could only limp along as fast as the slowest, smallest children. None of the young men paid any attention to him.

The party filed back through the jungle and entered the tunnel. The Godless women and children got progressively more excited the closer they got to home.

They talked loudly, laughed more, and everyone kept asking the men over and over again if the Red Riders really were all gone. Another air of celebration broke out when the party made it to the other end of the tunnel.

The four bands split up. The women and children from the other bands left to return to their own camps and their own territories. The women and children from Hangman's band kept chattering all the way home.

All the new people came with him, Blackjack, and Bone. The new people had nowhere else to go.

They got progressively more excited, too, as the journey neared its end. None of them could wait to finally settle down somewhere and start building their new lives.

Hangman couldn't enjoy their good mood. He didn't get progressively more excited about this. If anything, he became progressively more convinced that this would all go wrong in the worst possible way.

Chapter 25

Blackjack stood back and watched the new people enter the camp among the rocks. Quite a few women and children who had been out with Hangman accompanied the new people inside. The new people weren't completely surrounded by strangers.

Word spread like wildfire through the whole band when they heard the story. This group was nearly as big as the party of captives Hangman had brought back with him.

Kuvik stepped forward when he heard the story. "Come with me, all of you!" he called to them. "I joined the Godless after escaping from captivity by the Bounty Hunters. I can help you find places to stay where you can settle in and get everything you need."

The new people followed him. He took them to the other side of the camp and instructed them on how to build shelters for themselves. He sent the girls out into the jungle in the company of Godless children to gather building materials.

He gave all of the new people detailed descriptions of all things Godless. He told them all the rules, all the customs, and all the nuances they needed to get along in Godless society.

He also talked to them at length about all the band's stories of campaigns against other Clans, their journeys all over the country, and their battle against the Anglers to take this defensible valley where the bands could live in peace from their enemies.

Blackjack returned to his own shelter and sat down next to Narina. "This is a fine state of affairs," she remarked.

He sighed. "I'm starting to think Hangman was right about these people. There's something different about them."

"What is it? What's different about them?"

"I can't put my finger on it. I just have a bad feeling about bringing them here. They seem the same as the other captives, but they aren't the same. I can't explain it. Hangman knows them better than I do and he has a bad feeling about it, too."

"Why did you bring them inside the valley, then?" she asked.

"We couldn't leave them behind. He says some of them are good people. Maybe most of them are good people and only a few aren't. I don't know which it is, but I guess we have to find out the hard way."

She put her arm behind his back and stroked his hair. "I'm just glad we're home and we can all get our lives back to normal."

"Yeah." He got to his feet. "I need to go talk to my parents. Do you want to come?"

She smirked at him. "As long as it isn't a big secret."

"I have no secrets from you. You know that."

She got up and they crossed the camp to Hangman's shelter. He sat on the ground and leaned against the wall while Mora checked his injuries.

She bent over his leg first. "This is healing the way it should." She turned to his chest.

"Don't touch it," he told her. "Just leave it alone."

"Does it feel better?"

"It isn't as painful as it was. Just leave it. I can't face you taking the bandages off and then putting them all back on again. You'll know if anything goes wrong."

"At least take some more Gooji juice," she insisted.

"I don't need Gooji juice. I don't have an infection and I'm not going to get one if you keep the wound covered. The new people need Gooji juice more than I do. You should go check on them. Some of the women need your assessment to figure out what's wrong with them."

Like magic, some of the new people came over to Hangman's shelter just then. One of them was a man named Yiatu. Hangman had been telling Blackjack about him on the way back through the jungle.

Hangman had been telling Blackjack more than he ever wanted to know about which of the new men had conducted themselves correctly and which ones didn't.

Yiatu came with four other men. All of them belonged to Hangman's group of dedicated men who kept watch and stayed alert. These four had been conducting themselves with honor ever since they first showed up to ask for Hangman's help.

They all lined up in front of Hangman. "Is something wrong, brothers?" he asked.

"We....we need help," Yiatu blurted out and cast an awkward look around at Mora, Blackjack, and Narina. Thena came out of her parents' shelter right then to make the situation even more uncomfortable. "We don't know who else to ask, so we figured we better ask you."

"What do you need help with?" Hangman asked. "You only have to say the word. Whatever we have is yours. You're members of our Clan now. You'll always be members of our Clan as long as you keep dedicating yourselves to helping us in return."

Yiatu waved that away. "I'm not even sure if anyone can help us, but we have to ask someone."

"Name it," Hangman repeated. "What's the problem?"

Yiatu stepped forward out of line to approach the shelter a little closer. He pulled up his loose pant leg to reveal his bare thigh underneath. He hitched the fabric all the way up to his crotch and turned around so everyone could see the back of his leg.

Deep blade cuts slashed across the back of his thigh in multiple places. The cuts had damaged and indented the muscle. Red, raw, puffy, swollen, and some black, dead tissue surrounded the wounds going all the way down his leg.

Mora moved forward, squatted down behind him, and touched the wounds. "My God!" she breathed. "This is awful! What happened?"

"The Red Riders maimed us to stop us from escaping or fighting back." Yiatu pulled up the other leg of his pants and showed a series of cuts on his other leg, too.

He turned around just as fast, dropped both pant legs, and stepped away so he wasn't standing over Mora with her head at his crotch level. She responded the same way by standing up and returning to Hangman's side.

"We all have them and they're all in bad shape," Yiatu went on. "We don't know what to do about them."

"Do they stop you from moving around?" Hangman asked. "I haven't seen any of you limping. I don't know if you can run....."

"The wounds don't stop us from doing anything," Yiatu replied. "The Red Riders cut us when we were young—when they first took us as captives. Our injuries healed as much as they could. The muscles still work, but the wounds still cause problems. None of them has ever really healed right."

"I can treat them," Mora replied. "It will be painful and I won't be able to reverse the damage to your muscles, but I can get rid of the infection if you let me. The Red Riders don't use leaf paste or

Gooji juice on their wounded, so that will help a lot once we get rid of the infected tissue. The procedure will take time and you'll have to recover from it, but you'll be healthier in the end and the wounds will hopefully stop causing problems."

"That's what we want," Yiatu countered. "Some of the other captives have died from their injuries. Some of the women die from these injuries, too."

"Hold it," Mora interrupted. "The Red Riders injure the women, too? They never injured the other captives—not like that."

Yiatu waved that away. "You ask them. They'll tell another woman. They won't likely tell another man unless he already knows about it."

"This is what I was telling you," Hangman interrupted. "You should go check on the women. Some of them have problems—internal problems. You're the only one who can help them."

Mora nodded. "Okay. I understand. So....do all of you men have the same injuries?"

"Not all," Yiatu replied. "Some of the more compliant men got away without it. They didn't need it."

"I understand," she told him. "I'll take care of it. You can go back to your shelters now. I'll come over there and check on the women in a little while. I'll decide which of you is the most serious and work my way down from there. You men have been living with this for years. A few more days won't change anything."

Yiatu nodded. "Thank you."

He and the other men walked off. "I can't believe it!" Mora whispered. "I can't believe anyone would be so cruel!"

"You've heard the stories about the Bounty Hunters," Hangman told her. "The Red Riders are no better and might even be much worse. They use these women as breeders. God only knows what kind of damage the Riders did to them."

"I better go check on them." Mora picked up the bowl of leaf paste she'd been planning to use on Hangman.

Blackjack sat down next to his father. Narina excused herself and went back to her own shelter. A hum of peaceful, contented activity hung over the camp.

"It's good to be home, my son," Hangman murmured. "I have you to thank for this. I'm proud of you for handling the Red Riders. I knew you would. Now everyone knows you're Kral of this band."

"Not really," Blackjack replied. "You're still here. You'll always be Kral as long as you're still alive. I might take a more active part in running the band, but you're still Kral. Look at these people. They all followed you."

Hangman sighed. "I'm an old man just like Viking and the others."

"You aren't that old!" Blackjack countered. "You were in good shape before you got hurt. You'll get better."

"I'll never be what I was. The band needs a strong man—a stronger man than I am. The band needs you—not me."

Blackjack looked away. He didn't want to talk about that.

Hangman wouldn't stop, though. He murmured low under his breath so no one else would hear him. "The time is rapidly approaching, my son. The time is rapidly approaching when you will become Kral in name and deed. It will happen either when I die or I get too weak to act as Kral anymore. If that happens, I'll step aside and you'll take over completely. It will happen one way or the other. It's coming sooner than you think. Don't fool yourself about that."

Blackjack couldn't look at his father, so he looked down at his own hands. "I don't fool myself about it, but you can't expect me to be happy about it or to want to hurry the process along. I don't want that. I don't want you to go."

Hangman didn't smile. He rested his head back against the wall. "I will never get my strength back—not the way I had it when I was young. This body has taken too many hits. They're all catching up with me now. I will never go back to what I was. People will only ever call me Kral again from now on. They won't ever treat me like I am one because I'm not one. I will never be that again. My time is over. A younger man must rise to take my place and you're the best we have. It has to be you."

Blackjack didn't answer. He didn't want to think about his father dying or even weakening.

Hangman had always been the fortress that protected the whole band. He had been the bedrock on which this band built its future, its strength, and all its good fortune. He had been the architect of all of this.

The world didn't make sense without him as Kral. Nothing made sense without him as Kral. Blackjack didn't want to be Kral. He wanted his father back in the prime of his strength with the whole world eating out of his hand.

That would never happen. Blackjack knew that in the very core of his being the same way Hangman knew it himself. He wasn't young anymore. His body didn't spring back from these assaults. He could already barely move.

His own farseeing perspective told him the truth and he accepted the inevitable. He cared enough about his people to want the best for them even if he wasn't it. He had always been like that. He always put the good of his people first.

He didn't need recognition or honor or congratulations. He just wanted his family, his band, and his Clan to be as strong, as healthy, and as protected as they could possibly be.

He would gladly step aside for any man better qualified than himself. Hangman had been like that for as long as Blackjack had known him. Hangman was the most humble man alive. That's what made him such a perfect Kral.

Neither he nor Blackjack broke the silence. They sat side by side in the silent certainty that this would happen. One generation would pass while the other rose to ascendency. It was the natural order of things.

The father passed down his legacy to his son. The son married, had a family of his own, and became the father who passed down the legacy to the generation after him. Nothing could stop the turning of the seasons and the passage of time.

Blackjack could only ever hope to be a Kral as good as his father—and that meant doing what was best for the Clan. The Clan and the band needed the best Kral they could get—and Hangman wasn't it anymore.

Blackjack was a better Kral now. He was younger, stronger, faster, and just as cunning and determined as Hangman ever had been. Blackjack could lead the band against their enemies in ways Hangman couldn't.

Hangman had to step aside and yield to the better man. He was right about that. The time was rapidly approaching if it hadn't come and gone already.

Chapter 26

Mora came back to her shelter and sat on Hangman's other side. Bone showed up and sat with the family, too.

"How bad is it?" Hangman asked.

Mora made a face. "It's so much worse than any of us realized. I would say at least fifteen of those women are untreatable. They're so sick that nothing can save them."

"What's wrong with them?" Blackjack asked.

"They have internal infections in their wombs," Mora replied. "It starts off when a couple has intercourse and the woman gets an infection—probably because she's doing it with multiple men many times a day and those men aren't the cleanest if you know what I mean. Add on top of that that the men do it roughly and injure the women in the process. She gets an internal infection that travels up inside her womb and then spreads to the rest of her organs."

"Can't you give them Gooji juice?" Hangman asked. "Won't that kill the infection?"

"This has gone way past Gooji juice. This is why it's so important to give someone Gooji juice as soon as possible after they get hurt. Gooji juice can prevent an infection from starting. The juice won't kill an infection once it takes hold—especially not an infection as widespread as this. We don't have anything that can treat this. It's only a matter of time before these women die. The best we can do is give them a safe, comfortable place where they can spend their last days in peace."

"That's terrible," Bone murmured. "I had no idea it was that bad."

"Why do you think the same thing didn't happen to the first group of captives we rescued?" Hangman asked.

Mora shrugged. "Maybe because those men didn't go out to war. You made it sound like they were more interested in staying where they were in their camp and sending out everyone else to go after us. These men must have been traveling for a long time before they got here—which probably ran down the women's health at the same time. It was probably a combination of factors."

"There must be something you can do, Mother," Blackjack exclaimed. "We can't just let them die—just when they finally got their freedom."

"There's nothing we can do," she insisted. "These women would have died anyway in the Red Rider camp. They would have died if they'd gone out across the country on their own. They would have died either way. They're already lost."

Blackjack didn't know what to say, but a scream interrupted their conversation right then. His hand flew to his weapon and he and Bone both got to their feet. The hair stood up on the back of Blackjack's neck when Narina stormed around the corner of another shelter.

She clamped her mouth shut in a furious grimace of pure, murderous rage. She gripped two of the new women by the backs of their necks. She must have been gripping them hard enough to hurt.

They screamed and struggled, but she held them tightly enough to stop them from escaping. She stormed across the camp dragging these two women kicking and screaming toward Hangman's shelter.

The women's screams attracted the attention of everyone else in camp, both old and new. Everyone gathered around to see what was going on.

Narina got within twenty feet of the spot, hurled both women forward hard enough to knock them over, and both of them sprawled across the ground right in front of Bone and Blackjack.

The two women screamed when they landed and rolled onto their stomachs. Both women spread their arms and legs to break their fall.

"What the hell is going on?!" Blackjack demanded. "What are you doing to these women, Narina?"

She stormed forward and kicked both of them extra hard in their stomachs. "I just caught these two traitors talking behind one of the shelters over there." She pointed behind her. "They were talking about going out through the tunnel, finding another band of Red Riders, and telling them how to get into this place." She kicked both women again extra hard. "Weren't you?! WEREN'T YOU TALKING ABOUT BETRAYING US ALL?!!"

The women screamed too loudly to answer. Bone stepped forward. "Stop, Narina! Leave them alone!"

"Did you hear what I just said?!" she roared and turned around to bellow to the whole camp. "These two traitors just said they would go out there and bring the Red Riders through the tunnel to slaughter us all! Did you hear that?! These two want to sell us all to the Red Riders!" She spun around and kicked one of the women right across the face. "Didn't you?! DIDN'T YOU?!"

Blackjack couldn't watch this. He strode between the two women, got hold of Narina, and steered her the rest of the way to Hangman's shelter. Blackjack took her far enough away that she wouldn't be able to get to the two women.

Mora, Thena, and Bone all stood guard over Narina so she wouldn't be able to go after the two women again. Blackjack checked his wife more than once to make sure the others kept her under control.

Blackjack made a decision right then not to look at his father. This incident was Blackjack's business to handle. Hangman had no reason to do it. He would have to get to his feet to question everyone involved. Blackjack didn't want Hangman to get to his feet.

Blackjack strode around the two women and stood in front of them while they still floundered on the ground. Both of them groaned in pain. The woman Narina kicked in the face bled from her mouth. That side of her face was already starting to turn purple.

"Stand up, both of you," Blackjack snapped. "Stand up and face all of us if you have any honor at all."

Both women dragged themselves to their feet. Blackjack didn't even know their names. He decided in that moment not to learn their names—not unless circumstances somehow proved that they were innocent of this crime.

He wouldn't need to know their names if they were guilty of it. He'd known Narina for long enough. She was too practical to make a mistake about overhearing them.

She wouldn't have reacted the way she did unless she was absolutely certain of what she'd heard. She would have done anything to help these women reclaim their lives. She wouldn't turn against them unless they really betrayed the Clan.

The woman with blood on her lip pressed the back of her wrist to her mouth, looked down at the blood, and then glared at Blackjack. The other one looked like she might be about to burst into tears.

"Well?" he demanded. "What do you have to say about this? Did you plan to go out through the tunnel, find the Red Riders, and lead them back here? Is Narina's story true that you were speaking against our Clan?"

"NO!" the second woman whimpered. "We would never do that! I swear it!"

"Yes, we were!" The first woman turned her head and snapped at the woman next to her. "Just admit it, Nita. You can see they already know about it."

The second woman burst into tears. Her friend faced Blackjack and glared at him. "We were talking about it—and we would have done it if that witch hadn't caught us. We would have led the Red Riders here and they would have annihilated all of you."

He raised his eyebrows. "Why would you do that after my brother and his men freed you from them? You were captives—slaves. The Red Riders used you as meat. My father and the rest of our people have been helping you and taking care of you all this time. Why would you go back to the Red Riders and help them kill the very people who saved your lives?"

She snorted at him. "You're vermin. You're nothing. You all deserve to die—and the Red Riders will never stop hunting you until they kill you all."

Blackjack shook his head and turned away. "You're deranged—both of you." He waved to the uninitiated boys. Ghari and Urdis rushed forward. "You know what to do," Blackjack told them. "Don't bring them inside the camp. We'll stake the women outside so the ants don't enter the...."

Nita rushed Blackjack, grabbed his hand, flung herself on her knees, and howled with sobs against his legs. "NO!!" she screeched. "NO, PLEASE, NO!! Don't do that to me! You can't!"

"My father told you what would happen if you turned against us or put any of us in danger," Blackjack countered. "I was standing right there and heard every word he said. You agreed to his conditions when you came in here. Do you really think we would let you go free so you can shoot your mouth off to the Red Riders and risk all our lives?"

She tore away from him and hustled back to Hangman's shelter. She threw herself on her knees next to him and actually wound up partially landing on his injured leg. He grimaced in pain, but she was too far out of her mind to notice.

She grabbed his hand and groveled in the dirt in front of him. "Please, Hangman!" she wailed. "Please—have mercy! I didn't know! I won't do it again! Please—give me a chance! I'll do anything!"

He deliberately pulled his hand away from her, but he didn't move in any other way. He sat extra still to take it easy on his injuries.

"I told you before you came through the tunnel that you wouldn't get a second chance," he told her. "I told you we would show no mercy and that we would destroy anyone who put our people in danger. Look around you, Nita. Look at all those little children standing over there watching you right now. You would put all of them to death—and you don't even care. You're only here crying to me because you got caught. You would gladly stand aside and watch the Red Riders kill us all as long as you got away with it." He waved at the men standing around. "Take them both."

The men moved in and took hold of both women. Ghari and Urdis took off running into the jungle as usual. The men surrounded the two women and marched them out of camp.

The first woman walked out on her own legs. She kept glaring at everyone in defiance all the way there. Nita burst into a fresh fit of screaming, crying, howling, and begging for her life.

The men had to physically pick her up and carry her out of camp while she thrashed in their arms. She kept alternately trying to break away from them and reaching out to Hangman for help.

He didn't get up, not even when the men lugged her out of camp into the jungle at a distance from the rock entrance. The men pulled the first woman down onto the ground.

She cooperated with everything while they stretched her arms and legs to the four directions and staked her down into the dirt.

Nita fought the men all the way. She kept struggling so hard that more men had to come forward to restrain her while they finished tying her wrists and ankles to the stakes.

All the Godless left the camp and assembled in the treetops to watch. Godless law required that every member of the band bear witness to these traitors receiving their just punishment.

Blackjack climbed up with his men. Only Hangman and Viking stayed behind. All the new people crowded the camp entrance to watch from a safe distance. None of them knew how to climb the trees yet.

Ghari and Urdis came back pretty soon. They must have found their pollen and the ants pretty close by. The boys had to run to stay ahead of the ants.

The two boys scattered the pollen trail all the way to the two women and then a little farther beyond them to lead the ants away from camp after they finished off the two women.

Ghari and Urdis leapt into the branches and hustled back to rejoin the rest of the band. The ants overtook the two women in no time.

Nita screeched nonstop right up until the ants crawled on top of her and devoured her down to the bare dirt. Her friend gritted her teeth and only started yelling when the ants really started to devour her.

They muffled her cries pretty soon. She never built up to full-blown screams. Silence descended over the jungle while the ants finished off every trace of both women. The ants erased the two women from existence and then marched away into the undergrowth.

The Godless took their time to stare at the spot and then descend to the ground to return to the camp. Blackjack took that moment to address everyone, both the old people and the new people.

"If any of you is thinking about doing the same thing, let this be your last warning. You know what will happen when we find out who you are. You won't get away with anything. You'll perish the same way these women did. We'll punish all traitors with death. We have no choice but to keep our families and our Clansmen safe. We will never allow any of you to leave this valley alive—not until you prove yourselves loyal. Every person who pulls something like this makes it harder for the rest of you. I don't know why this should be so difficult for all of you to understand. You should be the first to root these people out and eliminate them so we don't have to. You should all be eager to prove your loyalty by exposing our enemies even if those enemies are right here inside this camp. Any of you who don't dedicate yourselves wholeheartedly to our Clan will die. We'll make certain of it. Any of you who truly dedicates yourselves to our Clan will do the same thing to anyone who betrays us, even if that person is standing next to you right now."

He waited for his words to sink in, but of course the new people didn't react. Any traitors hiding inside these walls right now—they wouldn't speak out. They wouldn't show themselves.

They probably thought they could sabotage the band from the inside the way Mora attacked the Red Riders from inside their camp.

He really didn't need to understand why these former captives would deliberately sell out and betray the people who saved them so these fools could run straight back to the brutal marauders who tormented, maimed, and enslaved these people.

None of that concerned Blackjack anymore. He turned his back on everyone, walked back to his father's shelter, and stopped in front of

Narina. Mora, Thena, and Bone stood right next to her where they could hear everything Blackjack and Narina said to each other.

Hangman sat on the ground against the shelter. He could hear everything, too.

"Are you all right?" Blackjack asked.

Narina nodded down at her feet. "I'm sorry I kind of overreacted. I should have checked with you before I did all of that."

"Not at all," he exclaimed. "You did exactly right. I'm proud of you for what you did."

Her head shot up. "You are?"

"Of course. I'm grateful to you for bringing them forward. You saved us all. Of course I'm proud of you."

Her features pinched. "I'm sorry! I don't know your ways!"

"You did everything right. You have nothing to be ashamed of. You're an asset to our Clan. You always have been. I feel lucky that I married you."

He cast a glance around at his family. He read their affection and approval in all their faces. He couldn't stay here. Narina needed him.

He put his arm around her shoulders, steered her out of their midst, and led her back to their shelter. He followed her inside and pulled her down on the bed to sit next to him.

He hugged her around the shoulders one more time. "You have nothing to worry about," he murmured. "It's all over now."

She covered her face and burst into tears. "I never wanted them to die! I'm so sorry! I never meant for them to die!"

"You didn't do this," he insisted. "They were the ones who did this. Hangman warned them. They knew exactly what they were doing. They came here to destroy us. They never planned to join us at all. These are our enemies. They don't deserve mercy or compassion. They deserve death. You killed the enemies of our Clan. That's exactly what you're supposed to do. You were supposed to kick them in the face. Nothing could be wrong with that."

She kept sobbing into her hands. He heard something in those sobs—something other than her apologizing for killing those women.

This was just the tension and nerves of capturing them and seeing the men feed the women to the ants. These tears were Narina's agitation over getting caught in a situation that should never have happened.

He put his arm around her and kissed the side of her head. He didn't try after that to stop her tears. He just let her cry herself out. This was all the natural part of her adjusting to life in the Godless Clan. She would get used to it. Everyone else did.

Chapter 27

Blackjack paced up and down through the camp and studied the men in front of him. Fifteen of the new men stood at one end of the line. Blackjack didn't worry about them.

These men included Yiatu and all the others that Hangman had determined were really committed and enthusiastic about joining the Godless. These men had proven themselves countless times in the month since they entered the valley.

Everyone in the band referred to these men as Yiatu's men. They stuck together, helped each other, and taught each other any skills any of them might know. They were starting to form their own little nucleus within the band.

The men went everywhere together including on hunting and scouting trips of their own. The men were becoming as invaluable and trusted as all the band's original men.

Mora had given all of these men extensive medical treatment. She had lanced and, in some of the worst cases, excised dead and infected tissue from their legs. The men took the pain well and didn't resist anything she did.

She'd been working all day every day applying leaf paste to their wounds and dosing all of them with as much Gooji juice as they could possibly drink.

The men had responded beyond anyone's wildest dreams and re-covered much faster than Mora predicted. The men were now as able-bodied as anyone could hope. They still carried the scars of the Red Riders' mistreatment, but no one could do anything about that.

The women with systemic infections had all died within the last month. No one could save them. The other women had buried their dead in the jungle according to their own custom.

Blackjack came to the other end of the line and grimaced at the rest of the new men. They had also been working to prove themselves to the Godless, but these men's efforts didn't come off so well.

The taint of Hangman's first negative impression lingered and left a sour taste in everyone's mouths. Blackjack didn't see himself ever fully trusting these men.

He had been starting to wish he could get over this prejudice and give them a chance because they really did try. Some of them just didn't know any better. They didn't know how to hunt or fight or even butcher or cook their own food.

He didn't blame them for that. Some of Yiatu's men labored under the same burden of ignorance. The Red Riders had used these men for other purposes and didn't teach them essential skills the men needed to survive.

Yiatu's men threw themselves into learning these skills. They worked around the clock to learn as much as they possibly could. They spent every day striving to their maximum to practice, improve, and put these skills into use.

Yiatu and his men tried to be a thousand percent Godless. They did everything the Godless men did only maybe not so well.

These others didn't try as hard. They didn't put as much energy into anything they did. They didn't seem to recognize the need to improve.

Mora had given them medical treatment, too. The men had recovered just as well, but they seemed to use their recovery as an excuse to lay around and relax.

These men stayed behind much longer than Yiatu's men even though some of Yiatu's men had been treated more brutally and suffered from more widespread infections and damage to their bodies.

Blackjack had been racking his brain about what to do about these other men. He didn't even know what to call them, so he had started referring to them by the same name that Hangman used for them.

He called them, "slackers" which is exactly what they were. These men would take any opportunity to avoid work, hardship, or exertion of any kind. They preferred the company of women, even women the men weren't in relationships with.

Blackjack had discussed the situation at length with his father. Hangman stayed out of the subject. He'd already executed the worst offenders. He left the rest up to Blackjack, now that the party had returned to camp.

Black had considered telling these slackers straight out that no one would ever respect them as long as they continued to act like this. Not even the women or children would respect men who sat around pretending to be injured when everyone in camp knew they weren't.

He went through the same quandary now while he stood in front of them appraising them for the hundredth time. He and the other men had planned to take the new men out on their first scouting trip outside the valley to search for any incoming Red Rider patrols.

The other part of Blackjack's mind considered doing nothing about these men, leaving them as they were, and letting the Red Riders or any dangerous creatures take these men when the time came.

The time would come. That was the thing. The Godless' enemies would come back and these men would have no choice but to go out to war with the others.

They wouldn't be able to survive if they didn't get good with their weapons and practice using them. Yiatu's men definitely understood this. They sparred with each other all the time when they weren't out hunting or scouting the countryside.

Yiatu's men didn't want to leave these precautions to the Godless. Yiatu's men wanted to find out for themselves if the Red Riders were coming back. Yiatu's men would go to any lengths to make sure the Red Riders didn't take the men back into captivity.

Yiatu and his men had all learned how to climb the trees. The men spent hours just traveling through the canopy and practicing to increase their speed so they could keep up with the Godless.

Certain Godless men would go out and race Yiatu's men. The Godless would travel as fast as they possibly could while Yiatu and his men tried their best to keep up.

These slackers hadn't even learned to climb as far as Blackjack knew. They hadn't even asked any of the Godless to teach them.

What did these slackers think they would do when the Red Riders attacked and all the Godless took refuge in the canopy? Then these morons would get stuck on the ground and it would all be over in a few minutes.

Blackjack made up his mind right then and there. He had no intention of wasting his time with these fools. He certainly didn't plan to take them on a sensitive mission like this—not when Yiatu's men would be traveling as one with the regular Godless.

Some of these fools actually walked around camp unarmed. They didn't even have the brains to come armed when Blackjack called all the men to meet him to come on this trip.

That on its own marked these men for death. They would go out into the jungle unarmed and meet their deaths from the very first creature that decided to come and investigate. Blackjack could only stand aside and bow to the inevitable.

Blackjack waved everyone forward to follow him and led everyone out of camp. He separated Yiatu's men from the others.

No one understood the vast gulf between these two groups better than Yiatu's men. They had been telling these slackers on a daily basis that they better change their ways real quick. The slackers still didn't listen.

Blackjack sent Kuvik, Bone, Chief, and Reaper with Yiatu's men to head for the tunnel and up to the top cliffs. Blackjack stayed behind with the slackers.

"Aren't we going with you?" one of them asked. Blackjack had made zero effort to learn these idiots' names.

Blackjack knew all of Yiatu's men by name and he knew their stories. They were good men who had seen the absolute worst.

"I want all of you to practice climbing the trees," Blackjack ordered.

The slackers gaped at him. "Climb....the trees?" the same man asked. "Why?"

"Because the Red Riders attack from the ground," Blackjack replied. "They don't climb the trees. The canopy is one of the few places we can protect ourselves from them. If the Red Riders attacked right now, every single one of you would be dead. None of you even thought to bring a weapon to defend yourselves. Your only hope would be to climb into the trees and you would need to do it quickly."

"But the Red Riders aren't attacking," another pointed out.

"Then what would you do if a Demonex attacked right now—or a Krakelow—or a Gorlock? You'll all go out to war with us if the Red Riders ever do come back. Do you think we'll ship you out to safety with the women and children? You agreed to defend this Clan in exchange for us taking you in. Now get up there and start practicing climbing the trees. If I come back and see any of you back inside the camp, you'll go out and not come back at all. Stay out and keep practicing until I return. I'll be asking around among the women and other men. If they see your faces inside the camp for the rest of the day, I'll find out about it and I won't be happy."

He shot away into the canopy and left them all standing there. He was rapidly coming to the end of his patience with these fools. No one in his band should waste any more precious time, food, or Gooji juice on these dopes.

He raced to the tunnel and caught up with the other men on the way up to the top cliffs. The men split up. Yiatu's party went one way. Blackjack and his men divided into three other groups and searched the area.

They didn't find anything, so they ranged for another thirty miles all around the area. The men still didn't find anything—not even any sign that the Red Riders had been nearby. Everything looked deserted.

The men rejoined at the top of the cliffs. "I don't like it," Bone growled. "I don't like it at all."

"They're out there," Chief agreed. "They might not be here yet, but they're here."

"Do you remember what that woman said before she met the ants?" Reaper went on. "She said the Red Riders would always come back. She said they would never stop until they destroyed us."

Blackjack nodded. "I remember and I feel it, too. I don't think there is a man in our band who doesn't feel it. That's why none of us celebrated after we killed those men at the bottleneck. We all knew it wasn't over."

"Maybe it will never be over," Cyclops suggested. "Maybe it will always be like this."

"I wouldn't be surprised. Maybe this is the price of freedom—that we always have to keep looking over our shoulders. Maybe the valley's only value is to buy us a little extra time to find out our enemies are moving in before they actually get near us. Maybe we're no different from every other Clan in that way." Blackjack turned away. "Let's get back to the camp. There's nothing here to find. We'll keep coming back and monitoring the situation."

He started to walk away when Yiatu stopped him. "Blackjack..... wait."

Blackjack turned around. "What is it, brother? Is something wrong?"

"We...." Yiatu waved at his men. "We want to help. We want to help monitor the situation—if you'll let us."

"Isn't that what you're already doing? You're already here. You're with us."

"That's what I'm saying. We want to come and search. We want your permission to leave the valley and scout the area—to keep watch for the Red Riders. You can send one of your men with us to supervise us. We just want to do whatever we can......"

Blackjack relaxed. "You don't need my permission to leave the valley, brothers. You don't need my permission to come and go as you please. You and your men have proven yourselves loyal and committed to our Clan. You're free to come and go anywhere you wish—as long as it's just you. Don't take any of the others."

"Of course not," Yiatu agreed. "We don't want to take the others."

"Then run your own band your own way and do what you have to do. Just let me know if you find anything."

Yiatu's men grabbed each other in delight at Blackjack's decision. They all grinned and shook each other.

"You men might consider taking your wives out of our camp and forming your own band," Blackjack suggested. "The camp is getting kind of crowded with so many extra people living in one spot. You should take your women and girls and establish your own territory somewhere farther south. Just consider it. You don't have to rush into anything, but you might be more comfortable there. Let me know what you decide."

Blackjack really did leave after that. He set off down the hill with the other men. Yiatu's band kept up easily. They had become a seamless part of the valley population. Blackjack didn't have to worry about them anymore.

The men headed down the mountain on their way back to the tunnel. Blackjack stopped halfway there when he heard voices. He and his men all stopped in the canopy to listen.

They only stayed there for a few minutes before three women came up the hill from below. Blackjack recognized them instantly. These women had been among the new people who'd entered the valley with Hangman and Viking.

Blackjack and his men stared at the women in silence. What in the wide world were these women doing outside the valley? They should have been terrified of venturing back into territory where the Red Riders might discover them.

The men didn't have to wonder for very long. The women stopped to rest right under the trees where Blackjack and his men sat listening to the women's conversation.

"You really need to toughen up, Vartha," one of the women told another. "You'll never make it all the way back to the Red Riders if you keep stopping to rest all the time."

"I just don't understand it." The other woman passed her hand across her sweaty forehead. "I just can't get my breath these days."

"Maybe you have something wrong with you like all the other women who died when they got here," the third woman suggested. "Maybe you're sick and you just don't know it."

"That's stupid, Midilia," the first woman fired back. "She can't keep up with us because she's lazy and never does any work. All she does is sit around and let other people do the work for her." The first woman turned to Vartha. "When are you going to start doing things for yourself? You can't let the Godless wait on you hand and foot all the time."

Vartha smirked at her. "The Godless don't do it. Kurian waits on me hand and foot."

The first woman grimaced. "That's just as bad. Does he even realize how ridiculous he's making himself by being your pampered little pet?"

"You should get one for yourself, Nalma," Midilia teased. "It would improve your mood."

Nalma snorted and got to her feet. "I don't need a man like that. No one does. You would never catch one of the Red Riders stepping and fetching for a woman. It's pathetic."

"He's sweet," Vartha exclaimed. "He's very caring and generous."

"He's generous with food supplied by the Godless," Nalma pointed out. "He doesn't provide anything of his own. He hasn't left the camp even once since we moved into the valley."

Vartha stood up, too. "It doesn't matter because he'll stay there and we'll go back to the Red Riders. I'll probably never see him again and good riddance."

The three women turned away and set off hiking up the hill again. Blackjack took a second to fully believe that these women really planned to leave the valley and return to the Red Riders. Who in their right mind would be that stupid?

He got up, moved through the canopy a short way, and dropped to the ground in front of the women. "Are you three going somewhere?" Blackjack asked even though he already knew.

The women stopped in their tracks. Vartha glanced at her two friends. Midilia blinked at Blackjack in confusion like she didn't fully grasp that he'd caught her. Nalma hardened her features into a murderous scowling glare.

Blackjack was beginning to understand that expression so much better now. No one had to explain to him what it meant. He already knew.

"Just do what you have to do and get it over with," Nalma snapped. "You'll all die."

"I don't think so." Blackjack waved at his men. "Tie them up hand and foot."

All the men moved in and obeyed him. Yiatu's men worked the hardest to restrain the three women and tie them up. Chief, Reaper, and Diamond were the biggest men here, so they slung the women over their shoulders and carried them back to camp.

Chapter 28

The camp burst into an uproar when the men came back carrying the three women bound hand and foot. The story raced like wildfire from mouth to mouth. Everyone assembled again, probably in anticipation of Blackjack feeding these women to the ants, too.

He didn't feed them to the ants—not right away. He ordered his men to separate the three women to three separate shelters. He sent Nalma to his own shelter, Vartha to Reaper's shelter, and Midilia to Bone's shelter.

Narina and the two men stood outside so no one would see them inside the shelters alone with these women. "What are you going to do?" Bone asked.

"I'm going to question them," Blackjack replied. "They might be able to tell us something about the Red Riders' plans and movements. This is the second time we've caught these women saying that the Red Riders planned to come back. These women might know something."

Bone's face drained of all color. "You aren't going to hurt these women, are you? I can't believe you would actually do something like that."

"I don't plan to hurt them, but I do plan to execute them. They already know what's going to happen to them. They might be willing to give us information if they think it will convince me to spare them."

Bone shook his head. "We shouldn't be doing this. We shouldn't be keeping any female as a captive—not even an enemy female. It's against Godless law."

"What do you suggest I do?" Blackjack asked. "How do you suggest that I get the information I want out of them?"

"Take them out into the jungle, stake them out for the ants, and question the women then. They'll know they're going to die. They'll be as likely to talk then as here—maybe even more likely to talk."

Blackjack couldn't argue with that and Bone was right. Holding these women as captives was against Godless law. Blackjack ordered his men to remove all three women and take them out into the jungle.

The band returned to the place where he'd executed the first two women. The men lined Vartha, Nalma, and Midilia in a row and cut their ankles loose so the women could stand up straight on their own.

Blackjack walked back and forth studying each of them in turn. "You were all caught attempting to leave and rejoin the Red Riders. Can any of you give us a reason why we should spare your lives?"

"We don't want you to spare our lives," Nalma spat. "We don't want to live with you!" She curled her lip at him in disgust.

"Why don't you want to live with us?" Blackjack asked. "Why would you want to go back to the people who help you as a captive?"

"Don't tell him anything, Nalma," Midilia interjected.

"Do you think I'm ashamed of it?! I'm proud of it!" Nalma turned to Blackjack. "We are Red Riders, you stupid fool. You're too blind and ignorant to see what's right in front of your faces—and *this* one is too innocent and soft-hearted to know anything about the world." She jutted her chin at Bone.

"What are you talking about?" Blackjack demanded. "Tell me plainly if you aren't ashamed of it. Why would you return to the Red Riders?"

"I just told you. We're Red Riders born and raised. We aren't captives. We never were. Your brother is just a boy. He didn't know what he was looking at. We blended in with the others and pretended to be captives. Nita and Asila weren't captives, either. Don't you realize that?"

Blackjack stared at her. Then his eyes darted to the two women standing next to her and his mind clicked. Most of the women Bone had freed carried the bruises, scars, and disabilities of countless injuries.

These three women standing in front of him right now—he didn't see a single bruise or scratch on any of them. They all glowed with health and beauty. So many of these people had entered the camp at the same time that Blackjack didn't pay attention to any single one of them.

He'd only noticed the people in the worst shape. The others blended in with each other. Come to think of it, Nita and Asila—they had both been in perfectly good shape, too.

He saw it all in the blink of an eye and understood exactly what Nalma was telling him. These women weren't captives. They had been born and bred as part of Red Rider society.

They might even have been the wives of some of the Riders that Blackjack and his men had killed—or that the Godless women and boys had killed.

He didn't need to understand anything else. He nodded to Ghari and Urdis and then to his men. The men took hold of the three women, staked them out on the killing ground, and the two boys ran off to get the ants.

Hardly anyone came out to watch this time. Everyone knew the drill. Blackjack only stayed because he was the one carrying out this execution. He had to stay.

At least none of these three cried and begged for their lives. They knew better by now. Vartha and Midilia whimpered in terror and looked around everywhere for the ants. Nalma kept glaring at Blackjack and baring her teeth in pure venomous hatred.

He could just hear the words passing through her mind. *They'll always come back. They won't stop until they destroy you.* She didn't have to say the words out loud. He already knew they were true.

The boys brought the ants and all three women screamed when the ants started to devour them. Only a handful of men stayed behind to watch. This whole procedure was getting old and Blackjack hadn't even started yet.

He waited until the ants moved out of the area. He had to stay long enough to make sure they didn't go near the camp, but the boys did their job too well. They laid a partial pollen trail away from the area so the ants followed it into the jungle.

The ants kept marching in the same direction. They never put the camp in danger.

Blackjack went back inside. All the new people went about their business at their own shelters or doing whatever they had been doing before this. He didn't see anything out of the ordinary, but that was an illusion.

He had to deal with all of them, but he didn't want to do it now. He went to his own shelter, but Narina wasn't there. He searched the whole camp and still didn't find her.

He went back to his shelter, but she hadn't returned from wherever she was. Did she go out into the jungle for something? Did she go for water? She should have come back by now.

He paced across the camp to his parents' shelter. Hangman sat outside in his usual place. He always sat there nowadays even though he had mostly recovered from his injuries. His ribs still hurt, but he could walk around almost normally.

He moved much more slowly than before. He didn't take risks and he never put himself in a position where he would have to run. He hardly ever left the camp anymore.

Viking had also become permanently disabled and could barely walk at all. He stayed at his shelter and didn't involve himself in camp business.

Blackjack pulled up in front of Hangman just as Mora came out of the shelter. She approached Hangman to tell him something just as Blackjack showed up.

Mora looked up. "Is everything all right, my son?"

"Did you find anything on the top cliffs?" Hangman asked. "Is anything up there."

"I didn't find anything. Have either of you seen Narina? I can't find her anywhere. She's nowhere in camp."

Mora burst into a grin. "She is in camp. She's here." She waved toward the shelter behind her.

"Why is she here?" Blackjack scowled at the shelter and then at his mother. "Is something wrong?"

"Nothing is wrong, my son. Narina is pregnant. She hasn't been feeling normal and she came here to ask me about it." Mora waved behind her again. "Why don't you go inside and see her?"

Blackjack hesitated while his world reoriented itself on its axis. Narina....pregnant....

What did Blackjack think was going to happen if he and Narina did it with each other—not just once but many times? They were married. Now she was pregnant.

He had to completely switch gears in his head to understand what that meant. He'd just been thinking this about Hangman only a few weeks ago. Blackjack had been thinking it about Hangman for a long time.

The father grew old. The son grew up and took over the father's position of authority and responsibility. The son took a wife and had children of his own. His children grew up and he grew old until one of his sons took over in his place.

That would happen to Blackjack the same way it happened to Hangman, Shadow, Silver, and all the men going all the way back until the dawn of time. It was inevitable.

Blackjack couldn't rise to become Kral without Hangman growing old, losing his old strength, and falling away. Blackjack would have to step aside or die someday so his son could rise and take over as Kral.

This child Narina was carrying right now—would it be a boy? Was this Blackjack's oldest son—the son who would be to Blackjack what Blackjack had been to Hangman—the son Hangman had been to Shadow?

Blackjack's mind reeled from all the interconnected implications of this moment. He saw so many shades of possibility going all the way back in time and all the way forward unto eternity. It would never stop.

He had to shake himself to bring his attention back to the present. His parents both smiled at him until he turned away and entered the shelter.

Narina lay on Hangman's and Mora's bed staring up at the ceiling. Her eyes widened in what looked like terror when Blackjack entered.

He sat down next to her and stroked her cheek. "Mora just told me," he murmured.

"You aren't angry, are you?" Narina quavered.

"Why would I be angry? You're my wife and I'm proud of you. We're going to have a family and this will be our oldest child. What could be wrong with that?"

She looked away and her features wrenched. "I don't know what's wrong with me! I don't understand myself! Everything seems to be going wrong! I don't know myself anymore!"

"That's okay," he breathed. "That's normal."

"No, it isn't!" she practically shrieked. "I've been around pregnant women all my life! None of them ever fell apart like this! I'm going crazy! What if something goes wrong?! What if something happens to me?! I can't even think! How am I supposed to survive this?!"

"Hey!" he breathed. "There is no normal for something like this. Is Mora satisfied that everything is okay?"

That's when Narina really started crying. "Yes! She says everything is fine and there's nothing wrong with me even though I feel like everything is wrong!"

He couldn't stand to see her in such distress—especially over something that should have been a happy occasion.

He bent all the way over and hugged her without picking her up off the bed. She clung to him sobbing in his ear. He had to pry himself off of her to straighten up and look down into her eyes swimming with tears.

"Listen to me," he breathed. "In fifty years, we'll be old like Hangman and Mora. We'll be grandparents and all our children will be grown with families of their own. We'll look back on this day and laugh that we were so young and foolish—okay? Everything is going to be okay."

Her features jolted all over the place, but at least she could nod in response.

"Maybe you should stay here for a little while," he suggested. "You don't have to go back to our shelter. I don't want you to think you have to take care of everything and do all your work—not right away.

Just take a little while to get your bearings before you go out there and face it. Okay?"

She nodded again. "I don't want to let you down! I don't want to let the whole Clan down!"

"You aren't. You're doing exactly what the Clan needs you to do. You're going to be a wonderful mother and our children are going to bless the day they were born to you. This is just the first hurdle. You've never been pregnant before. You don't understand what it feels like, so you're scared and confused. You'll understand it better and it won't bother you so much after you've had eight or nine more children."

She laughed in spite of herself. "Keep telling yourself that."

He smiled at her, kissed her once, and stroked her hair. "I have to go back out there. You stay here and relax as long as you need to. We have nine months to get used to this and things are bound to change as you go along. Don't worry too much if things get rocky at the beginning."

He kissed her one last time and left the shelter.

Chapter 29

Mora gave Blackjack an understanding look before he walked away. He didn't want to talk to his parents about Narina being pregnant. He would have plenty of time for that in the future.

He walked off to the other side of the camp, found Yiatu's shelter, and told him to round up the rest of his men.

"What's going on?" Yiatu asked when they all assembled around Blackjack.

"I need you all to help me go through the new people and find out which of them might be harboring loyalties to the Red Riders," Blackjack announced. "You men know these people better than I do. We'll start with the women, but I want all of you to give me your input on the men—if we can even call them that. I want to find out which of them are outright traitorous and which are just bone lazy."

"What are you going to do with them if they are just bone lazy?" one of the other men asked. His name was Sephus and he was the only man in the whole valley with a thick, full, black beard. He didn't cut it.

"I haven't decided what I'm going to do with them yet," Blackjack replied. "They're all too stupid to take a weapon when they go out into the jungle. I might just keep putting them in dangerous situations where their laziness and stupidity will get them killed. Maybe they'll wake up and learn and maybe they won't. I'm much more concerned with the traitors right now—starting with the women. I need all of you to give me as much information about them as you can. I want you to tell me exactly which ones suffered the worst, which ones you know were the victims of brutal Riders, and which ones got off lightly for whatever reason."

Yiatu nodded. "I can tell you most of those right now."

"Excellent." Blackjack took the group to the other side of the camp.

The members of the original four valley bands had camped over here. They had left the space clear when they moved out to their own territory.

Now all the new people had camped in one spot where they could help and support each other.

They had more space over here, but the Godless couldn't keep an eye on these new people. They could have been doing just about anything over here away from prying Godless eyes.

Yiatu escorted Blackjack through the camp. Yiatu nodded at each person in turn so he wouldn't outright point at them and make it too obvious that he was talking about them.

"That's Runa." Yiatu indicated a young woman barely nineteen years old. She still moved painfully from old injuries that hadn't healed correctly. "The Red Riders captured her when she was seven years old and turned her over to Segantu. He beat her ruthlessly and used her sexually even then. He liked it rough and he injured her badly. He didn't care what he did or even if he killed her. He could always get another captive. He eventually got tired of her and passed her off to his friends. She's been a captive ever since."

Blackjack looked away, but Yiatu didn't stop. He drew Blackjack's attention to each woman one after the other, told their names, and a shortened version of their stories.

The mistreatment these women had suffered turned out to be so much worse than even Blackjack feared. He didn't want to hear this, but he had to.

Yiatu talked for a long time. He filled Blackjack in on almost every woman in the camp until only ten remained. They just so happened to have camped in the same place in a line of shelters apart from everyone else.

The ten women in question went about their work the same as everyone else—with one distinct difference. Blackjack didn't see any injuries on them, either. Each of them was good-looking enough to get any man they wanted.

"I can't tell you anything about them," Yiatu finished. "I don't know any of them."

"This is what I don't understand," Blackjack remarked. "How did these women go with you without anyone realizing they were Red Rider women? How did none of you see that some of the Red Riders had brought their own women with them—and how did Bone not notice that these women weren't captives like the rest of you? Didn't he have to unlock the chains from all of you?"

"These women were wearing chains," Yiatu replied. "I don't know why. Maybe they heard your brother saying he had come to free all the captives and these women put chains on themselves to make themselves look like captives. I don't know that, but I do remember seeing these women come forward so your brother and his men could unlock the chains. I remember that—and the women had dirtied themselves to cover up that they weren't bruised. They cleaned themselves up after we joined with your father. Then everyone could see that the women weren't bruised—but I didn't think anything about it then. I just figured they had belonged to some other Riders I didn't know—like maybe these men kept the women chained up in their tents all the time. I didn't really think about it. I just accepted that the women were captives like any other. I didn't think they could be anything else."

Blackjack turned to the other men. "Was it like that for all of you?"

"We all had a little more important things to worry about then," Sephus remarked. "We were all so surprised and happy when your brother showed up with his men. Then he told us to arm ourselves and ransack the camp for supplies because we had to move out right away and put distance between us and any Red Riders. It was the middle of the night. None of us looked very closely at the women who were with us."

The other men nodded in agreement. Blackjack sighed. This didn't make it easy.

"You don't blame us for this, do you?" a third man asked. His name was Eman. He was significantly younger than all the rest of Yiatu's men, but no less staunch, brave, and determined to prove himself.

"Not at all," Blackjack replied. "I know you men didn't have anything to do with this. I know you took the job of protecting these women very seriously after my brother freed you. I admire you for protecting everyone the same way and treating them all as captives. You had no reason to think anything else. You stepped up and did the right thing. I'm proud of that. Yiatu, go over there and bring the first woman to talk to me."

Blackjack retreated to one side apart from the rest of the men. They stayed in a cluster where they were. The men didn't move out of the women's sight. The women could all see these men attending Blackjack while he questioned the women.

Yiatu brought the first woman over to confront Blackjack. Yiatu stayed there to listen and probably to guard the women. He and all of his men acted like they were the ones responsible for this disaster even though they had nothing to do with it.

"Is anything wrong?" the woman asked.

"That's what I'm hoping to find out," Blackjack replied. "What's your name?"

"Niri," she replied and glanced at Yiatu. "Am I in trouble?"

"That depends. What Clan are you from?" Blackjack asked. "Which Clan did you belong to before the Red Riders captured you?"

"Uh...." She opened and closed her mouth a few times. "I belonged to the Emerald Clan. Why do you want to know?"

"How old were you when the Red Riders captured you? How did it happen?"

She cleared her throat and threw back her head to shake her hair out of her eyes. She squared her shoulders and locked a ferocious gaze on him. He saw her bracing herself to tell a story she would just as soon not remember.

"I was in our camp with my family band. I was helping my mother and older sister butcher a Stalkion that one of my father's adult sons had killed. His first wife died and he took a second wife, so he had two sets of children—one older and one younger. I was his youngest and I was ten years old. The Red Riders attacked and carried off all the women in camp. My mother, sister, and the other women and older girls tried to escape that night and Red Riders hunted them down and killed them all. I and three of my cousins got lost in the undergrowth during the chaos. That's the only reason we survived. The Red Riders found us the next morning and took us back to their camp with them. That's how it happened."

Blackjack nodded. "Thank you for telling me. You can go back to your own business. I won't bother you again."

Chapter 30

Niri left and Blackjack waited for the next woman to come over. She was much taller than Niri and much better looking. This woman would have been a heartstopper in any Clan.

She moved with a subtle kind of grace like she knew how good-looking she was. She didn't act like she'd ever been afraid of anything in her life—much less the Red Riders.

She actually smiled when she came face to face with Blackjack. "Hello!" she exclaimed.

He tried to pretend that he didn't notice her giving him suggestive glances. "Hello," he replied. "What's your name?"

"Gara." She burst into a brilliant, glowing smile. "What is this about?"

"Which Clan are you from?" he asked. "Which Clan did you belong to before the Red Riders captured you?"

She only grinned more broadly. "Does that really matter? It was a long time ago."

"Humor me," he insisted. "Which Clan did you belong to?"

"I don't see why that should make a difference." She shot a glance at Yiatu and the men standing off to one side. "Are you going to throw people out based on which Clans they belonged to?"

Blackjack felt his temper rising. "My father already explained that we won't throw anyone out. Anyone who proves themselves loyal is welcome to stay. Anyone who doesn't prove themselves loyal will go to the ants as you've already seen. Now answer my question."

"Why should I? You aren't Kral of this band."

"Actually, yes, I am. Hangman is my father and he's too disabled to perform the functions of Kral. I was acting as Kral before he got hurt—but that isn't really any of your concern. Hangman went outside the valley with the women and children because he and Viking weren't able to participate in the campaign against the Red Riders. That's the only reason you met him first. I am still Kral and the decision about whether you live or die rests with me—not him. Now answer my question before I start to get the wrong idea about why you're acting so evasive. Which Clan did you belong to? How old were you when the Red Riders captured you? What were the circumstances?"

She burst out laughing. "It sounds to me like you're the one who has to justify yourself—not me."

Blackjack snorted and waved to his men. "Get her out of here!"

"Hey!" Gara started to struggle the minute Yiatu laid his hand on her arm. "Hey—leave me alone!"

"I gave you a chance to explain yourself," Blackjack told her. "What do you want from me? I asked a simple question and you gave me your attitude. Which Clan did you come from?"

"I don't remember, okay?" Her eyes darted around everywhere looking for someone to help her. Yiatu's men didn't move. "I was too young to remember."

"Which one of the Red Riders did you belong to?"

"What?" she asked. "What difference does that make?"

Blackjack compressed his lips and waved to Yiatu. "Get her out of here. Sephus, go into the camp and get the boys to bring the ants here...."

"NO!!" Gara practically screamed. "His name was Sakon! His name was Sakon! Ask any of the men. They'll tell you who he was. His name was Sakon."

Blackjack glanced at Yiatu and Yiatu nodded.

Gara burst into a rapid torrent of detailed, graphic descriptions of what Sakon used to do to her, including beating, stabbing, and torturing her. Her tirade went on and on without stopping.

Blackjack finally held up his hand. "Stop right there. Don't say another word."

"You said you wanted to know," she countered.

"Show me the scars."

Her eyes fell out of their sockets. "What?!"

"You just said he cut you with a knife. Show me the scars. Show me one scar—any scar. I'm not asking to see your body. Show me on your arm or your leg or your back."

She narrowed her eyes at him. "Are you calling me a liar?"

"Yes, I am. I'm glad we finally cleared that up. I'm calling you a liar, so show me the scars and prove you're telling the truth because, right now, you're on your way to visit the ants. I'm not going to listen to any more justifications. You're either lying about coming from another Clan or you're lying about Sakon hurting you. Lying to your Kral is a punishable offense either way. So show me the scars or you can kiss your life goodbye."

She blinked at him for a second and then relaxed her whole body. She actually smiled at him again. "I don't have any scars. He never hurt me. He loved me."

Blackjack only nodded and waved for the men to take her away. He didn't go with them this time. He had better things to do than waste his time with these filthy, rotten, stinking traitors.

He went down the line of shelters and interviewed the other eight women. He asked them all the same questions—which Clan they had originally come from, how old they were at the time of their capture, and the circumstances.

Four others besides Niri answered him directly, clearly, and filled in the details of their stories to his satisfaction. Two had been almost adult age when it happened and they remembered everything as if it had happened yesterday.

One of the others had been barely old enough to remember her capture. She didn't remember which Clan she belonged to, but she did remember her capture. She remembered the Red Riders fighting her male relatives and she remembered watching them die.

She had been so young that she didn't understand what she was seeing until the Red Riders had actually taken her to their camp. She had been too young for any of them to bother her back then.

The suffering of other captives had made a much deeper impression on her. She remembered that vividly—even more vividly than her own dead family.

Blackjack left her to her own business and turned to the last two women in line. He approached the ninth woman and got an even worse feeling about her when she smiled at him. That was never a good sign.

"What's your name?" he asked.

"Zosa," she replied.

"Which Clan did you belong to before the Red Riders captured you?"

"I belonged to the Followers Clan," she replied.

His head shot up. "Really? How old were you when the Red Riders captured you?"

"I was thirteen years old. I remember exactly how it happened."

Something in her bright eyes gave him another sinking feeling. He was becoming overly sensitive to people lying to him.

He studied the woman in front of him. She was also strikingly beautiful, healthy, and a little too happy about telling him her story.

She might have heard him asking these other women the same questions. Zosa had all the time in the world to come up with a plausible cover story for herself.

He thought it over for a second and made up his mind. He walked off through the camp to his father's shelter. Hangman looked up. "Is anything wrong, my son?"

Blackjack squatted down next to his father and rummaged in Hangman's shoulder bags. "I need to borrow some of your maps for a second, Father. I'll bring them back."

"Of course, my son. Whatever you need."

Blackjack found the map he was looking for and took it back to Zosa. Blackjack, Thena, and Bone had all studied these maps down to the smallest detail over the last five years.

Hangman and Mora had cut the maps up to make them fit inside Hangman's shoulder bag. This one section in Blackjack's hand right now had an index on the back listing all the town names and in which grids the viewer could find the towns on the map.

Blackjack held up the map in front of Zosa. "Read this," he ordered.

She frowned at him. "What do you mean? I don't understand."

He rotated over next to her, held up the map, and pointed to the index. "Read this. Read any of these words in this list. What does this word say?" he pointed to the word, *index.*

Mora had explained the concept of an index to Blackjack and his siblings—just in case they couldn't have figured out what it was. Zosa would have gotten enough of an education in the Follower Clan to understand what an index was.

She definitely would have been able to read these words. Mora said the Followers taught the littlest children to read. Any thirteen-year-old would have no trouble with this list.

Blackjack could read it and he hadn't gotten as much education as Zosa claimed to have gotten. She stared at the list and then her eyes darted all over the plastic-covered sheet. She had no clue what she was looking at.

Blackjack was all finished going through this whole song and dance with these foul liars. Who did they really think they were fooling with these flimsy, pathetic stories?

He turned around to call Yiatu's men forward. Blackjack didn't know if the ants were still out there or if the boys had already come back. He didn't care. He just wanted Zosa out of his sight.

A scream ripped through the air right then and startled him to high alert. "Aza!!" the women in the next shelter screamed. "Aza is gone!! Tazuna! Where are you?!" The woman burst out of her shelter and started tearing around all over the place. "My daughters! My daughters are gone!!"

Blackjack strode over to her. "What do you mean—they're gone? They could be anywhere in the camp."

"They never left the shelter! They were too afraid to go anywhere!" The woman broke away and raced around and around the shelter calling out. "Aza!! Where are you?!! Tazuna!! My daughters are gone!!"

Adrenaline started pumping through Blackjack's veins—and then he stopped where he was. Two children—two young girls—walking around alone out in the jungle—assuming they left the camp at all.....

The whole thing sounded way too implausible—almost like three women walking out of the valley and straight into the Red Riders' waiting arms.

Why would two young girls leave the camp or the valley—when those same girls had been too afraid even to leave their shelter before now?

Niri came rushing over just then and got in the distraught mother's face. "Rala! Rala! Look at me!" Niri practically yelled. "When was the last time you saw them?"

"I...." Rala took a minute to think clearly enough to answer. "I saw them.....a few hours ago. I left them in the shelter while I.....I was working out here. I didn't think to check on them.....and I just went inside just now....and they were gone!"

"Rala," Blackjack interjected. "Which Clan did you belong to before the Red Riders captured you?"

"What?!" she gasped and tried to turn away. "I have to look for my children...."

He overreacted, spun her around, and shook her a little too hard. "The whole band will go out to find your daughters as soon as you answer my question. Which Clan did you belong to and what were you doing when the Red Riders captured you? Answer my questions now or I'll know you're a traitor."

Her expression changed to a fierce glare. "Get your hands off me this instant! You have no right to interrogate me!"

"I'm the man who will send you to the ants if you don't answer. You're in pretty good shape for a Red Rider captive. You don't have any bruises or badly healed broken bones—not like Niri here. You were never a captive, were you? Were your daughters too afraid to come out of the shelter because they were scared of the Red Riders—or were they afraid of the Godless? Tell the truth!"

He shook her again, and when she still didn't answer, he shoved her toward Yiatu. "Take her and Zosa out and get rid of them. Then catch up with me and the other men. We have a much bigger problem on our hands."

Chapter 31

Blackjack rushed through the camp calling all his men together. He ignored the slackers. He didn't even tell them what was going on.

He barely took the time to give the map back to Hangman before Blackjack took the men out to hunt down the two missing girls. They had a head start.

It could have been a big head start. Blackjack didn't trust Rala to tell the truth about anything including when she last saw her own children.

She could have been the one to spirit them out of camp and send them out on their own. She could have planned to keep quiet to give them as much time as possible and put as much distance as possible between them and the Godless.

She might have only raised the alarm right at that moment because she saw Blackjack coming to question her. She might have thought the alarm over some missing girls would distract him from questioning her at all.

None of that mattered because he had to track down these girls at all costs. They must have grown up in the Red Riders. These girls didn't know how to conceal their footprints. They led the Godless straight to them.

The tracks indicated that the girls were about thirteen and eleven—old enough to hold some loyalty to their original Clan. Rala might have convinced her daughters that they should seek revenge for their murdered father against the Godless band that had killed him.

The girls couldn't have left the camp within the last few hours. They had already covered the distance between the camp entrance and the secret tunnel. Their footprints picked up outside.

Blackjack became more convinced by the minute that Rala must have sent the girls out much sooner than that. She might have sent them out last night or even yesterday or in the last week.

None of the Godless would have noticed the girls missing—especially not if they usually spent their time in their shelter. Everyone in the band had better things to do than keep track of someone else's children.

The men raced up the mountainside. They didn't catch up with the girls anywhere along that steep slope. The girls were nowhere to be found, but their tracks were. They had passed through here more than twenty-four hours ago.

The men didn't find the girls on the clifftop. The men continued to follow the girls' footprints. They had traveled a long way. The girls might have been out here alone for days.

Blackjack slowed when he started to see more signs of Red Rider activity in the terrain. He and his men traveled through the canopy and followed the girls' footsteps straight to a giant horde of Red Riders assembled forty miles from the cliffs.

The men hid in the branches and surveyed the enemy camp. The Red Riders brought all their comforts with them this time. The Riders pitched tents, constructed beds, and even brought plenty of captives to keep the men entertained between battles.

The Red Riders brought a much bigger army this time along with an equal number of Blastidons. The Red Riders must have brought a thousand men this time.

They didn't know yet that they wouldn't be able to take the Blastidons through the tunnel, but that hardly mattered. This many men would pose a great enough threat to the Godless.

The Godless would do better to engage the Red Riders outside the valley. Blackjack couldn't use the same strategy—assuming the Red Riders knew about the tunnel now.

The two girls' footprints joined up with this army. The girls must have come here especially to inform the Red Riders about the tunnel. Rala wouldn't have sent her daughters out here into such danger for any other reason.

Blackjack waited a long time. He didn't see the girls and he wouldn't have been able to do anything about it even if he had seen them. He signaled his men to retreat and they returned back along their route to the camp.

He stopped there in the entrance and surveyed all the people around him. They had been getting their lives back this last month.

Even the seasoned older Godless had to go through an adjustment period to get their lives back after the upheaval of the first war against the Red Riders. Now Blackjack's people had to go through the whole thing all over again.

Blackjack didn't look forward to telling them. He especially didn't look forward to waging this war without his father, Viking, and the other older men getting too slow and weak to take part. That was the worst part in all of this.

Yiatu came up to Blackjack just then. Yiatu and his men were just coming back from the jungle—without Zosa and Rala.

"What's happening?" Yiatu asked. "Did you find the missing girls?"

"Yeah. I found them. Round up all your men and arm yourselves, Yiatu. We're going to war against the Red Riders."

Yiatu's eyes widened. "Are they here—now?!"

"They aren't here yet, but they're moving in. The girls told them about the tunnel entrance, so we need to mobilize immediately. Go do it—now."

Blackjack walked away and grabbed the four uninitiated boys. He sent them out into the jungle alone to run south to the other valley bands and raise the alarm. Then Blackjack went through camp and informed every man present what was going on.

The younger men armed and came immediately. Hangman and Viking didn't move. Some of Red's men were getting too old to come out to war, too.

Kuvik came and so did Carnage, Jolt, and Burn. Red and Wildling came, but Blackjack pretended that the two men weren't there at all. He didn't much like their chances if it came to open combat against the Red Riders.

Blackjack simply couldn't bring himself to tell these men to stay behind. Red and his men had always been something like gods to Blackjack. It was bad enough that Hangman and Viking were out of action. Blackjack couldn't face losing Red and Wildling, too—not now.

"What are we going to do?" Chief asked after Blackjack told them about the situation. "We can't fight that many Red Riders. Our whole advantage to bringing them into the valley depended on them not knowing a way out of it. We don't have that advantage now."

"We're going out of the valley to camp outside," Blackjack replied. "We'll hold them outside the valley as long as we can. We'll continue to carry out ambushes on them to reduce their numbers and we'll do everything in our power to stop them from entering the valley. That's all we can do for now. Now let's go. Defending the tunnel will be up to us until the men from the other valley bands come to reinforce us."

The men took leave of their wives and left camp. Blackjack didn't linger to take a long farewell from Narina. He didn't know when he would be able to get back home. She might spend her entire pregnancy alone—and even then, he might not come back at all.

Chapter 32

Blackjack strode into camp and headed for his parents' shelter. Mora and Thena stood outside the door. Blackjack looked around. "Where's Father? Is he all right?"

"I'm right here, my son." Hangman came out of the shelter just then. He stumbled and then limped on his bad leg when he hobbled through the doorway.

He had been moving more and more slowly in the two years since the Red Riders had been besieging the valley. Blackjack had completely taken over all of Hangman's duties as Kral even though neither of them had made any official announcement about it.

Hangman straightened up in front of the shelter just as Bone rejoined the family. Blackjack turned to Thena. "Are you ready to leave?" He burst out laughing. "I can't believe my little sister is going to the gathering! You're all grown up, aren't you?"

Her cheeks turned pink and she looked away. "Stop it. It isn't that big a deal."

"It's a huge deal." He put his arm around her and kissed her on the cheek. "I can't believe I won't see you again after the gathering."

"You might," she returned. "We might be the only people there—or there might be only young women there."

"You won't be," Mora pointed out. "Fire from Yeoli's band is going to the gathering this year. You'll marry Fire if you don't marry anyone else."

Thena made a face. "I don't care if he is the only man there. I won't marry him. I wouldn't have to go to the gathering at all if I did want to marry him. I could just move to Yeoli's camp and spare us all the time and effort of traveling south."

"Don't worry, my love," Hangman replied. "Fire doesn't want to marry you, either."

"I know he doesn't," Thena countered. "We've hated each other for years."

The rest of the family laughed. "We better go if we're going to go." Blackjack crossed the camp to his own shelter. He found Narina standing there holding their two-year-old son, Mion.

Blackjack kissed her and then the little boy. "I'm going out now. I'll see you in a month or so."

Narina smirked at him. "Don't get married while you're down there, okay."

He laughed. "I'm quite sure I wouldn't find a woman as beautiful as you there. I'll come home to you and this little warrior. Don't worry."

She smiled and they kissed again before he left. He'd been coming and going for two years in between fighting the Red Riders.

He returned to his family and the party left the camp. No one else went with them. Hangman kept up with the others. He didn't slow anyone down.

Blackjack, Bone, and Thena could have traveled much faster without their parents, but Thena couldn't go to the gathering without both Mora and Hangman present.

Blackjack would conduct any negotiations as Thena's Kral, but the two parents had to be there just to say their last goodbyes to their daughter before she left home for good.

Blackjack didn't want to think about that. He didn't want to think about his sister leaving the band and maybe even the Godless Clan. He couldn't face it if she married into a Clan like the Followers. That would have been a disaster.

At least she knew how to read. She wouldn't be completely out of her depth there, but it would be much better for her to go with a Godless man—from somewhere.

The family met up with Fire's family as both parties approached the tunnel. Thena and Fire avoided each other. He had come from the very first group of captives that Hangman and his men had freed from the Red Riders.

Thena had made friends with and bonded with most of the women and girls from that group. She even got along with and liked most of the men and boys.

She and Fire repelled each other for some reason. They got along best when they had nothing to do with each other and each of them pretended the other didn't exist.

They traveled on opposite sides of the group while everyone else walked and talked together. Neither family suggested that Thena and Fire get together with each other. Everyone knew it was impossible.

Blackjack never would have consented to letting his parents travel all the way south to the gathering grounds if there had been any chance of Thena finding a husband inside the valley.

She would have no choice but to marry Fire if no other young men showed up at the gathering. That was the law. Every young woman had to pair off with a young man no matter who he was. Neither could pick and choose.

Mora and Hangman never would gotten together at all if anyone had given them a choice about it. Young people had a hard enough time finding spouses they weren't biologically related to.

Fire qualified, so he and Thena would just have to make it work whether they wanted to or not. Choice didn't enter the picture unless the people involved had more than one option.

The party exited the tunnel and ran into the Godless force standing guard outside the entrance. The Godless had stationed themselves halfway up the mountain so their presence wouldn't draw too much attention to the tunnel itself.

The Godless had been maintaining a base of operations here for the last two years and holding the Red Riders at bay. The Red Riders maintained their own base on exactly the same spot where Blackjack had first found them after the two girls had escaped.

The Red Riders probably thought the sheer size and numbers in their camp would intimidate the Godless. Instead, the Red Rider camp became their greatest liability. The Godless always knew where to attack the Red Riders.

The Red Riders stubbornly refused to move their camp even after two years of constant Godless harassment, ambushes, and unconventional attacks that dwindled the Red Rider numbers by the day.

The Godless continued their campaign of terror against the Red Riders, led dangerous creatures to attack the Red Rider camp, used all the same old poison darts, nighttime sneak attacks, and guerilla warfare that had kept the Godless alive all this time.

The Godless also killed countless Blastidons in the process. The Godless waged an even more vicious war against the Blastidons to stop the Red Riders from using the creatures against the Godless in combat.

The Godless never left any Blastidons alive whenever the Godless struck the Red Rider camp. Then the Godless butchered the dead creatures, took the meat home, and ate it. Why waste perfectly good food?

The Godless didn't eat the Blastidons that died by poison, of course. The Godless left those Blastidons to rot—which of course attracted ants and Abnormits to go after the Riders.

The Godless would have completely wiped the Red Riders off the face of the Earth if the Red Riders hadn't received regular reinforcements from the south. Blackjack really didn't care how many Red Riders they sent. The reinforcements wound up just as dead.

The Red Riders did still launch occasional assaults on the Godless position. The Godless always managed to hold the Red Riders off by using a combined strategy of frontal confrontation and unconventional flank and rear attacks to surprise and weaken the enemy.

The Red Riders' lack of creative thinking proved their undoing. They didn't adapt to the Godless way of fighting. The Red Riders had spent the early days of this war simply digging in to survive the Godless maneuvers by sheer force of Red Rider numbers.

The surviving Red Riders entrenched themselves to dig in and weather the Godless assaults. The Red Riders seemed to believe that they simply had too many men for the Godless to weaken the Red Rider force in any meaningful way.

The Red Riders approached their combat the same way. They simply ignored unconventional tactics and pretended they weren't part of the engagement. The Red Riders weathered them, too, even when these tactics were the one thing swinging the war in the Godless' favor.

Blackjack couldn't exactly say that he was swinging the war in the Godless' favor. He could only do that by completely eliminating the

Red Rider threat. He was no closer to doing that now than he was two years ago.

He and his men had held the Red Riders off. The Godless had stopped the Red Riders from setting foot inside the tunnel. Blackjack called that a victory in itself even if it wasn't a total, decisive victory.

Yiatu and his men had taken his advice, married women from the same group of freed captives, and left the camp in the rocks to form their own band.

All those men and women had children of their own now and so did all of Blackjack's men who were over the age of gathering. Everyone needed more space to grow and expand.

The stalemate between the Godless and the Red Riders gave all the Godless men a chance to go home and spend time with their families. The five Godless bands had developed a rotation within each band so some men stayed on guard while others went home.

Blackjack had to pay attention to the gathering right now. He was leaving the valley's defense to his men.

The journey went much more quickly than Blackjack expected. He expected Hangman to need extra time or for everyone to have to slow their pace to match his. He limped the whole way south, but he didn't stop or slow down.

He could move faster than usual when he really needed to. He used a sort of sideways hopping step. He would take a step on his bad leg and then skip two paces on his good leg. He could keep pace with any able-bodied person that way.

He couldn't travel through the treetops, so the party had to stay on the ground. Fire's father couldn't travel through the treetops, either. He'd suffered a head injury as a Red Rider captive. The injury had healed, but it affected his balance. He had to stay on the ground, too.

None of those obstacles slowed the journey. Blackjack, Bone, Fire, and Fire's younger brother Rogue hunted for the others and scouted the area for any sign of danger.

Blackjack usually couldn't stop thinking about everything related to the valley's defense. He usually had to work hard to block the situation out of his mind so he could pay attention to his wife and son.

Now he found all those concerns for strategy, maneuvers, ambushes, and enemy positions falling away. He only thought about the gathering. He would be the one responsible for negotiating with whoever Thena decided to marry.

Blackjack might not have to negotiate at all. The gathering might go quickly the way it went between Blackjack and Narina. Thena and Fire might be the only young people there. Then Blackjack wouldn't have to negotiate.

Actually, he would. He would have to make sure Fire understood his obligations to protect and provide for Thena even if they didn't like each other. Thena would have to understand her obligations, too. She had to give Fire children. That was the law.

They would just have to work together and figure it out. Hangman and Mora had more to overcome and they still did it. At least Fire and Thena were both Godless.

Blackjack actually liked Fire. He was a strong, steady, honorable Godless man who had distinguished himself in combat more times than Blackjack could count. Fire would take care of Thena. Blackjack never doubted that for an instant.

Fire did have a quiet, self-possessed nature. He didn't share his thoughts and feelings easily. He kept his own council and remained silent when others talked. Blackjack couldn't think of any other reason why Thena wouldn't like him.

Blackjack also didn't understand why Fire didn't like Thena except that he was too smart not to notice how much she hated him. He would have to be stupid not to notice that and act accordingly—and he wasn't stupid.

The two families enjoyed themselves apart from that. Fire got along with everyone in Thena's family. Hangman especially approved of Fire as a warrior. Even Mora liked Fire.

The journey south took a little over three weeks—less time than Blackjack and Hangman originally planned for it to take. The two families relaxed on the way.

"We still haven't seen any other people this time, either," Blackjack remarked on the families' last evening before the gathering. "The country is completely empty."

"It's strange, isn't it?" Fire's father Major agreed. "I wonder why. This country used to be full of people from all kinds of Clans."

"We've been living under the constant threat of enemy attack for so long," Hangman added. "It doesn't seem possible that we can have been living in the one part of the world that still has people living in it."

"The Red Riders are marauders," Mora pointed out. "They make their living by attacking other people and taking what they have. The Red Riders might have traveled a long way to find any people to attack. That may be why they're so intent on attacking us—because we're the only people around that they can attack. They may not be able to target anyone else because there is no one else."

Hangman raised his eyebrows. "Good point. I didn't think of that. I wonder if that means they have a limited number of men to send after us."

"They will have a limited number of men," she countered. "They have to. Their numbers can't be unlimited."

"I don't know about that," Hangman pointed out. "Look how many of those captives the Red Riders got pregnant. The Red Riders were reproducing themselves as fast as they possibly could."

"But not all those women gave birth to boys," Mora argued. "And of those boys the Red Riders did father, how many of them would really be willing to become Red Riders themselves and go out to battle for the Clan? Look at Hammer and his men. They loathed the Renegades, especially the Renegades who fathered them. Hammer and his men killed their own fathers in revenge for what the Renegades did to the sons' mothers. The Red Riders could expect the same thing. The number of sons born in captivity who would actually be willing to follow in their fathers' footsteps—it would be a tiny fraction of the children born in captivity."

"It's an interesting problem," Major agreed. "I wonder what it means."

"It means that we only have to hold out against them and keep killing as many as we possibly can," Blackjack added. "It means we can wipe them all out if we just stand firm and keep chipping away at them. If Mother is right and we're the only available target, then we're in the best possible position to eliminate the Red Rider Clan from existence exactly the same way we eliminated the Anglers. We just have to kill enough of them that their population can't bounce back."

Hangman frowned into the fire. "It does put a different spin on the problem to know that the Red Rider Clan is in such a weak and vulnerable position."

"Think about it," Blackjack went on. "They won't be able to reproduce themselves without captive women. The Riders won't be able to take captive women if there aren't any other Clans to take captive women from. The Red Riders mistreat their captives to the point of death. These women won't survive long enough to give birth to enough children to replace the Riders we kill. It's a game of numbers that the Red Riders can't win. We just have to continue to wage war against them until they lose enough strength for us to defeat them."

Chapter 33

Hangman limped into the gathering grounds and sat down. His leg hurt—a lot. The journey here didn't do his aching body any favors. Thena, Mora, Bone, and Rogue built a fire in the usual spot.

The two Godless families arrived first the way they had when Blackjack came to the gathering. Fire sat down with his parents. He didn't help the others—not with Thena there.

Hangman really, really hoped for Thena's sake that she wouldn't have to marry Fire. Hangman hoped she could marry someone she could make a fresh start with—someone she might grow to like and respect in future years.

Mora and the three young people built up the fire and sat down to wait for the other bands to show up. The hours passed and the sun went down. No one else came. Silence fell over both families as the inevitable truth sank in. It didn't look good for Fire and Thena.

Hangman hadn't wasted his breath telling Thena that she would have to marry Fire if no other young men showed up. She already knew that. She could hem and haw all day long and say she refused to marry him.

She wouldn't have a choice if it came to that. Fire knew it as well as she did. No one had to explain the law to either of them.

Hangman didn't mention it now, either. He wouldn't rub her nose in it—now when she faced her worst nightmare coming true.

The fire crackled. No other sound disturbed the silence. Fire's family fell into the same inevitable silence.

No doubt his parents really wished some other young woman would come to the gathering so Fire wouldn't have to marry Thena, either. They didn't want their son to marry a woman who hated him.

Hangman gave up waiting for any other band to arrive. It was too late already. He should just call on Major to accept the harsh reality so they could all start on the journey home.

Hangman took a deep breath to say those words. He didn't want to. He would have given anything not to say them, but at that moment, another band came out of the darkness from the west side of the plateau.

The Godless stiffened....and then Hangman's heart leapt when he saw that the newcomers belonged to Hammer's band.

He came with a large number of men, women, and young people. Hangman couldn't tell from here which of them was coming to the gathering and which just came in support.

Hangman's joy at seeing Hammer again drove Hangman to his feet. He had planned for Blackjack to negotiate on Thena's behalf, but Hangman couldn't stay sitting down—not with Hammer and his men sitting right across the fire.

Blackjack and Thena stood up in response to Hangman's movements. Major and Fire stood up, too.

Hammer burst into a massive grin when he saw Hangman's family across the circle. He got up and so did two young men and three young women. They were all too old to be Hammer's children—or any of his men's children.

"Let me go with Hammer, Father," Thena murmured out the side of her mouth. "Please, please, please! Let me go with Hammer! I'm begging you!"

"All right, my child," he breathed back. "I'll see what I can do. He has the only other young women here besides you. He has two men and three women. That makes four women and three men. One woman will go home alone. Which young man do you like?"

"Anyone but Fire." He heard her voice shaking. "Let me go with anyone but Fire. Please! I'll do anything!"

"Let me go talk to him." Hangman stepped out of his group and advanced across the circle. Major went with him.

They met up with Hammer in the center of the ring next to the fire. Hangman saw Hammer coming and couldn't hold back. The two men met in a powerful, crushing hug. Hangman felt himself starting to get emotional at seeing Hammer again.

They both pushed each other back and beamed at each other at arm's length. Hangman's throat hurt staring at this man and Hangman's face ached from smiling so much.

"We're both so old!" Hammer exclaimed and burst out laughing. "Look at you! Are you Kral now?"

Hangman shrugged. "I'm too old and slow. Blackjack is taking over for me, but I guess we can negotiate as friends."

Hammer burst into another big, blushing smile. "Yeah. We can." He glanced past Hangman's shoulder. "Is that Thena?! My God! She's gorgeous!"

"Who do you have over there?" Hangman asked. "These aren't your children. They can't be."

"They're the children of freed captives who came over to us and joined our band. The men have all initiated in good standing and the girls have all grown up Godless. The men are good men and the girls will make good wives to any man." Hammer turned to Major. "I'm sorry. I don't know you."

"This is Major," Hangman replied. "He's also a former freed captive from the Red Riders. He's a good man and highly respected in our band. So is his son Fire. He's strong, smart, brave, responsible, and well-respected. He'll make a good husband for any of your girls."

"Why didn't Thena marry him, then?" Hammer asked. "You could have spared yourself the trip down here."

"They've known each other for years and they don't get along. Neither of them wants to marry the other. They will if they have to, but they would both prefer someone else. That's why we're here—to see if they can find someone they both like better."

"One of our girls will have to go home and try again next year," Hammer pointed out.

"I would ask that you take Thena for one of yours," Hangman replied. "It's a long way to come for no outcome. We would rather not do it again next year."

"Actually, one of our girls doesn't want to marry at all," Hammer replied. "She had a hard time with the Bounty Hunters and she doesn't want to marry. We'll take her home and wait until next year. She came last year and we were the only band here, so maybe next year will be the same. She may get old enough that she doesn't have to come at all."

"She would have to marry a single man from your band," Hangman pointed out. "If anyone will have her."

"I'm not convinced that getting married would be the best thing for her, for her husband, or any children she gave birth to. We've seen some strange doings with these freed captives. I wouldn't want to end up with another disaster like the one that happened to Cheina—which is what might happen if I pushed this girl to marry someone against her will."

Hangman shrugged. "I've seen the same thing. You're her Kral, so it's your decision. So who do you want to pair off with whom?"

"Why don't we bring the six remaining young people together and they can talk to each other and decide for themselves?" Hammer suggested. "One of my girls and one of my men are willing to pair off with each other, but they want to see what else is available before they definitely decide."

Hangman nodded. "I guess that's as good a plan as any. Bring out yours and I'll bring out mine."

Hammer, Hangman, and Major returned to their places. Hangman told Thena what was happening and Major told Fire.

Hammer informed his own party and one girl sat down. She was extremely pretty, but Hammer knew her better than anyone. He'd also seen the worst that could happen to one of these women if circumstances pushed them too far.

Hangman wouldn't want what happened to Cheina to happen to anyone. It really would be better for the girl not to marry at all than to go through that—and to take her child through it, too.

The other six young people stepped out into the center of the circle. Hammer, Hangman, and Major stood off to one side while the young people talked amongst themselves.

Fire talked to the two girls from Hammer's party. Thena talked to the two young men from Hammer's party. Their voices combined so that Hangman couldn't hear what any of them were talking about.

He definitely saw sparks flying between Fire and one of the girls and between Thena and one of Hammer's men. The attraction couldn't be more obvious.

All six young people discussed and debated in a civil tone. No one got upset or jealous at all. Almost all of them nodded in agreement. Then they changed their configuration.

The man attracted to Thena stayed with her and the girl attracted to Fire stayed with him. The other man and girl from Hammer's party started talking to each other, but they nodded a lot, too. They didn't show any hostility or resentment at winding up together.

Hangman and Hammer exchanged glances. It looked settled from where Hangman stood.

He and Hammer stepped forward. "Are you all satisfied?" Hangman asked.

"Yes, it's all settled," the young man standing next to Thena replied. He stuck out his hand to Hangman. "It's an honor to meet you, Sir. I swear I'll take good care of your daughter."

Hangman shook his hand. "I'm sure you will. Any young man who has grown up under Hammer is good enough for my daughter."

"Are all the rest of you satisfied?" Hammer asked. "Buck? Neshi? Are you satisfied with this?"

The two young people from his party who had paired off with each other both nodded. "This is the best we're going to get," Neshi replied. "We already know each other. We know we'll be happy together."

"Fire?" Hangman asked. "Are you satisfied?"

Fire nodded. "Yes, I am."

"Then I guess we're done here." Hangman turned to Thena. "Travel safely, my love. I'll always cherish you in my heart."

She put her arms around him and kissed him on the cheek. "I love you, Father. Thank you so much for this. Come and visit me, okay?"

"I'll try." He stroked her hair once and tore himself away. He didn't want to make this a big emotional display.

Fire took his bride back to his family and they sat down together. Mora came forward and burst into tears when she said goodbye to Thena. Thena wiped tears off her cheeks, but she actually looked happy.

Mora turned to Hammer and hugged him, too. "Take care of my baby, Hammer. I'm trusting you."

"I will," Hammer murmured. "I sure do miss all of you. I'm so glad you're doing well in your own country."

Blackjack came forward to greet and hug Hammer, too. Then Hangman, Mora, and Blackjack went through the rest of Hammer's men, hugged, and engaged in the shortest possible reunion before they all had to leave.

Hammer's people welcomed Thena with open arms. The two remaining girls pulled her into their group and talked to her at length about their respective bands while the adults said their final goodbyes.

The parting came too soon for everyone. Hangman would have stayed all night and talked endlessly about everything Hammer and his band had been doing since they'd parted from Shadow.

They couldn't stay all night. Both bands had to travel back to their own territory. Hangman felt himself nearing the breaking point when he and Hammer came face to face for the last time. Tonight had passed far too quickly. Now it was over.

"You should come to see me if you aren't acting as Kral," Hammer murmured.

Hangman nodded and tried to swallow the lump in his throat. "I'll try, but it isn't so easy for me to travel anymore. This old body isn't what it used to be."

"All the more reason for you to come," Hammer insisted. "I would love to see you."

Hangman couldn't answer at all. He couldn't give voice to how much he wanted to see Hammer—and all his men.

Hangman didn't hold out any hope that he would ever see Hammer again—unless Hammer brought some more young women when Bone came to the gathering. That time seemed so far away right now.

The two men husked out a brief, broken goodbye and both bands walked off in opposite directions into the dark. Mora cried all the way to the jungle where the party camped in the treetops.

Major, his wife, Palea, Rogue, and Fire talked casually with Fire's new bride. Her name was Iaza and she was as Godless as anyone could ask for. She climbed well and settled right in with the new family.

Bone and Blackjack remained silent all evening. Mora sat there sniffing at Hangman's side. He found himself putting his arm around her to comfort her. Thena was gone and wouldn't come back.

At least she had gone to a good Godless band. Hangman didn't worry about Thena. Hammer would take good care of her. He wouldn't let her marry any young man who wouldn't treat her honorably.

Thena knew Vina, Sema, Eleph, and all the other young women who had left Shadow's band to follow Hammer and his men into their own territory. Those women would take care of Thena, too—and Cross was there. She wouldn't be alone.

Hangman couldn't ask for a better outcome for his daughter, but the dark cloud still hung over the whole family She was gone for good. Now only Bone and Blackjack remained.

Chapter 34

The two families continued their journey north on the way back to the Angler Valley. Iaza proved herself an enthusiastic, friendly, and helpful young woman. She proved herself every time the party made camp. She helped everyone and even offered to hunt.

She and Fire became more and more attached to each other the longer they spent together. They usually slept in each other's arms, but they didn't go any further than that where anyone could see them.

Hangman, his sons, and Rogue warmed to her. Mora absolutely adored her and so did Major. Palea didn't warm to Iaza. Fire's affection for his new wife poisoned his mother against Iaza.

Palea fell silent and became resentful on the way back to the valley. She refused to talk to anyone, especially her husband and sons. She would sooner talk to Hangman and his sons than her own family.

She glared, scowled, and snarled at Iaza whenever the younger woman went near her mother-in-law. Palea refused even to talk to Iaza even when Iaza asked Palea a simple question like inquiring if Palea wanted any more of the food before Iaza put it away.

Hangman started to feel extremely glad that Palea didn't talk to Iaza. Palea probably would have been saying all kinds of hateful, insulting things that Iaza didn't deserve.

Hangman also overheard Fire telling Iaza more than once that she never had to see Palea again once the family made it back to the valley. Fire would take Iaza to his own shelter where Iaza would be able to go about her business alone.

Fire insisted to his new wife that he wouldn't take her around his mother as long as she continued to act this way. He made it plain that he had no intention of subjecting his wife to this kind of treatment. He only put up with it now because they were traveling together.

Palea may even have heard her son saying these things and she still persisted in shooting death glares at her daughter-in-law right in front of her son. Palea continued this campaign of hatred even knowing it could cost her the relationship with her son.

Hangman didn't understand it at all. He only had to remember Mora's conduct toward Narina to see the startling contrast. Mora and Narina had hit it off immediately. Mora and Thena had welcomed Narina and made her one of their own.

Mora, Bone, and Blackjack saw all of this unfolding, too, but none of Hangman's family said anything about it. The party would make it back to the valley pretty soon. Then Fire would take Iaza away and the whole drama would be over.

Hangman didn't look forward to going home without Thena. The reality would set in once he and Mora returned to their shelter. They would have to face the harsh emptiness of knowing that Thena would never come back there.

Watching her grow up had been one of the singular pleasures of Hangman's life. He would have given anything for her to marry a man in one of the nearby bands.

Then Hangman would have been able to watch her raise her own family. He would have been able to be a grandfather to her children the way he was a grandfather to Mion. Now that would never happen.

Hangman didn't even know her husband's name. Did he have family back in Hammer's band? Did some of these young people's parents and siblings escape from captivity and take refuge with Hammer's men?

Their band sure did seem to be thriving. They got stronger, more numerous, and more self-assured every time Hangman saw them.

The party entered the valley system. Fire told Iaza all the old stories about how the band came to live in the Angler Valley. He told her about the tunnel before the party got there—not that she would have been able to find it on her own.

She had come from Hammer's band. Hangman trusted her for that alone. She was Godless through and through. He trusted her a lot more than the group of freed captives who had entered through the tunnel.

The party passed from one valley to another getting closer to the Angler Valley. Hangman looked forward to getting home—maybe for the last time. He probably wouldn't be strong enough to leave again—maybe not even to take Bone to the gathering.

Blackjack would have to take Bone to the gathering. Hangman might not even survive that long.

That thought barely crossed his mind before he heard the clang of metal ahead. The party was just descending the pass between one valley and another. The two families were nowhere near the Angler Valley—or near the Red Riders' camp.

The two families stopped in their tracks when they saw another reinforcing platoon of Red Riders thundering past on their Blastidons. These men headed north from somewhere off to the west. Hangman didn't see where the Riders were coming from.

They headed straight for the Angler Valley to reinforce the Red Riders stationed there. None of the Godless moved, but some of the

Red Riders saw them anyway. The Riders wheeled their Blastidons around to come after Hangman's party next.

"Get into the rocks, Mora!" he yelled out. "Take Iaza and Palea with you! Hurry!"

Mora sprang forward and grabbed Iaza's hand. "Come on!" Mora called. "This way!"

The two women scrambled into the high rocks. Palea took longer to clamber up there behind them. All three women got to safety before the Red Riders crossed the level ground and started riding up into the pass.

Bone, Blackjack, Hangman, Major, Fire, and Rogue all drew their weapons, but the men didn't stand their ground in the middle of the pass. That would have been suicide.

The men retreated into protected places in the rocks where they could flank the path and still engage the Riders. The Riders thundered their Blastidons up the path without realizing the danger—or they pretended not to care about the danger.

Maybe the Red Riders didn't think any people on the ground could pose a threat to them and their mounts. That was the thing about the Red Riders. They kept throwing away all their men in repeated attacks against the Godless.

The result was that none of the surviving Red Riders had any experience with the Godless' fighting style. None of the Red Riders found out the Godless' fighting style until it was already too late.

The same thing happened now. The Riders charged their Blastidons straight up the path and hit a blockage that the mounts couldn't navigate. The Blastidons were too bulky to fit through the rocks.

Hangman and the other men struck without mercy and stabbed the Blastidons through the sides and chests. Hangman lunged out of his hiding place and slashed his kukri across the nearest Blastidon's throat.

Blood gushed out onto the rock and the creature buckled onto its knees. The Rider barely sprang off in time before the creature toppled over and crushed him. Hangman dove back out of his hiding place to stab the Rider next, but the guy was too far away.

The Rider had already seen Hangman, rushed around the fallen Blastidon, and came after Hangman in the rocks. Hangman tried to retreat and wound up getting boxed in between rocks on both sides and behind him.

The Rider couldn't swing his axe very well in these cramped quarters. Hangman could fight better with his smaller size and smaller weapons, but not by much.

He deflected two strokes of the Rider's axe. The third smashed Hangman's kukri to a million shards of glass. The weapon had stood everything else since his initiation. Now it was gone.

He reacted lightning quick by stabbing the other kukri into the Rider's chest and twisting. The Rider bellowed out in mortal agony and chopped his hand down on Hangman's wrist.

The Rider's superior strength tore Hangman's hand off the blade. He was defenseless and the Rider didn't stop even with a kukri sticking out of his chest.

The Rider swung his axe in the only direction available. He swung it low and hacked it hard across both of Hangman's legs. The blade embedded itself in his flesh and shattered both his thigh bones.

Hangman buckled on the spot. He stayed conscious just long enough to see the Rider raise his axe to deliver the final killing stroke to Hangman's head.

Blackjack rushed up behind the Rider at that moment and slashed the man's throat before Hangman blacked the rest of the way out.

Chapter 35

Blackjack sat next to Hangman and stared down at his father's face. Mora had already spread leaf paste on Hangman's wounds, splinted his legs as well as possible, and given him multiple doses of Gooji juice.

"How will we get through the tunnel now?" Major asked behind Blackjack's back.

"We'll get through the same way we got out—by walking," Bone fired back. "This doesn't stop any of us from walking, does it?"

Blackjack should have told his brother to stay calm and polite, but Blackjack didn't feel like being either. This injury was the last thing in the world that Hangman needed.

This would finish him. That's all there was to it. He would probably never recover from this. He would be permanently crippled if he recovered at all.

"We'll carry him down the mountain ourselves," Bone grumbled under his breath. "You can take your family ahead for all I care. No one will stop you. You don't have to stay. The three of us will carry him. We'll make sure he gets home where he belongs."

"I didn't mean that!" Major countered. "I didn't mean we would leave him behind!"

Bone bared his teeth at Major and then went back to staring at Hangman in silent, dejected misery. Mora didn't look at or talk to anyone. She paid attention only to Hangman.

He'd regained partial consciousness since his fight against the Red Riders. He'd never come back to full lucidity. He might not. He might already be gone.

"What do you say, Mora?" Rogue asked. "Is it safe for Hangman to travel?"

"It isn't safe for any of us to stay here," she replied over her shoulder. "We all have to get into the valley. We should warn the men that the Red Riders are bringing in more reinforcements. The Red Riders always launch fresh attacks after reinforcements arrive."

"I mean is it safe to carry Hangman in this condition," Major went on. "Will traveling make him worse?"

"Nothing will make him worse," she murmured. "Nothing can make him worse—unless it's creatures or Riders coming upon us out here in the open. We have to go no matter what the consequences."

Bone got to his feet and left the camp without a word. Blackjack should have gotten moving, too, but he couldn't bring himself to move. He was looking at the end of his father right now. This was the end. This would finish Hangman if he wasn't finished already.

Bone came back with a freshly skinned hide from one of the dead Blastidons. He spread it on the ground and gripped his father's shoulder.

"Father!" Bone murmured. "We need to move you onto this hide so we can carry you home."

Hangman rolled his head from one side to the other. He didn't open his eyes. He just mumbled, "Do it."

Had he been awake through the whole conversation? Did he understand everything everyone was saying about him right now?

Bone exchanged a meaningful glance with Blackjack and Mora. The three of them had become connected by this silent thread of knowing ever since Hangman had gotten hurt. None of the three had to ask what the others were thinking.

Bone stood up, straddled Hangman's chest in a wide stance, and scooped him up under his armpits. Blackjack straddled Hangman's hips and took two big fistfuls of either side of Hangman's loincloth to move his hips.

He screamed out in pain when Mora scooped her arms under his splinted legs. Bone and Blackjack acted in perfect synchronicity. Both brothers picked up their father and slid him onto the Blastidon hide while Mora moved his legs.

Hangman collapsed sobbing and moaning in agony when they put him down, but at least it was over now. He didn't have to move. Blackjack went to the base of the hide. Bone and Mora each picked up a corner near Hangman's head.

Blackjack planned to carry Hangman's lower body by himself, but Rogue and Fire both came over to the hide and positioned themselves there, too. Rogue took the opposite corner near Hangman's other foot.

Fire positioned himself between Bone and Blackjack on that side. Iaza picked up the edge of the hide in front of Mora. That left Major and Palea. Major squirmed and shuffled his feet, but he couldn't do anything about it now.

The other six hefted Hangman off the ground. Six people carrying him made the load much lighter. They didn't have any trouble carrying him.

He winced and gasped in pain every time any of them walked over uneven ground and bumped the load out of place. Blackjack and the others just had to ignore him and keep going. They had to get to the Angler Valley at all costs.

Blackjack directed the party in a wide circuit away from the Red Riders' camp. The women had to stop more often to rest from the effort. That gave Bone, Blackjack, Fire, and Rogue the time they needed to scout the area.

The Red Riders weren't engaged in battle against the Godless at the moment. The party made it back to the Godless camp halfway down the mountain.

A horrified silence fell over the men when they saw Hangman's condition. None of the men spoke even to ask what had happened.

Blackjack called another halt there while he reviewed the defensive position. Kuvik, Yeoli, Chief, and Kavis were in charge at the moment. They filled him in on everything they'd been doing while the two families had been away.

Kuvik had been taking the ambushes, booby traps, and surprise attacks on the Red Riders much more seriously than anyone else. He had carried out multiple strikes on them recently and reduced their numbers.

Blackjack told him about the situation to the south and Mora's theory that the Red Riders might be attacking the Godless so strenuously because the Godless in the Angler Valley were the only targets available.

Kuvik raised his eyebrows. "That is an interesting way of looking at it. I didn't think of that, but it makes sense if the rest of the country is empty and we're the only people here."

"If it's true, then we can crush them by holding out and continuing to reduce their population," Blackjack went on. "They'll keep sending more and more men and we'll keep wiping them out as many as we can at a time. Eventually, they won't be able to send any more against us."

"That definitely gives me more reason to keep doing it—if you want me to," Kuvik returned.

"Of course I want you to. That's why I'm telling you. The more you kill, the better."

Kuvik nodded. "I can definitely do that. I'm good at that."

"I know you are. Just try not to get yourself or the other men killed in the process."

"Oh, I won't. Don't worry. I'll go alone if I have to. I'll be able to accomplish it better if I do it alone."

"Do whatever you have to do. I have to take my father and mother home. I'll come see you again as soon as I do that."

The six travelers picked up Hangman. He didn't rouse this time. He must have passed out. Blackjack and the others carried him through the tunnel.

They had to lift him up and over some of the machinery to fit him through to the other side. The party's actions would have knocked him out if he wasn't already unconscious.

Blackjack expected Major's family to take their leave on the other side of the tunnel, but Fire and Rogue insisted on carrying Hangman all the way to his shelter.

They even carried him inside, put him on his bed, and removed the hide from underneath him. He didn't wake up for the whole procedure.

The two families came face to face outside. Bone, Blackjack, and Mora thanked Fire, Rogue, and Iaza for their help. They shook hands as friends and Blackjack's family wished Fire and Iaza all the good fortune and happiness in the world.

Blackjack went through the motions of saying goodbye to Major and Palea and wishing them well. Mora did the same thing, but Bone didn't bother.

Major's family left. Now Bone, Blackjack, and Mora were all alone. "Can we do anything, Mother?" Blackjack asked. "Can we do anything at all?"

She stared down at the ground and shrugged. "No one can do anything. You two might as well go on about your business. You don't need to stay here. I'll take care of him."

"Don't hesitate to tell us if there's anything we can do—or if you want one of us to take over for you so you can go off by yourself for a while."

Mora looked around in wild panic. "Thena's gone!" she croaked. "She isn't here anymore! My daughter is gone!"

She started crying again. Bone and Blackjack moved in on her from either side and crushed her between them. Blackjack gave himself that moment to experience all the devastation of the last few days.

Thena was gone and now Hangman was gone, too. He would never be the strong, upright man he had been—the man everyone relied on when everything else fell apart. He had been a force of nature holding the whole world together—for everyone.

He would never be that again. The man he used to be would never come back—not ever. The old Hangman was already dead.

Chapter 36

The brothers pulled apart. Tears streaked Mora's cheeks and kept coming no matter how many times she tried to wipe them away.

Blackjack didn't say it out loud, but all three of them knew who she was really crying for. None of the three had any reason to grieve over Thena. She would live a good life with Hammer's band.

Losing her paled in comparison to losing Hangman. This whole disaster turned out to be so much worse than if he'd died in battle. Blackjack would much rather have faced that.

"You better go," Mora rasped. "Narina will want to see you."

Blackjack shared another one of those knowing looks with his brother, kissed his mother on the forehead, and walked off to his own shelter. The next generation needed him much more than the last one did.

He went back to his own house and sat down in front of it. He didn't want to see or talk to anyone. How long would it take before word spread that Hangman was at death's door and would probably never walk again?

Blackjack couldn't be the one to tell everyone that. He couldn't be the one to completely demolish the foundation of everything this band had built its future on.

He sat and stared at the ground while a million ideas collided in his head. He immediately started to think about the defenses again. Kuvik would be out there annihilating the Red Riders as fast as they sent in reinforcements.

Blackjack had to prepare himself and his men for the next Red Rider assault. It would come soon, now that the Riders had more men. He only hoped Kuvik would hit them before they launched their assault.

Kuvik might be able to take out all or most of the incoming Blastidons the night before the Red Riders' planned assault. That would slow down, delay, or possibly even derail the assault before it happened.

Or the Red Riders might launch the attack on foot. The Godless would have to defend themselves against that. Blackjack considered arranging for this battle to take place somewhere that the Godless could spring another ambush on the Riders.

That would take down their numbers even further. He would have to think of a good place and a good strategy to make it happen.

He couldn't think of anything right now—nothing but his father's condition. Hangman's latest injury overshadowed everything else. That was an unacceptable situation. Blackjack needed his head in the game to fight this war.

He just couldn't drag his thoughts out of the clouds no matter how hard he tried. He didn't want to fight the war. He wanted to help his father—but no one could. Mora knew more than anyone about how to help him. If she couldn't, no one could.

Bone and Blackjack hanging around constantly asking if she needed help would only make it harder for her. They could help her much more by keeping the valley safe for everyone.

The Red Riders had already hurt Hangman enough. The brothers couldn't let it happen again—to anyone.

Blackjack was still sitting there stewing over the whole nightmare when his little son Mion toddled out of the shelter behind Blackjack's back. The door slammed and the little boy burst into a mischievous grin when he saw his father.

Mion tottered over to Blackjack and practically fell over before Mion figured out how to stop. Blackjack had to put his arm around the boy to steady him.

Mion pointed in Blackjack's face still grinning like anything. "Baba!!" Mion gurgled.

"Hello, my precious son," Blackjack murmured. "Are you going on another scouting trip without Mother?"

Narina burst out from inside the shelter right then. "You rascal!" she exclaimed. "I told you not to run away from me like that." She glanced up and started to smile. Her face drained of all expression when she saw Blackjack. "What's wrong?"

Blackjack looked away. He could never keep anything from her. "Hangman got hurt again on the way home from the gathering. The Red Riders attacked us and broke both of his legs. We don't even know if he'll survive."

She gasped out loud and her hand flew to her mouth. "Oh, no! That's awful!"

"You have no idea. Mora is a mess."

"I should go see her." She got to her feet and then checked herself when she eyed Mion.

"Go," Blackjack told her. "I'm sure she would like to see you."

"Will you be okay?"

"Of course. I can take care of my own son."

She gave him a skeptical grimace and walked off toward Hangman's shelter. Blackjack didn't watch her go. He turned his attention to Mion.

The boy kept grinning like he already understood that he'd successfully evaded his mother's wrath. Blackjack sat back and watched the boy explore the area.

Mion kept pointing at Blackjack, grinning, and saying, "Baba!"

Blackjack laughed. Mion was such a cheery boy. Blackjack found it impossible to imagine this tiny child—almost still even a baby—as a grown, initiated man going to the gathering, bringing home a wife, and raising a family of his own.

It would happen. Blackjack would be lucky if he lived long enough to see it happen.

Hangman had enjoyed a long, fruitful life. He'd given his band decades of invaluable service, seen his children grow up, and lived to see his oldest grandson born. No one could ask for more than that.

Mion came back, tried a few more unsuccessful times to talk to Blackjack, and then tried to sit down on Blackjack's knee. Mion almost fell off into the dirt. Blackjack pulled the boy into his lap instead.

Mion kept leaning forward, picking up sticks and pebbles from the ground, holding them up, and trying to discuss them with Blackjack.

Blackjack treated the boy's indistinct babblings as real speech. "I know," Blackjack replied. "This one has a strange shape, doesn't it? It isn't round and it isn't quite oval, either, is it? Look at this bulb sticking out of one end. It reminds me of a person. What do you think?"

Mion launched into another string of unintelligible sounds mixed with gurgles and blowing bubbles in his own saliva. Blackjack enjoyed spending time with his son until Bone came over to sit down next to Blackjack.

Mion pointed at Bone and said, "Ohh."

"Good evening, little brother," Bone replied. "You're a mighty warrior, aren't you?" He turned to Blackjack. "Yiatu is asking to speak to you."

"Why doesn't he come and speak to me, then? I'm right here. He knows where to find me."

"He doesn't want to disturb you in case....you know....."

Blackjack made a face. "I'm not dead yet. I guess he can come and talk to me if he really wants to."

"I think you should call a meeting of all the other Krals," Bone suggested.

"I was planning to."

Bone's head shot up. "You were?"

"Of course. We've been fighting this war for two years and now it's cost us Hangman. We need to end it and that means exterminating everyone who knows about the tunnel."

Bone looked away. "Are you sure this isn't about Hangman himself?"

"I just said it's about Hangman. Are we going to wait around for the Red Riders to take out Kuvik next—or Red—or Yeoli? We need to finish these bastards—now. We've wasted too much time with them already."

"So how are you going to eliminate them all when they aren't all here?" Bone asked.

Now Blackjack was the one who looked away. "We have some business to attend to first."

"What business is that?"

"We have to initiate Urdis. Then we need to put some other preparations in place. We're holding the Red Riders at bay right now. We can keep doing that, but it isn't enough. We'll maintain our current state of defense while we maneuver our last puzzle pieces into position. Then we'll strike and the Red Riders will never recover."

"They'll bring in reinforcements while you wait," Bone pointed out. "You realize that, don't you? Every minute you delay makes them stronger."

"That's exactly why I am delaying," Blackjack countered. "You just said yourself that they aren't all here. The longer we wait, the more reinforcements they'll send. Then we can wipe out more of them when we finally do strike."

"You're Kral now," Bone blurted out. "You must understand that. Hangman is out—out completely. You're it."

"I know I am," Blackjack mumbled. "The rest of the band will need to hear it from him, though—as long as he's still alive. We can't do that now. His condition is too fragile. That doesn't matter, though. We need to make our preparations. That will give him time to heal at least a little bit—or not depending on how bad it is."

Chapter 37

Mora handed Hangman a bowl of freshly roasted meat. Black-jack, Narina, and Bone sat around the fire in front of Hangman's shelter while little Mion wobbled around from person to person.

He kept trying to talk to everyone, especially Hangman and Mora. Mion's language skills hadn't improved much in the six months since Thena had gone to the gathering.

He paused next to Hangman, rested his chubby little hand on his grandfather's shoulder, and pointed toward the camp entrance while Mion tried to tell him something.

"I completely agree with you, little brother," Hangman replied. "I couldn't agree more. The rocks offer the perfect defense against any mass invasion. The enemy can only get in one or two at a time. It was a stroke of genius on your part to choose this spot."

Mion gurgled with delight at this response and all the other adults laughed. "We should put him in charge of the war," Bone remarked.

Mora tapped Mion on the elbow. "Come over here and get some food, little grub. Leave your grandfather alone."

Mion stumbled over to her. She pulled him into her lap and placed another bowl of food in front of him. He started picking up the pieces of meat in his round little fist and stuffing them into his mouth as fast as he could go.

"You're such an expert, Mora," Narina remarked.

"You'll be an expert, too, when you get to be my age. It isn't complicated. It just takes years of practice."

"So what's your next plan, my son?" Hangman asked Blackjack. "Bone tells me you have some grand strategy in mind to exterminate the Red Riders."

Blackjack took a deep breath. "I want you to travel south to visit Hammer, Father. You can walk again even if you can't walk as fast as you used to. I want you, Kuvik, Red, and Wildling to travel to Hammer's valley and recruit him to bring the Ashtaws against the Red Riders."

Hangman's jaw dropped and he gasped. "Are you serious?"

Blackjack nodded. "We need an overwhelming force to wipe out as many Red Riders as possible. You and Kuvik know Hammer the best. I'm sorry for saying so, but you, Red, and Wildling are the least capable of participating in the war....."

"Why are you sorry for saying so?" Hangman countered. "We all know it's true."

"Well, the journey might take you some time to get there, but the Ashtaws would definitely swing this war in our favor. We could trample the Red Riders and at least eliminate a lot of them. We might even be able to drive them out of the country and scare them enough that they wouldn't come back."

Mora, Bone, and Narina gaped at Blackjack in horror. He didn't see them until he stopped talking.

"What?" he asked.

Mora gulped and looked away. She didn't want Hangman going anywhere, especially not on a long, dangerous journey with two men even older than himself and only Kuvik to guard them.

"He's....you know...kind of disabled for that, isn't he?" Bone asked. "He wouldn't be able to defend himself on the journey there."

"I can still defend myself," Hangman countered. "I might not be as mobile as I was, but I can still defend myself."

"You can't seriously be planning to go through with this!" Mora blurted out. "You can't seriously be planning to go on this journey!"

"Why not?" Hangman asked. "It's a great idea. The Ashtaws will be perfect for this. I wish I had been the one to think of it."

"Isn't it bad enough that you've just spent the last six months recovering from an injury that could have killed you?" Mora countered. "Do you really think I want you to die doing this?"

"Of course I don't think you want me to die, but I'm going to die one way or the other. At least this way I'll have a chance to help the band. I'm not doing the band any good sitting around here doing nothing—which is about all I'm good for these days. Hammer and I still have a connection. Whoever goes south should be someone who knows him. Who better than me? Besides.....I want to see him again—and I'll be able to visit Thena while I'm there."

"The journey will take time," Blackjack pointed out. "You'll travel slowly, so we'll just hold out until you get here."

"Of course," Hangman replied. "We'll try to get there as quickly as possible without putting ourselves in danger."

"And what if something happens on the way?" Tears sprang to Mora's eyes. "What do you think will happen to me?"

"I'm sure you'll be just fine without me," Hangman replied. "You've been working yourself into an early grave taking care of me while I've been recovering. You need a few months' break from that."

She looked away and refused to look at him again. He would do something like this—after he just spent the last six months relearning how to walk. Even now, he could barely hobble from one place to another.

A journey all the way south to the Ashtaw Valley would take ages. It would be long, hard, and painful—not to mention all the creatures the men would have to fight.

Red and Wildling were also slowing down. They might be able to help Hangman defend himself, but most of the hard work would fall on Kuvik.

This whole trip made Hangman way too happy. He wouldn't stop smiling at the thought that he would actually be able to participate in this war after all. He'd been out of action for almost all of it.

Blackjack saw how upset this made his mother. He got to his feet and brushed off his hands. "I'll go talk to the other men. You should leave as soon as you're all ready."

He kissed Narina and left. Bone made an excuse to leave not long after and Narina took Mion back to her house to get him ready for bed.

Hangman waited a long time before he spoke to Mora again. He slipped his hand into hers. "Don't be upset. You can't expect me to be happy sitting on the sidelines. At least I'll be able to do something. I'm not doing this to upset you."

"I know that!" she fired back. "I'm not upset because you're doing something or even that you're going into danger! You've been going into danger since we first met. You're always going into danger!"

"Then why are you upset? Don't ask me not to go. I have to."

"I wasn't going to ask you not to go! I just....." She bent her head, but she couldn't hold back her tears. "I don't want to lose you! I know you're going to die one day! I've been living with that for years. I just don't.....I can't.....I can't....."

He pulled her into his arms. She had to move toward him so he didn't have to move. That's how hurt he was. He couldn't even move out of his place to comfort her.

She collapsed against him sobbing hard. She really had been living with the reality of his imminent death since day one. She had always known he would die—probably sooner than he should have.

He just kept scraping through by the skin of his teeth. He should have died a dozen times, but he just kept surviving against all odds—just like this band he had created. He really was the living embodiment of everything strong and great about this band.

He kissed the side of her hair and pushed her back so he could see the tears streaming down her cheeks. He stroked her hair and used his fingertip to comb it out of her eyes.

"I love you," he murmured. "I never thought I would ever be able to stand to look at you. Now I don't know how I ever could have lived without you. You're everything good that has ever happened to me. I love you more than anything. I love that you're crying for me—because you're worried about me and because you want me with you."

She couldn't unclamp her lips to answer him. Of course she wanted him with her. Where else would she want him? How could she ever face her life without him after everything they'd gone through together?

She would have to face her life without him. He would die first. He was already so much closer to death than she was. He would leave her alone to face this life without him.

At least she wouldn't live long without him. Women her age never lived long in this world. Her sons would keep taking care of her for as long as she lasted, but she wouldn't continue to be a contributing member of this Clan anymore, either.

Everything good about her life had come from him. This band that she loved so much—her children and her grandson—all the wonderful people who had made her life such a blessing—they all came from him.

Those people accepted her, respected her, admired her, and listened to her because of him. They took her knowledge and used it to make this band great—because of him. None of that would have happened if not for him.

He might not come back from this trip. She really didn't see how he could. She had to be prepared for that.

He would go. He wouldn't stay behind. He couldn't. This drive to do something—to help the band—to protect everyone—he couldn't live without doing something. He would die so much more quickly and painfully if he stayed here just wasting away into nothing.

He cupped her chin and lifted her face so she had no choice but to look into his eyes. He could see all the love she felt for him pouring out in her tears. She never would have believed in her wildest dreams that she would ever feel this way about him.

She found it difficult to accept even now that she could feel this way about him—that so much of her life would come to depend on him—and that the thought of losing him would feel so much like the end of the world.

Watching him get hurt and not be able to bounce back—watching him age and crumble before her eyes—it stabbed her in the heart more than she ever could have imagined.

She had shared everything with him—the pain, the heartbreak, the disappointment, the hardship and struggle—he had been there through it all. He had encouraged her, supported her, and endured it with her.

She would never be able to replace him. She didn't want to. She actually wanted to die with him. She didn't want a life without him in it.

He kissed her again and that kiss burned with such bitter fire. He struggled to his feet and hobbled painfully into the shelter. He left her alone so he could go on with the business of getting ready to leave—as if he would do anything else.

He came out of the shelter and limped off into the camp to meet up with Kuvik, Red, and Wildling. Mora didn't watch him. They came back an hour later and Hangman told her he was going to go.

She stood up to hug him and kiss him goodbye. She wished him a safe journey and then did the same thing to his three companions.

She didn't tell them to take care of him. They would protect him with everything they had—and that still might not be enough to make the difference—for him or for them.

She watched the three men walk out of camp. They had to travel slowly to keep pace with Hangman, but a different kind of energy hung over the men now. All three of them buzzed with new purpose.

Hangman turned his head just as the men passed through the camp entrance. He grinned at his friends and they all laughed at something he said. She hadn't seen any of them this happy in a long time. He was the happiest of them all.

Chapter 38

Hangman stopped at the top of the Ashtaw Valley and looked down at the vast herds of giant creatures grazing in the sunshine. The place looked so unbelievably different than he remembered.

Dozens of people milled around down there feeding Fogpo leaves to the Ashtaws, petting them, talking to them, and tying bundles around their necks and harnesses around the creatures' heads.

Little children ran around yelling and playing between the Ashtaws' enormous feet. Some of the massive adults moved from place to place while they grazed. The children showed no sign of fear that the Ashtaws might step on them.

Some of these children even grabbed onto the Ashtaws' legs and held on to catch a ride when the Ashtaws walked somewhere new.

Men rode the Ashtaws in seat slings harnessed behind the creatures' heads. These men rode hundreds of feet off the ground, steered the creatures right and left, encouraged them to go and commanded them to stop, and called out instructions that floated on the breeze.

Hangman stared in awe at the sheer scale of the Godless operation going on in this valley. Hammer's people had established an extensive system for handling the Ashtaws, taming them, and training them to carry a rider.

Hangman strained his eyes to see everyone moving to and fro through the valley. He didn't see a single person he knew. Almost everyone here was far younger than he was.

"This is incredible," Red breathed. "He's a genius."

"It was like this when I came through last time," Kuvik remarked. "Only not so big."

"Do you know where their camp is?" Wildling asked. "We should probably alert one of these men that we're in their territory. We shouldn't just roll up to their camp unannounced even if we are Hammer's friends."

The four men turned away—and like magic, a group of strong, tall, powerful Godless warriors came running around the corner along the ridgetop path just then. Hangman didn't recognize any of them, either.

They skidded to a halt and some of them raised their weapons. "Who are you?!" one exceptionally tall man demanded. "You're invading our territory."

A second man elbowed his way out of the crowd. "Stop!" he snapped. "Put your weapons down! These are friends of our band." The young man turned around and extended his hand to Hangman. "Hangman! I'm Skin. Do you remember me? I'm Thena's husband."

"I remember you." Hangman shook hands. "We're here to visit Hammer—and Cross—and all the rest of their men—and you and Thena. We hope you don't mind us coming unannounced."

"You aren't," Skin corrected. "Hammer told you at the gathering that he would love for you to visit anytime. Follow me and I'll take you to our camp. I'm sure he'll want to see you right away." He turned back to the others. "Put your weapons down. These are our friends from another band to the north. Leave them alone. Go back on patrol, Crystal. You, too, Shark. You don't need to be here for this."

He turned all the way around, extended his arm between Hangman's party and the Godless patrol, and steered Hangman and the others away down the hill they had just climbed up.

Hangman had to be careful about his footing on the downward slope. Everyone had to wait for him.

Skin frowned at him. "Your legs are so much worse than when you came to the gathering. What happened?"

"I got hurt in a fight against the Red Riders. I guess I'm not as young as I used to be."

Skin burst into a grin. "I can't wait for Thena to see you. She'll be thrilled."

Hangman's heart turned a somersault. "Is Cross still alive?"

"Oh, yeah! The camp is crawling with his grandchildren." Skin frowned at him. "Do you know Cross?"

"He's my brother. Didn't you know? I'm surprised Thena didn't tell you."

Skin's eyes popped. "Oh, that! She greeted him especially when I brought her home from the gathering, but she was so busy greeting and reconnecting with everyone else she knew. I suppose I didn't see her doing anything unusual with him that she wasn't doing with everyone else. She has a special connection with him, but I guess it isn't that much different from her connection with Hammer and everyone else in this band. She never told me he was her uncle—but I guess it just never came up. We had so many other things to talk about."

"Where did all the new people come from?" Red asked. "Hammer has more people here than could have descended from just his original men."

"He brought in a bunch of freed captives from a few different groups—groups he and his original men defeated with the Ashtaws.

He brought in captives they freed from the Bounty Hunters....I don't even know how many they brought in."

"He said you came from one of those groups," Hangman pointed out. "Which Clan did you come from?"

"I don't think it was a Clan. It was a group of marauders who passed themselves off as Godless. They tried to be nice to Hammer at first while all the time scheming to take his territory, steal his women, and drive him and his men out of the territory. I remember the whole incident." Skin laughed. "Let's be diplomatic and say it didn't end well for the other party."

Hangman pricked up his ears, but he didn't tell anyone about the group of fake Godless that he and Mora had encountered in their travels.

Skin led the way down deep into a network of canyons south of the Ashtaw Valley. Hangman had to walk slowly there, too. The whole journey here had been like this.

Skin finally came to a stretch of more level ground along a river. "I think I should run ahead and tell Hammer that you're coming." He shot his eyes toward Kuvik. "Your friend knows the way from here, doesn't he?"

"Yes, I do," Kuvik replied. "Thank you for your help, Skin."

Skin nodded once and took off running into the jungle. He moved impossibly fast. Hangman had trouble remembering what it felt like to run that fast.

"He's a good man," Red remarked. "He's a good son-in-law for you."

"Yeah," Hangman murmured. "I wish I could get to know him better."

None of them had time to talk about anything else before Hammer, Cross, and a whole mob of their men came streaming down the canyon. Hammer and his men came long before Hangman's party got anywhere near the camp.

They all came to a halt there hugging and staring at each other in wonder. Hangman held his brother for a long, long time. Hangman didn't want to let go.

Cross looked so much older than Hangman remembered, but Cross was still the same steadfast man Hangman had always known.

Both brothers pushed each other back and feasted their gazes on each other with eyes swimming with tears. Hangman had never been so happy to see someone.

Chapter 39

Hammer's men distracted Hangman and Cross all too soon—and then Thena rocketed out of the undergrowth. She attacked Hangman so hard that she almost knocked him over.

He laughed while he hugged her. "Take it easy, little flower," he told her. "You'll break me in half."

"You're here, Father!" She held him at arm's length and stared at him up and down. "Are you all right? Are Mother and Bone and Blackjack all right? Is the band okay? Why are you here?"

"Everyone is fine," Hangman began.

"Slow down, everyone," Hammer interrupted. "Let's take this back to the camp. We can talk about everything there. We shouldn't do this here."

The whole party walked together through the jungle, but no one could stop talking. Hangman tried to hear what everyone else was saying. Hammer's men had a lot to say about everything they had been doing since they left Shadow's band.

Hammer led the way into a tall, narrow box canyon absolutely packed with shelters. "This is just our main camp," he informed Hangman's group. "We have seven other canyons all occupied."

"Are you Kral over all of them?" Hangman asked.

"Only for now. We plan to split everyone up into seven different bands, but we have to work together to manage the Ashtaws. The Ashtaws are a joint project—and we all share hunting territory. So it's going to be interesting negotiating all of that. We have a lot to discuss and decide before we break everyone up into different bands. Plus it doesn't work so well having one man as Kral over so many people. It causes issues of its own."

"We had that problem, too," Hangman replied. "That's why we split our people up. Now we have five different bands all over the valley."

Hammer waved toward his shelter, sat down, and then scowled when he saw how hard it was for Hangman to sit down.

"You're hurt," Hammer remarked.

Hangman shrugged that away. "I used to be. This is as healed as this old body will ever get. This is the best I can hope for now—and that's good enough. We all have to get old."

Hammer looked around him. Some of these people must have been his children and maybe his grandchildren. Hangman didn't want to ask about that.

"It's wonderful to have you here," Hammer remarked. "All of you. I'm so glad you came."

"Actually, this isn't a social call," Hangman corrected. "I'm here on business."

Hammer stiffened. "What business is that?"

"We have a problem in our valley to the north. The Red Riders have been besieging us for over six years. They've escalated their attacks and now they know a way to get inside our valley. They plan to slaughter us all—all except our women and girls, of course. My son Blackjack is Kral in my place, now that I'm too old, weak, and crippled to lead the band anymore. He asked me to come—to ask you if you would bring your Ashtaws to help us defeat our enemies. I know it's a long way to travel...."

"Of course we'll come," Hammer interrupted. "Don't say another word about it."

Hangman's jaw dropped. "You will?! Don't you even want to know the situation?"

"You just told me the situation. You said your valley is in danger from these people and you need the Ashtaws to defeat them. What else do I need to know to make my decision?"

Hangman opened his mouth and closed it. He didn't know what to say. He had expected Hammer to ask more questions and get more information before he agreed. Hangman hadn't expected Hammer to just agree right off the bat without any explanation.

He saw Hangman hesitate. "We're brothers. We agreed long ago that my band would help your band and that your band would help my band whenever we needed it. Didn't we? That agreement is still in force as far as I'm concerned."

Hangman looked away. "I'm the one who broke that agreement. I should have stood with you against Shadow."

Hammer made a face. "We both know you couldn't go against your own father. You traveled all that way to find him—and your mother and brothers were there—not to mention all your other relatives—Viking's wife—everyone. You always belonged with that band."

"No, I didn't," Hangman murmured. "I never belonged with them. I should have left with you. I would do it differently if I had it to do over again. I regret that now."

Hammer gripped his shoulder. "Leaving your father's band was the best thing that ever happened to us. I never would have become Kral of my own band if you had come with us. We wouldn't be where we are now if you had come. We wouldn't be in a position now to be able to help you. We're all married with families of our own because we left without you. We never would have gotten any of this if you had come. You did us a huge favor by staying behind. You did me the biggest favor of my life by staying behind. I can never thank you enough for that. I would have come to hate you and resent you if you had come."

Hangman didn't know what to say. Thena came back with Skin right then. She sat down on Hangman's other side. "You said you would tell me if Mother and everyone else was okay," she insisted.

"I told you everything is fine, my love," Hangman replied. "Nothing has changed."

She gave him a hard look. "You have."

He only beamed at her. "I guess I have."

"So do you plan to ride back to the northern valley on an Ashtaw?" Hammer interrupted. "Please tell me you don't plan to walk all that way."

Hangman blanched. "I don't know about that. I don't know about going anywhere near one of them."

"How long did it take you to get here?" Hammer demanded.

Hangman shrugged. "Six weeks I guess. How long will it take the Ashtaws to get there?"

"A few days at the most, I'd say. They travel fast when they want to."

"Will they give you any trouble if you take them out of the valley?" Hangman asked.

"Not at all. We've taken them out on maneuvers and strikes before."

Hangman grimaced. "I don't want to know what you mean by strikes."

"I mean we've used them to attack our enemies and flatten them. We've used the Ashtaws against Bounty Hunters, Renegades, marauders—everyone who gives us any trouble. We'll deal with these Red Riders."

Hangman studied him. "Can I ask you a question?"

"Of course," Hammer replied. "Please do."

"Have you seen many people in this country? This year is the second time we've come and gone to the gathering without seeing any people. The country is totally deserted."

"We've noticed the same thing. We haven't seen any people coming or going to and gathering. We were the only band there last year like I told you. The Renegades and Bounty Hunters have disappeared. We haven't seen anyone, either."

"It's so strange," Hangman remarked.

"What do you think it means?" Cross asked.

"Mora thinks the population keeps dwindling more and more every year. She thinks that's why the Red Riders are so insistent on attacking us—because we're the only target left."

"How do you plan to bring in new blood if there are no other people around?" Hammer asked.

"We have a lot of freed captives in our valley. Almost everyone there is either a freed captive or the child of freed captives. We don't need anyone to go to the gathering at all if they can find a mate from one of the local valley bands. We hold gatherings between ourselves inside the valley. If the young people find husbands and wives there and they aren't related by blood, we allow them to marry each other. If they can't find someone they want to marry or everyone available is related by blood, then we bring them to the gathering—like we did with Thena. My son Blackjack came two years ago and there was only one young woman there. They had to go with each other, but they liked each other, so it worked out. I suppose if we keep coming to the gathering and no one else comes, we'll just stick with our own for as long as we can."

"Our population keeps growing," Hammer remarked. "We should keep in touch with each other. We could start having gatherings between ourselves."

"It would work better if we lived closer to each other," Hangman pointed out.

Hammer laughed. "Which of us would move? We don't want to leave our valley and you don't want to leave yours."

"Maybe future bands would be willing to do it—especially if we eliminate all the marauder Clans. If the country is safe—or as safe as it can be with all the creatures around—maybe future generations will move closer to each other."

Hammer shrugged. "I suppose so. We should keep meeting at the gathering. We're coming up on a time when we'll have young people seeking husbands and wives every year. We'll always have to send someone."

"It's the same with us. If no one else is around, we could move the gathering grounds equidistant between your territory and ours. Then neither of us would have to travel so far."

Hammer beamed at him. "I like that idea."

"Let's at least wait a few more years to see if any other Clans come to the gathering. We should include them if they're there."

"I agree. Share a meal with us tonight. We'll leave in the morning. We should be back at your valley in a few days. You don't have to walk."

Hangman let it go. He wasn't ready to start thinking about riding on an Ashtaw, especially not all the way up near its head.

Wildling asked the next obvious question. "How do you ride the Ashtaws so high up there? How do you mount and dismount them?"

"Did you see the women and children feeding the creatures Fogpo branches?" Hammer asked. "We get the creatures accustomed to eating Fogpo from us every time we go to the valley. They lower their heads every time to sniff us, butt us around, and play games with us. They get used to putting their heads down every time we come to the valley. That's how we mount up. We use a combination of other commands to make them lower their heads. Taming and training the creatures was much easier even than Mora led us to believe. I wish she had come with you so we could show her our progress."

"Maybe you can show her when you visit the Angler Valley," Hangman suggested.

Hammer frowned. "What's an Angler?"

"It's a long story," Hangman replied.

Thena launched into the story before anyone could stop her. Everyone stopped their side conversations to listen to her.

She started with the story of Mora and her three children getting stranded in the valley, Hangman finding them, and their battle to escape that led the family to discovering the secret tunnel entrance.

She then went on to describe the family's journey to rejoin Shadow's band, Shadow's madness and vendetta against Hangman, Katha's death, the band leaving Shadow's territory, the Godless' first disastrous encounter with the Red Riders, Shadow's death, and Hangman's decision to lead the band north to the Angler Valley.

She finished by describing Hangman's and Blackjack's campaigns of destruction and mass death on the Red Riders, the battle to destroy the Anglers, and finally this latest war against the Red Riders after the two escaped girls informed them about the tunnel.

"That is absolutely incredible," Hammer breathed once she finished. "I didn't think anything could top our journey from Ceon to the northern mountains and then back south to meet up with Shadow's band, but that story definitely does top it. That is mind-blowing."

"So I guess you can see why I'm not in as good shape as I used to be," Hangman replied. "I suppose I've seen a few more miles than most Krals."

"You're the greatest Kral that ever lived," Cross interjected.

"Even better than Hammer?" Red asked.

Cross nodded. "I'm sure Hammer agrees with me."

"Of course I do," Hammer insisted. "After a story like that? I don't have anything that can hold a candle to that."

Vina, Sema, Eleph, and the other older women came over to Hammer's shelter just then. The women all greeted and caught up with Hangman's men. The women brought food for all the men and then sat down to eat it with them.

Everyone talked to everyone else about everything they'd been doing. The men talked about how they would use the Ashtaws to wage a counterassault against the Red Riders.

The old friends talked late into the night. Hangman didn't want to stop, but Hammer eventually ordered everyone to go to sleep so they would be able to function the next morning.

Chapter 40

Blackjack went through his men giving all of them their assignments. "Chief, I want you to take your men plus Bone and the others. I want you to circle wide to the south where the Red Riders won't see you."

"What do you want us to do there?" Bone asked.

"I want you to approach Red Riders from that direction and find out how many of them are moving into the area, how much of their population is coming north to try to take the valley, and I want you to intercept them from behind."

"Do you want us to engage with them?" Chief asked.

"I want you to carry out guerilla strikes on them, reduce their numbers, and interrupt the flow of reinforcements. The rest of us will carry out a bunch of quick, light strikes to occupy the Red Riders and distract them away from what you're doing."

Bone nodded. "That sounds like a good plan. We should be able to do that easily."

"Once we find out where they are, how many they are, and which direction they're coming from, we should be able to launch a much bigger assault on them and cut down their numbers even more."

The men split up. Bone, Rebel, Cyclops, Oracle, Pyro, and Chief took off south with Reaper and Diamond.

Everyone else stayed with Blackjack. He assigned the fighting men from the other valley bands to stand guard on the mountainside where the men could stop any Red Riders from getting to the tunnel.

Blackjack took Yiatu's men and everyone else from their camp and set off to scout the rest of the countryside. They started out by heading up the mountain where they intercepted another flank of Red Riders on their way down to attack the Godless position.

Blackjack and his men rushed in, carried out a sudden surprise attack, and immediately retreated into the undergrowth where the Red Riders couldn't follow.

The Red Riders took some time to regroup before they started another push south on course for the Godless position again. Blackjack struck a second time and he and his men killed a dozen Riders before the Godless vanished into the undergrowth.

The Riders took even longer to rally this time. These sudden, unexpected attacks never led to the kind of open conflict the Red Riders were used to.

Blackjack pulled all his men back to the highest canopy and split this group into three different prongs. Yiatu's men headed away toward the east to circle the Red Riders from the north.

The rest of the younger men went west. Blackjack kept Bantam, Lock, and the last few of Red's men along with Fortune, Cyclone, Iron, Torch, and Cloud.

Blackjack waited until the Red Riders started moving again. They anticipated another Godless attack and traveled much more slowly this time. The Red Riders tiptoed through the jungle hardly daring to advance at all.

Blackjack took his much smaller party to within a dozen yards of the Red Rider position. They didn't know enough to keep watch for any Godless hiding in the bushes.

Blackjack and his men attacked much harder and faster, and this time, they locked and engaged with the Red Riders in open combat. The Red Riders hesitated just long enough for Blackjack's men to wipe out another twenty Riders before the rest recovered.

They counterattacked with all their strength only to get hit again from the rear by Yiatu's men. Yiatu and his band had become blood-thirsty and ruthless toward their former captors.

Yiatu and the others considered this war their chance at revenge and they took full advantage of it. They slaughtered fifty Riders before the Red Riders recovered enough to turn around and defend themselves.

They had to split their formation and leave half their remaining men in the front to protect their comrades from Blackjack's party. The other half went at it against Yiatu's band—which left the Red Riders ripe for the young men coming from the west.

The three prongs closed the Red Riders from three sides and carved a path through the middle, only for all three Godless flanks to get over-run by another reinforcing wave of Riders coming from the north.

These men hadn't been part of the original enemy onslaught. These Riders must have stayed behind and only come out to back up their friends after the sound of battle drifted to the Red Rider camp.

Blackjack called his men to withdraw and they all retreated into the canopy. The Red Riders regrouped on the spot where both sides had engaged in the battle. The Red Riders went back to discussing their move against the Godless base of operations farther south.

Blackjack assessed this new force. He didn't have enough men to counter so many Riders. They came on foot this time after Blackjack's men had carried out another annihilation campaign against the Blasti-dons last night.

Blackjack glanced around. He might conceivably have been able to marshal enough men to attack these Riders a second time, but only if he pulled all the valley bands away from the tunnel. He wasn't prepared to do that—not yet.

He barely had time to think that before the men of the valley bands surged out of position of their own accord. The noise of battle must have brought them to get involved.

They brought enough men to overwhelm the Red Riders straight back. The assault would have turned into a bloodbath, but the Red Riders turned and ran for it.

They left the Godless in possession of the mountain the way they had been before. The Red Riders ran back northward, probably to return to their usual camp where Blackjack's men could hit them again.

Blackjack didn't want to do that right now, either. The Red Riders were too alert to Godless activity right now. He decided to wait until the Riders relaxed in their camp and let their guard down. Night was the best time to hit them. Early morning was pretty good, too.

He pulled his men back. The Godless returned to their base of operations where he ordered certain men to scout the area and make sure the Godless knew exactly where the Red Riders were at all times and what they were doing.

Then Blackjack went through the party to see who was injured and make sure they all got the treatment they needed. The shifts changed not long after that. Most of the men went home to their families while another group of fresh, rested warriors showed up to take over.

These new arrivals all wanted to go out immediately, attack the Riders, and take down as many as possible. Some of the men wanted to go spring another surprise attack on the Red Rider camp this very minute.

Blackjack had to stop the men from running off at the worst possible time. He was still talking to them about it when the scouts returned way too soon.

"They're to the south!" one of Yeoli's men gasped in a rush of panting. "They're gathering to the south along the riverbank. This whole thing—it was just a distraction!"

"Where are they?!" Blackjack demanded. "Show me."

That one man led Blackjack and his men south down the mountain and sideways along a curving pathway. It led to a series of rocky ledges jutting out of the mountainside. Blackjack could see the whole landscape from here.

A river snaked away to the south from the base of these mountains. The river wound through hundreds of miles of canyonlands the Godless hadn't explored yet. The valleys were too far away over vast areas of treacherous countryside.

The Red Riders had gathered in a mounted force of two thousand or more along one river bend. Blackjack wouldn't have believed so many people could exist in this country. People didn't gather in these numbers—not without attracting predatory creatures.

The Red Riders must have just gotten here or assembled from smaller groups from different areas. These Riders couldn't have come from the camp in the north that the Godless had been attacking all this time.

These Riders had too many Blastidons. Every Rider down there sat on a mount.

"What do you want to do about this?" Bantam asked in Blackjack's ear.

Blackjack glanced over his shoulder at his men. "You're the fastest runner, Arrow. Go back to the valley and bring out all our men—all of them. It still won't be enough and it will take time to alert all the valley bands, but go get them anyway. Tell them what's happening. We'll engage them down there—at a distance from the tunnel. That will buy the men time to get out here."

Arrow took off back up the mountain and Blackjack went back to surveying the landscape in front of him. The five Godless bands didn't have two thousand people in the whole valley, not even counting women, children, and newborn babies.

The Godless would never be able to rally a force big enough to defeat these Riders. Blackjack didn't have time to lay an ambush to defeat them all.

He couldn't even think of an ambush big enough that would defeat them all—not one that wouldn't wipe out the Godless into the bargain.

He didn't even have time to bring the ants. The river would block the ants on the eastern side and a whole army of ants probably wouldn't be big enough to eliminate this many Riders.

The men who had been standing guard over the tunnel entrance received Arrow's message first and showed up behind Blackjack to join his group. A hundred men came down the mountain to help him engage the Riders. That was all he had—a hundred men.

He saw the Riders' whole strategy in a heartbeat. The Godless had to leave the tunnel unguarded to come down here to face this Red Rider force. That left the Riders from the northern camp free to get inside the tunnel whenever they wanted.

Blackjack couldn't do anything about that. He wouldn't be able to stop this army from doing it. He couldn't even hope to slow them down.

The Red Riders took a few hours to get ready to make their move. Another hundred Godless men showed up from the valley bands. This wasn't all of them and it still wasn't enough.

The Red Riders finally mounted up and started riding north along the river to the base of the mountains. Blackjack didn't have to give the signal. All the Godless men surged forward and took off running down the mountain.

They headed straight for the river and cut south along its banks. All the men drew their weapons. The thunder of pounding Blastidon hooves shook the ground ahead.

Blackjack came to an open stretch of riverbank and pulled to a halt there. He didn't know why. His instincts told him to make his stand here.

He raised his weapons and all the Godless men spread out in a loose mob to blockade the riverbank. The Red Riders wouldn't be able to get past the men—not until their Blastidons trampled the Godless into the dirt.

Chapter 41

The Blastidons came barreling around the next river bend to the south. Blackjack couldn't even see all the Riders extending all the way down that line. He focused only on the Blastidons right in front of him.

They charged him. He raised his axes and chopped down the first creature that came near him. All the Godless around him struck at the same moment.

Those forwardmost Blastidons buckled and plowed into the ground. Their bodies created a barricade to the Blastidons behind them.

Countless creatures collided with the fallen bodies, pitched their Riders onto the ground, and the Red Riders wheeled to attack the Godless. Blackjack didn't see if other mounted Riders kept going up the mountain toward the tunnel.

Red Riders surrounded Blackjack both mounted and on foot. He fought them all through clouds of dust. Riders kept rushing him from out of the confusion, engaging him, and then spinning off somewhere else.

Blastidons appeared in front of him. He either attacked them, brought them down, or they charged off somewhere else. Some of them fell to other Godless combatants attacking from every direction.

The two sides battled in a chaotic jumble of different combatants coming and going from all sides. Blackjack couldn't see anything until a puff of wind blew through the jungle and swept the dust aside.

He could only see a few dozen Riders still mounted. The rest fought on foot, but this hardly leveled the playing field. The Riders outnumbered the Godless and drove everyone back north up the mountain.

Blackjack got too occupied to see what his fellow Godless were doing—not until ten Riders surrounded him. He couldn't fight them. He wound up backing into a group of Godless who joined up with more men from all down the line.

They left plenty of dead Riders and Blastidons on the field, but not enough. The Godless joined ranks to hold the Riders at bay, but that wouldn't last once the band made it to the mountains.

Not even backing as far as the tunnel would save the Godless. Blackjack counted down the minutes before the Riders made their final rush to wipe the Godless out of existence.

Blackjack took that moment to glance behind him. He searched everywhere for one place he could direct his men where they wouldn't get either cornered or surrounded. It was already too late. They already were cornered.

The Red Riders only had to circle their numbers from either side to surround the Godless. The Red Riders were already starting to curl in their ranks from the sides. It was all over.

The Godless saw the inevitable closing in on them. The men packed more tightly shoulder to shoulder to aim their weapons outward.

Blackjack still didn't see how this would help anyone. It would only make the Godless a more compact target for the Riders to annihilate.

At that moment, a different kind of thunder shook the landscape. This didn't sound like the pounding drumbeat of Blastidon hooves.

This resonated much more deeply through the very bedrock underfoot.

Blackjack didn't hear anything but a bone-shaking rumble almost below the threshold of human hearing. The rumble kept building until the whole mountain range quaked as far as he could hear. The sound even distracted the Riders.

They looked around everywhere, but no one could locate the source of the quake. Both sides came to a standstill and looked around. Some of the combatants even lowered their weapons.

Blocks of granite and giant slabs of rock dislodged from the highest mountain peaks. Boulders tumbled down into the valleys and all the combatants had to brace themselves to keep their balance.

Mora had told Blackjack and his siblings about earthquakes, but no one in living memory had ever experienced one. The Blastidons panicked, reared, and tried to run away.

Their Riders had to fight the creatures under control, but the Riders weren't much farther away from bolting in fear.

Some of them actually did rein their mounts away—and that was the moment when a massive herd of Ashtaws came stampeding over the nearby mountains. They pounded through one of the southern passes and charged down into the valley.

The battle had come to a standstill right there at the base of the pass. Blackjack couldn't possibly have known the Ashtaws would attack there, but the position worked perfectly in his favor.

The Red Riders had backed the Godless against the mountain while the Riders had positioned themselves directly in front of the pass. The combination of both mountains and open ground placed the Red Rider force directly in the Ashtaws' path.

Blackjack and his men surged back even farther and flattened themselves against the mountain side. The Ashtaws charged down the pass and into the open country along the river. The Ashtaws trampled hundreds or maybe thousands of Riders and Blastidons in their path.

The Blastidons squealed and shrieked in terror when they saw the Ashtaws coming, but the Red Riders' own overwhelming numbers stopped them from getting away.

They ran into each other, collided with each other, and blocked each other in so they all went down under the Ashtaws' feet.

Blackjack became aware of tiny black dots attached to the Ashtaws' necks right behind their heads. Not all the Ashtaws carried riders, but enough of them did to direct the stampede where the attackers wanted it to go.

The Ashtaws squashed countless Blastidons and Riders underfoot. The Ashtaws kicked the others to death in their haste to get through the pass and out into the open jungle along the river.

This valley offered plenty of open grazing land. The Ashtaws must have seen that and headed straight for it. Their riders didn't have to direct the Ashtaws anywhere. The Ashtaws didn't even see the tiny people and Blastidons clustered around their feet.

Blackjack couldn't breathe. He extended both his arms to either side and pressed his closest comrades back against the walls on either side of him to keep them out of the Ashtaws' way.

He wasn't the only one who did this. All the Godless men hung onto each other and pulled each other tight against the mountainside to avoid the danger. The stampede went on for a long time and kicked up an even bigger cloud of dust.

The Ashtaws all eventually charged over the pass, flooded into the valley, and spread out to graze. The wind blew the dust away to reveal a vast carpet of squashed, trampled, destroyed bodies on the ground.

Blackjack and his comrades took a long time to relax enough to let go of each other, much less move away from the mountain. Blackjack kept waiting for the Ashtaws to attack again.

They didn't. They hadn't attacked in the first place. They just stampeded in the most strategically advantageous way to defeat the Godless' enemies.

The Ashtaws rumbled low in their chests once they made it out to the grassy flats along the river. The creatures sounded contented there. They lowered their heads to graze and their riders dismounted.

Blackjack didn't shake himself out of his trance until he saw men moving around out there among the giant creatures. He couldn't recognize anyone from this distance, but they could only have come from one place.

He shuddered when he saw the dead Riders and Blastidons all around him. The Ashtaws had exploded their bodies and stained miles of countryside in gore.

He and his men skirted sideways and then up across the mountainside to avoid all of that. They descended a mile from where they started and then climbed down to level ground.

The Godless met along the river. Blackjack and his men came face to face with Hangman, Hammer, Kuvik, Red, and Wildling. Blackjack could only recognize his uncle Cross by the scars on his face. Cross had aged and become unrecognizable.

Blackjack didn't recognize any of the other men who came with Hammer—except for the young man who had married Thena.

"You're here!" Blackjack husked. "I thought you would take much longer to get here."

Hammer laughed. "These Ashtaws can cover the miles once they start a stampede." He glanced around. "Are any of the rest of your enemies causing you problems?"

"We....." Blackjack struggled to pull his head out of the clouds. "We don't know. We had to deal with this first." He remembered something and turned to the men from the other valley bands. "Get back up to the tunnel. The northern flank could be moving in on us."

Half his men split away. A bunch of others didn't ask his permission before they left to scout the area.

"We won't be able to take the Ashtaws inside the valley," Hangman pointed out. "We should leave them here in case we need them again."

Blackjack opened his mouth to say something and then stared at the Ashtaws. "They're incredible! I never thought I would ever get this close to one."

Hammer beamed at him. "Do you want to take a ride on one? Your father just did, so now it's your turn."

"Hell no!" Blackjack countered. "You won't get me near one of them."

All of Hammer's men laughed. "You might change your mind," Hammer replied. "You can come to the end of your life and tell your great-grandchildren that you rode on an Ashtaw."

Blackjack gulped. "I would just as soon come to the end of my life and say that I've never ridden on an Ashtaw."

Hammer's men laughed again. They found Blackjack's reluctance hilarious.

"We should get back up to the tunnel," Hangman suggested. "We can decide on our next move once the scouts return and tell us where the Riders are and what they're doing."

Blackjack nodded and turned around to head back up the mountain. He still had to think about it before he could walk away from all the dead Riders on the ground. Part of his brain kept trying to come up with a way to defeat such a vast army of enemy combatants.

He didn't have to defeat them. They were all dead at the base of the pass. The Ashtaws had wiped them out to the last man in a matter of minutes.

Chapter 42

Bone and his comrades raced through the jungle canopy heading east. They'd traveled south for two hours after separating from Blackjack's men.

Now Bone and his men approached the line of travel the Red Riders usually used to get from their own territory to the Angler Valley.

Bone didn't know how far he and his men would have to travel before they found any trace of the Red Riders. They usually approached and attacked the valley from the west. They might not be coming from the south at all.

He and his comrades first had to find out where the Red Riders were. Then the men would be able to decide what to do about it.

They came upon the Red Riders much sooner than any of them could have predicted. The men were traveling so fast that they almost stumbled onto the Red Riders.

The scouting party came to a halt in the canopy and looked out over the countryside at a giant Red Rider horde marching north. The Red Riders must have brought two thousand men from the south.

Was this all of them? How many more did the Red Rider Clan have down there waiting to move against the Godless?

The Red Riders had also brought all their captives with them. This group included plenty of captive men and boys, too. Bone didn't see why.

The Riders kept their chained captives together in the very rear behind the column. Mounted Riders surrounded the captives to guard them and make sure no one escaped. The majority of the Red Riders rode in procession in the front of the column.

Bone and his men crouched in the branches and watched for a long time. None of the men spoke or made any suggestions. Bone could hear his own thoughts racing through his comrades' minds.

This overwhelming force of Riders would end up at the Angler Valley. They would break the Godless defense, invade the valley through the tunnel, and not enough Godless would remain to defend the valley bands.

The Red Riders would take the valley and that would be the end of Hangman's dream of finding a safe haven for his people.

Bone and his men stood alone between the Red Riders and the destruction of the whole Godless Clan. That was it. Eight men. Eight men had to find a way to stop this horde from destroying everything Bone and his men held dear.

If Mora was right, then the Angler Valley could be one of the last bastions of Godless anywhere in the world—if not the very last. The Angler Valley might be the last bastion of peaceful people in the world.

The Godless had been living a dream life in the valley before the Red Riders came. The Godless could have that again if not for the Red Rider invasion.

The five valley bands could build up their population and spread to the rest of the country. These people could repopulate the world if they could only get rid of these filthy marauders.

Bone couldn't turn his back on this invading army—not even to run back north to inform Blackjack of the danger.

Bone and his men had to do something about this now. They had to at least reduce the Red Riders' numbers. He couldn't allow them to put his family and his people in any more danger than they already were.

Chief broke the uncomfortable silence. "How do you want to do this?"

Bone turned around. He was the youngest man here, but he saw in a heartbeat that Oracle wouldn't take the lead. Oracle, Pyro, and Chief had always followed Blackjack. Everyone did.

Bone wasn't Blackjack, but he made up his mind in a blink. "You take Oracle and Pyro to the other side of the column. We'll wait until they reenter the jungle up there—on the other side of that hill. Then we'll ambush the guards standing over the captives. We'll free the captives and send them on their way. Some of those Riders must have the keys to the captives' chains. The Riders won't make it to the valley anytime soon—and they always stop for the night. We can reduce their numbers that way."

Chief dipped his chin in one nod. He, Pyro, and Oracle took off heading farther south. The Red Riders made it easy by continuing north. The three men skirted behind the column of captive prisoners and mounted Riders standing guard.

The Godless followed at a distance under cover of another patch of jungle. Bone and his men stayed out of sight while the Red Riders filed over the hill. Bone's mind exploded with a million ideas about all the ways he could kill these guards.

He decided to fall back on one of Hangman's oldest tricks, clambered into the canopy, and raced alongside the column. The Red

Riders had to travel slowly to keep pace with all these captives. The Riders didn't gallop ahead on their Blastidons to get there sooner.

He found a nice, bendy sapling and lashed some vines around it. He didn't have time to braid it into a rope. He would just have to make this messy, but that didn't matter as long as the Riders wound up dead.

Bone happened to notice his friends perched in high branches all around him. They were all using the same trick. It was the quickest, easiest way to get rid of these Riders without actually going down there and attacking them.

Any other kind of ambush or creature might put the captives in danger. This method targeted one Rider at a time.

Bone lashed another length of vines around the first and rocked his weight against the treetop to bend it down toward the ground. The tree swayed farther and farther out of position until his weight finally bowed the top all the way down.

He rode it down, threw his length of vines around a Rider's neck, and the tree bounced back. The Rider jumped in surprise when the noose hit him—and then the tree yanked him out of his saddle and all the way up into the sky.

The man yelled out in fright as he sailed off into the wild blue yonder—and then he screamed when Bone pulled the second rope to release him at the very highest point of his swing.

The rope let the Rider go and he soared miles upward before he started to come down. Some of his comrades turned around to see what was wrong—but he wasn't there anymore.

They reined their mounts to a halt—and fell victim to Chief, Rebel, Pyro, and Diamond doing the same thing.

They eliminated the Riders in the very rear of the column. The captives looked around them in confusion when they realized no one was guarding them. They kept stumbling along with the others. None of these people could go away as long as they wore these chains.

Bone and his men raced alongside the column to keep up and overtake more Red Rider guards farther forward in the column. Reaper, Chief, Oracle, Rebel, and Cyclops used the sapling trick again and again to eliminate the guards.

Bone saw a problem with this and decided to change his strategy. He positioned himself above another guard. He didn't want to get too close to the mass of Red Riders at the front of the column. He didn't want them to notice what was going on.

He dropped out of the canopy and landed in a straddle behind the Rider seated on his mount. Bone grabbed the Rider before he could do anything and cut the man's throat.

The Blastidon squealed and reared, but the Rider held onto the reins well enough to control the creature. The Rider actually pulled back on the reins to bring the Blastidon to a halt.

The Rider tried to draw his weapon and turn around in his seat even as blood poured from his neck. Bone held onto the guy until the Rider weakened enough for Bone to pull him to the ground.

The Blastidon walked off following the rest of the column. Bone scrambled to search the dead Rider's body and found the keys tucked into the Rider's belt.

Bone grabbed the keys, sprang to his feet, and spun around to face the captives. He held his finger to his lips and approached the nearest captive who happened to be a man.

Bone got busy unlocking all the chains from every captive. They crowded around him all holding out their hands.

"Get into the jungle and get as far away from the Red Riders as you can!" Bone whispered. "Stick together and get away! Okay? Go on! You're free!"

They all tried to stay near him. Some of the women even tried to kiss him, but other captives pushed them out of the way so they could get near him instead.

His friends gathered in the canopy to watch and keep an eye on the other Riders. The column of fighting men kept moving north. Plenty of captives remained in the mob. The Blastidons hid what was going on. The Riders didn't notice anything.

The freed captives followed Bone's instructions and raced away into the jungle. Bone put the freed captives out of his mind. His recent experience with the captives in the valley changed his mind about trying to help these people any more than he already was.

He freed everyone behind him. That left a lot of captives still surrounded by guards and walking north on their way to the Angler Valley.

Bone hooked the keys to the waistband of his loincloth and scrambled into the canopy to rejoin his friends. They waited a while, but nothing happened. The Red Riders never stopped their relentless march north.

The Godless men kept pace with the column and pulled another identical ambush—or it would have been identical if Pyro hadn't pulled out of line and raced ahead.

Bone and his friends were in the middle of using their saplings to noose a few more guards when Pyro came back and dropped a collection of Krakelows onto the mounted Riders at the very front of the column.

They all came to a halt and had to retreat from the stricken Riders and Blastidons. A few injured men and Blastidons managed to fight their way out. The others couldn't save themselves in time and succumbed to the Krakelows.

Bone and his men worked their way through another group of guards. The rest got too preoccupied with fighting the Krakelows to notice anything going on with the captives.

Bone and his men used that opportunity to jump down on top of a few more guards and yank them off their mounts. The two sides got into a skirmish there before the Godless prevailed and finished off their opponents.

Chief and Rebel both took keys from their dead victims. The two men helped Bone free as many captives as they could before any other Riders noticed. All the captives in this part of the column were women.

The three Godless gave the captives the same message. "Get out into the jungle, hide yourselves, and then put as much distance as you can between yourselves and the Riders."

"They're on their way north," Rebel added. "You should be able to get away from them if you go south, east, or west. They won't come after you. You're free now."

"Stick together," Chief told them. "You'll be able to protect yourselves better if you stay in a group. You can meet up with the other captives. You can help each other and give each other protection. Then you can make your way home to your own Clans."

One young woman grabbed Rebel's hand. "Take me with you!" she pleaded. "Don't send me out there into the jungle! Let me stay with you!"

"You can't," he told her. "We still have to take out more of these Riders. We're on a mission here to protect our own people. We can't take you with us."

"Please!" Her face convulsed on the verge of despair. "Please don't send me out there alone! I won't survive."

"You won't be alone if you stay with the other captives," he insisted. "You can protect each other."

She clung to his hand and drew closer to him. "I won't feel safe unless I'm with you! Please don't send me out there! I can't face it! Please! I'll do anything! Just don't send me out there alone!"

Her words sparked a similar reaction in all the other captives. They all crowded around begging and pleading for the men not to send them away.

The men resisted for a few minutes and then started to exchange glances. That one young woman wouldn't let go of Rebel's hand. He didn't try to make her.

Bone saw his friends' resistance cracking. "This is a really bad idea," Bone insisted. "Do you remember what happened last time? We can't take them with us. We have to keep attacking the column. That's what we're here for—to slow these Riders down and stop them from going after the Angler Valley. Remember?"

"We can't just leave these women alone," Rebel pointed out. "None of them has a weapon. They won't be able to defend themselves."

Bone opened his mouth to say something else, but his friends were already leading the women farther south into the jungle. Rebel still didn't let go of that one young woman's hand.

She was quite good-looking in a sultry, exotic way. Bone overheard her telling Rebel that her name was Varsa. Bone got a very bad feeling about this when she hovered extra close to Rebel and stared deep into his eyes.

Bone glanced over his shoulder. The Red Riders had finally either dealt with the Krakelows or liven up trying to save their men and Blastidons from the creatures.

The surviving Riders circled the Krakelows, left the men and Blastidons for the Krakelows to devour, and continued the march north the same as before.

A few Riders had to execute their injured Blastidons. These men had to continue their journey on foot, but the column traveled slowly enough for these men to keep up easily.

Chief, Rebel, and the others led the captive women away. Bone lingered until the very last. He really didn't want to get involved with taking care of another group of captive women. His last experience left a bad taste in his mouth.

He would much rather have kept following the column and waging war against the Red Riders, but he couldn't do that by himself. He followed his friends at a distance.

The men confirmed his worst fears as soon as the group got out of sight of the column. All the women gravitated to the men and started getting close to them. Rebel became especially friendly with the young woman who had first asked him to take her with him.

Bone didn't go near any of the women. Some of them tried to get near him, but he pushed them away. These women immediately started to cling to the other men in his party.

They shouldn't have been acting like this—not so soon after getting free from the Riders. All his experience of these captives told him the opposite.

Normal captive women took time to get used to their freedom—especially when it came to attaching themselves to other men. This couldn't end well.

Chapter 43

Chief, Rebel, and Oracle led the freed women to a stream where the whole party came to a halt. "We'll stay here tonight and go on in the morning," Chief decided. "Then we can make another assault on the column."

"We'll need to take these women to safety before we go on," Rebel pointed out.

"You would have to take them miles away or even all the way back to the valley to take them to safety," Bone argued. "Don't you realize that? We can't take care of these women and continue our mission at the same time."

"Well, we can't leave them out here alone," Rebel countered.

"Why not?" Bone asked. "They wouldn't be alone if they went with the other captives."

"We're already here," Chief interjected. "We might as well spend the night here. We can decide what to do in the morning."

Bone opened his mouth to point out again that the men wouldn't be able to decide in the morning any better than they could decide right now.

He didn't get the words out before Varsa distracted Rebel again. She slipped her arm around his waist and he did the same thing to her.

Bone got a sick feeling in his stomach when all the men and women settled down to make camp. Reaper built a fire on the ground and everyone gathered around it. Bone kept a safe distance between himself and the women so none of them would get any ideas.

The women got the message, left him alone, and concentrated on the men who were more receptive. Bone didn't understand these women's behavior at all. They all seemed to be throwing themselves at these men so much faster than the men ever would have.

Night fell over the jungle. Diamond went hunting to feed everyone. Bone couldn't eat. He really wanted to withdraw into the canopy and sleep apart from all these people, especially when his men started hugging, touching, and kissing these women.

He tried again and again to open his mouth to protest. Every man in his party was underage. None of them could legally do anything with these women—not without life-shattering consequences.

Did these men really think they could get away with this just because they were away from the band? Blackjack was bound to find out. He wouldn't go easy on the offenders.

Maybe these men thought they could take these women back to the band and marry them. That would never happen once Blackjack found out they had done it before they were legally married.

Bone wouldn't be able to keep that secret from his brother. Blackjack was Kral now. Bone had grown up with these men. He'd always looked up to them, but he would be on a one-way trip to the ants if he kept that secret from Blackjack.

Bone didn't want to keep that secret. He wanted to stop this before the men did something catastrophic, but it was already too late. Some of them started touching the women through their clothes and then pulling the women down onto the ground.

Bone couldn't watch this anymore. He got to his feet and looked around in sinking horror. Rebel was already rolling on top of Varsa and weaseling his hips between her thighs. The other men weren't too far behind him.

Bone had a choice to make. He could walk over there, try to pull Rebel off of Varsa, and make one last hopeless effort to reason with him not to go through with this.

She was already starting to claw at his back, hips, and the ties of his loincloth. Her mews, moans, and sighs mingled with all the other noises coming from the rest of the party.

Bone's only other option was to withdraw into the canopy without saying anything. He jumped into the branches and retreated to a safe distance. He told himself not to watch. God knew he could hear enough even from this height.

Blackjack would be absolutely furious when he found out. What if he decided he couldn't trust Bone's story and came to believe that Bone had done it with these women in the same way?

Blackjack might exact the same sentence on Bone as the rest of the men. Then Bone would never be able to marry. That's what this was. That's what he was seeing right now with all those bodies writhing and thrusting down there around the fire.

None of these men would ever be able to marry anyone. Why in the name of God would they throw away a chance at lifelong happiness and the chance to build a family for one night of pleasure? It made no sense.

All of these men had grown up Godless. All of them had been raised with the same rules against getting involved with a woman before the age of gathering.

Most Godless men had to worry about themselves more than the young women involved. Young Godless women didn't throw themselves at men, especially not underage men.

The men kept apart in the company of other men until they married. They didn't mingle unless a man and a woman became attached to each other and developed into sweethearts who would later marry. They didn't fool around. That was forbidden.

Godless boys and girls grew up with these warnings ringing in their ears all their lives. Bone didn't have to explain any of this to his friends—so why did they do it?

The orgy around the campfire went on for a long time. The women's screams seemed to encourage all the other women. The noise definitely encouraged the men.

Both men and women let go and went into wild fits of carnal frenzy—much more than most Godless did on a regular basis. The noise and commotion went on for hours. Bone told himself to leave and go off into the jungle.

Maybe he should just go home right now. Maybe he should just head back to the Angler Valley alone, find Blackjack, and tell him everything before the other men came home.

Blackjack would be able to hear and understand Bone's predicament much better if Bone came back alone. Blackjack would be able to believe that Bone really hadn't participated in this.

Bone didn't want to travel with these men anymore. He didn't want to fight with them or call them comrades anymore. He wanted to get as far away from them as possible. Was he really thinking that? Was he really thinking of his own comrades as his enemies?

He should just abandon them, but he just couldn't bring himself to do it. He'd spent too many years fighting alongside these men and calling them his brothers.

He still considered them his brothers. He would have liked to save them from themselves, but it was already too late.

All the men and women down there had their clothes off by now. They rolled together, rode each other, and moved each other into different positions. Bone had never seen anything like this before. These women knew a lot more than Godless women did.

That on its own told Bone that this was all wrong. These women could only have learned these things from the Red Riders.

The debauchery finally eased off in the small hours of the morning. The energy wound down and the men and women collapsed together around the fire. None of them put their clothes back on.

Bone stayed where he was until the sky started to get light. Now what was he supposed to do?

He climbed down and approached the camp. These men would wake up to the cold, harsh reality of what they'd just done. Then one of two things would happen.

Either the men would continue their campaign against the Red Riders or the men would decide to take the women back to the Angler Valley. Bone didn't see how the men could do both.

He made up his mind then and there about what he would do. If the men decided to take these women to the valley, he would split away and travel there alone first to tell Blackjack what was going on.

Bone would only stay with his men if they separated from the women right now—this very morning. He would wait just long enough to see if these men realized their mistake and corrected it by sending the women on their way.

These men weren't the men he thought they were if they didn't do that. They already weren't the men he thought they were. These men were hardly Godless at all if they could go through with something like this.

He came to the edge of the trees and stared down at all the men and women lying twisted and tangled up together in a mass of bare arms, buttocks, and exposed body parts. They looked disgusting.

He took a deep breath to walk out there and.......and what? What exactly could he do? He simply refused to wake up any of his men. He would have to touch them to do that. Just looking at them made him feel sick and dirty.

He almost turned away right then, but Varsa started moving before Bone could do anything. She peeled herself out of Rebel's arms and sat up. Maybe now all the others would wake up and Bone could have his epic confrontation with his men.

Varsa didn't wake up Rebel—or anyone else. She twisted around and pulled the kukri from where he'd dropped his loincloth. She got to her feet still stark naked and plunged the blade into the back of his neck to kill him.

Bone froze and stared at the scene in horror. He couldn't accept what he was seeing. One other young woman did the same thing. She pried herself away from Diamond, took his axe, and hacked him across the back of the neck, too.

Both she and Varsa turned to the other men. They were all sound asleep and totally defenseless.

Bone launched himself out of the trees and sprang in to stop Varsa from attacking Chief. Bone didn't get there in time before she raised Rebel's kukri to strike.

Bone's rational mind shut down. These women were attacking his men. They would kill the whole party if Bone didn't do something.

He pulled his blades and instinct took over. He cleaved Varsa's head in half and dropped her right there. He spun around to face the other woman, but he stopped himself from attacking her, too.

"Stop right there!" he snapped. "Don't make another move if you want to live!"

"Get out of my way!" she fired back. "You have no right to threaten me!"

"I'll kill you if you take another step! Drop the blade—now!"

Their voices roused the rest of camp. Chief squinted up at Bone. "What's going on?"

"Get up, get dressed, and arm yourselves!" Bone snapped over his shoulder. "These women just killed Rebel and Diamond. Varsa was about to kill you, too, Chief! All of you get up! Hurry!"

His words roused the others, but not nearly fast enough. The men had to untangle themselves from the women, which woke them up.

"What's wrong?" one of the women asked. "What's the matter?"

"Get up—all of you!" Bone snapped. "Put your clothes on! You're leaving!"

"You can't leave us out here alone," the first woman insisted.

"You just killed my friend, you witch!" Bone spat. "You can go out into the jungle to die for all I care! You're lucky I'm letting you live at all!"

Some of the other women started crying. "We had nothing to do with this! Don't send us away because of them!"

"I don't care!" Bone roared. "We never should have taken you in the first place! Go meet up with the other captives like we told you to! Go on! Get over there!"

He herded all the women together in one place. He didn't try to go near the woman who had killed Diamond. She still held his blade stained with his blood.

Bone didn't care about that. She could keep it for all he cared. Maybe she would be able to use it to defend all the other women.

The men gathered behind his back. "What are you doing, Bone?" Oracle asked. "These women are defenseless captives. You can't just drive them out."

"Defenseless!" Bone pointed down at the ground. "Do you call that defenseless?! They killed Rebel and Diamond. Varsa was about to kill Chief before I intervened. These two would have killed all of you! Wake up! These women aren't helpless! They're your enemies!"

The men stared down at the three bodies on the ground—and right then, that one woman lunged forward to swing Diamond's blade at Bone. She took advantage of his men distracting him, but he anticipated her.

He raised his blade, deflected her swing, and she took a lot longer to recover than a trained warrior would have. He hacked his blade back the other way just as fast, embedded the razor edge in the side of her temple, and took her down.

He didn't hesitate a split second to disarm her. None of the other women were armed. He could finally face his men.

"Now do you understand?!" he snapped. "We're here to protect our families—not to screw around with strange women! None of you will ever marry now! Do you get that? You just squandered your entire futures for one night! Wake up before you destroy your whole lives and wind up like Rebel and Diamond here! We're driving these women out and then we're going to go on with our campaign the way Blackjack ordered us to! If you aren't with me on that, then we part ways right here! I warn all of you, though. I will make it back to the Angler Valley with you or without you. I will tell Blackjack what happened here last night and none of you will ever marry. That's the law. You can go out there and take your chances with another Clan if you don't like it. If you go back to the Angler Valley, you'll follow the law and take the consequences of your actions. That's my last word."

"You're right, Bone," Chief murmured. "We made a terrible mistake last night and we deserve that. We'll go with you and we won't fight Blackjack's judgment. That's the best we can hope for."

Bone watched the awful truth sink into each man's head. Things looked mighty different in the cold, clear light of day.

He turned around to face the women. "Go now," he told them. "Get out of here and go your own way. We aren't responsible for you anymore. You can take care of yourselves."

"You can't do this to us!" the same woman blurted out. "We'll die out there!"

"Then go back to the Red Riders for all I care," he fired back. "We freed you! Isn't that enough? You can whine and cry and say you had nothing to do with this, but how do I know you aren't lying to us the same way these two women did? We don't have time to go through all of you and question you about everything. We're on a mission here and it isn't to take care of all of you. We freed you. You can go anywhere you want. You can rejoin the other captives. They'll help you. We're done with you. You take care of yourselves now." He waved to his men. "Let's go."

Chapter 44

Bone and his men raced through the jungle to catch up with the Red Riders. They still had a few hundred captives in that column, but he didn't think about freeing them—not anymore.

Six men. The party only had six men left. They'd lost two to these traitorous women. He would have liked to feed them all to the ants, but even that would have taken too much time away from the campaign against the enemy.

Every minute cost precious time. Every minute brought the Red Rider force closer to the Angler Valley. Bone and his men had to strike now to make the difference between a Godless victory or extermination.

He no longer trusted these captives. His compassion for them no longer overshadowed his desire to defeat his enemies. The captives weren't his concern anymore.

The best way to help them would be to destroy the Red Riders. He couldn't be certain even then if the captives wouldn't cause the Godless more problems. He would just have to free them for the sake of the few good ones in the crowd.

He and his men pulled a few more ambushes to reduce the Riders' numbers. First, Bone and his men led parties of dangerous creatures to intercept the Riders. The Godless men did this with Demonex, Crushers, Krakelows, ants, and Stalkions.

Then Bone and his men used the poison darts to kill dozens of Blastidons, but whittling the darts took too long. The Red Riders always managed to travel too far away. Then the Godless men had to catch up.

He and his men scouted ahead and spotted a collection of Abnormit nests. Five giant mounds occupied one clearing with more nests in surrounding dead logs.

Bone floated a hasty plan to get in front of the Red Riders, attract them into following and running the Godless down, leading them to the Abnormit mounds, and then breaking the mounds to kill the Riders.

The Godless men dropped from the canopy right into the Red Riders' path. The Red Riders couldn't fail to see the men. The Riders spurred their Blastidons to charge and Bone and his men took off running through the jungle.

They didn't count on the Blastidons' speed. The Godless had carried out so many of these ambushes over the years. The Red Riders knew all the Godless' tricks.

Five Riders broke away from the others while ten of their friends hounded the men from behind.

Bone and the others had to keep running no matter what. The friends couldn't do anything to stop those five from outpacing the Godless and cutting them off from the front.

Bone and his men put enough distance between themselves and swerved off into the undergrowth. No other Red Riders came out to attack the Godless. The rest of the Red Rider force kept marching forward on their inevitable journey to the Angler Valley.

The Red Riders finally cornered Bone and his men. The Blastidons surrounded the friends. Bone and his men drew their weapons and closed in a circle to stand their ground.

The Riders charged in and the Godless men used the techniques their band had been developing all this time. Bone went down on one knee, pivoted sideways, and chopped his blade at a Blastidon's legs as it surged in to trample him.

The creature crashed face first into the ground and the Rider pitched off directly under the feet of another Blastidon charging inward from the other side of the circle. Bone launched to his feet just in time for another Blastidon to rush him from a few feet away.

He didn't have time to stop this creature, so he sidestepped, passed his blade across the creature's throat, and let it go right on charging into all the other Blastidons colliding, falling, and screeching all around him.

He took half a second to leap clear of the confusion only for the dismounted Riders to come after him on foot next. He couldn't fight men so many much bigger, stronger men than himself. All his friends were too busy fighting other Riders, too.

He tried to back away, but they encircled him—and then they rushed him. He ducked their axe swings and used the same combination of tactics against them that he'd used on the Blastidons.

He hacked at the Riders' legs, cut them under their arms, and stabbed and destroyed every time a Rider exposed any vulnerability. He got so consumed with his own fight that he didn't see what his friends were doing.

The noise and mayhem blocked out everything else. He barely took down one Rider before another appeared in his place. Bone couldn't even fight them anymore. He concentrated everything on just holding his own.

Another Rider stepped in front of him and raised his axe to strike. Too many other Riders surrounded Bone. He couldn't get away, and at that moment, a massive blade impaled the Rider through the chest from behind.

His eyes popped and he stared down in stunned shock at the blade sticking straight through his chest.

So did Bone. He didn't even think to defend himself against all the other Riders moving in to cut him down. Some raised their axes. He couldn't do a thing to stop them.

Blades impaled each of them just as fast—and these didn't stay in place. The blade penetrating the first Rider's chest slid out and the body collapsed to the ground. Bone found himself facing a big man—as big as any of the Red Riders.

This was definitely not one of the Red Riders. This man didn't wear reddish body paint or any of the Red Riders' other distinctive clothing or trappings.

The man wore his brown hair clipped short and a dark blue suit of clothing in a style that Bone had never seen before. The guy wore a black leather belt, shiny black shoes, and some kind of strange flat-topped hat with a narrow black brim.

Similarly dressed men attacked the Red Riders all over the area. These strangers attacked in a massive force, killed every Blastidon, took down every Rider, and then pounced on Bone's men.

Bone was still standing there staring at the stranger in disbelief when the guy surged forward, seized Bone by the arm, spun him around, and muscled him down on the ground.

"What are you doing?" Bone asked over his shoulder. "Who are you?"

"Shut up!" the guy snarled and bound Bone's wrists and ankles together. "Don't move or say a word."

Bone glanced around. All his friends lay chest down on the ground nearby. The strangers tied up all the Godless for some reason.

The strangers continued to wage war against the Red Riders, killed every Rider and mount they could find, and then attacked the column.

Bone stared in shock as dozens of these blue-suited strangers streamed out of the jungle from all over the place. Why hadn't he and his men discovered these strangers before on any scouting run? Bone had never even heard of these people before.

They attacked the Red Riders with brutal ferocity. The strangers used similar tactics to bring down the Blastidons. Then the strangers engaged the dismounted Riders in open combat.

Bone would have liked to get up and help these strangers fight the Riders, but the strangers didn't need any help. They fought with the same kind of square metal blades Hangman's band had stolen from the Renegade Clan.

Hangman's people didn't fight with those blades anymore. They didn't last long enough before they chipped, dented, and broke. Stone weapons lasted longer and the materials were more freely available in the landscape.

These strangers didn't seem to have that problem. They didn't use the blades to block the Riders' heavy axe strokes. The strangers' blades wouldn't have lasted five seconds doing that.

The strangers dodged every time the Riders swung their axes and then attacked the Riders' arms, hands, and bodies instead.

The strangers chopped at the Riders' wrists, fingers, and arms to disarm the Riders before finishing them off with stabs and hacks to the head, neck, and body.

Bone stared at the strangers in shocked disbelief. He had never seen anyone fight this way. The strangers had developed their own unique combination of techniques to compensate for the Riders' superior weapons.

The Riders weren't superior in any other way. The strangers overpowered the Riders and made short work of them. The strangers took down all the Riders who had been attacking Bone and his friends.

The strangers bound and immobilized these Riders, too. Then some of the strangers stood guard over the prisoners while the rest of the strangers charged off into the jungle to take on the column.

The noise of combat died out. No one moved for a minute until the strangers dragged Bone and his friends to their feet.

The strangers dragged the wounded Riders to their feet, too. Some of these Riders had nothing wrong with them except cuts or blade wounds on their arms and hands.

"Let's go. Move out," one of the strangers told Bone and his friends.

"Where are you taking us?" Bone asked.

"Shut up," the guy snapped again.

Bone didn't ask any other questions. The strangers cut the prisoners' ankles free so everyone could walk. Then the strangers marched all the prisoners away into the undergrowth. The procession headed west.

Bone hadn't seen the strangers coming from that direction. They'd appeared all around the combatants, but the strangers had to have come from somewhere.

He got stuck in the front of the group. He didn't see what the strangers or the Red Riders were doing behind him. The few glimpses he did catch of the party behind him only included his friends and the Riders they'd been fighting when these people caught them.

Chapter 45

The strangers in blue suits marched Bone and his friends into a loose, makeshift camp buried deep in the heart of the jungle. Whoever these strangers were, they didn't use tents or shelters or any other comforts on the march.

A few blackened firepits gave the only sign that this even was a camp—that and a few women walking around. They also wore blue suits, but they wore their hair long in two braids down the side of each woman's neck to hang in front of the shoulders.

The women and remaining men stopped what they were doing to stare as the attackers brought the prisoners in. The men who'd captured Bone and his friends shoved them down on the ground and rebound their ankles to stop them from running away.

The strangers pushed the captured Red Riders down into the same jumbled group with Bone and his friends. The Godless and the Riders glared at each other, but none of them could do anything about that now.

More men arrived behind that first party bringing all the weapons the combatants had been carrying at the time the strangers had captured them. Five men stacked all the weapons on one side of the camp. Another twenty stood guard over the prisoners.

The strangers brought in twenty Red Riders with Bone and his friends. More strangers showed by the minute leading more and more bound, captive Riders. None of them were armed or mounted.

The strangers posted more guards to account for so many extra prisoners. No one could get away.

Bone took the time to study these strangers in more detail. Their short hair made them look bizarre. Their blue suits didn't look like they belonged in the jungle at all. The strangers looked like they belonged to another race, but they were definitely human.

Bone didn't remember anything about Hangman's encounters with the Renegade Clan, but Blackjack had described them to Bone before. Blackjack had even drawn Bone pictures of what they looked like.

Blackjack had said the Renegades also cut their hair short, but they wore different clothing. None of their clothing matched—not like this. All these strangers dressed the same way. Even their women wore the same kind of clothing.

Their sleeves and pant legs came all the way down to the wrists and ankles. The strangers only showed bare skin on their hands, faces, and necks.

The strangers sure knew how to fight, though. Bone had to give them that much. The strangers brought in countless captive Red Riders. Most of them had minor injuries or none at all. A few of them resisted and the strangers cut them down in seconds.

The time finally came when the strangers didn't bring in any more Riders. The strangers left the prisoners sitting on the ground for hours. Plenty of the Riders glared at the six Godless men, but none of them could do anything about their situation.

Bone would have to think long and hard before he made any kind of alliance with the Red Riders even to help each other escape from these strangers.

These strangers obviously had an issue with the Red Riders and considered them enemies. Bone would have felt more inclined to join forces with these strangers if he could just convince them that he wasn't their enemy, too.

Night fell and the strangers lit their fires. Some of them went hunting and brought in their kills. The women butchered the carcasses and cooked for the men. Their movements and conversation reminded Bone of the Godless except that these people looked so different.

The women included some wrinkled old women, a few middle-aged women showing the signs around their hips and waists of having given birth, and a handful of teenage girls still under the age of gathering.

All the men treated these women respectfully. The women didn't walk around chained or bruised or in any distress. Every word the men said to these women the men spoke respectfully and evenly. No one mistreated these women.

A few more hours passed before some of the strangers standing guard pulled one of the Red Riders to his feet. The guards cut his ankles free, led the guy away, and he didn't come back. Then the same guards returned and took the next Rider away.

The process went on for a while. The strangers took five Riders away before Bone's turn came. He was the first Godless the strangers took.

He exchanged one last glance with his men before he lost sight of them on the other side of the strangers' camp. He didn't know what to expect. These strangers would probably execute all the prisoners. He had to prepare himself for that.

At least he could face his death knowing he'd done his best for his band and Clan. He would die in battle against his enemies. Blackjack and the others would take care of the valley.

Bone had done his best. He'd initiated in good standing and made his family proud in the time he had. He couldn't ask for anything better than that.

The strangers steered him between all the other strangers to the very far side of camp. They pulled him to a stop in front of another bonfire burning brightly at the edge of the trees.

A man sat in a chair behind a table there. It was the same big man who had saved Bone's life in the middle of the battle.

He looked so far out of place sitting in a chair behind a table in the middle of the jungle with nothing else around him. Bone knew what chairs and tables were because his mother had told him all about the ways of the ancients.

The family had studied a few ancient books in their travels. He knew enough to know what the interiors of their houses looked like. This was nothing like that.

A large book lay open in front of the man on the tabletop. He held what looked like a fountain pen carved out of a Ridgebeak feather.

He kept dipping the pen into a pot of black ink and scribbling in the book right up until the guards brought Bone to talk to him. The man looked up and locked his dark eyes on Bone.

"Where is your campaign headed?" the man demanded. "The Red Riders have been traveling north for years. Where is your column headed? I'll work my way through this group one man at a time until I find out, so you might as well tell me. Where are you taking all these captives?"

Bone took a second to understand the truth. "I'm not a Red Rider. I'm Godless. You can see I don't belong to the same Clan as they do.

We were in battle against them when your people intervened. My Clan has been fighting the Red Riders for a long time. They're traveling north to assault our valley. That's where they're heading. My men and I came south to intercept them, to slow them down if we could, and to reduce their numbers as much as possible. That's why we were fighting them. You can see from looking at us that we aren't Red Riders. You can ask them if you don't believe me. They'll tell you we aren't part of their campaign. We're trying to stop them....." Bone studied the man a little more closely. "You're trying to stop them, too, aren't you? You're enemies of the Red Riders. Who are you? We should work together. My men and I know a lot about their movements."

The man eyed him intently across the table. Then the guy's eyes dipped to the rest of Bone's appearance. This man was too smart not to notice the difference between Bone and the Riders.

"Why are they attacking your valley?" the man asked.

Bone ran through a brief explanation of Shadow's accidental blunder of taking the Godless women and children into Red Rider territory and Hangman's sudden assault to rescue everyone.

"That doesn't explain why they followed us all the way north," Bone went on. "My father and brother carried out a series of strikes and ambushes to eliminate Red Rider patrols that came after us. We left no man behind to tell the tale. We thought at the time that the Red Riders must be continuing their original plan to retaliate against us for killing their men. Then, as time went on, it became a point of contention with them to track us down and destroy us no matter how far away we went—at least, that's the way it looked at first. Now...."

Bone trailed off again. He didn't want to blabber and tell this man a bunch of information he didn't need to know.

The guy didn't stop staring at him. "Now what? What's the situation now?"

Bone shifted his weight to his other foot and tried not to squirm. "My mother originally came from the Follower Clan. She knows a lot about a lot of things. We've spent the last three years traveling south to the gatherings and we haven't seen a single person in the country. You're the first. She thinks the Red Riders are coming north to attack us because we're the only target left. They're marauders and they make their living by marauding and despoiling other Clans. We're the only Clan around—apart from you, of course—so they have to travel a long way to come after us. That's what she thinks, at least."

Bone shut his mouth and resolved not to say anything else unless the guy specifically asked him a question. The man sat in his chair staring at Bone so intently that Bone started to fear the worst.

"What's your name?" the man finally demanded.

"My name is Bone." Bone hesitated. "What's yours?"

"My name is Colonel Roland Kilpatrick. You may address me as 'Sir' or 'Colonel'. This is the 147th Regiment. Some people call us the Regiment Clan, but we aren't a Clan. We're a military unit and we've come a long way to hunt down the Red Riders. They attacked one of our outposts and killed a bunch of our people. They tried to carry off our women, but we tracked them down, eliminated the perpetrators, and got our women back. Our sworn mission is to wipe out all Red Riders everywhere. We plan to eliminate every man, woman, and child in the Clan to remove the threat both to ourselves and everyone else. We can't trust that any of them won't restart hostilities or harbor loyalties to the Clan. These marauders don't deserve to live on the planet. We're all better off without them."

Bone perked up. "Then....we could help each other. It would be easy for you to find the Red Riders if you came to our valley. All the Red Riders are going there. We've been waging war against them for years, but they always keep coming back. My brother wants to wipe them all out, too."

The colonel went back to staring at Bone with the same unblinking, unwavering stare. Bone couldn't read the colonel's expression except that he didn't just jump on board with Bone's proposal. Bone didn't expect him to.

The colonel finally waved to one side. "Stand over there. We'll deal with this later."

Chapter 46

The Regiment guards took hold of Bone's elbows and steered him to the edge of the trees. They left his hands bound behind his back and continued to stand guard over him while their friends brought in another Red Rider to face Colonel Kilpatrick.

The Rider was one of the men Bone and his friends had been fighting when the Regiment captured everyone. This particular man had been fighting too far away to fall from Colonel Kilpatrick or anyone who had been with him.

"Where is your campaign headed?" Colonel Kilpatrick snapped. "The Red Riders have been traveling north for years. Where is your column headed? I'll work my way through this group one man at a time until I find out, so you might as well tell me. Where are you taking all these captives?"

"None of your business," the Rider snarled back. "You can torture me or kill me. I won't tell you anything."

Colonel Kilpatrick waved at Bone. "Do you know this young man?"

"Godless scum!" The Rider spat on the ground at Bone's feet. "You'll all die!"

"How did this young man come to be with your party when we got there?" Colonel Kilpatrick asked.

"These Godless heathens have been attacking us for months!" the Rider fired back. "They don't stand and fight like men! They attack from the shadows to weaken us. They've already killed hundreds or maybe thousands of our men over the years."

"So how did it happen this time?" Colonel Kilpatrick asked.

"They dropped from the trees in front of us and we chased them through the jungle. We attacked them and they defended themselves. Then you showed up."

Colonel Kilpatrick nodded and waved to his men. They took the Rider away. Bone didn't know what that meant. Colonel Kilpatrick went on scribbling in his book.

Bone knew enough about ancient ways to recognize what the colonel was doing. Bone had never seen anyone doing it in person before. How strange the whole thing looked—especially out here in the middle of the jungle.

Colonel Kilpatrick scribbled in his book for a few minutes until one of his men came over to him, bent down, and whispered something in the colonel's ear. The colonel murmured something back that Bone couldn't hear.

The guards brought in another Red Rider. The colonel asked the same series of questions and got the same answer. Then the colonel asked the Rider if he knew who Bone was and how Bone and his friends had gotten into combat against the Riders.

The Rider confirmed Bone's story and the colonel sent that Rider away, too. The Colonel went through the same sequence with another ten Riders and got exactly the same responses from all of them.

They all spit on Bone, called him Godless scum or worse, and blamed him and his five comrades for all the Red Rider deaths going all the way back to Shadow's first unintended intrusion into Red Rider territory.

The guards took the tenth Rider away and brought in Chief next. He and Bone shared a significant glance across the firelight. Chief's eyes overflowed with questions, but he had to pay attention when Colonel Kilpatrick started to interrogate him.

The colonel asked Chief all the same questions and got all the same answers. Bone couldn't have informed Chief ahead of time about what to expect.

Then Colonel Kilpatrick asked Chief's name. The colonel frowned when Chief told him. The colonel asked why the Godless had such strange names.

Chief gave a long, detailed explanation of how Godless men change their names at initiation and that their original childhood names are thereafter considered an insult to the man in question.

Colonel Kilpatrick dismissed Chief with a wave of his hand. The guards pulled Chief over next to Bone. "Are you all right?" Chief whispered.

Bone nodded. He didn't get a chance to answer before the guards brought in the next prisoner. The sequence went on for hours. Colonel Kilpatrick questioned every single person exactly the same way.

He started by asking both Godless and Red Riders the same combination of questions. He worked his way through the other four Godless men and grouped them together to one side in between questioning all the Red Riders.

Bone listened closely. The Red Riders couldn't have informed each other about the colonel's questions, either. They all gave the same answers and confirmed that they considered the Godless their worst enemies—much more so than the Regiment.

Colonel Kilpatrick didn't finish interrogating the prisoners until almost midnight. He finally shut his book, screwed the cap onto his ink bottle, tucked his book under his arm, and stepped out from behind his table.

"You men come with me," he told Bone and the others.

Bone and his men followed Colonel Kilpatrick back across the camp in a different direction. He didn't return them to the same spot where the guards had confined the Godless men with the Red Riders.

Bone caught sight of the spot from a distance. None of the Riders were there anymore. Were they all dead? The colonel did say he wanted to wipe out all Red Riders everywhere.

He'd only kept them around long enough to get the information he wanted from them. In the end, Bone and his men were the ones who answered those questions. The Red Riders hadn't told Colonel Kilpatrick anything.

He stopped next to one of the fires. "Sit down," he ordered. "It's getting late. We'll all need to get some sleep before tomorrow morning."

Bone opened his mouth to say something, but some of the other guards came forward to free the prisoners' wrists. Bone rubbed the stiffness out of his hands. "Thank you."

Colonel Kilpatrick made a face. "Anyone who fights the Red Riders is a friend of ours."

Bone took a second before he sat down. He didn't sit too close to the colonel. Bone didn't want to start getting on friendly terms with this man.

"What's your next move against them?" Bone asked. "How many of them did you eliminate today?"

"Not enough," Colonel Kilpatrick snapped. "The survivors will regroup. Then we'll hit them again. That's the way we do it. We use an attrition model to reduce their numbers as much as possible, wait for them to regroup, and then hit them again to reduce them even more."

Bone nodded. "That's our approach, too."

Colonel Kilpatrick narrowed his eyes at Bone, but the colonel had to break off when one of the underage girls came over to serve him some food. He thanked her and started eating it while the girl passed around bowls to Bone and each of his men.

Bone saw the girl eyeing him and then smiling at him when she saw him watching her. He looked away. His memory of last night haunted him. He wouldn't forget that anytime soon.

"Why are you in charge of this party if you're the youngest of them?" Colonel Kilpatrick demanded as soon as she left.

"I'm not in charge," Bone replied. "I suppose Chief is in charge if anyone is. I guess....sometimes the other men follow my decisions because my father was Kral and my older brother is Kral after him."

"Is it true you're considered the same status as all the other men as soon as you initiate? That's strange."

"It's true," Bone replied. "I'm the same status as they are. If one of us has a good idea about how to do things, then the others listen and follow him. Age doesn't matter unless it's an uninitiated boy."

"So you have the same status as your brother and the older men? I find that hard to believe."

"No, not like that. They obviously have more status than I do, but we're the same among ourselves. I'm the youngest of this group since the other boys my age haven't initiated yet. Oracle, Chief, and Pyro are all older than my brother, so one of them would take charge if anyone did."

The colonel frowned. "I don't understand your ways."

"How do your people do it?" Bone asked.

"We don't do initiations. The boys aren't allowed to join the Regiment until they're eighteen...."

Bone gasped. "That late?! How can you function without using them sooner than that? They're capable of fighting long before that."

"Yes, they help protect their mothers and sisters, but the boys aren't allowed to take the oath until they're eighteen. Then they can join."

Bone shook his head. "I don't understand that at all. We have a hard enough time keeping the uninitiated boys out of it. My father and brother gave up trying and send the boys on their own maneuvers—as far as they're able to participate. They're too valuable to leave them behind."

"Your father and brother sound like interesting men," the colonel remarked.

"Maybe you'll meet them if you travel north to the valley. There are plenty of Red Riders there."

"We'll see." Colonel Kilpatrick looked away and set his bowl aside. "You should all go to sleep. We'll move out north in the morning." He got up and left the six Godless alone with their food and each other.

"This is bizarre," Oracle murmured as soon as the colonel left.

"Why is it bizarre?" Bone asked. "They want to wipe out all Red Riders. What better way than for us to lead the Regiment to the valley? They can kill all the Red Riders they like there. Forming an alliance with the Regiment will only benefit our Clan."

"I never thought I would meet someone more dedicated to slaughtering the Red Riders than we are," Chief remarked. "The Regiment even wants to wipe out women and children."

"Maybe the Regiment has tried to save the captive women and met with the same problems we have," Bone pointed out. "Maybe the Regiment knows by now that they'll never be able to completely weed out the traitors from the real captives."

"Thank you, Bone," Oracle breathed.

"What for?" Bone asked. "I just told him the truth."

"You didn't tell him about us. You didn't tell him about last night."

Bone cringed. "Why would I tell him that? It's none of his business as long as you still perform in battle. Last night is between you and Blackjack."

"Thank you anyway," Oracle went on. "You could have humiliated us in front of the colonel."

"I wouldn't do that. We're still comrades. You made a mistake and you'll pay for it. It isn't up to me to punish you for that, but it is up to me to be honest with Blackjack about everything that happened on this trip. I would be a traitor to my Clan if I lied to my Kral about something like this. I won't tell anyone else. You'll all come of age and you won't marry. That's all. No one has to know the reason why. I'm sure you won't be the first or the last single men in Godless history."

Silence fell over the group until Cyclops spoke up. "We should have listened to you, Bone. We should have distanced ourselves from those women. Then Rebel and Diamond would be alive right now."

"Anyone can make a mistake," Bone replied. "Now we better go to sleep like he says. We have a long way to travel before we get back to the valley. We're likely to engage more Riders before then."

Chapter 47

The 147th Regiment filed over mountains and passes, down into valleys, through jungle, and into other mountain ranges. Bone and his men walked along the ground with the rest of the Regiment.

The members of this unusual Clan referred to themselves as soldiers for some reason. Bone understood enough about ancient ways to know what Colonel Kilpatrick meant when he called the Regiment a military unit.

Bone also understood what a regiment was, what a soldier was, and what a military uniform was. He still found it impossible to think of the Regiment as anything other than a Clan like every other Clan in the country.

The Regiment had its own customs, attire, and way of thinking about everything. That was nothing every other Clan didn't already have.

The Regiment might have modeled itself on an ancient military unit with a bunch of soldiers serving under one commanding officer. The Regiment was still a Clan and Colonel Kilpatrick was still Kral of this band even if he called himself something else.

He kept Bone and his men near him all day so the colonel could question Bone about the situation at the valley. Bone explained all about Blackjack's strategy of holding the enemy at bay outside the valley to protect the women and children inside it.

Bone told the colonel about the Godless war against the Anglers, the freed captive women who had betrayed the Clan, and the escaped girls who had told the Red Riders about the only way into and out of the valley.

Bone told Colonel Kilpatrick about the tunnel. Bone had learned a lot about human nature in the last few months. The traitorous fake captives had taught him a valuable lesson about trusting his instincts when it came to people deceiving him.

He couldn't exactly say he liked Colonel Kilpatrick, but Bone got a feeling that he could trust Colonel Kilpatrick. The colonel struck Bone as far more interested in getting revenge on the Red Riders than on anything else.

Colonel Kilpatrick stated that his people had decided to annihilate the Red Riders to eliminate the threat the marauders posed to the Regiment and everyone else.

He stated that the Regiment had gone after the Red Riders after the Red Riders attacked and captured Regiment women. The Regiment wouldn't care about another Clan as long the other Clan kept to themselves, minded their manners, and left the Regiment alone.

Bone couldn't imagine a scenario where the Regiment and the Godless would come into conflict. They both hated the Red Riders. They could help each other wipe out the Riders.

Then the two Clans would go their separate ways. The Regiment wouldn't need to know about the tunnel, or if they did, it wouldn't matter because the Regiment wouldn't pose a threat to the Godless. The Regiment would be the Godless' allies.

Bone didn't think too much about it. His gut told him to tell Colonel Kilpatrick about the tunnel. Bone didn't think about it any more deeply than that.

None of Bone's comrades protested him telling some stranger the Godless' most closely guarded secret. The Red Riders knew about the tunnel. The situation couldn't get any worse.

Colonel Kilpatrick commanded a force of thousands. Bone never would have believed that any Clan could have this many people—much less that they would keep all their people in one place.

The Regiment traveled with a lot of women—a lot more than Bone initially realized. The women got all mixed up in the column. Their uniforms made them blend in and harder to spot. Only the women's long braids gave them away.

Bone could think of a lot of questions he wanted to ask about how the Regiment worked and if these people had any permanent home or camp anywhere in the world. They didn't seem to use any kind of shelters or structures. They just lived out in the open.

The Regiment trooped across country for the first half of the day before they overtook the survivors of yesterday's assault. The Regiment must have cut down a lot of Red Riders yesterday. A tiny fraction remained to regroup.

None of the Riders were mounted anymore, but they kept traveling north along with the remaining captives who had either survived or failed to escape yesterday.

Colonel Kilpatrick stopped on a hilltop overlooking the Red Rider force. No one could call it a column anymore. The Regiment had reduced it to more of a band and not a very impressive one.

Bone expected Colonel Kilpatrick to order the six Godless men to prove their story by engaging the Red Riders and at least helping to wipe them out. Colonel Kilpatrick didn't do that. He stopped Bone and his men there and kept them with him.

The colonel gave orders for his troops to attack the Red Riders while Bone and the others stayed on the hilltop with the colonel. Colonel Kilpatrick didn't even have to send his entire force out there. That would have been overkill.

Bone watched a party of two hundred separate from the Regiment. Those soldiers swarmed across the countryside at a dead run. They ran swift and sure just like the Godless. The soldiers just didn't use the treetops.

The Regiment overtook the Riders, brought them all down, and wiped out every last one of them, including the captives. Bone didn't know what to think of that. It wasn't his decision.

He could definitely see Colonel Kilpatrick's point about not leaving any of the women and children alive. That many captives would have been a burden on any Clan. No one understood that better than Bone.

The Regiment soldiers spread out and searched the countryside for any stragglers who may have escaped. The Regiment cleared the whole area and then moved on north along the same route.

Colonel Kilpatrick kept assigning scouting parties to search different parts of the landscape. He sent out more attack parties every time any of his people discovered pockets of Red Riders converging on the same line of travel.

"They always head north," he remarked after a while.

"They're probably coming to reinforce the Riders at the valley," Bone replied. "They're always sending out people to reinforce those we kill. There's never any shortage of them. Blackjack plans to just keep killing them all until they don't have enough fighting men to send after us anymore."

"I suppose that's as good a strategy as any. Your brother sounds like a great tactician."

"He learned from the best."

"So will your father take over as Kral again after your brother defeats the Red Riders?"

Bone looked away. "I doubt it. My father is too old and injured to act as Kral anymore. I don't know what will happen to him, but it won't be that."

"It seems a shame. I'd like to meet him."

"I'm sure he would like to meet you, too. He's always interested in meeting the Krals of other Clans, especially when they're his allies."

"You're lucky to have been raised by a father like him," Colonel Kilpatrick remarked. "He obviously raised you right."

"I know I am. He's the best Kral any man could ask for. All the men say so. I don't say anything against Blackjack. He's an excellent Kral, but Hangman is irreplaceable."

Colonel Kilpatrick frowned at him. "Where I come from, it's disrespectful for a son to call his father by his first name."

"It isn't among my people—and I don't mean any disrespect by it. Hangman....I mean, my father....he used to do it to his father. It's normal in my Clan."

Colonel Kilpatrick faced front to scan the countryside through narrowed eyes. "I've heard of the Godless Clan before. I heard they were barbaric heathens. It's not easy to reconcile that with what I see in you."

"We may be heathens, but we aren't barbaric. We don't go around attacking other Clans or marauding their women and goods or slaughtering them to take their land. We stick to our own territory. We only attack those who attack us first. We never take captives—either male or female. We kill our enemies. That's all we do. We mind our own business the rest of the time."

"Tell me more about your mother," the colonel prompted. "You said she used Follower knowledge to help the Godless. Tell me how she did that."

Bone spent the rest of the day telling the colonel all the old stories going all the way back to the Renegade Clan's first invasion into Godless territory, Mora's capture, and Hangman's journey to free her.

Colonel Kilpatrick listened to everything in silence except for the times when he broke off to send out different groups of soldiers to clean up any Red Riders still at large in the countryside.

Bone didn't finish talking until nightfall when Colonel Kilpatrick called his troops to a halt. All the soldiers got busy making camp and some of them went hunting.

The Regiment needed a lot of food to feed this many people. They hunted every night and never prepared anything for long-term storage. They always finished everything the same night the men killed it.

Colonel Kilpatrick kept Bone and his men near him. Bone's comrades hadn't been able to get a word in on the conversation all day. They let Bone do all the talking.

Colonel Kilpatrick finally invited the six Godless to sit down and eat with him. The same young woman came back to serve all the men.

"This is my daughter, Silloa," Colonel Kilpatrick announced to the whole group at large. "She's been helping me organize the campaign."

Bone thanked her when she gave him the food. Then he stayed quiet until she left.

"Is your daughter your only family?" Bone looked around him. "It feels strange not to have any kind of shelter to live in. Is it always like this?"

"We have fortified encampments at strategic locations," Colonel Kilpatrick replied. "We're on the march here, so we want to travel fast and light—and to answer your question, I have three sons in the Regiment. They deploy in other areas when I need them to. They're good soldiers. I'm proud of them."

Bone didn't ask about their mother. "Do you always travel with your women?"

"It depends on the woman and the men she's attached to. Some of these women are the mothers of soldiers in the Regiment. Some are the wives and daughters. It depends on each family. No one comes who can't keep up and contribute. Most of the men left their families behind, but a few come along."

"Do your women fight?" Bone asked.

"Only to defend themselves and their children. Women don't fight with the Regiment. Only sworn soldiers are allowed to fight in the Regiment and women don't join."

"They don't join or they can't join? Are they allowed to?"

"No, only men join the Regiment. Women can serve any other way, but they don't take the oath and they don't join."

Bone nodded more to himself than to the colonel. Bone was starting to understand these people better.

He hadn't seen any of these women carrying a weapon. Their uniforms worked better as camouflage. No enemy surveilling the Regiment from a distance would be able to pick out the women in the crowd.

Colonel Kilpatrick excused himself for a while. Bone and his friends talked while they finished their meal. Silloa didn't come back to collect the bowls, so the men stacked them in one place.

Bone's curiosity got the better of him, so he left the fire and wandered around among the other soldiers for a while. A few got close to the women camping nearby, but single men far outnumbered these couples.

The couples barely did anything in front of the other men. The couples barely kissed or even held hands. The camp offered no privacy at all for them to do anything more than that.

Everyone seemed to accept it as a matter of common decency for the couples not to flaunt anything in front of the single men and underage girls.

Bone never saw any of these people taking their clothes off or even exposing any skin above their wrists. The Regiment seemed to have an exaggerated sense of modesty—like the Followers.

Bone started to see himself in comparison to them. He and his men walked around in front of them wearing nothing but their loincloths and their shoulder bags. The Godless must look as outlandish to the soldiers as the soldiers looked to the Godless.

Did the soldiers think he was grossly immodest for dressing like this? Was this the reason the Regiment considered the Godless barbaric heathens—because they didn't wear the same kind of clothes?

He made it to the other side of the camp and stood there watching a bunch of soldiers sitting around their fire.

They talked about ordinary things like how to adjust their belts to make them more comfortable and how certain butchering techniques changed the flavor of certain animals' meat.

The men sharpened and repaired their weapons while they talked and ate. These were the most ordinary men Bone had ever seen. There was absolutely nothing unremarkable about them at all.

They were as human as any Godless. The soldiers just wore different clothes and cut their hair differently.

He listened for a while and then wandered out into the jungle by himself. He climbed into the treetops just so he could remember what it felt like to be Godless. The noise from the camp floated to his ears from a distance.

He eventually had to go back just to make sure his comrades were all right. He would have preferred to sleep in the treetops, but he didn't want to offend Colonel Kilpatrick.

Chapter 48

Bone climbed down from the canopy, approached the tree line, and watched the activity in the Regiment camp from a distance.

He wasn't a part of the activity or the camp. He wasn't part of the Regiment. He was a guest and maybe an ambassador. What these people did and thought didn't affect him.

He would go home to the Godless. Then people would surround him who did things his way and thought as he did. This was all temporary.

He was just about to walk out there when Silloa passed that spot and saw him. She stopped in her tracks, stared at him, and then approached him. She smiled again. He couldn't possibly mistake the subtext of that smile.

"Are you lost?" she asked.

"No, I'm not lost," he replied. "I came out here so I could think by myself."

"And what conclusion did you come to?"

He stepped around her to return to his men. "I came to the conclusion that I need to go find my friends."

She dodged sideways and grabbed his arm. "We're all alone here. No one is here. Don't hurry away."

Her touch set off an explosion in his mind. He couldn't stop think-ing about that night when all his men had defiled themselves with women they weren't married to.

He pulled his arm out of her grasp as gently as he could, but she held on and he had to do it harder than he should have. He said, "Excuse me," as quickly as he could and turned to leave, but she dodged in front of him.

"Why are you so rude?!" she demanded. "I just want to talk to you."

"I can see what you want to do." He tried to get past her again, but she blocked his path. He really didn't want to shove her out of the way. He didn't want to go near enough to touch her, so he backed off.

"What's the matter?" she fired back. "Don't you like girls?"

"You're underage and so am I," he pointed out. "I'm your father's guest. I'm sure he wouldn't like it if anything happened between us."

She burst into a grin. "So you want to. Admit it."

He shrugged. "I care more about following the law."

"What law?"

Bone frowned. "Doesn't the Regiment follow the law of gather-ing?"

"We don't have to. We have enough people from different blood-lines. If someone wants to marry, they can marry within the Regi-ment."

"But.....don't you have laws against people doing it before they're married—before they come of age?"

She burst out laughing. "Of course not! Anyone can do it whenever they want to. They don't have to be married."

His jaw dropped. "That's....that's impossible!"

She smirked at him. "Does that change your mind about me?"

His head cleared in another starburst of realization. She was inviting him to break the law with her—as surely as his men had broken it that night.

"I'm flattered that you think of me that way, but my people have laws against it," he told her. "We don't do anything until we're legally married at the age of gathering—which you aren't and I'm not. I would be breaking a serious law if I did anything with you—not to mention dishonoring your father's hospitality."

Her smile drained and her expression went stony. "Do you know how many men in this camp would kill to get together with me?"

"Then go with one of them. They understand your ways better than I do."

"I don't want them. I want you." She smirked again, took a step forward, and extended her hand to touch his bare chest.

He overreacted again and smacked her hand away before she could make contact with his skin. He actually considered turning around and running off into the deep jungle to get away from her.

She actually was really pretty in a strange, Regiment kind of way. He did find her attractive. That was the problem. He didn't trust himself around her.

Something drastic would have to happen before he outright walked away from her. He didn't want to offend her, either, even though he sensed that he already was.

She stared at him in fury when he knocked her hand away. Then she snorted at him, spun around, and stormed back to camp without looking back.

He followed her. He wanted to get out into the camp where all the other soldiers would be able to see him. She wouldn't be able to do anything there.

She barely made it past the tree line before she collided head-first with her father coming from one side. They were both walking straight and fast. They crashed into each other and bounced off.

He grabbed her arms to steady her—and then saw Bone following her. The colonel narrowed his eyes. "What's going on here?"

"Nothing," Silloa replied a little too quickly.

Colonel Kilpatrick turned on Bone. "Are you doing something with my daughter that I should know about?"

"No, of course not.....Sir....." Bone hadn't called Colonel Kilpatrick that before, but Bone had heard all the soldiers calling the colonel that. It seemed to be their standard way of showing respect for their commanding officer.

"Nothing is going on, Papa," she insisted, but her voice made it obvious that something was going on.

His expression hardened in a split second. He pushed her behind him. "Go back to camp." She opened her mouth to argue and he snapped at her much more harshly. "NOW!!"

She shut her mouth, turned away, and walked off without another peep of protest. Bone braced himself for a showdown.

Colonel Kilpatrick waited until she left before he confronted Bone. The colonel narrowed his eyes so dangerously that Bone trembled. He wouldn't get away from this man if the colonel really decided to retaliate. He could send the whole Regiment to hunt down Bone.

"Tell me what the hell is going on here—and it better be a really good explanation," the colonel barked.

Bone took a deep breath, but he found it impossible to stop his voice from shaking. "I was only explaining to your daughter that my people don't marry until the age of gathering. We don't do it with anyone other than someone we're legally married to. She said your people don't do it that way and anyone is free to go with anyone they want regardless of age. She said your people don't go to the gatherings because you have enough people inside the Regiment. She seemed to think......she seemed to think we could do it that way and she got offended when I said I couldn't because I was bound by different laws. I didn't mean to insult her. I was trying to be respectful of both her and your hospitality. That's all I said. She.....she tried to....." Bone looked away. "Well, she did something that would be considered a little too forward in my Clan and I might have overreacted by knocking her hand away before she could touch me. That's all. I tried to leave more than once and she stopped me. That's what happened."

Bone felt the weight of Colonel Kilpatrick's gaze boring into Bone's face from a few feet away. Bone couldn't hold the colonel's eye even though Bone hadn't done anything wrong.

He tried not to squirm in front of the colonel, but Bone's resolve might have cracked a few times.

At least he hadn't done anything he would be ashamed to tell his father and Blackjack about. Bone would rather offend both Silloa and her father than have to admit to his own people that he'd done something he was ashamed of.

Colonel Kilpatrick surprised Bone by speaking in a much softer voice. "You better go back to camp and get some sleep with your friends. If you're still interested in Silloa when you come to the age of gathering, you would be welcome."

Bone's head shot up. "You....you mean it?"

Colonel Kilpatrick nodded, but he didn't smile. "You're a good man—very polite and considerate. Just so you know, we do have the law of gathering. I don't know what she was thinking by telling you that—except that maybe she liked you and might have wanted to test you to see if you would actually go through with it. I'll talk to her about it. She won't bother you again."

"She wasn't bothering me. I just....." Bone frowned. "You don't?"

Colonel Kilpatrick smiled for the first time. "We don't go to the gathering because we already have enough people who aren't related by blood, but we do follow the laws of gathering. No one can marry until they come of age and anyone who does do it before then is barred from marrying at all. That's our law."

Bone frowned. "Oh. That's our law, too."

"I appreciate you sticking by your principles. I'll deal with her and make sure she behaves herself from now on."

Colonel Kilpatrick walked off and left Bone's head spinning. Of all the things the colonel had said, four words kept ringing in Bone's ears. *You would be welcome.*

He stumbled back to the fire and sat down with his friends, but he stretched out on the ground in a little while and stared up at the stars. Then he rolled over like he wanted to go to sleep, but he didn't. He couldn't sleep.

No other woman had ever shown any interest in him—not like this. He could take his chances at the gathering and possibly come away empty-handed—or he could go with the girl he knew was interested in him—and in whom he was interested.

She wouldn't be the first girl in history to come on to a guy while she was still underage. Plenty of Godless did it before they came to the age of gathering.

Their parents and Krals had to step in to insist that these young people follow the law and mind their manners until the right time. Bone couldn't fault her for that.

Her father would straighten her out. The Regiment followed the law of gathering, too—which meant her father would find out if she'd been fooling around with any other men on the side.

Her father wouldn't let her marry anyone under false pretenses. He would either tell the man in question about her past or her father would stop her from marrying at all.

None of that mattered because Silloa was so far out of Bone's reach that she was in another dimension. She was underage. She belonged to another Clan. Her father was Bone's host and the Godless' potential ally.

Bone wouldn't have anything else to do with Silloa—not unless something changed between them. It sure was nice to know it was possible, though.

It was nice to know he didn't have to spend his life alone—unless she did turn out to have violated the law. Then he would be better off without her.

Chapter 49

The Regiment continued its trek north. The journey went much quicker than Bone expected considering how slowly the Regiment traveled.

The soldiers could cover the distance more quickly because they didn't have any baggage or children with them. The soldiers broke camp at dawn every morning and left immediately. They didn't have to pack anything.

They didn't stop along the way. Some of them left the Regiment to carry out maneuvers in different spots while the rest of the crowd kept going. No one stopped until nightfall.

They re-entered the canyon country pretty soon, passed through a number of valleys, and finally came to a pass looking out over another valley.

"We're getting close to the Angler Valley," Bone told Colonel Kilpatrick. "We should skirt to the west and approach from that direction. That's usually where the Red Riders bring in their reinforcements."

Colonel Kilpatrick gave orders to his men to follow Bone's instructions, but before the party could move, Oracle shot out his arm. "Look! They're bringing in another army almost as big as the first."

The Regiment stopped there and watched a massive throng of Red Riders crossing the valley at a distance. They brought in just as many captives and mounted Riders as the Regiment had already wiped out.

"They must be moving their whole population up here," Chief remarked. "They must be planning to take the valley and make it their permanent territory."

"They're about to enter the jungle over there," Bone pointed out. "Let's spread out and take them down."

The six Godless men turned away to leave, but Colonel Kilpatrick grabbed Bone's arm to stop him. "You can't take out that many mounted men. They'll kill you in seconds. Let the soldiers go instead."

"We have a different way of dealing with them. Let us go first. You can clean up anyone we leave behind."

"We won't leave anyone behind." Now Reaper was the one who pointed. "Look."

Bone squinted at a ripple passing through the jungle. The undergrowth shivered in a long, broken wave stretching for miles in any direction.

Bone surged forward. "Let's go!"

The six men shot away running down the pass. Bone burst into the jungle, vaulted into the branches, and searched everywhere until he found a tree loaded with pollen.

He didn't have time to gather the pollen itself, so he hacked off a dozen branches and sprinted away cradling them in his arms. He caught up with his friends at the forward edge of a massive army of ants.

He handed a branch to each of his friends. They stayed in the canopy, stripped the pollen off the clusters of buds, and sprinkled the grains in front of the ants. They found it and followed the trail.

The six men spread out to cover the whole front of the wave. They turned the ants to intercept the Red Riders' line of travel. The ants picked up speed to gobble more and more pollen. The men had to run their fastest through the branches to keep ahead of the ants.

Bone spotted the Red Riders ahead. They could only walk their mounts at the pace of the slowest captives. The ants overtook the whole mob, swarmed the Blastidons, and the Riders vanished under the tide of black, crawling, gnawing bodies.

The captives screamed, but they couldn't run away with their chains on. They all went down under the sea of ants.

Bone and his friends watched the ants wipe the Red Riders completely off the face of the Earth. They left no trace that the Riders had ever been here except for all the pairs of chains and shackles lying on the ground.

Bone and his friends laughed and congratulated each other. "We can do it just as well as the Regiment," Chief crowed. "Maybe they'll learn something from the Godless."

The men stayed in the canopy to keep out of the ants' path and then returned to rejoin the Regiment. Colonel Kilpatrick scowled at the men. "We don't do things that way," he growled. "We face our enemies."

"You only say that because you have so many men," Bone countered. "You would have to do things differently if you had fewer people and found yourselves up against a more powerful enemy you couldn't defeat by conventional means. You would have to improvise and adapt. That's what we do. Who cares how we do it as long as we protect our families? You said you wanted to wipe out all Red Riders everywhere to stop them from threatening you or anyone else. Does it really matter which weapon or tool you use as long as you remove the threat?"

Colonel Kilpatrick didn't answer. He turned away and kept leading the Regiment on its journey north. He didn't talk to Bone or any of the other Godless for the rest of the day.

Bone didn't break the silence or say anything else to try to convince the colonel to see things differently. Bone really didn't care if the colonel or anyone else approved of the Godless' methods—or of Hangman's methods.

They weren't the Godless way, but they worked. These unconventional methods had kept the band alive for years. All these enemies would have wiped out Hangman, his family, and his entire band long ago if he tried to be brave about it and fight the old-fashioned way.

Everyone in his band had long ago gotten used to the reality that this was the only way. Adapt or die was the only rule that applied to warfare against any enemy.

Every enemy that came out against the Godless was stronger and more numerous. Hangman would have been stupid to fight them face to face. Blackjack knew it and followed in his father's footsteps.

Now it was Bone's turn. He respected his father and brother too much to second-guess their judgment. If these unconventional attacks were good enough for Hangman and Blackjack, they were good enough for Bone.

Viking, Red, Wildling, Carnage, and all the men who had fought with them and came after them—they all saw the wisdom of doing it this way.

No one in their right mind could tell Bone that these men weren't a thousand percent Godless. They were the most Godless men in existence and they all approved of this style of warfare. Bone respected them too much to question them.

He maintained his silence until sunset when Colonel Kilpatrick called a halt for the night. He kept apart from the six Godless men even then.

Bone prepared himself to break from Colonel Kilpatrick if necessary. He would either come around and see the light or he wouldn't. Bone didn't need him or the Regiment.

The Regiment would keep traveling north and attack the Red Riders. Bone didn't need to know anything else. He didn't need to be Colonel Kilpatrick's friend or to win his approval as long as they fought the same enemy.

Bone and his men settled down around the fire. One of the soldiers brought the men a slab of the Gorlock the soldiers had killed. Pyro put it on the spit to cook it.

Bone and his friends talked about what it would be like when they finally made it home to the valley. They were close enough to feel it. Bone wanted to hurry up and get there, but he wanted to bring the Regiment with him.

The Regiment could and would swing the war in the Godless' favor. This alliance would be worth the trouble of all these growing pains, but he was prepared to walk away if he really had to. The Godless would find a way. The Godless always found a way.

Pyro was just taking the meat off the spit when Colonel Kilpatrick showed up. He gave Bone a hard look. "Come take a walk with me. I want to talk to you."

Bone got up and left his friends without a word. This was it. This was the moment when he and Colonel Kilpatrick sealed their alliance. The rest of their friendly talk didn't mean anything until now.

They were bound to come to some conflict. The two Clans were too different from each other. They didn't share the same customs or the same ways.

They could only come to a true alliance once they brought all those differences out in the open. The alliance would have to stand in spite of the differences. No one could sweep them aside and pretend they weren't there.

Colonel Kilpatrick strode through the camp for a long time without saying anything. Bone didn't initiate the conversation. Colonel Kilpatrick had said he wanted to talk to Bone—not the other way around.

Bone refused to say anything until the colonel started. This was the colonel's show, not Bone's.

Colonel Kilpatrick faced front and didn't look at Bone. The colonel talked under his breath once he actually did start talking. He talked to himself more than to Bone.

"You're different," Colonel Kilpatrick murmured. "I knew you would be, but your intelligence and insight tricked me into ignoring it. I saw you as a smart, strong, determined man instead of a savage. I tricked myself into looking past the differences. Now I see that I can't ignore them anymore."

Bone still didn't speak. He didn't want to ignore the differences and he certainly didn't want anyone else to ignore them. He was Godless. He would never be anything else. He didn't want to be anything else.

If someone had a problem with him being Godless, then he and they were better off apart. He didn't want an alliance with anyone who couldn't accept the Godless for what they were.

Making an alliance with the Regiment didn't require the Godless to give up their ways or to change into something they weren't. That wasn't an alliance. That was conquest.

"I didn't think at first that I would be able to fight alongside you if you continued to use these methods," Colonel Kilpatrick went on. "I didn't think I could have anything to do with you or have you anywhere near my Regiment. I didn't see any way we could fight on the same side as long as you're doing things this way—but then I realized that you were right. You used the ants as a weapon—just like those bone blades of yours. We don't use those primitive weapons and we don't use the ants, but we fight the same enemy. We just do it differently."

"You heard what the Riders said," Bone replied. "We've been killing hundreds or maybe thousands of their men for years. We wouldn't have been able to do any of that without these methods. Everything we have we owe to my father changing his tactics and adapting to different conditions. I wouldn't be alive today if he had done things differently. Our whole band would be dead."

"I understand that." Colonel Kilpatrick started walking again and went back to talking to himself. "That's what I realized. You come from a different Clan—a different people. You have different customs and different styles of doing everything. You wear different clothes and wear your hair differently. You walk and talk and travel differently. Everything about you is different—so why not that? What do I care if you fight differently, too?"

Now Bone was the one who stopped. "So....you're okay with it?"

"I don't know if 'okay with it' is the term I would use for it, but I'm willing to let you fight your way while we fight our way. Isn't that what allies do? We take the strengths of both and combine them. We have numbers and strength on our side. You have cunning, speed, and all these unconventional tools at your disposal. Why not use both?"

Bone raised his eyebrows. "What are you saying? How would we use both?"

"I don't know, but I'm sure a way will present itself."

Almost like magic, one of the soldiers came up to them just then. "Sir! We just got a report from one of our scouts. The Red Riders are bringing in another force from the west. It's a big force—twice the size as the last one—and this is all fighting men—no captives."

Colonel Kilpatrick shot Bone a knowing look. "You see? This will be our chance. We'll try it and see what happens. What do we have to lose? We might just be able to take out a significant chunk of their fighting force if we work together."

Chapter 50

Bone and Colonel Kilpatrick stood at the top of another pass. The Regiment was only three valleys away from the Angler Valley—and it showed. The whole countryside teemed with Red Rider activity.

Multiple bands and patrols must have joined up from all over the place to form giant hordes of fighting men. Only some of these mobs brought captives with them. The horde in front of the Regiment right now didn't bring any captives.

"I'm starting to think your mother might have been onto something," Colonel Kilpatrick remarked. "They wouldn't come in such numbers and not bring captives unless the Riders were running out of captives. That must be why they want to take your valley—among all the other reasons. They want to capture your women."

"It will be a cold day in Hell before we let that happen," Bone muttered. "How do you want to do this?"

"That depends on what you're going to do to them and what method you're going to use to attack them. We don't want to bring in the Regiment if you're going to use the ants. We would rather stay out of the way of that."

"I don't think even the ants will be enough to defeat this army," Bone pointed out. "They must have two thousand men down there. That will be more than you can defeat on your own."

"That's why we need you. We need you to do something to either weaken them or reduce their numbers. What do you have in mind?"

"I don't know. I won't know until we get down there and see what's available. You take the Regiment around along the river there. Station yourselves at the next pass on the way north. We'll attack them in the jungle, reduce their numbers, and get them running toward you in disarray. They should be ripe for the picking by the time they get to you."

Colonel Kilpatrick nodded. "That's perfect. I'll see you over there."

He signaled the Regiment to follow him toward the river. Bone and his men headed into the jungle and raced through the canopy to catch up with the Red Riders.

They didn't bring captives, but they still traveled at a walk. They didn't gallop or charge or thunder in. Bone didn't see why. He didn't really care.

He and his men sprinted ahead of the Riders. Bone found what he wanted a few miles in front of the Red Riders. He and his men uncovered a Krakelow breeding nest in the trees.

As many as fifty Krakelows slithered around in the upper story along with a few thousand young, each one as dangerous as a fully grown adult.

Chief shuddered when he saw them. "I don't want to go anywhere near them—especially not with only six men."

"Station yourselves on the branches—there, there, there, and there." Bone pointed out each spot. "Wait for the Red Riders to pass underneath us and then bounce the branches to knock the Krakelows onto the Riders' heads."

His men nodded and each man took his position. They had to maneuver extra slowly, silently, and carefully to avoid attracting the Krakelows' attention too soon. That would have been disastrous.

Bone straightened up on his branch and inched down it as far as he dared to get the maximum bounce out of its springy foliage. He gripped another branch above his head to keep his balance.

All his men did the same thing, held their breath, and waited. None of the men dared to move in case the Krakelows attacked. Bone had never stood this close to a Krakelow except when he'd been in combat against them.

The Riders made a lot of noise coming through the jungle. They would have triggered a Krakelow attack if the creatures hadn't been so busy guarding their nest.

The Krakelows did slither a little faster around each other when they heard the noise. The Riders' voices agitated the creatures and made them more aggressive—which is exactly what the Riders would not want when the Krakelows fell out of the canopy.

Bone counted down the seconds before the Blastidons walked under the nest. None of the Godless dared to breathe—and then Bone nodded to his friends.

They all jumped on their branches and bounced the limbs as hard as they could. Countless Krakelows fell out of the canopy and landed right in the middle of the Red Rider horde.

Chaos erupted as the enraged Krakelows whipped, snapped, and shattered into thousands of segments flying everywhere at once. The Riders bellowed in horror, but they couldn't escape.

The young Krakelows coiled through the air faster. Their segments didn't do as much damage, but they flew farther and hit more Riders than the huge adults.

The adults pulled Riders and Blastidons to the ground, tied them up in knots, snapped their spines and limbs, tore off heads, rent bodies limb from limb, and sailed off somewhere else to do the same thing.

Bone and his friends watched in fascinated horror from the canopy. The Krakelows proved almost as destructive as the ants. The Krakelows took down half the Red Rider force, killed half of those, and maimed the other half.

The remaining Riders spurred their mounts and charged away. Some of the Riders and Blastidons carried segments with them already eating their way into the victims' bodies.

The noise of bellows, dying screams, and the Krakelows' characteristic hissing attracted other creatures.

Gorlocks and Crushers stormed toward the source of the commotion, snapped up mounts and Riders one after the other, and then a flock of Boultars swooped in.

They pecked the Blastidons off the ground and the Boultars tossed them down their throats Rider, Krakelow, and all.

Bone and his friends scrambled higher into the canopy away from the Krakelow nest to watch. This attack had worked out so much better than the men ever could have hoped. Only a remnant of the original horde made it to the pass.

None of the original horde made it through the pass. They ran into the Regiment there. The soldiers overwhelmed the Riders easily and took down all the rest of them in minutes.

The Regiment finished them off and left all the bodies lying there for the creatures to devour. Then Colonel Kilpatrick turned the Regiment away and marched everyone through the pass into the next valley.

Bone and his friends stayed where they were and watched the creatures finish demolishing the Red Riders. Good riddance.

Bone enjoyed the satisfaction of knowing his efforts were ridding the world of the Red Rider plague. None of these men would ever harm anyone again.

Soon the whole wretched Clan would go the same way. The world would be a better place without these men in it. Colonel Kilpatrick was right about that.

Bone and his men finally left the jungle, crossed the pass, and caught up with the Regiment when Colonel Kilpatrick called the halt that night.

A spirit of celebration broke out when the six Godless returned. Everyone congratulated the men and wanted to hear the whole story of how six men defeated such a massive army of Red Riders.

Bone and his friends had to tell the story more than once so everyone in camp could hear about it. The soldiers all laughed when they heard about the Gorlocks, Crushers, and Boultars joining in to take advantage of the Red Riders' misfortune.

Colonel Kilpatrick sent some of his men back over the pass to butcher any of the dead Blastidons the creatures hadn't already taken. Bone and his men finally returned to their own fire. The rest of the soldiers did the same thing and left the Godless men alone.

Colonel Kilpatrick came over to congratulate and thank Bone's party. Then the colonel left, too. Everyone had other things to do for the rest of the evening. The camp returned to normal except for this air of lighthearted victory lifting everyone's spirits.

The soldiers came back with the meat pretty soon. Bone went and collected a piece for him and his men to share, but walking around made him restless. He delivered the meat to his friends and then went off by himself.

He left the camp and climbed up into the high rocks to one of the nearby mountain peaks where he could look out over the countryside to the northeast. He could see the Angler Valley from here.

He sat down on a high, flat rock and stared at the valley in the distance. His family was all there. His whole life was there. He didn't belong out here. He ached to get back there, but now he knew for certain that the Regiment would come with him.

Whatever Blackjack and the others were doing to fight the Red Riders, the Regiment's presence would only help the Godless. The sooner the Regiment made it there, the better.

He was still sitting there when he heard footsteps coming up the hill behind him. He turned around and immediately faced front when Silloa stepped out from between the rocks.

He tried not to recoil when she sat down next to him and stared off into the distance. Did she even know what she was looking at or why he'd come up here? He certainly didn't do it as an invitation for her to join him.

"I'm sorry I tried to trap you," she began. "I shouldn't have done that."

He didn't know what to say, so he just said, "Okay. I can accept that."

"I respect you for sticking by your principles even when I said you didn't have to," she went on. "You're a better person than I am."

"Did your father tell you to come and apologize to me?" he asked. "Is that why you're here?"

"No, he didn't tell me to come and apologize to you. He just told me to stay away from you."

"Then you're disobeying him, aren't you?" Bone asked. He finally couldn't get over his curiosity. He turned to look down at her. "Why did you do it? Why did you lie?"

She shrugged. She only glanced at him for a split second before she looked away. "I don't know what I was thinking. I just....I guess I've been my father's daughter all my life. I've always been the one he and my brothers have protected. I've always done what he wanted me to do. I don't know. I guess I wanted to do something reckless—and I liked you."

"You could have thrown your whole future away—and mine."

"I know," she murmured. "I can only say I'm sorry so many times. It was a stupid thing to do and I'm sorry. I'm sorry I insulted you the way I did. I don't even care so much that my father came down on me. I deserved that. I care more that I acted disrespectfully to you—and you were so respectful back to me. It stings to know I could do that to someone."

"What do you mean when you say he came down on you? What did he say?"

She shrugged again. She didn't seem to be able to stop doing that. "He went off on me and told me that I had disgraced him and the whole family with my actions. He said it made him look at me differently—like now he had to wonder if I was out there doing it with every man in the Regiment." Tears sprang to her eyes. "That was the worst thing he said—and he's right. I wish I could take it back now."

"Are you? Have you ever done it with anyone else?"

"No." Her voice cracked. "I guess that's the problem. I never let myself think about it before. I couldn't try it with anyone in the Regiment because they all know my father and me and my brothers and my whole family. None of them would have gone for it. I had to try it with you. I'm not saying it was right because it wasn't. You asked why and that's the reason. I guess I just wanted to feel that and see what it was like—to see if a man would feel about me the way I feel about him."

"Feeling is one thing. Acting on it is another."

"I know," she murmured. "I know it was stupid and wrong."

He faced front. "Thank you for telling me. I appreciate it."

"He said more about you than he did about me. He said you were a good man and that any woman would be lucky to marry you. He said I could never hope to be good enough for someone like you if I could do this to you."

"I'm not good," he croaked. "I wish I was."

"What have you ever done wrong?"

"I let my friends down. I should have....I should have taken better care of them. I never should have let this happen to them."

"This? What's wrong with them? They look fine."

He shut his eyes and shook his head. "They aren't fine and it's my fault. I should have tried harder to save them. I shouldn't have let it happen—and I did let it happen. I stood by and watched and I said nothing. I should have dragged them away. I should have driven them away with my weapon before I let this happen to them."

She stared at the side of his face. He couldn't go on.

"I shouldn't even be out here," he husked. "I should be home with my family. I should be helping them...."

"Isn't that what you're doing?" She rested her hand on his shoulder and immediately pulled it away. "I'm sorry."

"You don't have to keep saying that. Anyone can make a mistake."

"My father is right. I don't deserve a man like you—and now I'll never get one. I'll marry someone from the Regiment and you'll marry a Godless girl who knows how to behave herself."

"We'll see," he replied. "You have a few years before you come to the age of gathering. What are you—seventeen?"

"Yeah. What about you? Are you seventeen?"

"Sixteen," he told her.

Her head snapped around. "You are? I thought you were older."

Now he was the one who couldn't look at her. He felt himself starting to slip into a state with her that maybe he shouldn't—or maybe he should.

She obviously knew right from wrong. Her father and brothers must have taught her. She had made a mistake. She just happened to make it with him—because she liked him and because he was available to her in ways no one else in the Regiment was.

He might have been willing to overlook that, but a lot could happen in two years before he came to the age of gathering. He couldn't marry anyone before then.

"Can I ask you something?" she asked.

"Of course," he replied. "What is it?"

"Would you ever marry me after what I did? Would you ever consider me—or did I completely mess it up?"

Now he was the one who shrugged. "I wouldn't rule you out because of that. I might rule you out for other reasons."

"Like what?"

"Like if you had ever done it with another man before this. I would expect your father to investigate that and take the appropriate steps if he found out that you did do it."

"He is investigating it. He doesn't believe me when I say I haven't."

Bone nodded. "Then I'm satisfied as long as he is."

She dove in and kissed him on the cheek. "I like you a lot, Bone. If you say it's possible between us, then I'll wait for you. I can't think of any other man I would rather marry."

She got up and hustled away into the rocks before he could answer. He went into another whirlwind of a million thoughts all crashing together in his mind.

He never expected to have a conversation like that with her. He never expected her to own up and come clean about her actions—and to take responsibility for them the way she did.

She didn't expect anything to develop between them. She wanted it to, but she accepted the consequences if her actions made it impossible.

The sensation of her lips on his cheek overpowered every other thought in his head. Her lips felt silky, warm, and blissfully soft. He could imagine turning his head just a few inches and vanishing into all that beautiful softness of kissing her back.

He had to push those thoughts out of his head before they spiraled into something much bigger and harder to resist.

At least she was there. She hovered at the edge of his awareness as a possibility now. He just had to find a way to get through the next two years without her.

Chapter 51

Mora stared out through the tunnel entrance at Blackjack and his men clashing in open battle against the Red Riders. The Riders had pushed the Godless almost all the way back to the entrance.

The Godless backed up the mountainside only to get trapped by Hammer's Ashtaws booming up the mountain from the river flats.

The Red Riders knew enough to anticipate that by now. The Ashtaws didn't surprise the Red Riders. The Riders only fell back for a second, dodged around the creatures' giant feet, and kept pressing forward to close with the Godless again.

Hammer and his men kept thundering the Ashtaws up and down the mountain trying to step on all the Riders, but the terrain worked against the Ashtaws now.

The trees got in the way and then the Riders pressed the Godless too close to the cliffs. The Ashtaws couldn't get close enough to make any difference.

None of Blackjack's men could break away to spring any ambushes on the Riders. Every Godless man in all five valley bands had to fight their hardest—and they still couldn't hold the Riders at bay.

Blackjack had to keep retreating. He fell all the way back to the cliff walls right outside the tunnel. The Godless had nowhere else to go but straight into the tunnel.

The Riders battled the men inside and all the way back to the machinery. Too few Godless could fit across the tunnel to hold the Red Riders back. Blackjack stood his ground until the very end.

The Godless crowded around the last tunnel corner before they came to the machinery. The Riders would penetrate the valley itself after this. Then the Godless wouldn't be able to stop the invasion.

The Godless turned the corner and the Riders surged forward to attack. At that moment, Mora and the other Godless women sprang out from the walls and fell on the Riders with countless weapons.

The women lined the walls in a gauntlet of hacking blades, axes, and stabbing knives. More and more Red Riders shoved into the tunnel. They all fell there in a pile on top of their friends. So many dead bodies filled the tunnel that they blocked the way to the machinery.

The Godless men and women fell back behind the pile, killed the few Riders who managed to crawl over, and eventually completely obstructed the passage with dead Riders.

The men and women squeezed through the machinery and stopped there on the valley side to catch their breath.

"Now what do we do?" Mora panted. "They'll dig out the dead and eventually get through to attack us in here."

"We need to work fast to come up with another solution," Blackjack replied. "We need to set up some surprise attack to wipe them out as soon as they come through."

"Do you have any ideas?" she asked.

He grinned at her. "We have some time before they get through. I want to go back to the camp and talk to Father about it. He can probably think of something. In the meantime, this machinery can act as a bottleneck. Half our men can stand guard while the other takes a break."

He gave orders to his men, split them into parties, set one half to guard the tunnel and kill any Riders who came through the tunnel, and ordered the others to make camp right there outside the tunnel.

Then he and Mora returned to the camp among the rocks where they reunited with Hangman. He sat outside his shelter as usual. Blackjack and Mora sat down with him.

"I think we should evacuate all the camps and move them as far south as we can," Blackjack suggested as soon as he finished explaining the situation to his father.

"That won't completely eliminate the problem," Mora interjected. "The Red Riders will only work their way through the men and then take the women and children after no more men are left to defend them."

"I didn't say the women and children would stay there," Blackjack corrected. "I mean we would move the women and children away from the conflict. We can hide the women and children in the jungle. As soon as the Riders enter the valley and spread farther south, we can move the women and children outside the valley."

Mora's face drained of all color. "You mean....leave the valley—after everything we've gone through to win this place?"

Blackjack shrugged. "What difference does it make as long as we're alive and safe? Isn't that why we came here—to keep ourselves alive and safe? The valley is useless to us if we aren't alive and safe. I would rather hand the valley over to the Red Riders than for any of our people to die or get hurt. That isn't why we're here."

"But.....that means wandering around out there again." Her voice strained. "We wouldn't even be able to stay in the canyon lands or in any of the other valleys. The Riders know about us. They would come after us and attack us again."

"Wouldn't that be better than dying?" Blackjack turned to his father. "What do you think?"

Hangman frowned and rubbed his chin. "You're right that the machinery creates a bottleneck to hold the Red Riders at bay, but it isn't a permanent solution. The only solution is to completely wipe out everyone who knows about the tunnel."

"What do you suggest?"

Hangman shrugged. "I'll have to think about it and see if I can come up with anything."

"Could you come up with it pretty soon? We're kind of in a bind here, you know."

Hangman smiled at him. "I understand that, my son."

Kuvik came over to talk to Blackjack just then. Blackjack got to his feet and walked across the camp to hold a conversation with him in private. That left Mora alone with Hangman.

She stared down at her hands as the truth sunk in. All these years—all this struggle—for nothing. Now the band would have to go back out into the wilderness and wander alone—maybe for years.

Hangman slipped his hand into hers. "Don't be sad," he murmured. "It's the way of things."

She fought back tears. "I don't want to leave! We can't leave! We can't just give up! This is our home! We fought hard for this place! We sacrificed too much. We shouldn't have to leave! No one should have a right to take it from us! It's ours by right!"

He pulled her into his arms and held her. "Blackjack is right. It's his job to keep the band safe no matter what it costs. Imagine if we had stayed in the northern valley. We probably all would have died there. We had to leave for our own safety. He's right that this valley is useless to us if we can't be safe and protected here. We would be better off out there in the wilderness than in danger from enemy invasion."

"We can't leave!" Tears streaked down her cheeks. Just looking at Hangman reminded her of all the hardship and difficulty it had cost the band to finally find a place of rest here.

He lifted her face to stare deep into her eyes. He was the only one who could talk to her like this. No one had sacrificed more than he had to give the band this sense of peace.

"Everything will work out in the end," he murmured. "You'll see. We'll defeat the Red Riders and we'll stay in the valley."

"How do you know?" she wailed.

"I just know. Our grandchildren will grow up here and our descendants will inherit this valley as their territory. The Godless Clan will continue to thrive and grow here no matter what happens with the rest of the population outside this country. We'll win this war. I feel it in my gut."

She tried to shake that out of her head. She didn't see how any of this could work out or how the Godless could win this war.

Blackjack came back right then, said he had to go back to the tunnel, and left.

"You better go with him," Hangman told her. "The other women need you."

She snorted and wiped the tears off her cheeks. The other women didn't need her. The other women needed a miracle. The Godless were all out of miracles. They'd played their last card. Now they were on the ropes with no way out.

She had nothing else to do but admit defeat and leave, so she got up and left the camp. She went back to the tunnel and helped the other able-bodied women make camp there. The band needed every possible person who could hold a weapon.

Everyone worked to construct shelters for themselves. No one would be going home until the Clan eliminated the Red Rider threat—if they eliminated it.

Mora felt herself slipping into a dark place of hopeless despair. She really didn't want to go back out into the wilderness. Hangman *couldn't* go back out into the wilderness. He wouldn't survive out there. He couldn't walk, run, or fight well enough to defend himself.

He wouldn't survive if he stayed right here in the camp in front of his shelter. He was already sinking into this life as a helpless cripple. He wouldn't last much longer.

Thinking that completely destroyed all hope she might have in life. She didn't want to leave without him. She didn't want him to leave at all. She cared more about him staying here than she cared about herself staying.

Staying in the camp would be the quickest way for him to get killed if the Red Riders invaded. Blackjack was right about that. Hangman would be better off out in the wilderness where he could take his chances with all the dangerous creatures out there.

She didn't see any way out. The darkness crowded in on her from all sides. It blocked out any chance of a brighter future.

Not even the possibility of seeing Mion and any other future grandchildren grow up could cheer her enough to look forward to whatever might come down the road for them.

Chapter 52

Hangman waited until Mora left the camp. Then he struggled painfully to his feet. He could still walk. It just hurt like hell to put his weight on his legs.

He crossed the camp to where Blackjack stood talking to Red and Kuvik. They were just wrapping up their conversation. Kuvik and Red left. Blackjack almost walked away, but he stopped when he saw Hangman coming.

"I want to talk to you about something, my son," Hangman announced and inclined his head toward the camp entrance. "Take a walk with me."

Blackjack raised his eyebrows at Hangman's legs and body. Hangman read volumes into that look. He wasn't what he used to be.

"Should you be walking anywhere?" Blackjack asked. "Why can't we talk over there by your shelter with you sitting down?"

"Because I don't want your mother to come along and hear what I have to say to you. Come on. You're going back to the tunnel anyway, aren't you? We can talk on the way."

Blackjack's eyes fell out of their sockets. "You want to talk to me about something and you don't want Mother to hear? This must be serious."

"You asked if I had any ideas about how to defeat the Red Riders. I do. I just didn't want to say it in front of her because she would freak out even more than she already is. She's been distraught about me ever since I got hurt. Now come on. Let's go before she comes back."

Hangman turned around and limped to the camp entrance. Blackjack hesitated, but he eventually came—of course. He waited for Hangman to hobble outside and Blackjack caught up in a few swift strides.

"So what's your idea?" he asked after an appropriate amount of time.

"My idea is that I lure some dangerous creatures to attack the Riders—either Gorlocks or Crushers. They'll follow me because they'll see that I'm injured and can't get away. You said the Riders can't get past the machinery—which means they'll move their camp down here to the tunnel. They already know that's the only way into the valley. They'll want to consolidate their victory, now that they've driven you back inside."

"So how does that help us?" Blackjack asked. "They're on the verge of invading the valley itself."

"It helps us because the Riders will all concentrate their numbers right there outside the tunnel. You can go through the machinery and engage them there—out in the open outside the tunnel. I'll lead the creatures to the battle and surprise everyone. You and the other men will already know about the plan, so as soon as the creatures arrive, you and the men will dive back into the tunnel where the creatures can't get you. The Riders will be trapped outside and the creatures will destroy them."

"This is a terrible idea."

"What else is there—apart from holding the Riders at the bottleneck for the rest of eternity? That isn't what we came here for—so our enemies could besiege us in our own valley. The Red Riders will never give up until they find a way inside. They could harness their Blastidons to the machinery, tow everything out of the way, and overrun us. We don't have a prayer of winning unless someone does something drastic to take out the Red Riders before they get inside. You said yourself we need to kill everyone who knows about the tunnel. What better way to do it than this?"

"That's one assault." Blackjack shut his eyes and raised his hand. "It doesn't matter because you aren't doing it. Even if it is a good idea—and I'm not saying it isn't—then someone else can go—someone who can actually run."

"That's exactly why I have to go," Hangman insisted. "This is exactly why you sent me to Hammer's valley. I'm not helping you defend the valley the way I am. I'm not doing anything except sitting there. The creatures will be more attracted to me than they will be to anyone else. More of them will chase me than would chase a healthy person who can run. It won't work unless I bring a lot of them."

"It won't work anyway because they'll catch you and you'll be dead!" Blackjack fired back. "This plan is doomed to failure! Don't you see that?"

"Not at all. I can make it....."

"How?!" Blackjack countered. "You couldn't outrun a fully grown Gorlock even in your prime! You wouldn't be able to outrun one now. You can't run at all—much less outrunning more than one! Please!"

"Give me a little credit, my son," Hangman chided. "I wouldn't try to outrun them. Don't you get it? I would outsmart them. I would dangle myself in front of them and make myself an irresistible temptation. They wouldn't be able to stop themselves from chasing me. I would duck and dart from one hiding place to another—just enough to keep out of their range and to stay in front of them. That's all I have to do—just long enough to get them to the battlefield. Then the creatures will see the Red Riders and lose interest in me."

"If you're right, then so many creatures will follow you that they'll go after you *and* the Red Riders," Blackjack snapped. "Did you ever think of that?"

"At least let me do something. Let me at least try. What can it hurt?"

"It could cost your life! That's what it could hurt."

"My life is already forfeit, my son," Hangman murmured. "I'll die if I go out into the wilderness. I'll die if I stay in the valley. My fighting and traveling days are over. This is the last and only thing I can do for the band—to try to end this war and give my people some peace. Just let me try. I'm a dead weight around your neck the way I am. The band won't lose anything if I die."

Blackjack gasped. "How can you even say that?! You're a hero to everyone in the valley—especially to me, Mother, and Bone! How could you even suggest throwing your life away like this?! How could you do this to us?!"

His voice cracked with buried agony. That sound stabbed Hangman in the heart, but he knew what he had to do.

"I wouldn't be throwing my life away, my son. I would be doing it to save you—all of you—and Narina and Mion and all your future children—yours and Bone's. If you ever loved me—if you ever looked up to me or honored me—then let me die trying to save my people one last time. I'm going to die anyway. Let me die doing it that way instead of sitting around waiting for the Red Riders to come along and finish me off."

Blackjack shook his head and turned away, but he didn't keep walking toward the tunnel. He faced out into the jungle with his back to Hangman.

Hangman knew when he broached the subject that Blackjack wouldn't take it very well. This was the reason Hangman didn't want to broach the subject in front of Mora. She would have a fit if she found out—when she found out.

She was bound to find out. Hangman needed Blackjack on board first. Blackjack was Kral. Hangman couldn't go at all if Blackjack didn't agree.

Hangman walked up behind his son. Blackjack was already taller than Hangman. Blackjack was a husband and father. He was every inch the man Hangman ever could have hoped for his son to be.

Hangman gripped Blackjack's shoulder from behind. "Let me go, my son. I have to. If I was ever anyone you could respect, then I have to do it. I have to be the person you all respect—and I can't be that sitting in front of my shelter while the rest of the band fights our enemies. I can't let my life end that way."

"Fine," Blackjack snapped over his shoulder, but he didn't try to hide the tremble in his voice. "I'll let you go, but you have to convince Mother first. I'm not going to be the one to tell her. You have to do it. You can only go if she approves."

Hangman's blood ran cold at those words. Was this Blackjack's way of stopping Hangman from going?

Hangman already knew it wasn't. Hangman would have to front up and tell Mora. This whole plan was Hangman's way of taking responsibility for the band's safety even if he wasn't Kral anymore.

He took responsibility for her, too. She was his responsibility as much now as she ever had been. He was responsible for telling her. He wouldn't let anyone else do it. He had to face her.

She would just have to understand why he had to do this. She knew him better than anyone. She of all people must realize that he couldn't just sit around and wait for the Red Riders to come and finish him off—not without taking one last shot at ending this war for good.

Hangman nodded. "All right. I'll tell her."

Blackjack threw up his hands. "I don't want to hear anything more about this until she comes and tells me that she approves of you going. I don't want to hear it from you. I want to hear it from her. Then we can talk about when, where, and how."

He walked off on his way back to the tunnel. That left Hangman to limp back to the camp. He lowered himself back into his old place.

He didn't want to sit here anymore. He never wanted to sit here ever again. He wanted to act. He wanted to fight. He wanted to get involved in whatever way this broken old body would let him.

He would have to be extra careful while he carried out this plan. He would have to make sure he survived to bring the creatures to the battlefield—which meant staying out of range of their teeth and claws.

They would have speed on their side, but he still had his wits. He would just have to outsmart them—and he would have to find them first. He would have to track down some location with a lot of Crushers and Gorlocks and.....

He had a flashback of the stories about Bone's initiation. Hangman really wished he could have been there, but the story was plenty impressive nonetheless.

That Gorlock nesting ground was inside the valley. Of course there had to be others outside the valley. It could take him weeks to hobble all over the countryside and he might still never find one.

He would have to get one of the boys or young men to find a Gorlock nesting site for him—and that someone would have to go through the tunnel with all the Red Riders sitting right there outside it.

Hangman put all those considerations to one side. Blackjack wouldn't let Hangman even talk to the younger men—not until Hangman convinced Mora. That was the first job.

He was still sitting there when she returned at sunset. She brought a piece of meat with her and cooked it for them to share for their evening meal.

"How are things going at the tunnel?" he asked.

She shrugged down at her hands going about her work. "They're about as good as they can be under the circumstances. The Red Riders haven't started digging the dead bodies out of the way yet. The tunnel is still blocked."

"I have an idea for how to defeat the Red Riders," he began. "Blackjack won't agree until I tell you what it is and get your approval."

She finally looked up and snorted at him again. She did that a lot lately. "Let me guess. It's something extremely dangerous and highly likely to get you killed. It involves putting yourself in deliberate danger—probably using yourself as bait either to lure the Riders into a trap or to lead some dangerous creature to attack them when they least expect it. Am I right?"

He couldn't help smiling at her. "You know me too well."

She snorted again and looked away. "Why do you need my approval? You're doing things like that all the time. Just go ahead and do it. You don't need to ask me."

"I need your approval because you're my wife and I'm a lot more injured now than I ever was when I did it in the past. Blackjack won't let me go until he hears from you that you're okay with it. He told me I had to be the one to tell you and convince you to let me go."

She raised her eyebrows. "Let you go? *Let* you go?! I don't let you do anything. I wouldn't be *letting* you go. You do whatever you want. You always have."

"Not anymore. Blackjack is Kral now. If he says no, then I won't go."

She snorted again. "This would be the first time."

"No, it wouldn't. There were plenty of times when I wanted to follow a course of action and didn't because Shadow or Butcher didn't agree. There have been more of those times than the times when I did what I wanted. I hardly ever do what I want."

"Well, you'll do what you want now. I'm sure you'll find a way to do it no matter what I say."

He could have said a lot of things to convince her. He could have repeated all the arguments he gave to Blackjack, but Hangman didn't repeat them.

Blackjack was a man. He could understand a crippled old man who had spent his whole life fighting and who came to the end of his life not wanting to spend his last hours alive sitting on his backside while the rest of the world defended his family from certain death.

Hangman clasped Mora's hands in his again. "I won't go if you really don't want me to. If you tell me not to go, I'll stay behind. I swear it. I won't do anything that would hurt you or dishonor you. If you say no, then I'll abide by your decision. You're more important to me than anything."

Tears sprang to her eyes again and streaked down her cheeks. She cried so easily these days. She took everything about this war personally—probably because she couldn't do anything to stop it.

She lowered her eyes and wouldn't look at him. He hated to see her so down even though he understood it perfectly.

"I love you," he murmured. "You're everything that makes my life worth living. I don't want to be this broken-down wreck of a man for you. I want to be worth something."

"You are worth something!" she choked. "Don't you know how much you mean to me?"

"Then let me be the man who means something to you. Don't let me sit here having you take care of me like a child. I don't want to be that to you. What else is my life worth if I don't do this?"

She opened her mouth and closed it again without answering. She would probably tell him that his life was worth something even without this, but she knew it wasn't. She knew it as well as he did.

His life was worth something because he did things like this. He had been doing them all his life. Those were the things that made his life mean something. His life didn't mean anything if he didn't keep doing them now.

"Fine," she mumbled through her tears. "You can go."

He leaned forward and kissed her on the forehead. "I love you. You're priceless to me."

She didn't answer. She only rested her head on his shoulder for a moment and then went back to cooking the food—the food she planned to serve him to eat.

She always served him—in every possible way. She knew him better than anyone and she served his purpose. She always contributed and supported whatever he wanted to do—even this. He probably wouldn't come home from this, but she still supported him.

She had to support him because she already knew he had to do it. He had to do anything to help the band. That drive was hardwired into his being. He never had to explain to her why he did so many things to put himself at risk for the band. She already knew why.

He sat in silence while she worked. She was beyond priceless to him. Every move she made rang out with such perfection and selfless loving care. She was the most perfect being in the world to him—and she was all his.

Chapter 53

Hangman, Kuvik, Red, Wildling, and Bantam stood on one side of the tunnel camp. That's what everyone called it now. It was the camp on the valley side of the tunnel leading to the outside.

The Red Riders had spent four days pulling the dead bodies away from the machinery. The bodies had already started to stink and gas out the Godless camp. Hangman could just imagine the fumes the Riders had been inhaling all this time.

The Riders had cleared the machinery only to run into Blackjack's bottleneck. The Riders couldn't get into the valley except by squeezing one or two at a time past the machinery.

This made them especially easy to kill—which created another blockage of bodies. These Riders died on the valley side of the machinery. The Godless had cleared these bodies right away, but the Red Riders didn't try again to get through the tunnel.

They had built their own camp right outside the tunnel the way Blackjack had anticipated. No one could get into or out of the valley at all now.

Hangman, Blackjack, and the other men had heard the Riders having long discussions about how to overcome these obstacles and get inside the valley. The Riders still hadn't figured out how to do that.

None of them had come up with Hangman's idea of harnessing their Blastidons to the machinery and pulling each piece out of the way. Hangman didn't want to wait around for the Red Riders to come up with a different plan.

"You remember what I said," Bantam told Hangman. "The Gorlock nest is three miles down the river. You can take all the time in the world you need to get there. Just be careful because you won't know it's there before you stumble on it. The Gorlocks guard the nest day and night, so make sure you don't stumble on a Gorlock before time whatever you do."

Hangman nodded. "I'll be careful."

"We'll start the battle when the sun first breaks above the mountains," Blackjack added. "Don't bring the Gorlocks or anything else before then. In fact, don't even show yourself until then. We can hold the Red Riders on the battlefield until you get there."

"I understand," Hangman replied. "I'll be there."

"At least take a weapon," Kuvik insisted. "Don't go unarmed."

"I won't be fighting anyone or anything, but I'm taking my kukri just in case." Hangman clapped him on the shoulder. "Don't worry about me. I'll be fine."

Bantam snorted. "I can't believe Mora let you go."

Hangman concentrated on Blackjack. "Is there anything else you want to tell me?"

"That's all. Just wait a while before you go out there."

The four men settled down by the fire. The heat made Hangman sleepy, so he stretched out and went to sleep. He would need it.

Kuvik shook him awake hours later. "It's midnight, Hangman. It's time to go."

Hangman got up and limped into the tunnel. Kuvik went with him as far as the machinery. "Are you sure about this?" Kuvik whispered.

"I'm sure. Stay here and take care of the band. I'll see you tomorrow."

The two men faced each other in the dim light coming from both ends of the tunnel. Hangman couldn't part from Kuvik without hugging him. Hangman hadn't said goodbye to Mora or Blackjack. Only Kuvik was here at the very end of the line.

The two men broke apart and Hangman wedged himself between the machinery. He slipped to the other end of the tunnel and tiptoed to the entrance. The Red Riders all lay asleep in their tents. They'd moved their whole camp from the mountainside down here.

Hangman surveyed the camp. It would have been so easy for some brave Godless warrior to go from tent to tent killing each and every Rider in his sleep. Maybe one of the men inside the valley was thinking and planning for something just like that.

That would be one way to eliminate all these Riders in one shot. Then the Godless could carry out the same procedure at regular intervals to eliminate the rest of the Red Riders.

That wasn't Hangman's plan right now. He couldn't be the one to carry out such a slaughter. He couldn't move fast enough to get from tent to tent to kill enough Riders to make it count.

That was okay. The Gorlocks would do it for him. He just needed to bring enough of them—which meant bringing them from a location with a lot of Gorlocks.

He couldn't think of any better way to get a whole crowd of Gorlocks to follow him than to assault or pretend to assault their nesting grounds.

He didn't go out into the Red Riders' camp. He scooted sideways along the cliff wall where the shadows concealed him. He inched one slow, painstaking step at a time to put more and more distance between himself and the Red Rider camp.

Bantam was right. Hangman could take all the time in the world to move as silently as he needed to. Getting out of the area without getting caught would be more important than getting there quickly.

He got far enough away to leave the cliff wall and head off into the jungle. Walking down the mountain hurt like crazy, but he pushed through it. He didn't come out here to take it easy on himself. He could have stayed at his shelter if he wanted to be comfortable.

He had to stop often. He could gasp and pant in agony all he wanted out here. No one would hear him.

He really did take all the time he needed to conserve what strength he had left. He would need it when it came to leading the Gorlocks back to the tunnel.

He had spent the last few days rehearsing exactly how he would do it—without getting munched, of course. That would defeat the whole purpose. He didn't come out here to get munched, either.

He didn't come out here to throw his life away. He came out here to save his Clan and destroy as many Red Riders as possible. He could only do that by staying alive. No one would save his Clan if the Gorlocks killed him.

The going got easier when he finally made it to the river. The ground leveled off and he could walk more easily here. He pushed on for hours, but he still made slow progress. This old body better not let him down when he really needed it to perform.

He spotted the Gorlocks moving in the undergrowth long before he got near their nesting grounds. Bantam had told Hangman all about the spot. The Gorlocks had chosen another huge stand of rock almost exactly like the one where Bone had initiated.

Gorlocks strutted around and around the rock to stand guard. Their heads stuck up over the surrounding canopy while they eyed the jungle for any sign of danger. The faint starlight glittered on the Gorlocks' feathers and flashed in their sharp beady eyes.

He couldn't climb into the branches, so he sat down under a tree to wait. He had made it past Red Riders. Now came the hard part.

He didn't plan to wait until the sun broke the mountaintop before he started his plan to lead the Gorlocks up to the battlefield. That would take too long, but he had to at least wait for daylight.

He might have dozed off a few times watching the Gorlocks patrol around and around their rocks. There were a lot more of them than he expected. This would get interesting.

He knew a lot about Gorlock behavior. He knew how they responded to someone running away in front of them. He planned to use his knowledge of their ways to his advantage.

He startled out of another doze and noticed the sky getting light. The shadows faded in the jungle and then daylight started to spread across the landscape. He got to his feet and inched closer to the rock.

The Gorlocks didn't rumble deep in their chests the way Crushers did. The Gorlocks made a clicking, chittering sound—and then he heard the young Gorlocks cheeping and screeching.

He hid in the undergrowth to watch them. The youngest hatchlings hopped around on the rock and into and out of their nests while their mothers stood guard. The older juveniles hopped down to the ground and explored around their male guardians' giant feet.

Some of these juveniles stood as tall as Hangman's head. Any of them could kill a person in one bite of their fangs or shred a person to death with their razor feathers.

Hangman counted down the seconds. He should have been more nervous. He should have felt jittery or maybe even thrilled to be out here taking part in the campaign against the Red Riders.

He never thought he would ever participate in anything like this again. He had come to think of himself as already dead and not really a part of the living world anymore—and he was right.

He was definitely already dead or as good as. He understood that while he stood there staring at the Gorlocks. If he lived or died today—if he ever went home after this—none of that mattered anymore.

He didn't expect to go home. He didn't belong in the camp anymore. His life was over one way or the other. He might as well make this count.

He stepped out into the open where all the Gorlocks could see him. His appearance produced an instant effect on them. They all spun around and screeched at him, but they didn't attack.

That was the thing about Gorlocks. They didn't attack unless something showed some sign of aggression. They didn't chase until something ran away from them.

He showed himself long enough for all the adults and all the juveniles to see him. The adults screeched at him. The juveniles copied the adults and then took a few curious paces toward him.

Their boldness spurred the adults to do the same thing. The Gorlocks advanced—until he stepped behind the tree he'd been hiding behind to begin with. The Gorlocks couldn't see him.

They halted in their tracks and stared at the place where he had just been standing. He wasn't there anymore. The Gorlocks weren't bright enough to understand how something could be there without them seeing it.

They might even be able to smell him. They had to actually see their prey before they attacked.

Their rumbling voices got closer to the tree. That was the moment when he made his move. He dove out of hiding and hopped, skipped, and limped as fast as he could to get away from the Gorlocks.

His movements triggered them to attack. They charged into the jungle. The adults darted their heads forward to snap him in half only to crash their skulls into the tree trunks.

The young ones moved faster and rushed forward. They closed the distance and came perilously close to catching him. He made it thirty yards and dove behind another thick tree trunk where the Gorlocks couldn't see him.

His sudden disappearance made the young ones hesitate. They glanced around in confusion and waited for their adults to catch up.

The adults had to fight their way through the undergrowth—and came up against the same problem. They couldn't attack what they couldn't see.

The creatures' noise escalated as their frustration and confusion built to the breaking point—and Hangman was nowhere near the battlefield yet. The Gorlocks would work themselves into a frenzy by the time he led them there.

The Gorlocks paced back and forth screeching and shrieking. They hunted around trying to find him—and that's when he darted out of hiding and hustled as fast as he could to the next hiding place.

This one was behind a giant rock. He scooted behind it, but he didn't stay in one place. He limped along its back side to the farthest corner away from the Gorlocks. The rock gave him cover to get farther up the mountain and put more distance between them.

Daylight spread and got brighter as he worked his way farther up the river and then to the mountain itself. The Gorlocks followed him every step of the way.

They always slowed down and then went through the same frantic searching behavior every time they lost sight of him. He made it halfway up the mountain before the sun broke over the highest peaks.

The battle started immediately. He heard crashing, screaming, bellowing, and the clang of weapons from here.

That sound infected him with the first trace of urgency and excitement. He had to get there and bring the Gorlocks with him. Twenty adults and at least thirty juveniles followed him up the mountain.

He broke out from behind his latest hiding place and made another sprint to another tree to hide, but at that moment, the deep booming pound of Crusher footsteps vibrated through the ground underfoot.

Ten Crushers stomped up the mountain to intercept the Gorlocks. The Crushers didn't see what the Gorlocks were chasing, but the Crushers knew the Gorlocks were chasing something.

The Crushers didn't have the same problem of needing to see something to attack it. They knew enough to circle their prey and trap it no matter where it was.

He couldn't stop now. He just had to keep going and hope for the best. He limped up the mountain as fast as he could, but he couldn't move fast enough to keep ahead of anything now.

The conflict between the Gorlocks and the Crushers saved his life. The Crushers swerved into line between him and the Gorlocks. The Gorlocks saw the Crushers moving in on their prey.

The Gorlocks shrieked in fury and vented all their frustration on the Crushers. Both species got into a scuffle right there until Hangman broke out from between some trees just then.

The Crushers caught sight of him and came after him. The Gorlocks did, too. They overtook him in seconds, but their hostility for each other got the better of them.

They crashed into each other and slashed each other with their fangs to drive each other away from him. They bought him just enough time to make it to the battlefield.

The Godless stood in ranks to defend the tunnel. They held the Red Riders off twenty feet from the entrance—right out in the open where the Crushers and Gorlocks would be able to see all the combatants.

The Red Riders fought with their backs to the incoming creatures. The noise and commotion of battle prevented the Red Riders from hearing or feeling the Crushers coming.

The Godless saw in time, but they still didn't break for the tunnel—not yet. They waited until the last second before Hangman stumbled between the two sides.

The Red Riders yelled out in alarm and scattered before the creatures. The Gorlocks and Crushers burst onto the field and attacked in fury. The young Gorlocks went wild slashing, biting, and ripping everyone in sight.

The Godless charged into the tunnel en masse. No one remained outside—except for Hangman. One of the Crushers accidentally kicked him with its foot as the creature rushed past him to chomp all the Red Riders.

The blow sent him sprawling onto his face on the ground. He was the last Godless out here with a whole ton of wild creatures in the middle of a feeding frenzy. The creatures tore the Riders apart all around him.

He glanced up and looked straight into the tunnel where Blackjack, his brothers, and all his friends stood watching him. None of them dared to come out here to help him. They couldn't and he didn't want them to.

He pushed himself up onto his hands and knees. His legs didn't want to obey him. He held out no hope whatsoever that he could get there before some creature took him down.

He had done the job. He had brought the creatures to kill the Red Riders. Now he could die.

He stumbled to his feet and took the first lurching steps toward the tunnel. He made it ten feet before one of the adult Gorlocks rushed him from behind. The creature opened its mouth to cut him in half.

A Crusher charged in to grab him at the same moment and the two creatures' heads collided with him at the same instant. The impact hurled him off his feet. He sailed across the gap and smashed into the cliff wall full force.

The blow knocked him out and he slammed down on the ground, unconscious.

Chapter 54

Blackjack and Kuvik took advantage of a break in the fighting to dive outside the tunnel entrance. The Gorlocks and Crushers had brought down countless Red Riders. Now the creatures battled each other for the scraps.

The young Gorlocks weren't interested in eating the dead Riders nor were the young Gorlocks interested in fighting any Crushers. The young Gorlocks raced back and forth through the jungle hunting down any Red Riders still close enough to catch.

None of the Crushers or Gorlocks noticed when Blackjack and Kuvik each grabbed one of Hangman's legs and pulled him back inside the tunnel. The men surrounded him.

"Is he dead?" Calv asked.

"He's still breathing and he doesn't seem to be bleeding anywhere," Kuvik remarked. "He just got hit hard. He might have re-injured himself. We won't know until he wakes up."

"We have to take him back to camp," Blackjack decided. "One of you go out there and bring in a Stalkion hide so we can carry him. The rest of you get through the machinery and stand guard on the other side in case any Red Riders decide to take refuge in here."

Everyone got busy—everyone except for Kuvik. He stayed there kneeling next to Hangman's body. Kuvik examined him all over.

"Can you tell anything about what's wrong with him?" Blackjack asked.

Kuvik shook his head. "Only that he's still alive."

Blackjack straightened up and let out a shaky sigh. "I can't believe he actually did it. It actually worked."

"Did you really doubt him?" Kuvik stood up. "He's far too determined to let something like this beat him. He never planned to die out there."

"Still," Blackjack countered. "I know he's a great warrior—he still is even now. I just never thought he could pull off something like this—not in his condition."

"The question is what we're going to do about it. The Riders will regroup eventually."

"We'll have to wait and see....."

"Don't wait and see," Kuvik insisted. "Bring your men out here and establish your camp outside the tunnel. He gave a lot to buy you this space. Take advantage of it. Don't wait for the Red Riders to come back and stake out the tunnel themselves. Let them know this is your land and you won't tolerate them being here."

Blackjack nodded. "You're right. I will—but we'll take care of him first."

"*I'll* take care of him. You stay here and see to our defenses."

Blackjack grinned at him. Kuvik was one of the few men who could actually contradict Blackjack without causing any offense.

"*You* stay here and see to our defenses," Blackjack ordered. "I'll take my father home and then come back and help you."

Kuvik shut his eyes and inclined his head. "Who am I to argue with my Kral?"

"You just did, Kuvik. Don't lie."

Kuvik laughed, but they had to break off their conversation when the men came back with the Stalkion hide. They loaded Hangman onto it and hefted him over and around the machinery the same way they did last time.

"We really have to stop letting him get hurt," Red muttered on the way back to the camp in the rocks. "When is he going to learn?"

"Probably never," Blackjack replied. "We're the ones who need to learn to stop letting him."

"Letting him?" Red snorted. "No one *lets* him do anything. He makes up his mind and does it."

The men talked all the way back to camp about Hangman's latest victory. He had carried out a mass slaughter of the Red Riders and nearly gotten himself killed in the process.

He had broken the blockade on the tunnel. The Godless could go outside now and stake their claim on the mountain. The tunnel belonged to the Godless again.

Mora only snorted when the men brought Hangman in unconscious and Blackjack told her what had happened. She only compressed her lips, shook her head, and got to work taking care of him.

The men put him on his bed and left him in her care. None of them could help him. They would all find out how bad his injuries were once he woke up—if he woke up.

Blackjack went back to the tunnel. Kuvik had ordered the men to move their camp back outside the tunnel to the very same spot where the Red Riders had just been camping.

The Crushers and Gorlocks were out there devouring the dead Riders, so the Godless men couldn't move the camp right now. They worked in a fever to pack up everything.

They were just starting to dismantle their shelters when Blackjack arrived and threw a wrench in the works. "Leave the shelters here. The second shift will camp here. The first shift will stand guard out there. You won't need shelters."

No one acted too surprised by this change of plans. The first shift went through the tunnel and stood guard inside the entrance.

The young Gorlocks could get inside the tunnel, but they gave it up when the men jabbed their weapons at the creatures and injured a few of them. They went back to eating the dead Riders.

The Abnormits were already starting to move in. They cleared the area by the end of the day and left nothing behind. The men waited for the Abnormits to leave before they went outside and stationed themselves at strategic spots around the area.

Blackjack paced up and down making sure he'd covered every possible angle. He met up with Kuvik at the entrance. "What will our strategy be when the Red Riders come back?" Kuvik asked.

"We'll send out our scouts to find out where they are and how many men they have," Blackjack replied. "Then we should go on the offensive, hit them hard, and reduce their numbers again. They might be camping somewhere. We can make another night raid and kill them while they sleep."

"I have an idea," Kuvik announced.

Blackjack groaned and covered his eyes. "Oh, no! Not another idea! I don't want to hear any more ideas ever again for the rest of my life. I'm not taking any more ideas."

Kuvik pretended not to hear him. "We should do it again."

"Do what again?" Blackjack made a face. "Why do I even ask?"

"I mean we should repeat what your father just did. Someone should go to the Gorlock nesting grounds and lead them up here to attack the Red Riders a second time."

"That won't work. The Red Riders won't fall for it."

"They won't have a choice. They'll attack again sometime. It's inevitable because they'll always want to get inside the tunnel. Then all of you will fall back to the tunnel and the Gorlocks and Crushers will attack the Riders and wipe them out. Your father did it when he could barely walk. It would work even better if the person could actually walk and even run."

"I don't like the sound of this," Blackjack muttered. "In fact, I hate the sound of it."

"You let your father go. Let me go."

Fortunately for Blackjack's sanity, he didn't have to answer that right now. He was getting really sick and tired of these older men coming up with these suicide plans to throw themselves in front of dangerous creatures to lead them to kill the band's enemies.

Hangman had been doing that for decades and look where it got him. Blackjack didn't need to get one of his most valuable and trusted warriors hurt or killed doing the same thing.

The Red Riders didn't come back or even show themselves, so Blackjack sent out a scouting party to locate the enemy. The Riders had returned to their former camp on top of the northern ridge.

They didn't seem to be doing anything up there except licking their wounds, so Blackjack returned to the camp to check on Hangman. Blackjack found Mora sitting next to his bed. Hangman was awake. God, he looked old!

Blackjack sat down on the floor and squeezed his father's shoulder. "How are you feeling, Father?"

"Sore—sore and tired," Hangman rasped. He fought to focus his eye on Blackjack. "What's the situation outside?"

"The Riders have retreated to their old camp. We're setting up outside the tunnel to guard it. We won't know anything until they regroup. Then we'll decide what to do."

Hangman shut his eyes and turned away. "It worked. The creatures drove them out."

"Yeah," Blackjack murmured. "It worked."

Blackjack caught his mother making eye contact with him. He didn't need to ask how bad Hangman's injuries were this time. Getting hit like that could never be good for him considering the condition he'd been in before.

Blackjack didn't ask that or talk about anything else. He just sat here and spent time with his parents. How much longer did he have with them?

He sensed the time slipping through his fingertips. Hangman couldn't last much longer if he wasn't dying already. Mora would last longer, but Blackjack would lose her one of these days soon, too.

He really wished Bone was here. Blackjack would never find out what had happened to his brother. Bone and his comrades could all be dead out there somewhere. Blackjack would never see them again.

Then Blackjack would be all alone with Narina and Mion. Blackjack didn't want to face that. He didn't want to face down the grim, harsh reality of losing his whole family.

Narina came over to Hangman's shelter to talk to Mora about something. Narina entered with Mion and discovered Blackjack there. She sat down next to him and he filled her in on everything that had been happening with Hangman and everything else.

Mion played around the shelter like it was his own. He chatted to Mora and Hangman about everything.

His language had finally clicked and now he never stopped talking about literally everything. He wouldn't keep quiet from the minute he woke up in the morning until he crashed out at night.

"Was I like that?" Blackjack asked Mora.

She laughed at him. "God, no! You were born an adult in a little boy's body. You were the most serious child I've ever met. You couldn't wait to grow up. You hated being a child. None of you children talked this much."

Blackjack and Mora enjoyed Mion's company while Narina took a break and went out for a walk by herself. Hangman rested with his eyes closed except when Mion tried to talk to him.

Then Hangman opened his eyes long enough to answer until Mion got distracted and went off somewhere else. The sun went down outside. Narina came back and the two women cooked for the family.

Blackjack spent the evening with his family and then went home with Narina and Mion. She put Mion to bed and lay next to him until he fell asleep. Blackjack stretched out on her other side and waited.

She rolled over to face him after Mion fell asleep. Blackjack pulled her into his arms and held her, but he didn't feel like taking it any further even though he wanted to.

Hangman had bought this night for Blackjack to enjoy with his family. Hangman had bought this night with whatever small degree of mobility and health he had left. Was it worth it?

He considered it worth it, so it must have been. Blackjack just couldn't escape the sinking realization that his father was dying. Hangman had played his last hand.

Everyone probably thought he'd been all finished before this. Now he really was finished—for good. He would never go out and do anything like this again. He would probably never walk again. Blackjack would be very surprised if Hangman did walk again.

He had lived a long, hard, storied, legendary life. He had become a hero to his people at a young age and stayed one right up until the end. That's what he'd been trying to tell Blackjack all along. Hangman couldn't end his life any other way. It had to end like this.

Every fiber of Blackjack's being rebelled against Hangman's death. Of course Blackjack knew it was inevitable. Everyone had to die. Hangman was no exception.

Blackjack just couldn't face it—not like this. He couldn't be here lying in bed with his wife while his father lay dying right on the other side of camp.

Blackjack let go of Narina and rolled onto his back. He couldn't even explain to her why he couldn't connect with her tonight.

She didn't ask any questions. She just scooted in next to him and pressed her body against him while he held her with one arm around her shoulders. He couldn't do anything else. His mind stayed fixated on Hangman.

Blackjack couldn't even think of anything else. Blackjack had to bear silent witness to the greatness of a man passing out of life in the fullness of time. That was the least Hangman deserved for his efforts.

Chapter 55

Blackjack paced through his men checking them all, but they had all brought as many weapons as they needed. They were as ready as they were going to get to engage the Red Riders again.

Hammer and his men occupied one flank of the group. The Godless force had separated itself by band affiliations. All the men of each band stuck together with the people they knew from their own bands.

Blackjack hadn't planned it that way, but he didn't try to change it. He didn't see that people keeping separate interfered with the warriors' effectiveness.

If anything, it made them more effective. They fought alongside the men they knew and helped each other when they needed it.

Each band separated itself by age group, too. The younger men of similar ages stayed together and so did the older men.

Hammer's party did the same thing. He seemed to be following Hangman's example of letting the younger men establish their own leadership structure within the band. This looked like the new way of doing things. ,

They had implemented this strategy because it worked. The younger men would need their own leadership structure when they got old enough to run the band and the older men moved out of the way for the younger generation to take over.

What better time for them to learn and develop that structure than when they were young and under the guidance of older men?

The younger men didn't need any guidance that Blackjack could see. They did just fine on their own without any help from anyone. Blackjack would have been perfectly happy to let any of those younger men take over and run the campaign in his place.

He hardly had to organize anyone. They all knew what they had to do and how to do it.

He stopped next to Kuvik. Kuvik, Red, Wildling, Bantam, and Lock were the only older men coming on this campaign. The others were all too old, too slow, and too weak. Red and Wildling weren't far behind them.

Kuvik, Bantam, and Lock were the last truly able-bodied older men. Blackjack had been coming to realize why Hangman valued Kuvik so highly and why they had become such great friends.

Blackjack considered Kuvik something like a third uncle. Bantam and Lock might be Blackjack's real uncles, but Blackjack relied on Kuvik for guidance in ways Blackjack would never rely on Bantam or Lock. He never relied on them for guidance.

The men were just going over their weapons again when Calv and Urdis came running down the mountain. They pulled up all out of breath in front of Blackjack.

"They're there!" Calv gasped. "They're still there—in the same spot and the same number! They haven't moved!"

Blackjack called to the rest of the men. "Let's move out!" He pointed at the boys. "You boys fall back inside the tunnel and stand guard on the other side of the machinery. Kill any Riders who try to come through. You boys will be the last line of defense if we break and the Riders try to invade the valley. Understand? Don't leave your posts and definitely don't come out to help us. You have to stay inside. You'll be the only ones protecting the rest of the bands."

Urdis nodded. "We understand. We won't let you down."

Blackjack nodded and turned away. All the valley bands had sent their uninitiated boys to the tunnel to guard it on the inside while the men went out to launch this offensive against the Red Riders.

Blackjack didn't like leaving the whole valley's fate in the hands of boys, but he couldn't spare any initiated men to stay behind and stand guard. He needed every man to join the assault.

The men didn't wait for him to lead them up the mountain. Every man here had gone on some scouting party to check the Red Riders' position. They still occupied their old camp.

Only a tiny fraction of Riders had survived Hangman's maneuver to bring the Gorlocks and Crushers to slaughter the Riders.

The Riders hadn't launched another attack against the Godless. The Riders didn't have the numbers to do anything, especially against such a large, combined force of Godless in one place.

Kuvik cut away from the others and took off running away into the jungle heading south along the river.

Blackjack put Kuvik out of his mind. Blackjack pretended that he and Kuvik hadn't made a plan for Kuvik to bring any dangerous creatures to use against the Red Riders. Blackjack couldn't rely on that.

The Godless traveled along the ground and made no effort at all to conceal their approach to the Red Rider camp. The men didn't talk, but they didn't stop themselves from stepping on branches, crashing through undergrowth, and making all the noise they wanted.

It probably wouldn't make any difference. The Red Riders didn't observe or listen to the surrounding jungle the way the Godless did.

The Red Riders didn't act like they knew or cared if anyone was sneaking up to attack them. No one had attacked them before the Godless started doing it.

The Godless slowed down and did start to be quiet when they got near the Red Rider position. The Godless force assembled in the undergrowth and spread out to surround the camp.

The Red Riders lounged and relaxed in and around their tents. They didn't notice a thing. Blackjack didn't have to give the order to attack. The Godless rushed in from multiple sides. The Red Riders didn't grab their weapons in time.

The slaughter began with the Godless working their way through the camp one Rider at a time. The Godless showed no mercy and cut down every Rider no matter who or where they were.

The Godless worked inward toward the center of camp. Those Riders who did get to their weapons in time gathered there and closed together in a cluster to defend themselves.

The Godless force surrounded the Riders to wipe out every last man. The Godless outnumbered the Riders by five to one. Not every Godless could fit in the inner ring to face the Riders. The rest had to stay outside.

Blackjack watched from a distance and found himself looking over his shoulder. More Red Riders would come. Did they know about the tunnel, too? How could they communicate with each other over such distances to pass that information to their comrades?

He would just have to keep waging this war for as long as it took to eliminate them all and stop them from invading his territory. Being Kral meant keeping a constant watch on everyone and everything.

Almost as if his thoughts made it happen, a distant rumble vibrated through the ground just then. This wasn't the steady thump of

Crusher footsteps. It kept drumming in an unbroken hum of noise and vibration.

He knew that sound even before he heard or felt it. It was the sound and vibration of Blastidon hooves—a lot of Blastidon hooves.

The other Godless heard it, too. The warriors surrounding the Red Riders hesitated to listen and feel the vibrations coming up through their feet from the ground.

The Red Riders heard and felt it, too. They burst forward in a sudden rush of new energy and counterattacked, but they couldn't stand up to so many Godless.

The Red Riders' actions set off an answering counterassault from the Godless. The men collapsed inward and cut all the Riders to the ground, but it was too late. A massive horde of Riders swept over the mountain's brow right at that moment.

Blackjack and the rest of the Godless stared at the tide of Blastidons thundering down the mountain. They overflowed the pass and the torrent never stopped. None of the Godless had seen a Red Rider force this big before.

The Blastidons picked up speed as they ran downhill. They shrieked in a combination of excitement and fear as their own momentum started to carry them away. None of them could slow down or stop on their headlong charge for the camp.

None of those Riders could have known ahead of time that the Godless were there, but the Riders sure acted like they did. They raised their weapons to strike.

All the Godless leapt back into position and formed ranks to meet the Riders. The Riders charged into the Godless ranks and tried to chop the Godless down.

The Godless attacked the Blastidons first, pulled the Riders to the ground, and the battle disintegrated into a chaotic jumble of both sides all mixed up with each other.

Enough Blastidons survived that first wave to drive the Godless back. The Godless retreated back down the mountain in the direction from which they'd come. Both sides wound up reforming together into two flanks facing off against each other.

Chapter 56

The Red Riders tried again and again to charge the Godless, only for the Godless to take out more Blastidons and bring the Riders down to the ground. The surviving Riders had to fight on foot.

They couldn't get near the Godless line—not with so many Blastidons in the way. The Red Riders brought in more mounted fighters than the Godless could tackle—and more mounted Riders kept coming over the pass even as the battle engaged.

Blackjack didn't see any end to the Red Rider force. Was this all of them? Did the last remaining Red Riders finally join into one overpowering force that could finally wipe the Godless off the map?

Blackjack would never find out if this was all the Red Riders. He would never defeat a force this size. He didn't have to tell his men to fall back. They all saw the end closing in on them.

The dismounted Riders retreated to the back and formed a second flank behind the Blastidons. The Godless would never bring down this many Blastidons. Even then, the Godless would have to fight the dismounted Riders. The battle wouldn't last long.

The Godless kept retreating. There was nowhere else to go but back inside the tunnel. At least the Blastidons wouldn't be able to get past the machinery. The Godless could always make a stand behind the machinery—for as long as that lasted.

Hangman's words kept coming back to haunt Blackjack in his private moments. The Red Riders could harness their Blastidons to the machinery and pull it out of the way. Then nothing would stop the Riders from invading the valley.

The Red Riders would be able to accomplish that so much more easily with this many Blastidons. The Red Riders might not be the most creative people in the world. None of them was as creative as Hangman, but one of them was bound to think of it sooner or later.

Blackjack had to come up with some trick to stop this catastrophe from happening, but he couldn't think of anything. He and his men backed away as far as their first camp halfway down the mountain.

They couldn't even make a stand here. They would never be able to make a stand anywhere—not against this many Riders.

Kuvik came running back just then and intercepted the Godless force at their old campsite. Two dozen Gorlocks run after him.

He maneuvered their approach so the Gorlocks intercepted the back of the Red Rider force. The Gorlocks overtook plenty of Riders to eat. The Gorlocks never put the Godless in danger.

The Red Rider horde was too big even for the Gorlocks to make a difference. The Godless drew back faster to put more distance between themselves and the Gorlocks. The Godless left the Gorlocks to feast on as many Riders as the creatures could catch.

They favored the Riders who had lost their mounts. The Riders couldn't get away, but the mounted riders only surged forward to keep pace with the Godless.

Enough mounted Riders remained to keep pressing the Godless down the mountain. The two sides didn't change their positions at all.

Blackjack took that moment to glance behind him again. He could see the tunnel from here. Now what was he supposed to do? He really didn't want to go in there. He could have used the bottleneck, but he would rather stop the Riders here.

This many Riders were bound to find a way through the tunnel. He wasn't even sure the bottleneck would work anymore—not against this many. They might be able to get through fast enough to force the Godless away from the machinery.

Then the Godless would have to fight the Riders inside the valley. Blackjack didn't like the Godless' chances if that happened—not against an enemy force this size.

He had to face front and pay attention to all the Blastidons charging him again and again. He couldn't cut them down fast enough to make a dent in their numbers.

Were even more of them still coming over the pass at this very moment? Did their numbers even stop after they pushed the Godless down the mountain? Would the Red Rider numbers ever stop?

At that moment, another pounding drumroll of vibration came from a different peak of the same mountain range. It didn't sound or feel the same as Blastidon hooves. This sounded softer and quieter but no less overwhelming.

The Riders must have realized the difference, too. Some of them turned around to see what made that sound.

Every combatant on the field stopped and stared at a completely different horde of people streaming over another pass to enter the valley. These people were not mounted. They came on foot.

They almost looked like ants in their full suits of dark clothing. The men cut their hair short. They didn't look human next to so many Red Riders and Godless.

The strangers swarmed the valley by the thousands and overran the Red Riders from behind. The newcomers even pulled down the

Gorlocks, slaughtered them right then and there, and moved on to the Riders.

Blackjack caught one glimpse of his brother in the crowd. Five of his men fought alongside him in the heart of the swarm. Blackjack didn't need to see anything else. He didn't know who these strangers were, but they must be Bone's allies.

Blackjack bellowed out in rage and plunged straight back into the fight. The strangers went after the Riders with frightening brutality. The strangers even put the Godless to shame.

The strangers teamed up in mobs to overpower Blastidons, pull them to the ground, and annihilated mounts and Riders in seconds. The strangers worked their way through the Red Rider force by sheer power of numbers. The Riders didn't stand a chance.

The Red Riders obviously didn't have a clue who these strangers were, either. The Riders turned their mounts around to fight back—and fell victim to the Godless attacking from the other direction.

The battle swung the other way instantly. The Godless represented only a tiny drop in the ocean of all these short-haired, blue-suited strangers. They didn't need mounts. They slaughtered Blastidons left and right. The Riders didn't survive for long.

The Godless wound up with no one left to fight. Blackjack came to a standstill with his men around him. They stopped fighting and just watched in awe as the strangers wiped out the rest of the Riders.

Bone and his men worked side by side with the strangers. Blackjack never would have known that these six men were Godless except that they looked different and fought with different weapons.

The strangers showed no sign that they considered Bone and his comrades any different from themselves. Bone and the others must have been traveling and fighting with these people all this time.

The strangers finally finished killing all the Riders. The strangers worked their way through the sea of bodies to kill off all the enemy wounded, both Riders and Blastidons.

Bone and his men happened to notice Blackjack and his men standing there watching. Bone eyed his brother across the battlefield and then split into a massive grin.

Bone and Blackjack strode out to meet each other in a giant hug. Blackjack didn't even care that his brother was covered in the blood of other men.

"What are you doing, little brother?" Blackjack couldn't help but laugh in pure happiness when he pushed his brother back and held him at arm's length. "Where did you find all these people?"

"They found me." Bone waved behind him and a different group of the blue-suited strangers came forward. "This is Colonel Roland Kilpatrick. He's in command of the 147th Regiment. They've sworn to wipe out the Red Riders to the last man, woman, and child, so I figured...." Bone shrugged. "What better place than here for them to find plenty of Riders to kill?"

Blackjack turned to the tall man Bone indicated. The guy eyed Blackjack through narrowed eyes. Blackjack understood fighting men, especially those who commanded other fighting men.

Colonel Kilpatrick came forward and stuck out his hand. "You must be Blackjack. Your brother has been telling me all about you."

"Thank you for coming to our aid," Blackjack replied. "Your timing couldn't be better."

Colonel Kilpatrick ignored the compliment and curled his lip at all the dead Riders at his feet. "I don't suppose this will be the last of them. We'll stick around out here and intercept any other parties that come to this valley."

"Do you know of any other parties that are coming to this valley?" Blackjack asked.

"Not yet, but I'll send out my scouts. The Riders all seem to be coming from the south. We'll scout the terrain, find them, and intercept them before they come this far." Colonel Kilpatrick squinted at the surroundings. "This is a good country. We might decide to stay here."

He turned around and leveled Blackjack with another hard look. Colonel Kilpatrick struck Blackjack as a hard, unbending man who didn't waver when he put his mind to something.

"We obviously wouldn't stay in *your* territory," he went on. "We would have to negotiate the most favorable location as long as we stayed out of each other's way."

"Our territory is the next valley over. We don't claim any of the land around it. You could choose from the whole mountain range." Blackjack made a snap decision. "Why don't you come to our camp? We can talk more comfortably there."

Colonel Kilpatrick nodded. "Thank you. I'd like that. Just give me a minute to give orders to my people."

Colonel Kilpatrick made some gesture to Bone and the two men retreated to a distance out of earshot from the rest of the Godless. Blackjack couldn't help noticing his brother talking to this man as an equal.

"Can you believe this?" Red murmured in Blackjack's ear. "I thought we'd lost those men. Now they show up with a whole army of fighters who are sworn to wipe out the Red Riders. I never would have believed it."

Colonel Kilpatrick finished his conversation with Bone just then and walked off to give orders to his men. Bone returned to rejoin Blackjack's party.

"What was that about?" Blackjack asked. "What did he say?"

"He only said he wants me to come with him when he goes to your camp. He doesn't know you—any of you. He doesn't like going into an unknown Clan's territory alone or even with a smaller group of his men. He wants me to go with him as his escort. He wants me to help him negotiate with you. He knows me and he trusts me. He doesn't know or trust you. That's all he said."

"That's all right, then." Blackjack found himself studying his brother. "What happened to you? We thought you were all gone."

"We skirted the Red Rider force trying to reduce their numbers as usual," Bone replied. "We got into a fight against them and the Regiment attacked. They thought we were Riders at first. Then we all realized we were fighting on the same side. We've been traveling here ever since. I told them they could find Riders here. That's why they came."

Blackjack shook his head. "It's amazing. You've done very well for yourself." He turned to the other men in Bone's party. "All of you have. I'm proud of you."

Bone gave Blackjack a strange look and Bone's eyebrows came together in the center. Blackjack knew his brother too well not to recognize that look. Bone had something else to say—something important.

Chapter 57

Colonel Kilpatrick came back with ten of his men and three women. Blackjack didn't recognize any of these people.

The women all wore their hair in two braids hanging from either side of their heads and draped in front of their shoulders.

Bone introduced three of the men as Colonel Kilpatrick's sons and one of the women as his daughter.

Bone kept referring to the members of the Regiment as, 'soldiers'. They used ancient military titles left over from eons past. Blackjack didn't understand why, but he let it go.

He decided to treat the Regiment's ways as the strange customs of another Clan. They had their own way of doing things that didn't concern him. He wasn't here to change their ways.

The two parties joined. Enough soldiers remained on the battlefield and none of the Red Riders had survived. Blackjack didn't have to worry about leaving the battlefield.

He still found it hard to turn his back on the Red Riders even after they were dead. His instincts told him to stay out here, to send out scouts to track down any Red Riders in the area, and attack them again.

He didn't want to offend Colonel Kilpatrick by seeming to imply that the Regiment couldn't do all of that—or that Blackjack didn't trust the Regiment to do it competently and thoroughly enough to locate the Red Riders first.

Blackjack didn't know or trust the Regiment, so he decided to trust Bone. Bone would have told Blackjack if the Regiment wasn't competent enough to locate the Red Riders first.

Blackjack could see how competent the Regiment was. They were certainly competent at killing Riders.

The Regiment numbers created an impenetrable wall between the Angler Valley and the outside world. No Red Rider horde would be able to get to the valley—not without going through the Regiment first.

That would at least slow the Riders down enough for the Godless to do.....something. Blackjack didn't see that the Godless would be able to do anything—not compared to what the Regiment could do.

He led the way back to the tunnel. Bone introduced Colonel Kilpatrick to Hammer, Cross, Kuvik, Red, Bantam, and all the other men. Bone explained all the connections between these people.

He talked to Colonel Kilpatrick all the way to the camp and pointed out a bunch of different details of the landscape and the Godless' strategic position.

Bone had obviously told Colonel Kilpatrick a lot about the Godless history in this valley and beyond. Bone explained about the machinery when the time came for the men to wedge themselves past the machinery to get through the tunnel.

Bone stopped Colonel Kilpatrick halfway up the tunnel. Blackjack and his men listened in silence while Bone pointed to long, parallel grooves on the wall. He explained how Mora had surmised that the ancients had used the machinery to carve out this tunnel.

Bone explained that not even Mora could figure out why the ancients had left this machinery here. He explained that she could only guess that the people who had carved this tunnel must have planned to come back and use the machinery later.

Bone kept talking on the way out of the tunnel and through the jungle to the camp in the rocks. He went on to discuss Mora's ideas about how the Anglers had gotten into the valley in the first place. It was one of the great unsolved mysteries of the band's history.

Blackjack listened in silence. He found himself marveling at how smoothly Bone handled Colonel Kilpatrick. The two men were obviously on close social terms. Colonel Kilpatrick chimed in with questions and comments at the right times.

None of Bone's men interjected, either. They followed and listened in silence, too. Had it been like this the whole time the men had been traveling with the Regiment?

The party entered the camp and Bone led Colonel Kilpatrick to Hangman's shelter. He sat outside in his usual place. That was as far as he'd gotten after his most recent injury. He couldn't move much except for taking a few steps between his bed and his usual spot outside.

Bone introduced him to Colonel Kilpatrick and gave Hangman the briefest possible explanation of the outcome of the battle.

"Please sit down." Hangman waved to the ground nearest him. "Thank you for coming to our aid."

Colonel Kilpatrick sat down next to him. Blackjack sat on Hangman's other side.

"It's a pleasure to meet you at last." Colonel Kilpatrick replied. "Your son has been telling me all about you—and the rest of your people. This is an impressive valley you have."

"It isn't so impressive when our enemies know how to get inside," Hangman returned. "Our plan was to eliminate anyone who knew about the tunnel entrance. Now it seems that everyone knows about it."

"Does it matter if your friends and allies know about it?" Colonel Kilpatrick's voice took one an extra edge of steel. "We would never take advantage of that to put you in danger—not unless you made yourselves our enemies."

"We have no intention of making anyone our enemies," Blackjack interjected. "We only came to this valley to live our lives in peace. These enemy Clans tracked us here to wipe us all out. We wouldn't be fighting them at all if not for that."

Colonel Kilpatrick turned to face Blackjack. So this was how it would go. Bone must have told Colonel Kilpatrick that Blackjack was Kral of this band—not Hangman.

Colonel Kilpatrick understood that only too well. He could be as polite as he wanted to Hangman. Colonel Kilpatrick didn't try to negotiate with him.

"Your brother has explained to me that the Godless Clan doesn't take captives or go out to war against any Clan who doesn't make themselves your enemies," Colonel Kilpatrick replied. "I don't see that the Regiment would ever become enemies of your Clan if that's true. We only went after the Regiment because they came after us first. We recovered our captured women and girls from them, but they still wouldn't leave us alone. That's when we swore to wipe out their Clan—not in revenge but to remove the threat they posed to us and everyone else in the country. That's why we're here. We have no interest in fighting another Clan that's peaceful toward us."

"We feel the same way," Blackjack went on. "I see no reason for us not to form an alliance……and I wholeheartedly approve of my brother telling you about the tunnel entrance. You would be free to come and go as our friends and brothers if you chose to settle in this area. We could hold combined gatherings to introduce new blood into both our Clans."

Colonel Kilpatrick stiffened when Blackjack referred to the Regiment as a Clan. Blackjack watched Colonel Kilpatrick's expression carefully, but the colonel let it go just as quickly. He didn't make an issue out of it.

Colonel Kilpatrick narrowed his eyes at the rest of the camp. Hardly any of the fighting men came back with the group. Almost everyone here were women and children—and a few old men too weak to do anything.

"Your brother says you break up your people into smaller bands," Colonel Kilpatrick replied. "That's smart. I wish we could do it that way. We would attract fewer creature attacks."

"Maybe you could do it that way if you settle in this country," Bone interjected. "These mountains have countless valleys, each one as rich as this one. You could split up the Regiment into different bands, each with its own valley territory. The Regiment's presence would deter enemy Clans from invading. You could rejoin into a unified force if anyone did invade. Then you would be as strong as ever. You would be even stronger because your people would be able to grow and expand their population to fill the valleys. No one would be able to stand against you."

"What about you?" Colonel Kilpatrick countered. He started by talking to Bone and turned back to Blackjack. "Do you plan to expand outside this valley?"

Blackjack shrugged. "I suppose we have enough people now that we would have to consider it. We have five bands living in this valley. It's already becoming too populated. Someone will have to leave soon. I suppose we'll move into the adjacent valleys, too. We would have to survey the country and decide which part of the mountains belonged to you and which belonged to us."

"I don't see that we need to make it as complicated as that," Colonel Kilpatrick countered. "We can just expand as long as we're all friends and allies and neighbors. If someone wants to split off and form their own band, they can move into a valley that no one else is living in. A Godless band wouldn't be able to move into another band's territory even if they belonged to the same Clan. We can treat each other's bands the same way. The new band would have to choose a territory with no one in it regardless of where the territory is."

Blackjack spread both hands. "You're right. I appreciate that you want to live with us as neighbors. We welcome your people."

Colonel Kilpatrick gave him another hard look and went back to narrowing his eyes at all the women, children, and families working around the camp.

"Is something wrong?" Hangman asked. "Tell us if something is bothering you."

Colonel Kilpatrick replied over his shoulder without turning around to face any of the three Godless men. "Nothing is bothering me—nothing you need to concern yourselves about. It's just....strange. Your son and his men are so different from us. Their ways are different. Their fighting style is different. Everything about them is different—and now I find myself in a country full of the same kind of people—where all his ways are normal."

"Is anything wrong with that?" Hangman asked. "Your ways are different to us, too."

"No, of course nothing is wrong with it." Colonel Kilpatrick finally turned around, but he had a hard time making eye contact with any of the three men. "It just takes some getting used to. I'm not used to it. It's been hard enough getting used to your son. He belongs to another Clan. It's strange to be the outsider in another world where everything I know no longer applies."

Bone interjected. "You mentioned that your people live in fortifications to the south and west of here. Would you build them here in your chosen valleys?"

Colonel Kilpatrick nodded. "That's our way. We could never live in these temporary camps the way you do—not unless we're on the march. When we settle, we settle for good."

"Would you want us to participate in joint maneuvers with your men?" Bone asked. "Or would you want us to keep our maneuvers separate until the time comes for us to face a common enemy?"

Colonel Kilpatrick's expression hardened even more if that was possible. He fixed Bone with a piercing stare, but that look didn't bother Bone. He acted like he was used to it.

Colonel Kilpatrick lowered his voice even more dangerously, but Bone didn't react to that, either. He responded as though Colonel Kilpatrick was struggling to control his voice—not that he was trying to threaten anyone here.

"That's exactly what I'm trying to say," Colonel Kilpatrick growled. "I think we should keep our people separate as much as possible. You have your ways and we have ours. We're allies and friends. That doesn't mean we'll start living together. Your fighting style is too different from ours. You travel in the trees, scout from the trees, and camp in the trees. We don't do it that way. I don't think it would work for us to go on joint maneuvers. If we come together to fight a common enemy, you'll fight your way and we'll fight ours. We won't mix."

"I understand and I agree with you," Bone replied. "I think it's a good plan."

"So.....you don't have a problem with us establishing ourselves in the surrounding valleys?" Colonel Kilpatrick asked.

"You mentioned that you planned to stake out the territory to the south and east to intercept any other Red Riders moving into the area," Blackjack added. "It sounds like you're already planning to occupy valleys at a distance from us. It isn't as though you plan to set up in the very next adjacent valley where we would run into your people on scouting trips."

"No, of course not," Colonel Kilpatrick replied. "I wasn't planning to."

Chapter 58

Mora came over to the shelter she shared with Hangman. Someone somewhere must have gone hunting.

She brought a huge chunk of freshly roasted meat, laid it out on a clean piece of cured hide, and divided it up to serve to all the surrounding men, including the men from the Regiment.

Blackjack couldn't decide if her arrival interfered with the men's conference or not. He would have considered sending her away if she wasn't already handing out bowls of food to Colonel Kilpatrick and his men.

Bone didn't miss a beat. "This is my mother, Mora—the Follower woman I told you about. Mother, this is Colonel Roland Kilpatrick. He's in command of the 147th Regiment that is making an alliance with the Godless in this valley."

She looked up, smiled at Colonel Kilpatrick, and raised her greasy hands all covered in meat juice. "It's a pleasure to meet you, Colonel. You'll forgive me if I don't shake hands."

"Not at all," he replied. "Your son is a credit to you—to all of you. You should be very proud of him."

She beamed at him and then shot Bone a glance. "I am. I'm very proud of both my sons."

Bone interjected by steering the conversation back on track. Blackjack found himself once again in awe of his brother's statesmanship. He was a born negotiator, diplomat, and liaison between the two Clans.

"Did you plan to break up the Regiment right away?" Bone asked. "You have enough people to occupy multiple valleys. I didn't think the Regiment's cohesion was shaky enough for that. I didn't think it was shaky at all."

Colonel Kilpatrick followed Bone's lead exactly. Colonel Kilpatrick had asked Bone to come here to intercede between the Godless and the Regiment. Now Bone was doing it and Colonel Kilpatrick let him.

"I wouldn't call it shaky," Colonel Kilpatrick replied. "We just have way too many people to establish ourselves in one place. We would only put ourselves in danger. I wouldn't split up the Regiment if I thought we would face any more enemy resistance."

Blackjack's head shot up. "You mean none? You really don't think the Red Riders will offer any more resistance?"

"I mean not enough to justify keeping such a large force in one place. Even one of these valleys wouldn't be enough to support us. We need to divide if we're going to settle anywhere." Colonel Kilpatrick frowned. "Is that going to be a problem?"

"Not at all," Blackjack replied. "We weren't planning to send any new bands out into the area anyway—not anytime soon—not soon enough to interfere with your plans. You can occupy whichever valleys you want. We'll take what's left when the time comes."

Colonel Kilpatrick looked away and went back to watching the Godless going about their work. Mora finished serving the food, picked up the hide, and left without a word.

"It's going to take me a while to learn how to settle down and live in one place like a real man again," Colonel Kilpatrick muttered under his breath. "It's been so long."

"Have you been on the march ever since the Red Riders first attacked?" Bone asked.

Colonel Kilpatrick nodded. "They took my wife and oldest daughter. My sons and my younger daughter escaped. We formed the first Regiment with the other men who had lost their wives and daughters to the Red Riders. We went after them and got the women back, but it was too late. The Riders injured my wife. She died four months after we brought her back. My daughter......" He trailed off. "She was too distraught over what happened. She said she didn't want to live after that and that she could never marry or look at another man. She took her own life."

"I'm sorry," Bone murmured. "You never told me."

"I haven't talked about it since it happened." Colonel Kilpatrick kept his head turned. He refused to look at anyone. No one else said a word. "Everyone else in the Regiment already knew about it, so I didn't have to talk about it. You're the first people I've met who don't know."

"I hope you can find peace here," Bone went on. "Don't hesitate to call on us if you need us."

Colonel Kilpatrick finally turned around. His expression didn't soften at all. He compressed his lips. "I appreciate your friendship and your hospitality. I think I better go out to the Regiment now. We can meet in the coming days if we need to discuss anything or re-negotiate our alliance."

All the men stood up. Blackjack extended his hand to shake Colonel Kilpatrick's. "You would be welcome in our camp anytime. Please let me know if you need anything or if you encounter any problems we can help you with. We're in your debt after today."

"You did us a favor by attracting the Red Riders to one place where we could attack them," Colonel Kilpatrick replied. "We're glad to make friends with anyone who considers the Red Riders the enemy."

He withdrew and took his people with him toward the camp entrance. Blackjack considered escorting the soldiers back to the tunnel or maybe sending some of the Godless men to do it.

Colonel Kilpatrick's parting words seemed to indicate that he didn't want anyone to escort him. He had made it pretty clear that he wanted the two Clans to continue to live apart even if they occupied the same country as friends, allies, and neighbors.

Blackjack couldn't exactly fault him for that. The Godless and the Regiment wouldn't mingle any more than any other Clans did. They would come together for gatherings and then separate. That was the way of the world.

Bone followed the party to the exit. The men filed out into the jungle. One of the women stayed behind. It was Colonel Kilpatrick's daughter. Blackjack didn't remember her name.

She shared a murmured conversation with Bone for a minute before she left with the rest of her father's men. Bone returned to Hangman's shelter.

Blackjack didn't ask what was going on between Bone and Colonel Kilpatrick's daughter. It was none of Blackjack's business.

"You did very well, my son," Hangman told Bone. "We have you to thank for this alliance."

Bone shrugged that away. "The country is big enough for all of us, I suppose. We can expand into other valleys without intruding on each other's territory."

"This will give more bands permission to leave the valley," Blackjack pointed out. "The Godless and the Regiment will be able to protect each other much better this way."

"The Regiment will eat well tonight," Bone went on. "They have all that Blastidon and Gorlock meat to share between them. None of the soldiers will have to go hunting. They already have enough."

Blackjack faced his brother. "Did you want to tell me something, little brother?"

Bone winced. "Not here."

Blackjack waved to his parents' shelter. "Step inside."

The two brothers went inside. Bone told Blackjack in a halting undertone about what had happened with Oracle, Chief, Pyro, Reaper, Diamond, Rebel, and Cyclops—and about Rebel and Diamond's deaths.

"I should have stopped it," Bone husked. "I blame myself."

"You have nothing to blame yourself for if you didn't do anything." Blackjack hesitated. "I have to say this, brother. You know I love you and I respect you too much as a Godless man not to tell you the truth out front. I have to tell these men as their Kral that they can never marry, but I also have to ask them to confirm that you didn't do anything. Please don't take offense, but I have only your word that you didn't when all the others did. I have to ask them. I have to get their confirmation that you're innocent."

Bone looked away and nodded. "I wouldn't blame you if you barred me from marrying, too. I deserve that."

"No, you don't. If you didn't break the law, then you have nothing to blame yourself for. You're the one man of the whole party who didn't break the law. Why should you suffer the same punishment when you did nothing wrong?"

"They're my brothers and my friends!" Bone blurted out. "I should have stopped them! I should have done something! I should have driven those women away....."

"They're captives—or they were. We've been saving and freeing captive women all this time. The others probably started out by wanting to help and protect these women. It all spiraled from there. You did help them and free them and save them—and they betrayed you. You couldn't know ahead of time that they would betray you. They probably seduced the men on purpose so the women could kill them later."

Bone looked away again. "I don't know what to think anymore. I don't know if I can ever marry or trust a woman after that."

"You seem cozy enough with the colonel's daughter."

Bone grimaced. "'Cozy' isn't the word I would use for it."

"Use whatever word you want. A lot can happen in two years. You may feel differently then. You may decide it would be pretty nice to have a wife and a family of your own. You don't have to marry her. You could marry a nice Godless girl you already know and trust. Then you wouldn't have that problem."

"Can we not talk about this anymore?" Bone asked. "The men are all still out there standing guard over the tunnel. We should send them home until we know for sure that we're under threat again."

Blackjack nodded. "You go do that. Go tell them to go home to their families."

Bone left and Blackjack went back outside. None of the other men were around and neither were the women. He had nothing else to do, so he sat down next to his father.

"Our fortunes seem to have taken a sudden turn for the better," Hangman remarked.

Blackjack glanced at him and looked away. "It would certainly seem that way."

"This Regiment seems like a strong ally. We're lucky to have them."

"Yes, we are," Blackjack remarked. "I hope it works out the way we talked about today. That would be ideal for everyone—especially us."

Silence descended between the two men. Blackjack found himself looking around at the women and children. Godless men started to slowly trickle back into camp the longer he sat here.

He didn't have to get up or organize anything or check on anything. The country was finally at peace. Enemy Clans might invade this territory again someday, but the Godless wouldn't have to face it alone—not ever again.

Chapter 59

Blackjack glanced over his shoulder. He sat in conference with Colonel Kilpatrick, Hangman, Red, Hammer, Cross, and the other older men, but Blackjack barely heard their conversation.

Another conference was taking place across the camp—a conference Blackjack wasn't a part of.

Silloa Kilpatrick, her three older brothers, and half a dozen other Regiment people sat around with Bone, Skin, Fire, and a whole crowd of Godless young people from a dozen different bands, both inside the valley and from Hammer's people.

Blackjack already knew what the younger generation was talking about over there. Bone had told him ahead of time that these people were going to meet and what they planned to talk about. Blackjack wouldn't have known otherwise.

They were over there sealing a permanent alliance between all their Clans and bands. The Regiment wasn't a regiment anymore. The throng of soldiers had already broken up into dozens of bands, each with its own commanding officer acting as Kral.

Hammer planned to do the same thing as soon as he got home.

Skin and most of the younger Ashtaw Valley men had already consolidated their loyalties with each other. They had already decided which of them would go out as their own bands and which men would act as their Krals.

Each of these men had to negotiate with all the others as equals. Blackjack didn't know which of them were Krals. It didn't really concern him—not until they came to negotiate with him.

He didn't think about it too much. He wasn't in charge of anything that happened outside this valley or even anything that happened outside this camp—not anymore.

He was Kral of one band out of dozens. He held no authority over anyone that any of these other Krals didn't also hold.

The safety and prosperity of all these bands and even Blackjack's band depended more on these young people than it did on him. He was already passing into history with another generation rising behind him to take over.

He couldn't help but feel a surge of pride for all those young people, especially his brother. Everyone in all these bands trusted and respected Bone. He had earned it by being one of the smartest, most insightful Krals of the whole younger group.

That's what he was. He was a Kral. The men who'd gone out with him to make allies of the Regiment—those men already treated him as their Kral. They accepted his word as law and obeyed him to the letter. No Kral ever had more loyal men.

The conversation between Colonel Kilpatrick, Hammer, Yeoli, and the other older men drew Blackjack's attention back to the people in front of him. He had to turn his back on the younger men's conference, but he already knew what was going on over there.

Colonel Kilpatrick pointed to some of Hangman's maps spread out on the ground. "This is our closest fortified encampment. It isn't that far away from equidistant between the Ashtaw Valley and these mountains. I say we establish a permanent gathering place here—in this valley. It's on the very border of the canyon lands. All three of our peoples should be able to get there easily—or equally easily."

Hammer frowned at the map. "You're right. That isn't far away at all. It will be easier for us to get there than the official gathering ground in the south."

"It isn't the official gathering ground if no one is using it," Blackjack pointed out. "We have more people up here than in all the south country put together. It makes sense for us to gather on our own."

"Do you still want to keep having internal gatherings between ourselves?" Hammer asked. "You have a lot of people. We have a lot of people. The Regiment has a lot of people. I'm sure our young people will prefer to marry within their own Clans. They shouldn't go to the gathering at all if it isn't necessary. That will only put their families in danger."

"I agree," Colonel Kilpatrick replied. "I see no reason to go to the gathering as long as our young people can find husbands and wives within their own people."

"I agree, too," Blackjack added. "We have too many people as it is and they're all having children. The gatherings would get too crowded and chaotic if we took everyone. Some of these young people will pair off before the gathering. They might as well stay home and spare everyone the effort and confusion."

Colonel Kilpatrick frowned at the maps. "I wish I could find some of these. They would be so useful to find out more about this part of the country."

"You can take them and study them if you want to," Blackjack told him. "We aren't using them."

Colonel Kilpatrick's head shot up. "You mean it?"

"Go ahead. I'm sure you'll keep them safe. We could send some of our men south to collect more of them." Blackjack glanced over his shoulder again. "I'm sure some of our younger men would be happy to take a trip south. They could bring back copies of these maps for all of us—for every Kral in the canyon country."

"That would be great." Colonel Kilpatrick gathered up the maps and got to his feet.

Then came the long, laborious process of everyone saying goodbye to everyone else. Bone and the other young people did the same thing. They stood up and everyone hugged each other before they left.

The two generations met up to exchange the last few ideas. Mostly they just hugged, promised to see each other soon, and spent a long time expressing their affection for each other.

Hangman stood up, too, but he didn't move through the crowd. His closest friends came to see him. He spent a long, long time saying goodbye to Cross and Hammer. All three older men got tears in their eyes when they hugged each other.

Colonel Kilpatrick led the Regiment people out of the camp, but he wasn't in charge anymore, either. His sons had each taken over as Kral of one of the outlying Regiment bands.

Not even Silloa lived with her father anymore. She'd gone out with one of her brothers' bands. She and Bone spent a long time standing nose to nose, holding a murmured conversation between themselves, and even holding hands.

They had to steal these few isolated moments before they went back to living on opposite sides of the mountain.

Those days were rapidly coming to an end. She'd already come to the age of gathering. As soon as Bone came to the age of Gathering, she would leave her family and go to live with his band.

Hammer, Cross, and their men finally took their leave from Hangman, Red, Wildling, and the other older men. Hammer's men rejoined with Skin and the other younger Ashtaw Valley men.

They went through another procedure of saying goodbye before the men left to go home. They would mount their Ashtaws down by the river. The men would make it home in a few days at the most.

Hangman didn't move away from his shelter to escort his friends out of camp. He could barely walk at all these days.

Blackjack accompanied the guests as far as the camp entrance. He didn't escort them to the tunnel. His allies knew their way in and out of the Angler Valley. These men had been coming and going whenever they pleased.

All the surrounding Regiment bands knew their way through the tunnel, too. The Godless had no reason to keep the secret from their closest friends and allies.

Bone went with Blackjack to say goodbye to Hammer's people. Hammer, Cross, Skin, and the others raised their hands to wave and then vanished into the jungle.

Blackjack stayed where he was. He didn't want to turn away. He didn't want to face what he knew was coming.

Bone turned away first and faced Blackjack. "It's time for us to go, too," Bone murmured. "Give me your blessing."

Blackjack had no choice but to face the inevitable. He turned aside and stopped in front of his brother. "I know you're going to be great. You already are. I'm proud of you and...." Blackjack felt himself choking down a rush of painful emotion. "I'm gonna miss you."

The two brothers met in a crushing hug. Blackjack felt his eyes sting. Bone crushed Blackjack just as hard as Blackjack crushed Bone.

Blackjack really didn't want to say goodbye to his brother, not even when Blackjack knew this would be the best thing for Bone.

Leaving the band and striking out on his own with his own people—this was the threshold that made Bone's greatness possible. He couldn't grow into his strength if he stayed here in his brother's shadow all the time.

The two brothers broke apart. Blackjack's throat hurt too much to say anything. The crooked, trembling smile on Bone's face told Blackjack all he needed to know. This parting would be as hard for Bone as it was for everyone else.

Blackjack didn't want to make it harder by getting sappy about it. He didn't want to hold his brother back. Bone had to follow his own destiny. He deserved that.

He turned away from Blackjack and made his way through the rest of the camp saying goodbye to everyone else. Bone spent a long time taking his leave from Hangman.

Mora came out of the shelter and burst into tears when she said goodbye to Bone. The family had discussed this at length. No one understood better than Hangman and Mora did that Bone had to leave.

Leaving would be the best thing that had ever happened to him. It was the beginning of the rest of his life—his life as Kral of his own band.

He finally tore himself away from his mother, said goodbye to Hangman one last time, and approached the camp entrance where Blackjack stood waiting.

Bone's men joined him along with four other couples who would go out with him. Oracle, Pyro, Chief, Reaper, and Cyclops had all accepted Bone's judgment that they would never marry.

They had dedicated themselves to him as their Kral. They would form the core of his loyal fighting men who protected and provided for the rest of the band.

Bone had already negotiated with five other Regiment couples who wanted to join his band as soon as they came to the age of gathering.

Then Silloa would join them to form the nucleus of families who would raise the next generation.

Blackjack got a sick, sinking feeling in his gut watching Bone lead his new band out of the camp in the rocks. None of those people had ever looked happier to embark on their new lives.

Bone looked the happiest of all. Blackjack never would have wanted to rob his brother of that.

Blackjack didn't even know which valley Bone and the others planned to establish as their territory. Bone and the others had been negotiating that with the other Regiment bands. They didn't include Blackjack in their discussions. It was none of his business.

Bone and the others vanished into the jungle. They were gone. The past was dead.

Blackjack turned away and returned to Hangman's shelter. Hangman was sitting down again and Mora sat next to him. Narina had come over with Mion. Narina was pregnant with her and Blackjack's second child.

Mion talked as much as ever. Hangman and Mora chatted with him and kept him entertained while Blackjack and Narina sat next to each other in silence.

This camp was going to start looking and feeling awfully different without Bone here—and without all the visitors here. Blackjack hardly recognized it anymore.

Actually, the camp still looked and felt exactly the same. All the other families kept doing the same combination of activities. Nothing ever changed.

These old people would die. Viking was already dead and buried out in the jungle. Blackjack and those his age would get old. Mion and the others would initiate and take over running the band their own way.

Blackjack already felt himself drifting into that distant place where he watched all of this happen from a distance. It happened outside himself as if he was already too old, weak, and slow to keep track of what the young people were doing and planning.

Blackjack and Narina stayed with Hangman and Mora for the evening. The whole family shared a meal together.

These wouldn't last, either. Then Blackjack would be the last of his family still living in this camp—the camp they'd established when it was just the five of them living here all alone. He never could have predicted then that this would be the outcome.

He never could have predicted that thousands of people would come to live in the Angler Valley and the canyon country around it—and that this would become one of the most prosperous and densely populated areas in the whole country.

He never could have predicted back then that their family—Hangman, Mora, Blackjack, Bone, and Thena—would be the seed that led to the rebirth and revival of such a thriving population.

Would this wave of growth keep spreading across the country? The Angler Valley Godless, the Regiment, and the Ashtaw Valley Godless were already on their way to forming a sweeping tide of interconnected population.

Their territories combined with each other through a shared gathering ground. More bands would spread. They would make the gathering process easier for themselves by settling closer to the gathering ground from both sides.

Soon the distance between them would close and disappear. New bands and new couples would have no choice but to expand outward. They would have to establish new gathering grounds, new alliances, and new lines of defense against enemy Clans.

Blackjack had always seen himself as the leader in this band. His people had put him in charge. They all listened to him and obeyed him.

That time was over. He was just a man like any other. He raised his family. He hunted to provide for them. His children would grow up and move away. His daughters would marry into other bands and disappear out of his life, only to build new families somewhere else.

Life looked so much better when he saw it like this. He could appreciate its beauty and perfection when he looked at it from the outside as an observer.

He glanced over at Hangman. Hangman kept casting soft, loving glances around the camp in between playing with his beloved grandson. Hangman saw the world, the camp, the Clan, and all of humanity like that now.

He saw them from the outside. He could appreciate their beauty, perfection, and prosperity—now that he wasn't really a part of it anymore.

He cast those loving glances at his family, too—what was left of it. That love extended to all the valley bands, all the Regiment bands, the Godless bands outside the Angler Valley, and farther afield to Hammer's people on the distant horizon.

Their struggles, battles, difficulties, and hardship—nothing could be more perfect than that. The difficulties bound them together in an unbreakable connection that would never end. It would pass down from father to son and mother to daughter—forever.

Chapter 60

Mora hugged Narina. "You remember what I told you." Mora sniffed back tears. "Drink that bark tea morning and evening. It will help with the vertigo until it passes."

"I remember," Narina murmured.

Mora turned away to stop herself from seeing Narina's expression, but that only brought Mora face to face with Blackjack saying goodbye to Hangman.

The two men held each other for a long time before Hangman pulled away.

"Are you sure about this?" Blackjack's voice broke. "It isn't too late to change your mind."

Hangman only nodded. "Yes, it is. I'm sure."

Hangman turned aside first. Blackjack's features twisted. He struggled to hold himself together.

Hangman limped over to Mora. This was the furthest he'd walked since his last injury outside the tunnel. Every step caused him excruciating pain. Everything caused him pain these days. Even sitting in one place caused him pain.

He gave Mora one hard look, cast the most passing glance at Narina and Mion, and kept going toward the camp entrance.

Hangman walked extra slowly. Mora barely had to walk at all to keep up with him.

He didn't look back at Blackjack's family watching Hangman and Mora leave. Mora stopped at the entrance and raised her hand once. Blackjack and Narina did the same thing.

Mora felt herself falling apart. She couldn't look at Blackjack and Narina anymore—not without completely dissolving in tears.

She saw both of them on the verge of despair, too, but Hangman was right. It was all already over.

He hobbled out of the camp. None of the others came to say goodbye. He'd already said goodbye to the very few friends he had who were still alive. They would all be gone soon, too.

Mora followed him out into the jungle. They took all day to cross the valley to the tunnel. They didn't get there until sunset.

The two of them sat on the ground inside the tree line. She carried a bundle of supplies for both of them and shared out some of her dried food with him. They didn't talk except when Hangman thanked her. He barely looked at her.

They slipped into a deeper silence than they'd ever entered before. He'd always asked her about everything going on in the camp and farther outside it in the rest of the valley.

He'd involved himself at least in an unofficial capacity in all the negotiations between Blackjack, the Regiment, and all the other allied bands. He'd always wanted to know and understand everything that was happening.

Not anymore. He groaned in agony when he and Mora stretched out on the ground and went to sleep. Then he groaned in agony when they woke up in the morning and he had to struggle to his feet.

They left through the tunnel. Both ends were deserted. Mora didn't see a single person anywhere. All the surrounding bands sent out scouting parties to protect the area, but they weren't here now. No one hung around the tunnel entrance anymore on either end.

Hangman turned south and followed the river. The surrounding bands had developed a policy not to establish territories in adjacent valleys.

They left a buffer around each other so they didn't encroach or even come close to encroaching on each other's territory. That might change in the distant future when the country became more heavily populated, but everyone had plenty of space for now.

Hangman traveled so slowly that it took him and Mora a week to travel all the way down the river. She hunted small game to feed the two of them. That was all she could handle at her age. She wasn't mobile enough to hunt anything else.

The river flowed into the next valley system to the south, but Hangman didn't go that way. He turned off and started climbing into the mountains.

Mora followed him. She had to stop every few paces, wait for him to limp ahead, and then catch up with him. He never turned around or acknowledged that he was slowing her down. He just kept going no matter what.

He stopped every few minutes to catch his breath and to gasp in pain. Every move cost him a massive effort. He winced every time he put his weight on his legs.

Sitting and lying down in the evening racked him in torment, but getting up in the morning was the worst. He had to fight for every movement and usually wound up drenched in sweat by the time he got to his feet.

Mora watched in silence while he struggled through it. She didn't try to talk him out of it.

He took another two long, slow, agonized, painful weeks to climb all the way to the top of the mountain—or almost to the top. The couple left the jungle and hiked across barren, rocky passes to another hilltop between the highest peaks.

This hilltop had some sparse trees growing on it. Hangman and Mora could look out over the canyon country from here. They could see the Angler Valley with its distinctive cliff features.

Hangman stopped at the brow of the hill looking down on the whole countryside. He wavered on his unsteady legs. Silent calm fell over him, now that he'd finally made it up this far.

He stood there in silence for a long time before he glanced around and finally lowered himself painfully to the ground.

Mora got busy, put her bundle down, and started constructing a shelter. She built it behind him so he only had to scoot a few feet to lean against its outer wall. He let out another shaky breath once he got into that position.

His gaze remained locked on the valley in the distance. Both he and Mora knew everything that was going on inside it and all around it.

She went hunting again, lit a fire, and cooked for both of them. Mora settled into the comfortable silence. She didn't feel the need to break it. Maybe nothing would. Maybe she and Hangman wouldn't talk to each other again.

They both already knew everything they might say to each other. Whatever they might say to each other fell into the same category as things going on in the valley. They belonged to the other time—the time before now.

She took the food off the fire, divided it, and handed it to him. "Thank you," he murmured.

She barely glanced up at him. She even hesitated to acknowledge his thanks. What did he think she was going to do—not provide for him now that he couldn't provide for himself?

The fire in his eye stopped her from looking away. He stared at her with all his old intensity. The weight of his stare held her gaze in an unbreakable grip.

He slipped his hand into hers and squeezed. "Thank you," he breathed. "For everything."

Tears sprang to her eyes when she realized what he was saying. What did he think—that she wouldn't have done all of that—that she wouldn't have done her absolute best for him all these years?

She'd only ever tried to do her best for him—and she couldn't even say those words out loud. She still only wanted that. She never wanted anything but to be good enough for him—to make him proud.

She'd spent her life just hoping against all odds that she could somehow find a way to be what he needed her to be.

She didn't have to ask if she was. She already knew she was—and he'd told her countless times that she was and that he was proud of her.

This feeling still burned in her heart—the ache to be good enough for him.

He squeezed her hand and rubbed the back of her knuckles with his warm, rough, gnarled fingers. His hands had seen it all.

"I love you," he murmured.

She picked up his hands and kissed the weathered skin and twisted knuckles through her tears. She couldn't even say the words—not now. There were no words anywhere in any known human language for this moment between them.

He smiled at her and then pulled his hand away to turn back to his meal. She did the same thing, sat next to him, and they both looked out over the countryside while they ate.

This was the only activity left to them now—watching the rest of the world pass them by. Hangman had been doing it in the camp, but he didn't want to do it there anymore.

He didn't want to sit there like a useless lump while everyone watched him crumble and die. He wasn't a part of the camp life anymore. He was already gone, so he had no reason to stay there and every reason to leave.

Now he and Mora would watch from here.

They finished eating. She took his bowl and her water skins. She had to hike a long way down the back of the hill before she found water. A small stream ran through the ravine behind the hill. This was the closest place she could get water.

She returned to the shelter, handed Hangman one of the full skins, and went back to her own work while he stayed where he was. She unpacked her bundle. She didn't have much food left. She would have to hunt again pretty soon.

She and Hangman hadn't brought any other skins to act as a bed. They would just have to make do with the ground for now.

She didn't plan to hunt anything big enough to get her any skins, either. Having enough skins to make a bed was a luxury she and Hangman couldn't afford anymore.

She went hunting and found a clutch of Gurlgs in the undergrowth. One was a mother with seven chicks, but the chicks were all essentially fully grown now.

Mora couldn't figure out why any of them were still spending time with each other. The chicks should have gone off on their own a long time ago.

The seven former chicks even acted like chicks. Their mother scratched for insects and seeds on the jungle floor and made all the same noises as if the chicks were still small.

Mora didn't look forward to fighting these creatures, so she climbed a tree and used a sapling to noose one of the chicks. It was a huge male almost bigger than his mother.

The sapling carried the bird far enough away that the others didn't see where it landed. She lowered it to the ground. The noose had broken its neck. She only had to cut up the dead creature and carry the pieces back to camp.

Hangman didn't comment when she set up a tripod to dry the meat for their long-term food supplies. She worked into the evening, cooked some of the meat for her and Hangman to eat, and went back and forth to the stream to clean her hands and tools.

She was still working when Hangman shifted away from the shelter wall, stretched out on the ground next to the fire, wished her good night, and thanked her again for everything she was doing.

She smiled at him. "Sleep well. I'll see you tomorrow."

His lips twisted the wrong way when he tried to smile back at her. "Don't stay up too late, okay? Get some sleep tonight."

"I'll try."

He groaned when he lowered himself to the ground and gasped when he curled up on his side and pulled his knees up. He folded his arm under his head, shut his eyes, and let out a shaky sigh.

She kept casting sidelong glances at him and smiling at him. She would have liked to make him more comfortable, but nothing could accomplish that.

She returned to her work, turned the meat over on the tripods, and took the scraped bones and offal out into the jungle for the creatures.

She gathered up all the Gurlg feathers and carried them into the shelter to make a bed. That would be a more comfortable place for Hangman to sleep, but she didn't wake him up. He could sleep there tomorrow night if he wanted to.

She finally finished hanging up all the meat, sat down by fire, and ate her own food. The firelight made her sleepy, but she stayed up a little longer anyway.

Everything about this life felt easy, comfortable, and inevitable. She could continue in this silence forever if she had to. She didn't need it to be anything more than it already was.

She eventually took Hangman's advice, put some more wood on the fire, and curled up on the ground nearby to go to sleep. The night noises sounded peaceful and comforting. They confirmed everything she already knew.

She slept soundly and woke up in full daylight the next morning. She pushed herself up and stretched out her hand to check the meat to see if it was dry enough.

Hangman lay asleep in the same place where he'd curled up last night. He'd rolled onto his back during the night.

She barely glanced at him—and froze. That one glance told her more than she ever wanted to know. He lay too still. He wasn't breathing.

Other than that, he looked asleep. One of his arms lay across his chest. He looked comfortable with a neutral, sleeping expression on his face. His eyes were closed.

She stared at him for a long time before she could bring herself to turn away. She stumbled to her feet and blundered over to the hilltop. The country lay before her as always with the valley in the distance.

She'd known when she came up here that he wouldn't last long. The journey from the camp to here would be his last. He hadn't lasted even twenty-four hours after he made it this far.

At least he could rest now. He wasn't in pain anymore. She slumped onto the ground staring out at the distant countryside. Now it was her turn. She would stay here until she fell asleep and didn't wake up. She was already gone.

She'd been telling herself for months and even years that she didn't want to live without him. Now she didn't have to.

She would have to take his body out into the jungle, but she wouldn't do it now. She already felt herself disappearing into the landscape. If she was here or if she wasn't here—did it really make a difference in the end? No one could tell the difference and neither could she.

Time slipped away from her. The sun traveled up into the sky. It cast tiny shadows behind each pebble on the ground. Those shadows swung around, shortened, and then started to lengthen as the sun arched to the other side of the sky. One day. One day out of many.

Nothing moved her from this spot. She might sit here for another year—or five years—however long it took. It didn't matter anymore.

She was still sitting there in mid-afternoon when a scouting party crossed an adjacent hill in sight of her shelter. The scouts were all young Godless men barely the age of gathering or maybe even younger. They belonged to one of the southern valley bands.

They climbed up from behind the hill to survey the surrounding terrain. They saw her sitting there and watched her for a minute.

Their eyes ranged over the shelter, the tripods, the fire, Hangman's body, and her sitting at the edge of the hilltop.

She saw herself from their point of view. They didn't recognize her. They didn't know who she was. She was just any old woman who had left her camp to come out into the wilderness to die. She wasn't part of the life of the valley anymore—or life in general.

They studied her for a few minutes and then left down the other side of the hill. They left her alone in the silence—where she belonged.

Her gaze migrated out to the canyon country again. This country didn't need her and Hangman anymore. They'd spent their lives giving everything they had to make this country what it was. They'd succeeded.

Life had given them everything they could ask from it. They couldn't ask anything else and life couldn't give anything else. Their transaction had come to an end, but this moment had never felt so sweet.

It was the fulfillment of every desire and every promise she and Hangman had ever made to each other. They'd faced everything together, endured everything together, and enjoyed everything together.

Now they would face this together, endure this together, and enjoy this together, too—the way it should be. Neither of them had to go through it alone.

Life wasn't made to live alone. She couldn't have chosen anyone better to go through all of that with her. She couldn't think of anyone she would rather do this with, too. Now she didn't have to.

<u>The End.</u>

Keep Reading

 rideland Series

When a rescue mission goes disastrously wrong.....

Lieutenant Dina Dyer and her team find themselves held captive on an alien planet—the prisoners of an unstoppable power they never could have imagined possible: a race of sentient cats that keeps people as pets, slaves, and as prey for the hunt. In a world where every friend can become an enemy and nothing is as it seems, Dina must find the courage to escape before time runs out.

Caught in a toxic cocktail of attraction, politics, intrigue, and danger, her journey to freedom navigates the depths of human darkness where destinies collide and survival is the only reward worth fighting for. With the fate of millions hanging in the balance and betrayal surrounding her at every turn, can one woman become the firebrand that brings an entire planet out of shadows and into the light of freedom?

You can find it at your favorite book retailer.

Sign Up Once--Get all Theo Mann's free books including brand new releases

S ign Up Once--Get all Theo Mann's free books including brand new releases

In a world where everything is out to kill you, humans must fight for survival every day against huge dangerous creatures and enemy Clans. The Godless Clan has enough to worry about already. They don't need to fight their own.

Sixteen-year-old Shadow knows exactly what to do when he discovers a girl from an enemy band hiding in the jungle. He takes her captive as a prisoner of war, but the Godless have a strict code of honor when dealing with women—even enemy women.

He and Katha will have to fight for their very survival and overcome generations of mistrust before they make it back to their people—who just might be the most dangerous enemies either of them has ever faced.

Sign up at www.theomann.com to read it for free

About Theo Mann

I write 70 books per year—and yes, before you ask, all these books are my original creative work. Nothing written under my name is AI-generated or ghostwritten because I write better than AI and any ghostwriter out there.

People don't read fiction for entertainment or to escape from reality. People read fiction to see their humanity reflected in another person's character and story.

This is my promise to you. When you read my books, you'll see your own humanity reflected in the characters and stories. I take this commitment to my readers very seriously. My books are an intimate form of communication between us. I would never disrespect my readers by turning that over to a machine or another writer. This is my bond between me and you as my reader.

I write 20,000 words per day as my daily work output. If anyone with a public platform would like to challenge me to prove this in a controlled environment, feel free to contact me on this website's contact page.

I worked as a professional ghostwriter for fifteen years. Now I'm on a mission to set a Guinness World Record by writing 700 books over the next ten years and 1400 books over the next twenty years, all originally written by me. See my website for the full book list.

I'm also the author of *Proof for the Existence of God* and the *Crimes Against Fiction* blog. You can find all my nonfiction work at www.crimes-against-fiction.com.

If you have a story idea, or if you would like me to explore a series in more depth, or if you'd like me to explore a character by writing a spinoff series about that character or world, leave me a message on my website's contact page. I answer all reader emails, so ask me anything, tell me what you liked and didn't like, and let me know where you'd like your favorite series to go. I would love to hear your ideas and find out what you'd like to read next.

Find out more at www.theomann.com.

Also by Theo Mann (so far)

<u>Standalone Novels</u>

Kingdom of Heaven

The Verge

<u>Series</u>

Onyx Series (Books 1-6)

Prideland Series (Books 1-4)

Ultra Meridian Series (Books 1-7)

Hellhounds Series (Books 1-7)

Battlefleet Series (Books 1-4)

Highland Heroes Series (Books 1-6)

Battalion 1 Series (Books 1-5)

The Network Series (Books 1-6)

Corrupted Coil (Books 1-5)

Rise of the Giants Series (Books 1-10)

The Edge of Chaos Series (Books 1-5)

The White Series (Books 1-7)

9 781991 425454